Name & Address
Withheld

JANE SIGALOFF

was born in London and, despite brief trips into the countryside, she's always been a city girl at heart. After studying history at Oxford University she entered the allegedly glamorous world of television, beginning her career as tea and coffee coordinator for Nickelodeon U.K. After she progressed to researcher and then to assistant producer, her contracts took her to MTV and finally to the BBC where she worked for over three years.

Since 2000, Jane has enjoyed a double life as a part-time P.A., which has given her more time to write and feel guilty about not going to the gym. She lives in London with her laptop and ever-expanding CD collection. She has never consulted an agony aunt.

Name & Address Withheld is her first novel.

Name & Address Withheld

Jane Sigaloff

RED
DRESS
INK
™

First edition December 2002

NAME & ADDRESS WITHHELD

A Red Dress Ink novel

ISBN 0-373-25022-3

Visit Red Dress Ink at www.reddressink.com

Printed in U.S.A.

ACKNOWLEDGMENTS

You wouldn't be holding this book
if it wasn't for the incredible support and encouragement
I've received over the years, and I'd like to
thank everyone who has stood by me through
the thick (and not-so-thin) versions.

Naming a few names, special thanks and love
must go to: Susie, Anthony, Peter, Paul and Omi—
for years of unconditional love, support
(emotional and financial), for believing in me
and for never being disappointed that I didn't get
a real job. Carole Blake—for picking me out of
the slush pile, continued encouragement
and for never doubting it would happen
(or not telling me if you did!). Also to Isobel
and the whole team at Blake Friedmann.
Sam Bell at Red Dress Ink—for seeing what the
others didn't and helping Matt realize his potential.
Kate Patten—for all your invaluable advice on everything,
for endless cups of tea, mutual appreciation and for
such happy days at no.95. Charlotte Cameron—for
spectacular sounding-board properties, wise words,
SoCeLo, mix tapes and martinis. Louise Hooper—
for high-energy positivity and fast-talking since 1979.
Melissa Andrewes—for pedantic proofreading and for
encouraging me to exercise. Alice and Stuart Morgan—
for the temporary roof over my head and boundless
enthusiasm. Chris Gore—for so much support
at the outset and for almost as many pizzas
as I got rejection letters.

Many thanks also to:
Steve, Jan, Tanya, John and Tracy Arie, Gemma Brown,
Elton Charles, Camilla and Sue Codrington, Sarah Cohen,
Marten Foxon, Mary Ann Graziano, Mandy Key,
Hilary Love, James Meikle, Fred Metcalf,
Mandy Moore, Siobhan Mulholland, Patsy Newey,
Notting Hill and Ealing High School,
The Parises, Sandy Paterson, Chris, Lavender,
Laura and Alice Patten, The Smails, Julia Stones,
Annabelle Tym and Lizzie Tyrrell.

And finally, to the creators of *Sex and the City* and
The West Wing—for making British winters a little less gray.

For Edward & Dora

chapter  1

*W*hy *is it that we always want what we can't have? It doesn't matter whether it's that Prada bag, Nike's latest offering to trainer culture, Jennifer Aniston's hair, Jennifer Aniston's husband, George Clooney or the senior school sweetheart; there are times in our lives when we think—no, we know—that life would be complete if only we had the item in question. By the same token it is a human failing that we rarely realise what we do have until it is no longer ours to keep. Both have happened to me more often than I would care to remember.*

Mark was all I ever wanted between the ages of fifteen and sixteen. My school exercise books were littered with his name, hearts with our initials carved by my lust during double English and, most importantly, our percentage of compatibility which I once worked out to be eighty-four per cent. A miscalculation. I should have spent more time paying attention in maths. When he finally asked me out the week after my seventeenth birthday—because, I now fear, he had asked everyone else out already—I thought I was going to burst with pleasure. It was a match made in heaven—I had the soft-focus daydreams to prove it.

For five weeks it was the real hand-holding thing. My months of background research paid off and I had all the right answers to his questions and all the right cassettes in my collection. I was In Love. Then the object of my misplaced affection stole my virginity before chucking me publicly and unceremoniously just before the end of term. My life ended as quickly as it had begun. I wept and fasted, and wept and fasted some more. Then came the hunger and I ate like never before. My adolescence would certainly have been less traumatic without him, but I would have laughed in the face of anyone who'd tried to tell me at the time. Adult lesson # 1 learned; the hard way...

'There you go, love. Have a nice evening.'

Lizzie looked up from the magazine. She'd been so busy checking her weekly column for mistakes that she'd momentarily been transported back to her teens. A fist of nerves settled in her stomach as she realised that she'd arrived at her destination.

Four hundred people were expected to celebrate Christmas and a successful first year in which City FM had been put on the radio map and, as the station controller Richard Drake liked to tell her, as their newest recruit she was an important part of that. Lizzie wished he was there to remind her just once more for the record as her self-confidence temporarily vanished and she fought an increasingly strong urge to melt into the Soho crowds and disappear. Just because it was a work do, it didn't mean that it was supposed to feel like an assignment, and she couldn't help feeling that anything referred to as a 'do' should always be a don't. There was, of course, the develop-a-mysterious-24-hour-bug tactic, but from previous experience Lizzie knew that two painful hours at the office party were worth their weight in nights out on the beers for the rest of the year.

As the taxi pulled away from the kerb, having deposited its perfumed payload on the pavement, a familiar ringing noise caught her attention. Saved by the bell? She prayed it was an emergency. Nothing life-threatening, just party-threatening.

Lizzie rummaged for her mobile, which for several rings eluded her grasp despite the smallness of her bag.

'Hello?'

'It's nearly quarter to ten, for God's sake. Shouldn't you be paralytic by now?'

Lizzie smiled. It was Clare. Best friend, flatmate and chief party outfit adviser.

'I've literally just got out of the cab.'

'Well, hurry up and get yourself to that bar. It's one thing being fashionably late, but if you leave it much longer no one will even remember you were there at all. Just remember you're gorgeous, witty, intelligent, beautiful and sober...well, relatively...an inestimable advantage at this stage of the evening. You'll be able to impress them all by still being capable of pronouncing words of more than one syllable. Leave your nerves in the cloakroom and get yourself a drink.'

'Thanks. I will...' A few ego-bolstering words of support and Lizzie's attitude had done a U-turn. 'And thanks for all your top fashion advice earlier. Thank God for you and your wardrobe.'

Way back, B.C. (before Clare), Lizzie had endured a couple of outfit *faux pas*. Now she was practically a D-list celebrity she couldn't afford to rock any boats with her choice of partywear.

'No problem. Couldn't have you rocking up in pin-striped skintight stretch drainpipe jeans!'

'Listen, you, that photo was taken in 1984. Anyone who was anyone had a pair. Probably even Madonna.'

Clare ignored her. Her job was done and, besides, she had a restaurant to run.

'Lots of love...catch up with you in the morning for a debrief.'

Lizzie snapped her expensively compact mobile shut. Giving herself a sultry smile, she pulled her shoulders back, instantly adding breasts to her outfit, and despite the newness of her shoes managed to sashay the requisite twenty metres to the door retaining both her composure and the full use of both ankles.

'Lizzie Ford.'

Sullenly the bouncer checked his list before slowly un-hooking the rope that stood between her and the rest of the evening. While the stretch of red curtain tie-back cord at mid-calf level wouldn't have stopped anything—with the exception, perhaps, of a stray sheep—from getting in if it really wanted to, it was all about the image of exclusivity. Judging by the re-lief Lizzie now felt at being on the right side, it was working.

She smiled amicably at a couple of semi-familiar faces as she swept—well, stepped—into the party, which was already in full swing. Parties had been much more fun when she could waltz up to people who knew nothing about her, might never see her again, and didn't know where to find her. Now, with her own jingle and her own show, she had forfeited her right to anonymity.

Matt hated big work parties. Pressure to look good. Pres-sure to provide jocose and scintillating conversation even if the person you were talking to had nothing of interest to con-tribute. Pressure to network... It was no wonder that people ended up incredibly drunk, determined to start digging their own professional graves by discarding all tact and diplomacy and fraternising with people that they were normally—and often for good reason—intimidated by.

He spotted Lizzie the minute she walked into the busy bar. He knew who she was. Listener research showed that she was already one of their most popular presenters, and thanks to Lizzie Ford an agony aunt with sex appeal was no longer an oxymoron. *The Agony and the Ecstasy* was outstripping its ri-vals in the ratings, and she brought a unique blend of under-standing, sympathy and the odd soft rock track to their airwaves. Rumour had it she was going to be a big star. Watch-ing her work the room, he had no reason to doubt it.

What he really needed was a night in, a pint of Ribena, a balanced meal and a video. But instead he was pouring yet more beer and canapés down his iron-coated alimentary canal. To make matters worse the bloke opposite him had been bor-ing him rigid for the last ten minutes.

Here was a graduate with high hopes who hadn't yet had his enthusiasm dampened by a few years in the workplace, and Matt knew he should have been flattered by the attention. After all, he'd only wanted an insight into the 'creative wizard' that was Matt Baker. He'd never been called a wizard to his face before. Maybe it was time to invest in a pointy hat, or at least sew a couple of stars onto his Ted Baker shirt. Matt smiled to himself. Unfortunately this was interpreted by his co-conversationalist as a green light to continue. Matt was barely listening. His eyes were fixed but not focused.

Professionally it had been a good year. On the domestic front it was becoming easier and easier to forget that he had a wife. Five years down the line they shared a mortgage and a bathroom, but little else. He'd always known she craved success. Ambition was one of the things he'd found so attractive about her. A fiery determination, which he had no doubt would pay off, and a professional self-belief that could be incredibly intimidating whether you were her bank manager, her boss or just her husband. But now it felt as if he was irrelevant. Last season's must-have accessory. Taking a swig of his beer, he willed his intoxication to move on to the wildly happy mad-dog phase. Alcoholic introspection was not conducive to the festive spirit.

Lizzie went through the motions and, her inhibitions soon buried at the bottom of a glass, worked her way round the room air-kissing, hand-shaking and nodding enthusiastically. Once she'd made contact with Richard Drake, done the small talk thing with the other big bosses, pretended to be interested in the station's main advertisers and concentrated on saying the right things to the right people at the right time she made a bee-line for her producer, Ben, and joined the rest of her production team—who were apparently intent on sweating away the remaining hours on the dance floor.

As the physical effects of her non-existent dinner, multiple G&T, high-heeled dancing evening started to kick in, to her relief she spotted a recently vacated leather sofa and, sinking into the cushions, still warm from their previous occupants, slipped her shoes to one side, flexing her aching arches.

The bar was packed with people in various states of alcoholic and narcotic distress. Several public displays of affection were taking place in what had earlier been considered the darker corners of the venue, but now, thanks to intermittent bursts of strobe lighting, their indiscretions were clearly visible, if a little disjointed, giving their liaisons a pop video feel. The thumping music was loud enough to create an atmosphere in that everyone almost had to shout to make themselves heard, and overall it was decadent enough to ensure that it would be described over e-mail on Monday as a great party. Those whose recollections were sketchy would probably go so far as to say it had been fantastic.

She was miles away when the drive-time DJ, Danny Vincent, slithered into her personal space, instantly activating her built-in quality control alarm by resting his arm along the couch behind her in a semi-territorial manner. He was reputedly as smooth as the voice that calmed many frayed tempers in traffic jams, and certainly at this too-close range Lizzie could see that his teeth were too white and too perfect to be his own and that his shiny designer satin jeans were at least one size too small.

'So, what's a beautiful, young, successful woman like you doing sitting alone in the corner?'

His voice was indeed a phenomenon. Somewhere between a growl and a purr. But it was the most interesting thing about him by a considerable margin. Lizzie wished she'd left before he'd gatecrashed her party.

'Resting. People-watching. Taking a breather on my own.' She pointedly left longer pauses than natural between the last three words to make her point. A cue for him to leave. But Danny was far too thick-skinned to notice.

'But this is a party.' He said it like 'pardeee'. 'A chance to meet new people, to road-test a few colleagues and get to know your new station family.'

Things were going from bad to worse. Lizzie was trapped in the corner with a station jock who was suggesting 'road testing' colleagues. Her stomach tensed involuntarily, but Danny was bankable talent with a long contract and way above her in the pecking order, so provided he kept his pecker to himself she would just have to be civil.

Twenty minutes later he'd barely paused for breath, peppering his egocentric monologue with innuendoes just to check Lizzie was listening and smiling in the right places. Lizzie couldn't stand him, but, thanks to his body position, she couldn't stand up either. He hadn't even offered to buy her another drink, even though she'd made sure that she'd drained her glass dramatically three times in as many minutes. His eyes were glazed with self-love; hers with self-pity.

Lizzie started to pray to the god of Interruptions and Small Distractions while desperately looking for someone she knew to rescue her from drive-time hell. Not only was there no one familiar on the horizon, but as she gradually sank into a dark leather sofa abyss, her eyeline was currently at most people's ribcages and rapidly falling to suspender level.

Matt was at the bar—again. As he picked his way back to his workmates he spotted Lizzie in the corner and, watching her as he distributed his round, he decided that her body language said, *Help...Rescue me.* Leaving his colleagues midsentence, he strode over to do the decent thing.

'Lizzie Ford—Matt Baker. Pleased to meet you.'

His confidence was alcohol-assisted and, while she had never set eyes on him before, Lizzie stood up gratefully to shake his hand. Danny looked less than impressed at the interruption, especially as Matt obviously had no interest in talking to him or getting his autograph.

'Matt?'

Lizzie smiled warmly and Matt grinned back, his tiredness forgotten. She really was very pretty. Her brown eyes seemed to radiate energy, and right now that was just what he needed.

Subconsciously he ran his fingers through his hair. It wasn't, Lizzie noted, self-consciously long enough to suggest that he was growing it to prove that he still could, nor was it so short as to suggest that it had been shorn to disguise a rapidly receding hairline. Illuminated by stray rays from the dance floor, there were times when it almost took on a Ready-Brek glow. Divine intervention.

'Yup...I'm a copywriter, responsible for those unforgettable slogans advertising City FM that you see on buses and bill-boards.'

Lizzie thought for a moment before starting to reel them off. '"Because it's hot in the City". "Tune in to City life". "The City that cares..." Wow, they actually pay someone to come up with those! It must be a full-time job...'

'OK, so they don't really work out loud, at a party, but re-search has shown that...'

Matt tailed off mid-sentence. Lizzie was smiling mischie-vously and now he regretted having been so defensive. One day he'd have a career that made a difference; until then copy-writing would have to do.

Danny, no longer the centre of attention, sloped off. The coast was clear.

'Thanks so much for coming over. I thought I was stuck with him for the rest of the evening.'

Matt adopted his best deep Barry White voiceover tone and faked an American accent. 'Danny Vincent...loving him-self...on City FM.'

Lizzie laughed as she imagined the new jingle being played in at the intro to his show. 'I'm not sure he'll go for it...'

'Hmm...maybe it needs a bit more work... Anyway, I spot-ted you from the bar, and I was getting the SOS vibe, so I thought I'd better respond to the international distress call be-fore you gave up the will to live.'

'I owe you one.' Lizzie was pleased that the god of Inter-ruptions and Small Distractions had obviously been at tea with the god of Good-Looking Specimens when he'd received her distress call. No wedding ring either. 'Can I start by getting you a drink? I'm gasping—not that motormouth noticed!'

Motormouth? Had anyone used that expression in conver-sation since the late seventies? Lizzie wished she could be a little bit more articulate when it mattered. In an attempt to dis-tract Matt from her retro turn of phrase she turned her empty glass upside down to demonstrate the urgency and Matt—apparently undeterred by the motormouth moment—raised the bottle of beer which he'd barely started and nodded.

'Same again, please. Thanks.'

He really didn't need another drink, but he didn't want to go either. As far as he could remember from the press release he'd seen when she'd joined City, she wasn't married and was a couple of years younger than him. Old enough, then, to remember the TV programmes and references to pop music that were wasted on the combat trouser-wearing members of his department...or cargo pants, as they seemed to be called these days.

As he watched his damsel, now distress-free, weave her way to the bar he checked his shirt buttons and flies automatically. All present and correct. Good. No reasons for her to stare at him unless she was interested in what he had to say. He, on the other hand, was overtly staring at her back when she suddenly turned unexpectedly, and quickly he jerked his head round and focused on something non-existent on the dance floor. He didn't dare look back just in case she looked over and caught him staring again.

As Lizzie elbowed her way to the bar she glanced back at Matt, who was nodding his head in time to the beat, pretending to be absorbed by something happening on the dance floor in order to avoid the stigma of mateless party abandon. Very cute. She shoved a couple of drunken partygoers out of her way impatiently. She wanted to get back before he changed his mind and wandered off.

'Here you go.' Lizzie handed Matt two bottles of beer. 'They were doing buy three, get one free, so I thought I'd join you. I'm sure we'll get through two each.'

'Thanks.' Matt wished he hadn't already had at least six already. How was he supposed to impress her if he was in danger of losing the ability to enunciate properly?

After a synchronised swig from their bottles they both started speaking at the same time.

'So...'

'So...'

'You first...'

'No, you...'

Another swig...

...and a smile.

He had very good teeth, she couldn't help noticing. Her step-father had been a dentist and had left a legacy of interest in incisors, canines and premolars for her to deal with. She'd always believed that clean nails and nice teeth were important indices of personal hygiene.

Matt, unaware that he was under observation, was off to a good start. He decided to break up the meaningful look competition and took charge.

'Shall we find a table?'

'We could stay on the sofa if you promise to protect me from Danny.'

'Right.' My pleasure, he thought. But thankfully for his credibility it remained unsaid.

As they sat down, Lizzie sighed with relief. 'I've decided I hate office parties.'

'Me too. Can't stand them. You spend the whole evening pretending that everyone you work with is your best friend. The fact that you don't have anything to say to them when you're sober doesn't seem to stand in your way...until the next day, when you realise that you've arranged to go to the cinema, to go on holiday with them or something equally unlikely—all because you drank too much the night before.'

'Exactly.'

'Or you spend the next working week trying to work out whether the member of senior management that you felt the need to be excruciatingly honest with remembers your conversation and is going to hold it against you.' Words were tumbling from his mouth and it appeared that Matt was powerless to do anything about it. Alcohol had loosened his tongue. He closed his mouth in an attempt to reverse the process.

Lizzie giggled. He was right. 'It's even worse for me because, as an agony aunt, I'm somehow not supposed to be the person who takes her top off on the dance floor, who downs a pint the quickest or snogs people randomly. If you like, I'm the token parent at the party—and that, I must say, is one of the only disadvantages of my job.'

'Probably saves you a lot of embarrassment in the long run.'

'Maybe.' Lizzie wasn't interested in sensible conversation. She was flirting, obviously so subtly that Matt hadn't noticed yet, but she was out of practice. Most people in advertising that she knew, including Clare's ex-husband, were hooked on creating the right image, modelling themselves to fit whatever was considered to be of the moment. Matt, however, was a natural. He was charming without being smooth, boyish yet well worn, tall but not gangly and solid without being chunky. Lizzie wondered what the catch was. Maybe he wore briefs or Y-fronts?

'So how does it feel to be on the up? This has been quite a year for you, hasn't it?'

Oh, no. Now he'd thrown in a proper question while she'd been hypothesising about the state of his underwear drawer. The first test. And an answer that required a careful combination of articulacy and modesty—neither trait enhanced by a cocktail of gin, tonic and lager. Lizzie was bashful. This year had certainly marked a step in the right direction, but there were still plenty of boxes unchecked on her list of ambitions and, as far as City FM were concerned, she was still the new kid on the radio block.

'It's great. I'm loving doing the show...and my column...but it's hardly brain surgery...' Lizzie stopped herself. What exactly was the self-deprecation for? 'So far so good. It's quite a fresh approach, and the listeners seem to like it...radio awards here I come...' Much better. Positive without being cocky. But now she was babbling so much that she had noticed Clare's raised eyebrow even though she wasn't even at this party. It was a side effect of beer. Probably something to do with the bubbles. She reined herself in. Clare would have been proud.

'How about you?' Masterfully done. The ball was back in his court now, and she was much less likely to bore him if he was the one doing the talking. She might have been trained to fill any silences on air, but she knew that silences in day-to-

day conversation were not only natural but to be encouraged
if you wanted to retain any close friends.

'I've had a fantastic year professionally. My best ever. My
slogans have even won a couple of awards.' Matt silently chas-
tised himself. Next he would be trying to impress her with his
A-level results. What was the matter with him?

'Really? So how did you get into copywriting?' Another vol-
ley straight back. Lizzie was still trying her best to be flirtatious, but it didn't seem to be working. She'd even bowed her
head slightly, and had been trying to look at him out of the corner of her eye in what she had thought was a coy fashion. But
what if he just thought she had a weak neck and a slight squint
and was too polite to mention it? Seduction was bloody hard
work. Matt clearly had no idea what she was up to.

'Well, I had a one-liner for everything from a very early age.'

'You must have been a precocious kid.'

'How dare you?' Matt put his hand on his hip in mock in-
dignation before leaning closer to Lizzie in a pseudo-whisper.
'But if the truth be known, I was—a bit.' He smiled, amused
that he was being so candid. In fact, he was really enjoying
himself. 'I was the youngest and my mother and father doted
on me. Drama lessons. Music lessons. Tennis lessons. I had
them all... But like most little boys I was happiest watching
television. ITV was my channel of choice, and I always looked
forward to the adverts—even though the best ones were always
on at the cinema.'

'Pa-pa-pa-pa-pa-pa-pa-pa-pa...' Lizzie, to her horror, had
suddenly started singing the Pearl & Dean theme tune that had
haunted the cinema trips of her youth. She was about ten seconds in before she realised what she was doing and stopped
herself at once. Singing to a stranger in public. Certifiable behaviour. Lose ten points. It was too late. Matt had noticed and
spontaneously finished off the tune for her.

He was thrilled. So Lizzie had been brainwashed by advertisers too. And what a relief to have met someone who was just
comfortable with herself instead of being totally preoccupied
with saying what she thought he wanted to hear.

'I'd be that child singing jingles in the back of the car. I remember getting into trouble once for singing the telephone number of our local Ford dealer all the way to Devon, and I think my father was ready to strangle me with his bare hands when I finally moved on to the likes of the ever so catchy, ever so irritating "Transformers...robots in disguise" campaign... By then I was well into my teens.'

Lizzie smiled, genuinely entertained by the man beside her and desperately trying to put the Pearl & Dean moment behind her. Matt was very engaging and, while she knew it was pure cliché, his face really did light up when he spoke. She had better pull herself together before she allowed the moment to go all soft-focus around the edges. She decided that more questions were the best option. That way she could just look and listen.

'So how did you get into it then?'

'To my parents' delight I left university with a degree in English...'

Which university? When? With what class of degree? Lizzie could feel the spirit of her mother tapping on her shoulder and chose to ignore it.

'...but to their disappointment I had no real focus or motivation, and ironically I sort of fell into advertising by accident. Once I was there I was hooked. If you think about it, trends are always changing—and it's my job not only to reflect what's out there but to try to anticipate new ideas, or even fuse a couple to create fresh styles.'

He looked across. Lizzie seemed interested enough, but then again she made a living out of listening to other people. Matt decided to give her a 'get out of jail free' option just in case.

'Promise you'll just stop me when you get bored. Yawn, stand on my foot, stare at some bloke at the bar—that sort of thing. I don't want to be a fate worse than Danny.' But Matt knew that right now he had a lot to thank the king of slime-time for.

Lizzie glanced down at Matt's legs. Relaxed-cut dark jeans. No stretch satin in sight. She looked up a little too quickly to be discreet and hoped Matt didn't think she'd been staring at his lap. Their eyes locked.

'It's interesting. Really.' Suddenly self-conscious, Lizzie looked away and pretended to rummage in her little bag for nothing in particular.

'I guess I'm just trying to justify my existence. If only I was a heart surgeon and could gain instant respect. You know—just add boiling water and stir gently.'

'Hmm?'

'For instant respect...'

'Oh—I get it.' Lizzie did, but only a nanosecond after she'd said that she already had. 'Anyway, justify away. Believe me, you'll know when I'm bored...'

Matt hesitated. He wasn't convinced.

'...and I've still got a beer and a half to go.'

Lizzie was more than happy to let someone else do all the talking. It made a nice change.

'Well, OK, then...if you're sure you're sure...'

'I'm sure I'm sure.'

'Remember, I did warn you...'

'Yes. Yes.' Lizzie was impressed that he'd even stopped to think about whether she was interested or not. Her recent experience had definitely indicated this was a dying trait.

'Right...'

Matt's whole intonation changed as he verbally rolled up his sleeves and prepared to address Lizzie as a student of his craft. He wasn't being patronising. Just passionate. Lizzie was mesmerised, although if she was being honest she couldn't only credit her interest to the topic under discussion.

'If you just think about things in a different way you can see where we were at certain times in our lives, and where we are now, by what we eat, drink, wear and by the adverts that we see around us...'

He really was very desirable. Lizzie was glad that tonight had been a G-string occasion. She always felt at her most seductive and unnervingly saucy when she was wearing one. Irrationally so, really. Until her second or third drink she usually just felt as if her knickers had ridden up and got stuck between the cheeks of her bottom.

'...most of it's subliminal at the time, but looking back it's all quite clear. Look at the minimalism of the late 1990s: less was more, everything was about stripping away the excesses, getting our autonomy and power back. Natural everything. Neutral plain colours. Cotton and cashmere, not nylon and polyester. In fact very little artificial anything—a reaction to the multicoloured, additive-laden 70s and 80s. Fashions change. Who in the late 1970s and 1980s would have thought that we'd be eating rocket salad...who even knew what rocket was...?'

Matt paused for effect and she snapped out of her daydream at once. Had he been talking about salad? Impossible. Bugger. Lizzie scolded herself. She really had to learn to pay attention when people strung more than two consecutive sentences together.

Not requiring a response to his rhetorical question, Matt continued unfazed, much to Lizzie's relief. From now on she would treat everything he said as a listening comprehension.

'You'd have dismissed it as faddish if anyone back then had suggested that we'd be drinking cranberry juice with vodka in bars—indeed, drinking cranberry juice in Britain at all, where cranberries have traditionally been teamed with turkey at this time of year. The world is becoming a smaller place. You only have to look in your kitchen cupboards: ginger, lemon grass, chilli, vanilla pods, couscous. But these new trends are only replacing the old. In the seventies it was frozen food. If you couldn't freeze it, it wasn't worth eating. In the late eighties it was microwaves and ultra-convenience. With our go-getting attitudes, the revolutions in micro-technology and generally higher standards of living why would we want to have spent any more than five or ten minutes cooking? In the nineties it was back to basics. Organic and fresh was best and cooking made a comeback, as did gardening. But fashions are left behind. They're superseded by new choices and new theories on the way we should live our lives. Who now can even remember what disk cameras and Noodle Doodles looked like? Who in the late 1990s would have even have considered wearing a brown and powder-blue acrylic tank top—unless, of course, they were doing the whole Jarvis Cocker retro thing? But then maybe I'm just bitter because powder-blue isn't my colour...it just doesn't do anything for my skin tone...'

Matt feigned camp and Lizzie laughed. This time she had been listening and, while she could no longer claim objectivity, it certainly was a positive departure from discussing football teams, gym attendance, holidays and other people's heartache.

'So is what you're saying that nothing happens by accident? We all choose to eat things, decorate our homes in a particular way, travel to certain places, because subliminally we've been told to?'

'Precisely.' Matt briefly wondered why it had taken him so long to say exactly that.

'Isn't that just a little bit frightening?'

'I suppose a little. But we're not all clones. Free will and independent spirit will always prevail—plus a natural rebellion against the norm, which will spin off new ideas for people like me... I mean look at this...' Matt held up his bottle '"Ice" beer. Colder? Maybe. Smoother? Maybe. Better? Maybe. And "Light beer". Less sugar and more alcohol? Or only because you wouldn't get guys asking for a Diet Budweiser?

'And to think there I was accusing you of just writing cheeseball slogans.'

Matt smiled, 'Well, to be fair, nine times out of ten I'll be poring over a computer screen as the client deadline approaches, desperately trying to come up with something innovative, witty, punchy and memorable. I'm not usually contributing to or capturing a moment in time. Shaping cultural history is for politicians and pop stars. And even they are just absorbing eclectic influences. It's pretty much impossible to have a totally new idea.'

Lizzie concentrated on draining the last of her beer from the bottle in what she hoped was possibly an attractive fashion. Matt used the moment to round up.

'Plus, I've been lucky. Doors have swung open at the right times and all that. Personally, it's been a bit lonely, but I'm not sure that you can have everything. Something has to give... Oh, God...Lizzie....are you OK?'

Lizzie nodded and blinked back a few tears as Matt reached over and gently rubbed her back. The dregs of her lager had frustratingly slipped down the wrong way and she'd been trying not to draw attention to it, but the more she had tried to disguise her discomfort the more she had felt her chest tightening. She'd been drowning in a mouthful. She coughed a few times, restoring a clear passage for air to reach her lungs, and did her best to smile and relax. Fucking hell. Thirty-two years old and she couldn't even swallow properly.

'Fine.' She rasped her response and closed her mouth just in time to stop a stray burp escaping noisily. 'Only choking.' She smiled at her Christmas cracker level of humour and tried to ignore the fact that she could still feel his hand on her back—even though it was holding his beer bottle now.

Matt grinned. 'I get the message. Lecture over.' He quickly snuck in a question, just in case Lizzie was thinking about using her near-death experience as an excuse to move on. 'What about you? How did you get into the whole agony aunt thing?'

Whenever Lizzie wasn't looking directly at him, he stole a glance at the whole picture. Even without his beer goggles on she would've been very attractive.

'Well, it wasn't exactly a planned career. Sure, like most girls under sixteen I pored over the problem pages in magazines at my desk at breaktime and between lessons, but I would have died of embarrassment if I'd had to say clitoris out loud, let alone to a total stranger on the radio in front of more than a million people.'

Matt laughed.

Lizzie could feel herself blushing under her foundation. Clitoris. Out loud. In conversation. With a man. A man that she found attractive. Nothing like building up her feminine mystique. Maybe she should issue him with a map to her G-spot while she was at it. It could only save time later. Honestly. She could have punched herself with frustration. She moved on quickly in a totally transparent attempt to change the subject.

'I did a degree in sociology but always wanted to get into journalism, and I started writing for a magazine when I left college. When I moved to *Out Loud*, problems became my thing. Then about nine months ago my editor there put me in touch with these guys and I developed some pilots for a new type of phone-in show. The rest, as they say, is history. I still do my page and a weekly column and I'm amazed at the number of letters, calls and e-mails I get every week. It's not like I have a perfect relationship track record...far from it.'

Lizzie stopped herself. She didn't want to go into her relationship history. Fortunately, despite the fact he was nodding assiduously, Matt seemed to have zoned out of the conversation.

So he hadn't been hanging on her every word? Hmm. But then again who was she to talk? Thanks to his tactical positioning on the sofa, Matt could see that Danny had returned to the bar and was now hovering dangerously close by, no doubt hoping to launch himself at Lizzie again and resume where they had left off. But Matt wasn't even going to let him try. When they'd sat down he'd promised to protect her and he was taking his new role as chief of security very seriously. It was an emergency, and so he suggested something he rarely enjoyed.

'Let's dance.'

Matt was up on his feet and Lizzie, designer heels forgotten, leapt up to join him. She loved dancing. It wasn't her greatest talent, but she was certainly an enthusiastic participant whether it was garage, disco, salsa or overly energetic rock 'n' roll. She'd watched The kids from *Fame*, *Footloose* and *Dirty Dancing* more times than she would care to admit, and as she'd aged had learnt to forget about being self-conscious and just allowed the rhythm to take over. There was something so very exhilarating about two people communicating through music. It didn't have to be over the top stuff. Just a few side steps or symmetrical arm movements as groups of people mirrored each other to bring them together. She didn't understand people who just stood at the side and watched.

Matt was inspired by Lizzie's ebullience on the dance floor. He was no Patrick Swayze, but here in the semi-darkness he was enjoying what was usually the worst part of any evening for him. Thankfully the thumping dance music was soon replaced by songs with words and a hint of a tune, and when they were both hot and tired, to their relief, the slow numbers kicked in. Matt pulled Lizzie in for a couple of close ones before she could think to protest, and to his delight halfway through the second song she relaxed, resting her head on his shoulder. He breathed deeply in an attempt to get his heart-rate down. He was sure that Lizzie must be able to hear the pounding in his chest and didn't want her to think that he was geriatrically unfit or that she had landed the over-excited teenage virgin at the school disco.

At one-thirty someone with a twisted sense of humour turned all the lights on, illuminating what, seconds earlier, had been a den of iniquity as brightly as an operating theatre. Fortunately Matt was insisting on staying with her until she found a cab and, despite her self-assured protestations of independence, Lizzie was delighted that he hadn't just wandered off when the music stopped.

They walked all the way to Trafalgar Square and then along the Strand until they reached the taxi queue now snaking across the cobbles and out of the gates at Charing Cross Station. Good old Brits. Drunk as everyone was, the queue was perfect.

By the time they finally reached the front Matt had decided that he'd share her cab. Lizzie wasn't sure whether this was chivalrous or lecherous. She certainly hadn't got coffee in mind, or waxed her bikini line in the last few months...but then it seemed that he really was just being friendly. Had she really lost her ability to give out the it's-all-right-if-you-kiss-me vibes? She looked across at her fellow passenger who was staring resolutely out of the window. She couldn't exactly ask him. Lizzie crossed her legs and sat back in the seat, hoping that tight cornering on the journey would send them sliding across the leather banquettes into each other.

Matt didn't know what he was doing. He knew he couldn't

have left her in the West End taxi-hunting on her own, and it had seemed silly to risk another twenty minutes in the cold when they could easily share hers. That was all he was doing. Right. But he hadn't had such a relaxed evening in one-to-one female company for years, and now he was feeling a frisson of excitement that he'd almost forgotten existed. He released his grip on the handle above the door and slipped back into his seat. Just at that moment Lizzie slid into the side of him as the driver took a corner Formula One style. He put his arm around her shoulder to steady her. And left it there.

As Lizzie directed the driver to her door Matt knew that, while he was still sailing on the crest of a lager wave, he really wanted to kiss her goodnight, and even with his rusty dating dial he knew that she wouldn't resist him. As the taxi slowed to a pant Matt gave the cabbie the postcode for his onward journey before sliding the interconnecting window closed and turning to face Lizzie who, to his amusement, was taking ages to gather her non-existent belongings together before opening the door.

Taking her hand, he leant forward to give her a goodbye peck on the cheek and, to his delight, Lizzie moved her mouth to meet his. Like a couple of love-struck teenagers they kissed. His synapses buzzed with the excitement that passed between them as he felt her lips touch his, just lingering enough to be meaningful. In a moment she was gone, and for a second he'd never wanted anything more than to still be with her.

Matt's mind was a mess as the driver pulled away from the kerb.

'Where next, mate? Well done. She was lovely.'

Lizzie had come down off her cloud by the time she'd unlocked the front door. She shouldn't have kissed him. True, she'd had a much better evening than she could have imagined, but he was a work colleague...sort of...and she'd had a lot to drink. Alcohol had diluted her inhibitions and now, sobering up at home, the self-justification process was starting in earnest. But no one was going to be having meetings with the advertising people until well into the New Year, by which time Matt might have forgotten all about it.

About what, exactly? They'd had a couple of beers, chatted, danced, chatted, and then, for about ten seconds, they'd kissed each other goodnight. If she'd been eighteen years old she would've just put it down as a good night out, so why, fourteen years later, was she torturing herself? Lizzie hated her carefully camouflaged romantic core. It caused nothing but trouble. That was why she'd made the decision to bow out of the relationship arena and focus on her career instead. Professionally she berated herself. What if he'd been hoping for a kiss and tell with a B-list—make that E-list—agony aunt? But then there wasn't exactly anything to kiss and tell about, was there? She was single, pissed, and at an office party. Nothing scandalous about that.

She wished that the gland responsible for providing her with this level of adrenaline would take a break. All these hypotheticals were in danger of giving her a headache. Life was all about taking opportunities and seizing the moment, and tonight that moment had been hers. In fact, if she was totally honest with herself, part of her wished she'd taken a bit more.

Lizzie performed her ablutions noisily, and even gargled a couple of times with some vintage Listerine that she found on a shelf, hoping that Clare would wake up for a debrief. Wide awake, Lizzie climbed into bed. How could she possibly sleep now?

Across London Matt looked out of his kitchen window as he poured himself another pint of water from the filter jug which she insisted was better for them. He was disconcertingly sober. For the first time in his life he had been unfaithful: to his wife, to himself and to Lizzie.

He should've said something. It might only have been a kiss, but in his mind it was already a whole lot more. His marriage might be dead, but why should she believe him? It was the oldest line in the book. Now it was rapidly approaching 3:00 a.m. on Saturday morning and he was about to creep into bed claiming to have lost all track of time at the party. Hopefully she wouldn't wake up. She was certainly unlikely to have missed him. If she had, it would be the first time in months. He picked up his glass and left the kitchen, confused.

chapter 2

Rachel rubbed her eyes and was appalled to feel that her incredibly expensive all-weather mascara was now crusty. As she swallowed and winced at the furry stale oral aftermath of her Shiraz Cabernet and Marlboro Lights session, fragments of her evening started to return to her memory. She must have drunk a lot to have been smoking. Enough to forget that she had given up last month. A token attempt to try and keep at least one of her vices under some sort of control. She cupped her hand and exhaled into it. Her breath smelt as bad as it tasted.

'Bollocks.'

Now she was talking to herself. Not a good sign. She fell back onto the cushions. It had only been a few drinks with the team after work, but, coupled with a long boozy client lunch earlier in the day, it had obviously got a little out of hand. Now that she had a sofa in her office this was becoming an all too frequent occurrence.

Almost dizzy with the effort, Rachel rummaged in her capacious bag for some breath-freshening gum, paracetamol and her mobile. She held the display close to her face while her eyes refocused to inspect the small screen. No missed calls and no messages. Relieved or disappointed? She wasn't sure. She could call and tell him that she was on her way, but phoning at this point would be tantamount to admitting she was in the wrong, not just at the office. Hopefully she'd manage to slip into bed undetected and be vague about the time of her return if he asked in the morning.

As she located her shoes, she shivered in the unfamiliar cold of the office. In two days she'd be here raising hell like she always did on a Monday morning when deadlines looked as if they weren't going to be met, and tomorrow she'd be back to tie up a few loose ends and do the real work that was near impossible to achieve while she was playing hard at project- ing the image of being in control.

Next week she would finally know whether she had won the account they'd all been working so hard for. She could already picture the banner headline in *Campaign*: 'Anti-drugs offen- sive taken on by Clifton Dexter Harrison', and her publicity shot alongside. It was high-profile, and a huge social concern, and once you'd made a name for yourself the industry didn't forget. The account director on the last AIDS awareness cam- paign was running his own agency now. This could be her big break. The culmination of all the late nights and early morn- ings of the last few years. She'd sacrificed everything for this moment.

Rachel felt a pang of remorse. She'd always had a selfish streak—single-minded, she preferred to call it. But she couldn't sit back and relax until she'd made a name for her- self. Rachel was a here-and-now girl. Moments were for seiz- ing and unwinding was for watches—all part of her 'take now and pay later' attitude to life. But this could be it—her very own meal ticket. Then she'd set about fixing her relationship. She was sure that with a bit of effort and a couple of surprise weekends away it could all be back to normal again. Rachel didn't do failure. Fingers crossed, she would make her New Year strategy the anti-drugs offensive followed by a quick-fire campaign to save her marriage.

The issue addressed, her mind returned to rest and now fo- cused on getting her some beauty sleep as soon as possible.

By waving her arms as she locked her office Rachel managed to trigger enough motion sensors to illuminate her exit route from the building, and successfully startled the security guard who she suspected must have managed to nod off against the cold marble wall of their smart reception area. She wondered how much they were paying him to sleep in the upright position.

The house was pitch-black and, jaw clenched to prevent her teeth chattering, she tiptoed up the stairs. As she stared into the dark of the bedroom she could see that the curtains were still open and the bed was still made. He wasn't back yet. Her concern was only momentary as her tired memory saw fit to remind her of a message she'd picked up when they'd left the bar. He had another Christmas party.

Relieved that she wasn't going to have to explain her late return, have sex or yet another conversation about nothing in particular, Rachel flicked the lights on. She cleansed and toned in record time and was dead to the world when her slightly smoked and pickled husband collapsed into bed beside her. The room was quiet as their breathing patterns united and they lay beside each other, together but apart.

chapter

3

George Michael and Andrew Ridgely were crooning away on the radio for the umpteenth December in a row. It never seemed to be their Last Christmas.

Lizzie was lying in bed, staring at the ceiling, waiting for the cacophony of mushy sentiment and sleigh bells to come to an end. It was Saturday morning. Five days before Christmas. No wonder so many people found the festive period depressing. The contrast with the high of the night before was almost too much. But the evening had surpassed all her expectations and now the weekend was just the same as it would have been whether or not she had kissed Matt. It just felt worse. And it certainly wasn't being helped by the hangover that was starting to roll in from somewhere behind her ears.

Clare must have been watching her from a hidden camera, as she chose this moment to wander in breezily with a cup of tea. As if she had just happened to be passing with a spare mug. Lizzie wondered how many times she had walked past her door in the last couple of hours, desperate for some sign of life.

'Morning. How was last night, then?'

'Great...'

It was a unique delivery. Lizzie's voice rumbled and squeaked into action and her first syllable came out grudgingly. Her tones were definitely less dulcet than normal, and she could only just hear what she was saying. She must have done more shouting in smoky atmospheres than she had realised. She coughed a couple of times in an attempt to restore her more familiar range before continuing.

'...a lot of fun, actually...' Her voice was a unique tribute to Eartha Kitt.

'Really?' Clare's voice was laced with expectation. Eager for details, she perched on the edge of Lizzie's bed just as her flatmate leapt to her feet, impressively grabbing her towel from the chair in one single movement.

'I'll fill you in after my shower.'

Lizzie surprised herself with the buoyancy of her tone, especially as her whole body was wobbling with the effort of reaching a vertical position. Heart beating faster than normal, she half-walked, half-skipped to the bathroom just as Macy Gray's 'Winter Wonderland' replaced Wham. She didn't know why she hadn't just confessed there and then. For some totally irrational reason she was suddenly embarrassed at her behaviour.

She was standing on the bath mat drying herself when Clare knocked.

'For goodness' sake. You never get up after ten on a Saturday. I've been pacing up and down in the kitchen, cleaning surfaces, just waiting for you to wake up—and then you decide to have a shower first. Since when have you been so obsessive about your cleanliness? Unless, of course, you're washing a man right out of your hair...'

Lizzie refused to be goaded into a confession. All in good time. She swapped her now damp towel for her bathrobe, and as she opened the door Clare practically fell into the room. She must have been leaning right up against it.

'Well, I spoke to all the bosses without saying anything incriminating, boogied the night away with Ben and the team, drank lots of alcohol and then got stuck in the corner with Danny Vincent—possibly the most self-centred, boring, slimy drive-time DJ in the history of broadcasting. It was terrible. To make matters worse my head feels too heavy for my body, and right now I'm not sure whether I'm going to make it through the next few hours without being sick...' Lizzie didn't remember being exceptionally drunk at any stage of the evening, but her body was telling a different story. 'Maybe I'm coming down with something...'

'Poor you...' Clare empathised fervently.

This was why, Lizzie mused, she was her best friend.

'...but I think you'll find it's just a good old-fashioned hangover. So, did he make a move?'

Lizzie shuddered at the thought of those whiter than white teeth and tighter than tight trousers.

'No. Thankfully, just when I thought there was no way out, I was rescued by a different bloke who had spotted my predicament from the bar.'

'I see.'

Lizzie was being so pseudo-offhand that Clare now knew there was a whole lot more to this than she was being told at the moment. This was typical Ford behaviour. Whenever Lizzie had anything interesting to divulge she just tossed it in ever so casually at the point in the conversation where you had as good as stopped listening. Clare decided to play it cool for now. She knew from experience that this coy moment couldn't last long. Lizzie meanwhile, freshly energised by her shower, was just burbling on.

'Anyway, just the usual, really. Lots of drinking, chatting and dancing, and then I got a taxi home. It must have been nearly 2:00 a.m. when we finally found one.'

'We!' Clare picked up on the discrepancy at once. Ha! Lizzie had let her guard down. Such a careless mistake. Amateurish, in fact.

Lizzie could have kicked herself. It had all been going so well. But Clare was her best friend. She was entitled to the full story—and besides, it wouldn't feel real if Clare didn't know. Yet now she felt sheepish. Since her divorce Clare had been so generally anti-men that Lizzie felt somehow she had let the side down.

'OK. So I shared a cab with him.' Lizzie looked at her feet awkwardly.

'With...'

The intensity of Clare's stare was currently boring a hole in the side of her head. Lizzie felt sure that Clare would be able to bend spoons if she put her mind to it.

'With Matt.' Lizzie looked up. She was going to take this on the chin. She had nothing to be ashamed of. It wasn't as if she met people every weekend. In fact she couldn't remember the last time...

'The guy who rescued you from the clutches of the delightful Danny?' Clare grinned at her use of alliteration, just in case Lizzie had missed it.

'Yeah.'

'You shared a cab all the way to Putney? Does he live round here, then?'

Lizzie hesitated as she realised that she had no idea where he lived. She vaguely remembered Matt telling the driver where to go next, and she even remembered listening, but she had no recollection of what he'd said. Her mind had quite clearly been on other things.

'I'm not sure...I got out of the cab first.'

'So the taxi didn't terminate here, then?'

Clare was now striding back and forth across the landing, casting a cursory glance at Lizzie from time to time. Lizzie attributed this increasingly irritating habit to the surfeit of dog-eared John Grisham novels on their bookshelves and one viewing too many of *A Few Good Men*, which seemed to be playing on a loop on one of their digital channels.

Clare adopted her best quasi legal tone.

'Miss Ford, in the early hours of Saturday December twentieth did you, or did you not, bring a Mr Matt to 56 Oxford Road for a night of wild abandon?'

Lizzie was stalling. Nothing like building nothing into something. One kiss had become headline news in south-west London. They really had to get out more.

'It's a simple enough question. Did you bring a man back to our apartment last night? Yes? Or no?'

Apartment. She'd definitely been reading another American legal thriller.

'No.' All of a sudden Lizzie was feeling very self-conscious and very naked underneath her bathrobe.

'But at any point on the night in question did you engage in the activity of kissing? Were salivary juices exchanged?'

Clare certainly knew how to make an ostensibly romantic moment seem very clinical. But the I-know-I'm-onto-some-thing look now plastered all over on Clare's face was making Lizzie laugh. She stopped fudging her answers and, between giggles, confessed.

'Yes. Guilty as charged. We kissed in the cab. He left. Happy?'

Lizzie didn't want to get on to the fact that she hadn't got his number and didn't know when, or even if, she would be seeing him again or, more interestingly, the fact that she knew she'd quite like to. Clare was bound to say something dis-paraging, plus it always seemed like tempting fate. It was time to move this conversation on. Lizzie was determined to develop her enigmatic side, and now was as good a time as any—plus, once she admitted that she liked someone things always seemed to go awry. However humorous Clare thought she was being, this was Lizzie's life they were mocking, even if right now there was more material than normal.

'I suppose I'd better get on with my day...'

Clare looked at her watch. 'Your afternoon...'

'Afternoon, then... God, you can be pedantic.'

'Takes one to know one. You've taught me everything I know. Anyway, now you're up I must just pop to the shops. Do you need anything? I shouldn't be long but I don't have to be at the restaurant until five...' Clare waited for Lizzie to process the information. If she knew Lizzie as well as she thought she did, she'd offer to cook them some lunch. She could almost hear the cogs grinding into action.

'Right... Why don't I cook us some lunch? Take advantage of the fact that we're both in the flat at the same time. Novel, I know. Spaghetti Bolognese OK for you?'

Bingo. Clare loved the way that Lizzie's mind always

worked the same way. It was one of the most male things about her personality.

'Great. Is two o'clock too late for you?'

'Perfect. I'm sure I can manage on tea and toast until then.'

'Bit peckish, are you? Was your tongue sarnie not very filling?'

Lizzie was already on her way to her room. Thanks to Clare, though, she was smiling.

Clean, dressed, and well on her way to physical and emotional recovery, Lizzie headed down to her study. She wanted to at least start work before lunch, so that it would be easier to return to later, when the call of the shops would be strongest. Surrounded by her post, she switched on her computer and then, to order her thoughts, made one of her famous 'to do' lists. Scaring herself into action, she started by printing off her e-mails and adding them to the letters pile for immediate attention.

Her concentration was coming and going in waves but, focusing on the screen in front of her, she forced herself to keep typing. She had almost succeeded in blocking out her surroundings when the phone rang. The shrill electronic bleat cut through the silence and nearly prompted an instant coronary. Lizzie just stared at it. Could it be?

Caught up in the moment, she overlooked the fact that she hadn't given him her home phone number, that she was ex-directory, and that there was no one in the office that morning to give it to him and so, after flicking her hair back with her hand, she answered in a semi-flirtatious fashion.

'Heylo?'

'Liz, it's me...'

'Me' being Clare. Lizzie did her best not to actually sound disappointed.

'Clare.'

'I'm in Waitrose. Do you need me to pick up the stuff for our lunch?'

'Yup, that would be great...' In her hungover state Lizzie had completely forgotten about the whole needing ingredients in order to cook lunch thing. Thank goodness one of them was living in the real world today. 'The usual...and don't forget—'

Clare interrupted her. 'Mushrooms and red peppers. I know.'

'Thanks...' Clare really was the perfect flatmate at times. 'And a couple of tins of chopped tomatoes.'

'No problem. See you in a bit.'

'Bye.'

But Clare, anxious not to waste even a few seconds of her free call time, had already gone.

Lizzie was rereading her notes in an attempt to recall her train of thought when the phone rang for a second time. Again she leant back in her chair, ran her fingers through her hair, and, ever so casually, slightly slurred her greeting.

'Heylo?'

'Liz, it's Mum. Can't be long. I'm on the mobile in the Sainsbury's car park.'

'OK.' What was this? The phone a friend from a supermarket half-hour?

'I hope I haven't interrupted anything...'

Chance would be a fine thing. 'It's fine, Mum. I'm working, but...'

'On a Saturday? You are conscientious.'

A compliment. Only, the way she said it, almost an accusation.

'What do you need?' Lizzie could feel herself snapping without meaning to and pulled herself up. She'd always believed what goes around comes around, and didn't want to jeopardise any chance of her and Matt getting together in the not too distant future by upsetting her mother now. It was perfectly clear female reasoning.

'That Thai curry you were telling me about...'

'Mmm...'

'What was the fresh herb you needed?'

'Coriander. Lots of it. Ignore the recipe and put loads in. If you buy too much you can always freeze it.'

'Thanks, darling. It's just I left the list at home.'

'No problem.'

'Listen, must go. This phone's giving me a headache. I'll call you soon. We haven't had a proper chat in ages.'

'OK. Speak to you later.'

'Bye.'

Lizzie shouldn't be allowed to cook when she was feeling hungry. While she might not be about to admit it, this mountain of pasta was comfort food. Clare knew her cravings for spaghetti, shepherd's pie and lasagne all came on days when Lizzie was feeling vulnerable. It was as if the food of her youth represented a surrender of her adulthood. When things got really bad, butterscotch and chocolate Angel Delight would follow for dessert.

Clare tactfully kept the conversation away from parties and instead talked weekend turnover tactics. Union Jack's was a restaurant that thrived on word of mouth. Its modern British cuisine was raved about by its regulars, but they were still a long way off becoming a household name or selling a tie-in cookbook. A few *Evening Standard* recommendations had helped to put it on the map, and occasional visits by celebrity local residents meant that other Londoners were happier to go out of their way just on the off-chance that they might eat alongside someone they had seen on TV or an album cover, but the challenge was to fill the place at weekends when, Clare imagined, most of their patrons visited friends in the country, jetted off for glamorous weekends or entertained in their interior designed, feng-shuied living spaces in fashionable West London.

They were strategising hard when the doorbell rang. Clare was mid-mouthful, so Lizzie drew the short straw. At 3:00 p.m. on a Saturday it could only be the tea towel and oven glove salesman, or possibly the Putney branch of Jehovah's Witnesses. Lizzie whooped as she looked at the screen integral to their state-of-the-art intercom—essential security kit for two women living on their own and a sound investment made after being taken in by the persuasive sales patter of a not unattractive salesman at the Ideal Home Exhibition. This way they could hide from persistent exes, uninvited relatives and the aforementioned tea towel sellers without passing up any opportunities to flirt with cute delivery men or missing out on bona fide guests.

The cause of Lizzie's excitement was a man on the doorstep. A least she thought she could see someone behind the huge bow and...what was it? Frustratingly, even with her eyeball almost resting on the screen, she couldn't quite see. She took the stairs two at a time, arriving back in record time clutching a large wicker basket laden with all things wicked. Moist chocolate brownies, assorted mini-muffins and huge soft cookies were piled high on gingham napkins. Heart racing—along, Lizzie hoped, with her metabolic rate—she inhaled a couple of mouth-watering samples before tearing off the accompanying card.

'Well...?' Clare joined her on the sofa, licking her fingers as she tucked in. She couldn't believe that Lizzie hadn't read the card downstairs. This demonstration of will-power was very out of character. 'What does it say?' Clare leant up against her shoulder so that she could read the message simultaneously. Lizzie was being painfully slow and insisting on opening the envelope carefully so as not to tear it.

All the card said was 'Call me,' followed by two phone numbers. An 0207 number and a line of digits with more eights and sevens in it than were healthy. It looked long and confusing enough to be a mobile number.

Lizzie was beaming, and reprimanded herself silently for having doubted him earlier. How long should she wait before she called? As if she could read her mind, Clare decided to ask her outright.

'So when are you going to call?'

Clare was scraping their now abandoned lunch into the bin. They had both already eaten more than enough to exceed their total recommended calorie intake until tomorrow lunchtime.

'Mmm. In an hour or so?' Lizzie feigned nonchalance. She wasn't sure what was wrong with straight away, but she knew that Clare saw every man as a recipe for disaster. Lizzie, on the other hand, couldn't help being an eternal optimist. One day she hoped to be rewarded for her dedication to an often disappointing cause.

'So keen. You are, of course, assuming that they're from Matt.'

'Well, when Mum wants me to call she tends to use the phone rather than sending an edible carrier pigeon.'

'Maybe they're from Drive-Time Danny.'

Lizzie was hit by an instant wave of nausea totally unrelated to the amount of sugar she had just ingested, and for a few seconds her perfect moment evaporated. But Danny probably didn't think he had to send anything to anyone—except perhaps a signed photo of himself. They had to be from Matt. Had to be.

Clare hadn't meant to sound negative. And she had to admit sending cookies, muffins and brownies was a sweet—and sure-fire—way to Lizzie's duvet.

'I suppose there's no harm in giving him a call this afternoon...' Clare knew that Lizzie would do whatever she wanted to, but by giving Lizzie her endorsement she hoped she would be seen in a less negative, spoil-sporty light. She couldn't help it if she had been let down one time too many. 'Why don't I make us a cup of coffee and then you can ring him? Or, if you'd rather wait until I go to work, I'll be out of here by four-thirty.'

Lizzie had drained her mug long before Clare, and now had cold feet. Clare had been teaching her to live life without her heart on her sleeve and Lizzie admired her style. She was now inclined to leave it until Monday, but then she might have missed the moment altogether, and she couldn't honestly see herself doing any work until she had got this out of the way. Besides, it was what she told her readers all the time. Be yourself and don't play relationship games, because unless both parties know the rules you'll lose every time.

Right. Time for her to take some of her own advice. She picked up their walkabout phone, dialling and wandering simultaneously, and tried the 0207 number first. It went straight to answer-phone. The voice on the message didn't really sound like the one she remembered from last night, but it didn't sound like Danny either. She left her name and number before hanging up, just in case it wasn't his voicemail at all.

As she dialled the mobile number she prayed that the scribe at Muffin HQ wasn't dyslexic or innumerate. All her nerves needed now was for this to be a wrong number. With each ring her heart edged a little bit closer to her mouth, until finally the phone rang out, irritatingly diverting to voicemail.

'Hi, you've got through to Matt Baker...'

Lizzie could have jumped for joy at the relief that the delivery had definitely been from the right man.

'...I'm sorry I can't take your call right now, but please leave your name and number and I'll get back to you as soon as I can.'

Lizzie hung up and held the phone to her chest. What should she say? After a few moments of pacing she decided less was more and rang back, obediently leaving her name and number but no message. Now she would have to make sure that her phone was free to ring by not using it.

When it rang five minutes later both Lizzie and Clare nearly fell off the sofa. After a great deal of arm-waving on Lizzie's part Clare answered it. Lizzie knew her behaviour was pure fifteen-year-old. Of course it wouldn't be Matt. It was far too soon.

'Annie. Hi. Yes, thanks...'

Her mother. Again.

'I'll just get her for you... Don't keep her too long...' Clare smiled mischievously '...only she's waiting for an important call. I know... I know...'

What did she know?

OK. Yes, I'll tell her. Fine. Thanks. Hope to see you soon. Right. Bye for now.'

Whose mother was she anyway?

'She says you can call her later. Apparently you arranged to have a chat?'

Lizzie rolled her eyes. 'Hardly. I just said we'd speak later. You know—Some Time Later, not Within Three Hours.' Her mother still didn't understand that some adult children didn't speak to their parents several times a week, a day or an afternoon. But Lizzie knew she got lonely on her own, especially at weekends.

Clare had barely put the phone down on the sofa next to her before it rang again.

'Oh, well, maybe she's forgotten something...' Clare chucked the receiver, still ringing, at her flatmate. 'She's your mother...and I've got to get ready.'

'Yup?'

'Lizzie?'

Damn... She should have known. The one time today she hadn't answered the phone with her 'heylo' hair-flick and it was him. Bloody typical.

'Matt! Hi! Thanks so much for my food parcel. It's wonderful.'

Too effusive? But Lizzie had never really been able to do 'aloof', and she wasn't about to start now. She leapt to her feet, instinctively wandering out of earshot to her bedroom.

Clare turned the radio down and occupied herself with silent chores, listening out for any nuggets of information that might waft down the stairs. She knew she shouldn't be eavesdropping, but she and Lizzie didn't do the secrets thing and hearing it first hand would only save time later. As Clare strained to hear she was only managing to pick up the odd word, so she crept a bit closer to the stairwell which brought her instant rewards.

'...oh, right... Are you feeling better...? Great... I know...I know. There seems to be a lot of it about.'

A lot of what? Clare wondered to herself. Syphilis? Flu? Office-party-related shagging? Now Lizzie was laughing. Now more talking. Clare paid closer attention.

'Work in the morning...on a Sunday? Poor you. Mmm... yes...I see what you mean. Mind you, I've only got a hot date with my post bag...wild, crazy thing that I am.'

Clare balked. Sympathy with a hint of empathy. Lizzie was spiralling into the romantic quagmire as usual. She never was quite as hard to get as you would think from reading her column.

'Lunch tomorrow? OK... Yup... Better than OK—great.

Where shall we meet? ...don't mind...I eat everything...usually all at the same time...' Lizzie laughed out loud again.

Clare smiled at Lizzie's 'joke'. Matt might think she was being witty and spontaneous, but if he stuck around for long enough he would discover that it was one of Lizzie's standard lines.

'OK. Perfect. See you at 1:00 p.m. Bye.'

Clare returned to the kitchen as quickly as she could without actually running, and faded the radio up while clattering pans together in the sink. She busied herself with scrubbing the Bolognese pan and waited for Lizzie to report back.

Lizzie rang off and would have flick-flacked to her study had she ever got higher than the shoulder-stand BAGA level of gymnastics. Instead she whistled her way there, and happily immersed herself in work.

Clare was happy for her. Just as long as Matt wasn't going to let her down. The trouble was, despite the hundreds of letters she received each week alerting her to the contrary, Lizzie did have a tendency to look for the best in people. With a failed marriage behind her, Clare was more cynical. When your perfect husband is unfaithful six months after he says 'I do' it affects your perspective. Her rose-coloured spectacles definitely had a darker tint than most.

chapter 4

Thump... Thump... Thump...

Her pulse was currently reverberating around the inside of her cranium in Surround Sound. Her joints were aching and her eyeballs were hot and dry in their sockets. It wasn't a hangover. That meant only one thing...but she couldn't be ill. In thirteen years of schooling she'd only been absent for a handful of days, postponing any ailments for the lengthy holidays when she wouldn't be missing out or overtaken by any of her classmates. She knew she was fiercely competitive—whether it was careers, gym attendance or just a Christmas game of Monopoly. It was in her DNA. As she struggled to the bathroom in an attempt to begin her daily routine and kickstart herself into action Rachel knew that today she would be forced to admit that she was human. It was a grand admission.

At least it was a Saturday. Work could wait twenty-four hours. They wouldn't have official confirmation until Monday, but she was sure they'd won the account. Rachel smiled into the mirrored cabinet above the washbasin as she imagined telling the partners. She'd be walking on air.

It now appeared that all that air was in her eyelids; she'd

never seen them looking quite so puffy. A quick prod of her neck and underarm area confirmed that her glands were up, and after sticking out her tongue and making the traditional self-diagnostic 'aaaaah' noise she searched the shelves for suitable drugs. Adding a couple of soluble aspirin to a glass of tepid basin tap water, she weakly swooshed the water round in the hope that the resultant whirlpool effect would speed up the fizzing process. It might only be 9:30 a.m. but the day already felt as if it was slipping away.

Rachel stared into the mirror, pawing in disbelief at the pallor which must have descended in the dead of night—along with the contrasting purple shadows which stretched under her eyes and shaded the sides of her nose. As she downed the grey aspirin suspension she grimaced at the nostalgic familiarity of the bitter bitty aftertaste. From the sad day that she had out-grown Calpol, aspirin had always been administered by her mother at the first hint of a temperature. Rachel shuffled back to bed and, teeth now chattering, crawled under the duvet, her breathing shallow to conserve heat.

She hadn't had a sick day for at least a year, and had been working six-day weeks for almost as long. She simply didn't do colds and minor afflictions. At least she was alone, free to doze in front of the television without interruptions. Her husband had left earlier, to tidy some things up in his office, and she knew where to find him—not that she did the needy wife thing very often. It wasn't her style—although she did wonder whether he might prefer it if she was a little bit ditsy and less competent occasionally. This was the downside to a day in bed: too much time to think—and there was plenty in her personal life that merited attention. But she'd managed to dodge her problems for months, and she certainly didn't want to face up to them when she was feeling as shitty as this.

After channel-surfing for over an hour, Rachel knew she must be seriously ill. Twenty minutes of morning television was usually enough to persuade even the most apathetic couch potato to rise from the cushions and do something with their life other than fantasise about remodelling their neighbour's garden. Exhausted, she finally succumbed to unconsciousness, and when she next opened her eyes her body was on fire. Feverish strands of hair stuck to her scalp and her cheeks almost stung with the intensity.

Momentarily disorientated, she soon noticed a note on the floor. She craned her neck in search of the alarm clock: 14:07. Which day and which year she couldn't be sure. Her brain was definitely lagging behind at the moment.

> *Rach*
> *Didn't want to wake you.*
> *Thought these might help while away the afternoon. You might as well celebrate your temperature with an overdose of trash, fashion and recipes!*
> *Off to Banbury to brainstorm with a client. Back later. You can get me on the mobile if you need me.*

Beside the bed there was now a pile of magazines and a bottle of his cure-all—Lucozade. In all the years they'd been together she'd never once professed to like it, but she knew it was the thought that counted. Ironically, she didn't appear to have the strength to open the bottle. It promised to be an energy provider—but only if you could get past the plastic seal.

Rachel's palms were ribbed with the pattern on the cap when she finally heard the fizz and collapsed back into the pillows. Pathetically she sipped at the orange sticky solution and wrinkled her nose as she dramatically swallowed each mouthful as if it were her last. While she waited for the sugar to pervade her bloodstream she half-dozed while her mind wandered. He'd always been the thoughtful one, and she was always too busy to notice. Maybe she should book them a surprise holiday somewhere glamorous.

Rachel closed her eyes. She could do with a tan, and that feeling of the sun warming her skin as the sea breeze whipped over her bare tummy...

She'd barely seen him recently. Just the familiar shape of his back as she crawled into bed and the routine noises of his exercise bike, shower and toast ritual every morning. She hid behind her eyelids until he left for work at seven—that way she could focus on her day without having to make interested conversation while he brushed his teeth. She did love him in her own way, even if she had trouble demonstrating it.

Rachel pulled a face. The thought of physical intimacy was a total turn-off. She just had too much on her mind. Thank God she was married. At least there wasn't pressure to be out there sleeping around and regaling the team with tales of random sex in unusual places. But there had been a time when they'd made love whenever their paths had crossed, day or night. Now they barely made cups of tea for each other.

In her fluey haze Rachel suddenly became preoccupied with the fact that he'd made it all the way to her side of the bed while she was asleep. In theory someone could have broken in and stolen everything from around her before pumping her full of bullets and she wouldn't even have woken up. She really should stop watching *Crimewatch*. She'd always been terrified of being burgled when she was in the house, and this quality thinking time wasn't helping. In a minute she'd have to get up and check the house for unlocked windows just in case. In a minute.

As another chill spread through her bones Rachel snuggled down in her now sweaty, fever-ridden T-shirt. Sport seemed to be dominating the television, and she turned it off assertively. Somehow her head couldn't cope with the combined noise and bright light from the screen any more. Even on the lowest volume setting it felt as if everyone was shouting. Rachel realised that this could be turning into a whole weekend in bed. If anything she was feeling worse, not better. Just as long as she was back in the office on Monday morning... She might even manage a couple of hours tomorrow if she was feeling a little less wobbly...

Rachel flicked through the selection of magazines. This was a rare treat. She never actually had time to read the ones lying around the office, and they were only really there to monitor rival campaigns. She was impressed with his choice. Some of her favourite titles plus a selection of the newer British shelf-fillers. The fashion pages had always been one of

Rachel's must-read sections of a magazine, but as she leafed through next season's essentials she observed that the models seemed to have got younger and thinner since she'd last looked... Thirty-six next birthday, yet it only seemed like yesterday that she had been celebrating her twenty-fifth. Now she was sounding old. She was starting to think things that she had heard her mother say years ago.

Rachel read the copy printed alongside the pictures. It would be far more useful for the reader if they could be just a fraction more honest: Cristalle—it was all about the name; you just didn't get catwalk models called Joanna or Jane—wears a trench coat that you will never be able to afford and that will never look this good on you, probably because you won't wear it over your best underwear to nip to the supermarket. Gypselle has been airbrushed to look good in that bikini. Petra pouts for Peckham in an outfit worth the GNP of a small developing country...

Half an hour of ludicrous fashion suggestions, a few potential new looks, an innovative way to apply eyeshadow and several irrelevant horoscopes later, Rachel found herself reading a problem page. They'd always been the most interesting part of a magazine when she'd been at school. Educational, voyeuristic and at times aspirational. All the girls had pored over the pages and learnt a great deal about G-spots, blow jobs and old wives' tales—all stuff they'd claimed to have known about years before as they'd committed the information to memory before hurriedly stuffing the magazines into their desks at the first glimpse of a member of staff on the horizon.

Over twenty years later Rachel was still gripped. It appeared that agony aunts had come on leaps and bounds. Normal, humorous, down-to-earth and practical advice. Not evangelical or hypothetical. She squinted at the photo. This one wasn't unattractive either, and, at a guess, was about her age. Rachel digested the page and accompanying column in minutes, before sitting back on the pillows. She didn't need to pay a shrink to tell her that the reason she was so interested in other people's problems was because she had several of her own.

For all her denial and self-justification, Rachel knew that

every way you looked at it she was taking him for granted. But she simply didn't have the energy to spoil him at the moment. She'd read the marriage repair articles, she knew it wasn't about grand gestures but just about doing things together, but time was the one commodity that she couldn't spare and it was impossible to fit a weekend away into a Sunday afternoon.

She was sure that in a few weeks things would calm down at work—but wasn't that what she'd said in July? And now it was December. And if she was doing a bit more taking than giving at the moment surely she could make it up to him in the long term...wasn't that what this lifelong partnership deal was all about? He'd tried to get them to 'talk'. He'd said she didn't listen. That everything was always on her terms. They'd laughed about that. But what if he'd given up?

Rachel shook her head. He adored her. Everyone said so. He'd always run to his work when things weren't going well. She'd taught him to. Besides, if it kept him occupied what was the harm? At least if he was busy she didn't feel quite as guilty.

Part of the problem was her lack of an available sounding board. Her mother would tell her to reassess her priorities, but then her mum could single-handedly set women's emancipation back one hundred years in one afternoon with her traditional take on married life. Rachel knew she didn't approve of her daughter's lifestyle. And she adored her son-in-law. Their friends all saw them as some sort of golden couple and outsiders saw a good-looking, high-earning, well-dressed couple—people will excuse almost anything if you are aesthetically pleasing—out there getting what they wanted from life. It was a masterful deception. Rachel knew that she should swallow her pride and well-disguised insecurity streak and just call one of her older mates, but she couldn't help but see it as a weakness that she couldn't cope.

It must have been a combination of these reasons, coupled with her abnormally high temperature and a strange heaven-sent force, that drove Rachel to do something that she had never thought she would ever do. Taking the 'Ask Lizzie' column to her study, she wrapped herself in a blanket and flicked on her computer. It was as if an alien force had entered her body. She half expected Mulder and Scully to appear shouting in the doorway, just as it was too late to save her, but something compelled her to sit down at her computer and type out a letter.

It flooded onto the page. Rachel couldn't get the sentences out fast enough. Seeing the words on the screen was cathartic, and much less expensive than hiring a therapist, and somehow it was a relief not to have to say any of it out loud. She could admit to herself that she was a bit of a selfish, self-centred control freak with workaholic tendencies who had taken her husband for granted via a keyboard, but actually vocalising it would be a whole different ballgame.

One long, convoluted paragraph later, Rachel looked up. There it was—her life in black and white. She added a few commas and full stops before signing it without thinking, then deleted her name and, remembering the problem page etiquette of her youth, typed 'Desperate Matt Dillon fan, London'. Smiling, Rachel replaced the pseudonym with the more credible 'Name and Address Withheld' and pressed print quickly, before she lost her nerve.

Deleting the document from her hard drive, she held the only hard copy above the wastepaper basket for a few moments, resisting the urge to scrunch it into a ball, instead folding it and putting it in a self-seal envelope. She hadn't enclosed her address. She didn't really want or need an answer. But by sharing everything with a total stranger at least now she felt she'd been proactive. She addressed the envelope and slipped it into her briefcase. Maybe she'd post it. Then again she could always shred it tomorrow at the office if she changed her mind.

As she clambered back into bed Rachel closed her eyes and promised herself that she would make more of an effort. Five years of marriage were worth fighting for. She was far too young to be a divorcee. These agony aunts are fantastic, she mused. She felt tons better already.

chapter 5

Sunday morning dawned a little earlier than usual at 56 Oxford Road. Lizzie had been wide awake for a good half-hour, pinching and tensing various body parts and wondering whether it was physiologically possible that she had put on a visible amount of muffin-related weight since Friday night. If she concentrated hard she was sure she could feel a spot on her nose. Perfect timing. A first-date outbreak. She resisted the overwhelming urge to wipe her t-zone on the duvet cover and finally conceded that more sleep was out of the question. Time wasn't going to tick by any slower if she got up.

Soon Lizzie was languishing in her second bath in twelve hours. Last night's had promised to detoxify her and this morning's foaming oil was supposed to be sensual, although it smelt more like a melted down throat lozenge than an aphrodisiac to Lizzie. Maybe that was where she'd been going wrong all these years.

A strange transformation was taking place. Over the last couple of years, via a gradual process of attrition, Clare had introduced a new dimension to Lizzie's cleansing ritual. A quick splash with soap and water had been outlawed, and while at first she had complained about the complexity and expense of it all, Lizzie now secretly enjoyed her ablutions. Her brother might have taught her how to spit bathwater a very long way, but he hadn't given her the inside track on exfoliation and soap-free cleansers. Thanks to Clare, Lizzie now had a beauty 'routine' of sorts.

Fifteen minutes ago she had decided to administer an amateur mini-facial to her over-cleansed pores in preparation for lunch. Only now, reading the small print on the back of the tube, it appeared she needed a muslin cloth. But where on earth did you get a muslin cloth before eleven on a Sunday? And what did you do with it the rest of the time? Her bathing idyll shattered, she hurriedly washed the mask into the bathwater and pulled the plug.

Once safely returned to dry land, she inspected her shins slowly to check she hadn't missed any hairs on her earlier shaving spree while debating what to wear. At least if you met someone after work there was only so much you could do in a maximum of five minutes with mascara, a hairbrush and a hand towel in the Ladies'. Sunday lunch usually called for the 'girl next door' look, but this was proving difficult to plan as she didn't know where Matt lived or where they were going. As Lizzie moisturised all over she couldn't help wondering whether this was all a waste of time. The more effort she made, the more disappointing the date usually turned out to be. But the pampering was for herself. Honest.

Back in her bedroom, Lizzie stood in front of her chest of drawers, the towel tied round her waist gradually loosening itself, forcing her to gyrate her hips slowly as if trying to keep an invisible hoop aloft. Clare must have thought this was some sort of pre-date limbering up process when she chose that moment to bring Lizzie yet another cup of tea. Maybe it was a thinly disguised attempt at sabotage. Lizzie was sure that she had read somewhere that tea was bad for cellulite. The towel finally fell to the floor.

'Great, Liz, he'll love it. The nude look is really in this year. You might think about a few accessories though.'

Lizzie reclaimed the damp cold towel and tied it firmly

round her body, using her armpits to clamp it in place before taking her tea from Clare.

'Ha-ha...' A slight edge of panic crept into her voice as she just stared into the open drawer. It might as well have been empty for all the inspiration its contents were currently emitting. 'What on earth am I going to wear?'

'Why don't you start with underwear?' Clare climbed into Lizzie's bed to watch her getting ready. She'd given up on dating. She didn't want to have to think about putting a loo seat down when she stumbled to the bathroom during the night, and her days of removing pubic hair embedded in the soap because Mr Shag didn't believe in using a sponge were over. But if Lizzie was still determined to give men the benefit of the doubt then at least Clare could experience the first date build-up vicariously, and of course she was there to give Lizzie all the sartorial and moral support she needed.

He could do the justification. The fact he was entitled to a little bit of happiness. The fact he wasn't having what most people would call a relationship with his wife these days. The fact that he'd found someone to have some fun with. The problem was that, whether it was in name only or not, he was married. Fact. No matter which angle you approached the situation from, he only came out of it one way. As a two-timing, unfaithful lowlife.

It may be a cliché, but Lizzie really was different. And when he'd woken up yesterday he'd felt fresh for the first time in months. He'd walked round London with his eyes wide open, invigorated by the smells of life and the sounds of the capital. Everything appeared to have more colour. Now he was sounding like some sort of love-struck teenager in a creative writing class. There really was no hope.

Matt knew he was being selfish, but being fair hadn't worked that well for him so far. It wasn't that he resented his wife's success, her hours or her focus. Quite the reverse. He'd never done needy. And he'd been so proud of her. Objectively, he still was. He wouldn't care if they barely saw each other if, when they did, it was special. Now it wasn't even mediocre.

And she wasn't prepared to try. That was the problem. One-way traffic. Their relationship wouldn't have passed even the most relaxed quality control.

Yet, even with all the excuses, devious just wasn't his style. He was a nice guy, not some Lothario, and frustratingly he seemed to be at the mercy of his principles which apparently weren't interested in keeping a low profile. He was going to tell Lizzie over lunch. She was an agony aunt; she knew life wasn't perfect. He'd just have to trust her to understand. And hope she didn't run a mile.

By the time the doorbell rang at nine minutes past one Lizzie had been pretending to read a magazine on the sofa for the last twenty minutes, but not a word had sunk in. Instead it appeared that the glossy pages were simply reflecting her nerves straight back at her. She didn't know what she was worrying about, and it had been so long since she'd last been on an official 'date' that she couldn't remember whether she'd always felt like this.

Clare had finally—and thankfully—gone to work just over an hour ago, but that had left Lizzie with nothing to do except sit, sit, sit, check her appearance in the mirror and then go to the loo again. Her clothes said relaxed and weekend but not scruffy, and she'd put enough effort into her accessories and eye make-up to signify effort without trying too hard. At least she was waiting at home and not pacing up and down in the cold, round the corner from where she had actually arranged to meet him, in order to try and be a couple of fashionable minutes late.

She left a few seconds after the buzzer went before sauntering over to the intercom while her stomach looped the loop a couple of times. There he was. Fantastic. She grabbed her keys and cast a quick glance over the radiators. All set for a possible post-lunch coffee. The sitting room was a knicker-free zone.

As she opened the door she wondered...to kiss or not to kiss? Awkward moment number one, and they hadn't even said hello yet. Dating hell had begun. This was, she reminded herself, why recently she had opted for the being single option. That and the fact that there hadn't been a long line of eligible or desirable suitors to hand...not even a short line.

'Matt.' She was bright, breezy, and hoped her choice of perfume wasn't too overpowering. Nothing worse than burning your first date's nasal hair within seconds of meeting. He seemed unfazed, and didn't sneeze. All good signs. To her disappointment he resisted the urge to kiss either her cleansed and toned cheeks or her freshly moisturised and glossed lips. She pretended not to care.

'Lizzie, hi...you look great.' She really did. In actual fact 'great' really didn't do her justice. Matt could feel his good intentions slipping away. 'Sorry I'm a bit late. I had to shoehorn my car into a tiny space up the road.'

He had driven. So he wouldn't be drinking much. Lizzie wasn't sure if this was good or bad.

'What do you drive?' Lizzie craned her neck to look at the row of wing mirrors jutting out into the pavement at waist height.

Matt resisted the urge to answer 'a car'. Sometimes the oldest lines were not always the best.

'A Karmann Ghia....'

'Wow.' Not Lizzie at her most articulate. But definitely one of her favourite classic cars of all time. Very stylish. A sign? An image of Clare shaking her head appeared. Of course not. Just a car.

'It's one of my weaknesses, I'm afraid. I spent my last bonus on having her resprayed.'

'Convertible?' Lizzie knew the answer before she'd even asked the question.

'Of course. Vital for the approximately thirteen sunny days we have every year.' He grinned, proud of his male logic.

Lizzie laughed. Excellent. He could tease himself, and hadn't even tried to drop engine statistics into the conversation.

'Such a great shape. Obviously designed when wind tunnels hadn't been invented to ensure maximum fuel efficiency.'

Matt nodded. 'We'll have to go for a spin in it some time.'

A spin? *A spin?* Matt's cool temporarily deserted him. No

one had gone for a spin in forty years. Was embracing your parents' vernacular all part of the ageing process?

'That'd be great.' Lizzie hadn't registered 'spin' per se, only the allusion to a follow-up outing before they'd even left the doorstep. Excellent. 'So where are we off to, then?'

Lizzie managed to sound much calmer and more offhand than she felt. She could feel her blood coursing through her veins and was trying to breathe deeply and slowly without it being apparent to anyone but herself. She didn't want Matt to think she was about to break into an aria as they were walking along.

'I've booked a table at that flash-looking restaurant on the river. I thought we could probably walk from here. It's a perfect day.'

'Fab.' A man who felt happy eating somewhere that wasn't a pub, a Café Rouge or a Pizza Express. And he was right, it was a perfect day. Lizzie inhaled deeply as they walked down the road. It smelt like December. That fresh, clear, cold and slightly smoky smell which even in London made you think of log fires and snow-covered copses.

Winter was probably Lizzie's favourite season. On the days when the pale yellow sun shone brightly in a clear blue sky and frosty grass crunched underfoot, life was good. There was something ethereal about wrapping up in jumpers and fleeces and walking until the tips of her ears and toes froze only to be rewarded with a steaming mug of hot chocolate, or lunch with a mysterious new man...

Matt broke into her reverie. 'I love days like this. All we need is a bit of snow and a few Alps...'

Yippee—same wavelength.

'An open fire...logs crackling...and blankets.' She had meant it innocently enough. Only out loud it had overtones, undertones and *double entendre* at every turn. Matt fortunately hadn't picked up on it. He was happily chatting about the positive effects of sunshine on the UV-challenged British public.

As they strolled down towards the river Lizzie sighed contentedly. It was at times like this that she felt the relief of finally being an adult without all the hang-ups and put-downs that had dominated almost every conversation on dates in her twenties. So her dates were further and fewer between these days—at least they had some potential when they did happen. A complete contrast to the grab-any-guy-to-prove-I'm-still-attractive approach that had kicked in after her last serious relationship crashed and burned. No one was going to tell her who she was and what she wanted any more. Love me, love my CD collection. Gone were the days of hiding *The Best of Erasure* in the depths of her underwear drawer. It might have taken a while, but it seemed she had finally learnt her lessons well.

Lizzie managed to eat her herb salad without splashing her face with balsamic vinegar or resorting to the Ermintrude display-a-leaf-between-your-lips approach, and didn't spill anything on herself or the tablecloth during the other courses. From their table by the window they watched rowing crews glide past, a reminder of halcyon days when sportsmen hadn't felt the need to don shiny sportswear plastered with the marks of their sponsors. The tranquillity was interrupted intermittently by the idiosyncratically speedy and noisy afterbirth of fibreglass bathtub launches and loudhailers as the coaches tried to keep up with their oarsmen.

The distraction was welcome as they hadn't drunk nearly enough to move onto the searching questions round, and so their conversations were dominated by dissections of work and Friday night. Lizzie was doing her best to fill any silences, and it was due to this, coupled with an over-attentive head waiter who appeared silently to check on them at inopportune intervals, that Matt hadn't got round to mentioning his marital status. He'd now decided to wait until there weren't people sitting at tables only a few metres away desperate to eavesdrop on other people's lives because their own were so dull. He didn't feel the need to provide a floor show. Nor was he impatient to ruin the moment.

The light was fading rapidly by the time they'd finished their coffees, and it was Matt who suggested that they cross the bridge and go for a walk in Bishops Park. He took a deep breath as he followed Lizzie out of the restaurant. It was now or never.

He was just rehearsing his confession in his head when he realised that Lizzie must have asked him a question and was, as is customary in a conversation, now waiting for an answer. Her eyes were glistening, and to his amusement he noticed that perfect crimson circles had formed on her cheeks, which were now rosy in the style of *Noddy Goes to Toytown*. He smiled slowly, stalling. It was no good; he was going to have to admit that he had been thinking about something else instead of hanging on her every word.

'Well?' Lizzie was getting a little impatient.

'Sorry, Liz... What did you ask me?'

'I just wanted to know if you do this often.'

'What?' Matt wondered if the word had come out as defensively as he thought it had. Lizzie didn't seem to have noticed anything strange. But then she didn't have a guilty conscience screaming silently at her.

'You know—pick up women on a Friday night, play the chivalrous man, whisk them home in a cab, send them a basket of cakes, and then do a Sunday lunch date?'

Matt laughed despite himself. Nerves had always had an unpredictable effect on his emotions. There must have been a short circuit somewhere that had permitted this particular reaction.

'No, to be completely honest I'm a bit out of practice. This is the first date I've been on in years.' Matt felt his chest tighten. It was about time he was completely honest about a few other things as well. He had just deftly dodged the perfect opportunity and he knew it.

'Really?' Lizzie was pleasantly surprised. So there were eligible men out there who could cope with being on their own... Just wait until she told Clare. Her afternoon was improving by the minute. As they came to the rail by the river Lizzie closed her eyes for a minute, savouring the moment and resting her eyes from the now biting wind. Matt stood behind her and she leant back, resting her head on his chest.

Matt was incredulous. It felt as if they had known each other for years. It couldn't have been going any better. And the better the afternoon got, the less he wanted to spoil things. Why couldn't he have mentioned his foundering marriage on Friday night? The longer he left it, the more calculating he appeared. And how on earth did you drop having a wife into conversation without ruining everything? You just didn't see films where the guy got the girl after a 'Hey, I'm married, but not happily...now kiss me before you think about it too much' moment. And the last thing he wanted to do was upset her. Bit late now, he thought grimly. But maybe if he had a chance to explain... As he stood there, Lizzie's head resting on his jacket, the chill wind burning his nostrils and filling his lungs with the floral scent of her freshly washed hair, luckily the icy gusts could take full responsibility for the water that had suddenly appeared in the corners of his eyes. How could his life have become so complicated in less than forty-eight hours? Matt wrapped his arms around Lizzie from behind her, in a reverse bear hug, and luckily couldn't see the enormous grin on her face as they stood gazing at the river in silence.

Matt was desperately searching for the words to continue. Eventually he managed to produce something that resembled a voice, albeit not really his own.

'Lizzie?'

'Mmm.'

'I'm having a lovely afternoon—you know that, don't you...?'

'Yes, I do...' Lizzie felt a flush of pride '...and I'm having a great day too. I take it all back. Office parties are fabulous.'

She was effervescent in her enthusiasm. Matt's heart plummeted to his stomach.

'The thing is—look, I'm afraid I've got some bad news. I should've mentioned it on Friday night, I suppose, but I just never got round to it.'

'What is it?' Lizzie tensed and turned urgently to face Matt.

His heart, now back in the right place but beating faster than normal, melted.

'It's just that...well...you'd be bound to find out sooner or later...I just wanted to tell you myself... It's not very good timing, I'm afraid...' *Come on, Matt,* he berated himself. *Come on...*

Lizzie was just staring at him. Aside from the wind that was whipping through her hair, animatedly fanning it out behind her, she was totally motionless. He couldn't do it.

'The thing is...I'm off skiing on Tuesday for two weeks, so I'm afraid I won't be around after tomorrow until the middle of January. I guess that rules me out of the whole holiday season as far as you're concerned. But, if you can wait, I'd love to see you when I get back.'

Lizzie shook her head in disbelief. Matt could see the tension in her face dissipate. Finally she smiled.

'You are a funny one, Matt Baker. I thought you were going to tell me that you were married or gay or only had a couple of months to live or something...' Relieved, she turned to face the river again. 'Believe me, Christmas is overrated. You have to spend the day with close family on pain of death. You eat too much, try and wash it down with too much alcohol, and then top it off by watching a usually highly unsuitable film and having to pretend not to be looking when anyone shags or swears in case your parents or great-aunt are still awake on the sofa next to you. Alternatively, the evening is spent arguing over the annual game of Trivial Pursuit. I'm not sure what's worse, actually. As for New Year's Eve—well, that was obviously invented just to make everyone feel that they lead really dull lives. Year after year everyone feels that they are the only person who hasn't been invited to the party of the season. I get hundreds of letters every January from disappointed people who are thoroughly depressed after the Christmas build-up turns out to be a load of old hype...'

Lizzie was rambling. And Matt wasn't really listening. Lizzie might not be a weekly dater these days, but even she could tell that his eyes were now glazed. And she wasn't even facing him. His muscles were locked and he was standing stock still. Maybe he had frozen solid.

She decided to test her theory...

'I mean you'd be depressed if you were forced to spend three weeks every year on a beach in California, wouldn't you?'

'Mmm...'

It was an automatic response. Inserted at the first sign of a pause. He definitely wasn't listening.

Sure enough, Matt was miles away. In a place where he was watching a slow motion replay of the conversation that had just happened. The one where he had failed to bite the bullet. Let the moment pass. It was playing on a loop. And with each repetition he felt more foolish. This was atypical behaviour. Not big. Not clever. Not good enough. It was a professionally executed lie, surprisingly easy—masterful, in fact, if lacking a little in the imagination department. A perfect demonstration of the use of tactical truth economics.

He *was* going skiing for a week with a few guys from work for New Year, so there was an element of truth in there somewhere. He could even send her a postcard... He shook his head silently. By the time he got back from his 'fortnight' on the slopes he would make sure that he could give Lizzie what she deserved or be honest and face the consequences. Maybe this was the impetus he needed.

Lizzie was looking at him expectantly again. This time she had folded her arms and was tapping her toe in a comedy fashion. Again he apologised, and again he had no clue what she had been saying. With a bit of luck she'd dump him in a minute for failing to pay attention to her. At least then he could feel sorry for himself. Right now he was busy hating himself to his core.

'Well, quite frankly, Matt, I'm beginning to take it a wee bit personally. I mean, it can hardly be a great sign if I'm boring you already. It's true, I do have a tendency to gabble—especially when I'm a bit over-excited. Clare, my flatmate—you know, the one who owns the restaurant that I was telling you about earlier...?'

Matt nodded. 'The restaurant in Notting Hill...' See—he had been listening most of the time. Lizzie acknowledged his response with a nod, but barely drew breath.

'Well, she's always telling me off for going on and on, and I'm trying to retrain myself, I'm really trying, but it's a long drawn-out process. It doesn't help that I get paid to ramble for a living. See, I'm doing it again. Right, that's it. I'm stopping. Right...now.'

She pretended to zip up her mouth, and this time Matt was listening and ready with something to say.

'Sorry, Liz. Please don't take it personally. I've just had a really tough couple of days and I've got a lot on my mind.'

Lizzie stared at Matt blankly. He stared back. Now what? He was sure he had said that last bit out loud.

'Permission to speak?'

'Granted.' Matt laughed and took her arm. 'You're barking, do you know that?' Thirty-two going on twelve, he thought to himself. A vast improvement on the people he usually met, most of whom were far too busy taking themselves incredibly seriously to see the funny side of anything.

'I prefer eccentric. It conjures up fewer images of antiseptic bluey-grey linoleum corridors and men in white coats.'

'Yup, more like monocles and dandruff...'

Lizzie poked his arm playfully.

'Well, at least I don't think up slogans for a living. I think that's madder than what I do...at least I help people.'

'I help them too. I help them remember which brand to buy. Imagine how stressful supermarket shopping would be and how long it would take if you had to weigh up the pros and cons of each item while you were standing there with your trolley before making a decision.'

'So what you're saying is that you've helped by brainwashing them into picking Ariel over Persil, Country Life over Anchor or vice versa?'

'Something like that.'

'Mmm...really helping. Shouldn't be long before you find yourself on the New Year's Honours List. Arise, Sir Matt— Lord of the Brand. Helper of the Decisions, Knight of the Supermarket Shopper... I can't wait.'

Matt grabbed Lizzie's arm and pretended to punch it amicably before linking it with his own.

They strolled back over the bridge very much together. It was truly a black and white Robert Doisneau photo moment. Had he been there with some film in his camera Lizzie felt sure that they would have adorned the walls of thousands of students in years to come. Immortalised arm in arm, the river behind them, eyes shining, in first-date heaven.

As they walked past the cinema Matt stopped at the 'Showing Now' poster selection. He didn't want to head home just yet, but he didn't want to have to do all the talking either. He checked the screening times with his watch. They were in luck.

'Fancy an early film before we head back?'

'Why not?' Lizzie loved spontaneity, and she was in no hurry to say goodbye. Clare would be at work for ages yet, so there was no point in rushing home to report back. She'd only end up calling her mum, who would be bound to rush round for all the gossip before trying to set one date to meet Matt and another one for the wedding. Better not to invite the kiss of death into this relationship yet.

Lizzie panicked. What was she thinking? Relationship was far too strong a word. It was barely a first date, even if it did feel as if they had known each other for years.

They stood in silence reading the posters. Lizzie knew what she wanted to see. There was a romantic comedy that everyone else had been talking about for ages. You know the sort. Boy meets girl. She loves him. He hates her. He shags someone else and she pretends not to care before he realises that the first girl is the one he really loves by which time she, of course, has finally moved on, has shacked up with someone totally unsuitable and is trying to put him behind her. He pursues her until she finally succumbs to fate just before the final credits... Fate being that the two really good-looking, well-paid, A-list movie stars end up together. But there was a thriller on too. A stylish film, critically acclaimed, but not what Lizzie would have chosen for a Sunday afternoon. Still, she was sure that the man in the image business currently holding her hand would pick it.

'Well, Liz, what do you think? I'm up for the romantic comedy if you are...or have you already seen it?'

For once Lizzie was speechless. He'd even referred to it as a romantic comedy and not as a 'girlie film'.

'I know the thriller's supposed to be a cracker, but I'm not in the right mood now. Besides, I've always been a big fan of the everything-works-out-in-the-end genre...' Matt's conscience inserted a pause. He overrode it. 'In fact I've learnt a lot from romantic comedies. Some of my best girlfriends have been picked up with lines that I've borrowed from Andrew McCarthy, Tom Cruise...even Tom Hanks... And girls love it even more when I quote Julia Roberts or Meg Ryan at them.'

Lizzie resisted the urge to propose there and then. A man who confessed to liking Julia Roberts and Meg Ryan vehicles was a rare find. Secretly she was impressed, but outwardly she played it down.

'You smoothie, Matt Baker. Using "lines" to pick up girlfriends? But I suppose in the interests of you learning a few new ones I can probably force myself to sit through it. I've been meaning to see it for ages but never got round to it.'

'Me too. It's been out for weeks. We must be two of the only people who haven't seen it yet. It's a sign.'

'A sign? It's a sign? Don't even try and go all spiritual on me. I can't believe you just said that. The only sign is that neither of us go to the cinema enough.'

'Lizzie Ford, a cynic...I'm not convinced. Secretly I think you love a good line. All women do!'

Lizzie smiled. Enigmatically or in a stupidly happy way? She wasn't sure and didn't care.

Between the trailers and the feature the cinema was momentarily plunged into total darkness, and to Lizzie's delight Matt leant over and kissed her. She kissed him back and then, like teenagers, they snuggled up and watched the movie in silence. It was perfectly predictable, with a feel-good soundtrack to distract the viewer from the linear plot. Luckily the storyline was far from complex. Lizzie was only half watching and half wondering what might happen next...

As they turned into her road Lizzie looked at her watch for the first time since one o'clock. It was nearly seven.

'Thanks, Lizzie. I've had a great afternoon.'

Had. Surely he wasn't thinking of going home yet? Granted, they'd already spent six hours together, but it wasn't as if either of them had Sunday night homework deadlines to meet. And besides, she'd tidied the flat especially.

'Do you want to come in for a quick coffee before you head off?' Was that too keen? After all he was only driving across the river, not embarking on a transglobe expedition. Lizzie wished she could remember what time Clare had said she'd be home. Not that it really mattered, but she didn't want Matt to feel that this was a heavy 'meet my best mate' moment.

'Well...' Matt hesitated. 'Only if it's Nescafé.'

'Kenco, I'm afraid.'

'Hmm.' He furrowed his brow in mock concern. 'Well... I suppose I could make an exception on this occasion. Although I have to say I'm surprised at you. Everyone knows that Nescafé is the instant coffee of romantic comedy fans... I mean, their drinkers are always having close encounters of an intimate coffee breath nature...just look at their ad campaigns.'

'My Kenco is the "really smooth" blend, though.'

'But of course.' Matt grinned.

'And just because you work in clichés doesn't mean you have to live in one.'

'I'm just teasing. I said yes, didn't I?' He knew he should really be going, but he quite wanted to kiss her again before he left.

Lizzie smiled and rummaged in her bag for her door keys as Matt continued.

'Don't you think it's strange that coffee is seen to be seductive? Personally, the aroma of instant coffee always makes me think of teachers in duffle coats standing around in wet playgrounds, their hands wrapped round those brown-tinted Pyrex coffee mugs.'

She knew exactly what he meant. The world according to Matt Baker was a familiar place. Lizzie could picture the scene now.

'Not very romantic at all, in fact...'

'I haven't had a duffle coat for years,' Lizzie added apropos of nothing as she unlocked the front door.

Matt's train of thought hadn't reached the next station yet. 'Well, I think you'll find that they drink the "primary and secondary" blend. I've heard good things about the "really smooth" option, though...'

Matt wandered into the kitchen while Lizzie was boiling the kettle and, having laughed a little too hard at the photo collage of Clare and Lizzie's fashion and hairstyle retrospective in the clip frame on the wall, caught himself staring at her back as she stirred milk into their drinks. He stopped himself before she felt the intensity of his gaze and, sheepish at his behaviour, reverted to his preferred defence mechanism—humour. He didn't have to look far for inspiration.

'So which one of you is the smoker, then?'

Lizzie wheeled defensively, surprised at the line of questioning.

'Neither of us. Why?'

Matt pointed at a box of Tampax which had been left lying on the kitchen table next to the box of matches she and Clare used to light their large candle collection.

Lizzie reddened in a very teenage 'oooh-it's-a-tampon' fashion and distractedly shoved them into the utensil drawer out of sight. As old as she got, being blasé about Tampax in the presence of the opposite sex was still an effort. She must have missed the box during her earlier tidying frenzy. She and Clare didn't even register things like tampons any more. They were no more unusual or scarce than Biros, and often turned up in just as many unexpected places.

She turned to offer an unnecessary apology but, seemingly unruffled by their sanitary tableware, Matt had taken their coffees over to the sofa and was now relaxing cross-legged, his head resting on the cushions, eyes closed. Lizzie sat down next to him and he opened his eyes and turned to face her. In perfect synchrony they both reached for their coffee, took a sip, and returned their mugs to the table.

Christmas was now in danger of becoming Lizzie's favourite time of year. She stifled the urge she suddenly had to hum 'White Christmas' and instead allowed the silence, now laden with anticipation, to play havoc with her heart-strings.

Matt studied Lizzie's face with real affection before leaning forward to kiss her. Their lips met for the third time in forty-eight hours and this time it was minutes before they prised themselves apart.

Lizzie was lost in another world. A world which was a hell of a lot more exciting than the last few months had been. As they fell back into the outsize cushions Lizzie relished the weight of his chest against hers. She could feel herself spiralling deliciously into a whirlwind of male musk and intensity.

As they started to shed a few layers Lizzie got the giggles. She felt like a Russian babushka doll. She'd been doing her utmost to be sultry, but so far, as Matt removed each layer from her top half, it was only to discover another one underneath. At her laugh Matt sat up and smiled sheepishly.

'OK. What is this? Pass the parcel? How many layers are we talking, here?'

'It's all about layers in December. You're nearly there now.'

'Thank God,' he muttered as he resumed his challenge.

It was only a few more moments before Lizzie was delighted to hear him murmur approvingly at her cleansed, toned, perfumed and moisturised chest and stomach. She mentally thanked her mother for her years of indoctrination in the there-is-no-such-thing-as-too-much-preparation approach to dates. She breathed in for good measure and shivered with sheer delight as his tongue explored the surface of her skin.

Somewhere in the back of her mind she knew this was all a bit soon. But, hey, he was off on holiday in a couple of days and why shouldn't she give him something to remember her by? She knew his name. She had his mobile number. In *Sex and the City* the women had sex with totally random men all the time and didn't seem to feel guilty. She was thirty-two, for goodness' sake. She pushed her conscience to one side and indulged herself in the moment. As she watched Matt kissing her tummy she knew what was going to happen next. She decided to make the move to her bedroom just in case Clare came home early and didn't fancy a floor show. From the way his hips were pushed up against her own, and the change in the fit of his jeans in the button fly area, she knew he wouldn't say no.

chapter 6

It couldn't have been more than fifteen minutes before Matt was smoking his proverbial cigarette. While no one would argue against the fact she'd been having a great time a few moments earlier, she could also feel a little disappointment creeping in. Folding her arms across her chest, she rolled over, annoyed.

This never happened in films. The sex was always amazing. The guy was invariably a great lover with a comprehensive knowledge of innovative ways to drive you wild. It wasn't as if Lizzie brought men home very often, and when she did, she expected the world to move. Unfortunately their first encounter wasn't even going to register on her Richter Scale, even if he was just about to drift off with a smile on his face. In fact, thinking about it, Matt had been the first for...over a year. Not that she was counting. Over a year. That had just crept up on her. Not a statistic she was going to be shouting from the rooftops.

Matt groaned before rolling over to nestle behind her and resting his chin on her shoulder. 'Sorry, Lizzie.'

He was going to have to do better than that.

He kissed her neck. Despite her crotchety mood, she could feel his lips on her skin long after they had left it.

'Um...all a bit embarrassing, really. Couldn't help myself. You were just too good. I couldn't wait any longer.'

'Hmph.' It was cute. A nice try. But ten minutes was short by anyone's standards. Especially for a first time. And the foreplay bit had been going so well.

'I'll make it up to you, if you'll let me.' There was a smile in his voice.

Matt had started stroking her tummy lightly and was now running his hands up and down the front of her thighs. Despite herself Lizzie could feel a whirlpool of excitement spreading through her. Maybe she would have to give him one more chance. It was only fair. Lizzie Ford, queen of self-sacrifice, she was not. She rolled over and turned to face Matt, and as she wrapped her arms and legs around him he picked her up and seemingly effortlessly sat her up on the edge of her bed. He must be stronger than he looked. Second time lucky...

He was forgiven. Especially as he was now encouraging pillow talk. Lizzie loved chatting as she drifted off to sleep. It brought back memories of the rebellion and companionship of sleepover parties. At the same time, though, it was strange. They had just consumed each other from head to toe and now they were comparing ages, star signs, backgrounds and ambitions. Either way, a total contrast to Lizzie's normal bedtime ritual, when she drifted off to sleep alone and in silence, her mind racing to make 'to do' lists for the following day.

Lizzie felt naughtily saucy. She wasn't normally a yes-on-the-first-proper-date kind of girl. But, curled up in his arms, she didn't regret it at all. She hadn't met someone with as much potential as Matt in years, and she was looking forward to helping him fulfil it.

Matt slowly moved his wrist to try and find an angle where he could catch enough light on his watch face to make out the time. 12:08. He watched Lizzie sleeping beside him. Totally naked and relaxed. Her musky smell lingered in the bedclothes around them. A lump formed in his throat. He had to leave. Gingerly pulling himself to the edge of the bed, and almost sliding out to avoid rippling the mattress, he picked up his pile of clothes, found one shoe, and eventually its partner, as he tip-toed to the bedroom door. He stood there for a moment. Everything was quiet. He held his breath and opened the door.

As he removed his hand from the handle there was a slight clunk and Lizzie stirred. Matt froze in his half-taken step. To his relief, after a little somnolent murmuring she slept on, leaving him free to creep off uninterrupted.

He was ashamed. Matt Baker was a fraud. A con artist of the highest calibre, a charlatan, and yet he wanted to do it all over again. It was Monday morning and he wasn't at home. He'd have to pretend that he'd fallen asleep on the sofa at his office again. It had genuinely happened to him recently, but this time he would have to lie.

The frosty calm silence of nocturnal suburbia was instantly shattered as he turned his key in the ignition and the classic engine rumbled into action. It harked back to a time when cars made less of a purr and more of a roar, and Matt sank as low as he could into the seat, craving anonymity. As the heater melted the ice on the windscreen just enough for him to be able to see where he was going he disappeared into the night.

chapter 7

Lizzie woke up languidly and revelled in the feeling of her nakedness against the cool Egyptian cotton of her duvet cover. The all-pervading and unbeatable aroma of fresh toast teased her nostrils and, eyes still closed, she ran through the edited highlights of the last twenty-four hours.

It was only when she finally turned to gloat a little at her conquest that she discovered she was alone. Her pulse suddenly racing, she scoured the bedclothes and surrounding surfaces for a note. Nothing. Moreover, his clothes were no longer in a heap on the floor...unless he had something to do with the cooking smells that were wafting up the stairs.

Lizzie lay back on the pillows, removed the sleep from the corners of her eyes and ran her fingers through her hair a few times, removing her centre parting. She didn't want to miss the breakfast in bed moment if it was just about to happen. She'd bet he was a cereal man. And his tipple? Peter-Pan-complex-Frosties? Real-men-eat-Shredded-Wheat? Or leave-those-love-handles-at-home muesli? Judging by the current state of affairs, maybe it was Cheerios.

While she was waiting Lizzie rummaged in her bedside debris for the remote control and, turning on the radio, was horrified to discover that it was just about time for the eleven o'clock news bulletin. By Lizzie's standards this was a lie-in of gargantuan proportions. Disappointment lurked in the wings. Matt had gone from doting breakfast chef to typical male in less than sixty seconds. He must have left hours ago.

Hauling herself out of bed in an attempt to distract herself from the crap inevitability of it all, Lizzie busied herself with the emergency tidying to be done before Clare waltzed in.

In a whirlwind of light-headed activity, Lizzie found and folded her clothes, located all the bits of condom wrappers and pieced them together just to ensure there wouldn't be any telltale Durex logos lurking on the carpet. This was the seedy aftermath of the night before and Lizzie collapsed back onto the bed feeling hot, bothered and decidedly unsexy.

Within nanoseconds she was back in the bolt upright position and rummaging through her make-up bag. This was when she was glad that she'd decided to stay on the Pill, even though she presently had sex less often than the England cricket team won a Test series. As she knew from her letters, condoms weren't always to be trusted, and taking the Pill had become a habit. Somehow it made life a little easier and, although she knew she shouldn't be popping hormones on a daily basis, it prevented her skin and monthly mood swings returning to their teenage ferocity. Anyway, it was one of the few things in life which was still free, and in the prolonged barren months between men it helped to remind her that some people had sex regularly.

Lizzie wrapped herself in a towel and set off for the bathroom to restore herself to her formerly feisty incarnation. On the bright side she'd had a great day and sex—twice. On the down side she didn't like to think that he made a habit of this...

And to think that she'd already been thinking of it in relationship terms. Would it take a lobotomy for her to learn? She'd jinxed it all by herself by daring to think long term. Men definitely had a sixth sense about that sort of thing. Her instinct had said genuine last night, and she was usually quite a good judge of character, but then he was unlikely to have had 'love 'em and leave 'em' printed on his boxer shorts. For all she knew he was a serial sex-on-a-first-date merchant. Still, Lizzie had vowed in the past that she would no longer live with her heart on her sleeve. She could be pragmatic. Right. It was just sex. In which case everything was going according to plan. Well then. Much easier to deal with now.

Lizzie had barely put one carefully painted toenail over the threshold when she saw Clare standing at her bedroom door, a slice of half-eaten breakfast in her hand. The 'phantom' toast-maker was indeed at home. For once Lizzie wished her flatmate had a nine to five job. Clare's knowing smile was making her feel like an attraction at a Victorian circus. Roll up. Roll up. Come and see the woman who had sex twice in an hour with the incredible disappearing man.

'So I take it you had a good afternoon and evening with Mr Matt? Coffee too this time. What progress.'

Lizzie was beginning to wonder whether Clare had installed CCTV before she realised they had abandoned their mugs on the coffee table. There was no point denying anything.

'Yup, we went to the cinema after lunch and he came back for a coffee before heading home. What time did you get in?'

'Oh, not until half-one. I ended up drinking the world to rights with a few girlie mates...just for a change. You must have done your usual pass-out-on-the-sofa-before-staggering-to-bed trick. You left all the lights on. I know I'm a sad old nag, but we don't need to leave the hall, landing and sitting room lights on while you're in bed, so if you could just try and muster enough energy and co-ordination to hit a few switches as you stumble past I'd appreciate it.'

'Sure. Sorry.'

Lizzie didn't even remember turning the landing light on, and smiled esoterically when she realised that Matt had probably put and left it on when he got up to leave...which meant he must have left before Clare got back. Which meant—her smile evaporated—he hadn't exactly hung around. Clearly she wasn't as irresistible as she had previously thought. And to think that she'd entertained the possibility, albeit fleetingly, that he might be making her toast this morning...

Clare was quick to notice the split second when the corners of Lizzie's mouth turned up.

'Lizzie Ford. You...you...you pulled, didn't you?'

Lizzie hated that word. It was so unromantic, and didn't sound like anything she ever wanted to be involved in. She wished that for once Clare could be just a touch more tactful and a fraction less direct. She was feeling more than a little emotionally fragile this morning.

'Well, isn't Matt a lucky boy...?'

For the first time since she'd woken up Lizzie was glad that he wasn't in her bed, listening to Clare going on and on...and on.

'So...' Lizzie was refusing to make eye contact. Clare couldn't bear it any longer, and she couldn't wait for Lizzie to tell her in her own time either. 'Well...did you? Did he...? Is he...you know...? Well...?'

Lizzie wasn't helping. It was going to have to be the direct approach and it was now or never. 'Well...did you shag him?'

The pause that ensued was pregnant—with twins. Lizzie reddened, Clare had her answer and, despite her flatmate's broad, almost proud smile, Lizzie felt a little cheap. About £4.99.

Clare decreased her volume for dramatic effect, bypassing her normal speaking tone in favour of a clipped half-whisper. She had just one more question.

'In which case, where is he now?'

'How would I know?' Lizzie tried to sound flippant and failed miserably. Her presently folded arms indicated only one mood: defensive.

Clare knew that Lizzie was incapable of emotionally de-taching herself from this sort of situation. Maybe she should have adopted a more softly-softly approach, but the trouble with that was that she never got any answers. Lizzie always started out trying to be coy about relationships. Clare usually only got the real truth after copious amounts of alcohol or after the final whistle had been blown on the whole thing.

'Ahh. So he didn't exactly say goodbye, then?'

'No. I just woke up this morning and he had gone. No note. Nothing.'

Clare scolded herself for being so insensitive. She was seriously cross with Mr Matt. She changed her whole tone and demeanour at once, and replaced accusatory with sympathetic.

'So that's it, then?' She went over and gave Lizzie a hug and stroked her cheek affectionately. 'Just a one-night stand?'

'Yup, that's it. Just a bit of festive fun.' It sounded logical to Lizzie, even if it didn't feel fun right now. She wished Clare would stop being so nice. It was only making her feel tearful and crying wouldn't achieve anything. If she was feeling hurt, it was her own fault for letting him get under her skin.

'Was it worth it?'

Lizzie blushed. Clare had her answer. She could have told Lizzie that she should have waited, but it was a bit late now and no one needs a told-you-so, smart-arse flatmate at a time like this.

Lizzie was sitting in her study, staring at her computer screen trying to work, when the doorbell rang. She had no idea what time it was. The day had been doing its best to drag its heels since she'd got dressed.

'I'll get it!' Clare shouted.

Fine with Lizzie. She didn't want to talk to anyone. The front door slammed and was shortly followed by a tentative knock at her study door.

'Yes?' She didn't even look up. She wasn't in the mood.

'Liz. Good news...he obviously has shares in delivery services.'

'Hmm... What?'

Lizzie looked over her shoulder. Clare was standing there with a huge bunch of flowers.

Her cloud of depression suddenly lifted and Lizzie gave Clare's arm an excited squeeze as she took the bouquet and headed to the kitchen in search of a big vase and card-reading privacy. It was a tasteful arrangement, wrapped in expensive brown paper and tied with fashionable rope instead of pink ribbon, an interesting mixture of warm winter shades and, most importantly of all, not a carnation in sight. They were almost certainly the nicest flowers she had ever received—not that she was biased or anything. She dared to hope who they were from.

Darling Lizzie...

Woo-hoo.

Please forgive me for disappearing. Thanks for last night. Have a great Christmas and see you next year, when I get back from the slopes.
Lots of love, Matt xx

Darling! Some might say that was over the top, but Lizzie imagined Matt saying it and knew that it was perfect. She could feel herself blushing. She reread the card before pinning it onto the kitchen noticeboard and then looked up to see that her privacy had only been momentary. Clare reappeared, obviously about to leave for work, and glanced over to the card.

'So, he's a skier.'

'Apparently so.'

'But not a poseur.'

'Definitely not.'

'Right. Well I'm off, then... See you later—*Darling Lizzie.*' Clare raised an eyebrow and smiled as Lizzie blushed for a second time. She had returned to her teens.

As she saw Clare off the premises Colin, the good-looking man who owned the garden flat, arrived home laden with Christmas shopping and Lizzie waved a hello. Lizzie and Clare knew Colin about as well as anyone in London knew the people that lived above, below and next door to them. They weren't best friends, like Chandler, Rachel, Phoebe, Ross, Joey and Monica, just real-life neighbours stepping in to water the odd plant when their holidays didn't coincide. A neighbourly alliance and general level of friendship which was certainly preferable to worrying about whether Hannibal Lecter rented the flat underneath theirs.

In the absence of a spare arm to wave with he tilted his head in recognition and helloed back.

Colin brought colour to the street. His steady stream of male visitors gave them plenty to gossip about and, in the summer months, provided plenty of eye-candy as they sunbathed in the tiniest of shorts. But right now she had a phone call to make and, taking the unilateral decision against going down for a gossip, gave Colin a huge grin so that he wouldn't take her shutting the front door in any way personally.

All she wanted to do was wish Matt a good holiday. And in order to dodge any further questioning, she wanted to give herself the pleasure of phoning when she had the house to herself. She dialled his mobile before she'd even thought about what she might and might not, should and shouldn't say. He answered after half a ring.

'Matt... It's me—Liz.' *Darling Lizzie*, she thought to herself, and smiled. 'Thank you so much for the flowers, you old smoothie.'

'Hey, less of the old, if you don't mind! It was a pleasure. I really enjoyed yesterday.'

Matt took a step out of the shop he was currently standing in. Trying to buy his wife a Christmas present when they'd barely had a conversation in months would have been hard enough. Trying to choose a present the day after he'd slept with someone else was pretty much impossible. He had no idea what she wanted any more. It was difficult to tell. Her moods were exhausting and he couldn't even remember the last time they'd had a real laugh together, and certainly not when she was sober. She didn't need new jewellery; she needed a new husband. A yes-man. Someone who didn't want a soul mate.

'Me too.'

There was now the briefest of pauses as their minds flashed back.

'So, where did you slope off to in the middle of the night? I had visions of a lazy breakfast in bed this morning.' Lizzie knew she should have gagged herself. He'd apologised on the card. That should have been enough for her, but, no, she had to ask him again. How to put a man off after one date...sound like a wife or mother... She was doing a great job so far.

'I couldn't sleep. You were snoring so loudly...'

Lizzie was mortified. 'I wasn't...was I?' God, had she been? It'd been so long since she'd had overnight company that she might well have developed chronic nocturnal habits without realising.

Matt couldn't help but laugh at her shocked tone. 'OK, you win. You weren't...' Relief flooded through Lizzie's veins. 'I was just kidding. It was more of a distant rumble...'

'Oi, you.'

'I just woke up and decided that I'd be better off going home and getting an early start rather than being led astray by you in the morning. You, young lady, were fast asleep—beautifully silently, I might add—and so I crept off. Have you had a good day?' Matt changed the subject as quickly as he could without inviting suspicion.

'Not bad. Plenty of work to keep me out of trouble. Just thought I'd call to say thanks for the flowers...they're great... and have a fantastic time skiing.' Not too much pressure now, Liz, she reminded herself. Be fun. Do not under any circumstances be neurotic.

'I'll try. Snow, sunshine, schnapps...it's a tough old life. I'll give you a call when I get back. I'm home on sixth of Jan, I think.'

Morning? Afternoon? Evening? Lizzie wanted to ask but knew she absolutely couldn't. So they'd had sex; it didn't entitle her to a copy of his itinerary.

'Great. Well, have a great time. Look after yourself, and I look forward to more adventures and romantic comedies in January.'

'Me too. Take care.'

'Bye.'

'Bye.'

That was it. End of conversation. And while in the final analysis there were plenty of positives in there, Lizzie could have burst into tears as she hung up. Two weeks was nothing.

But two weeks over Christmas and New Year was a mini-life-time. And considering they had only been dating for three days—if you were being generous—anything could happen—which was why, Lizzie reflected, life was much simpler, if at times less exciting in that reckless, rip your clothes off sort of a way, if the only person you had to worry about was yourself. Objectively her situation was very simple. Either she would see Matt again or she wouldn't, in which case she had great sex, muffins and flowers to remember him by. From her postbag, she knew that was more than some people ever had.

The campaign was Rachel's. There'd been champagne and plenty of back-slapping and now she was celebrating with a designer spending spree. Her fortunes were changing and, despite her cumulative exhaustion, there was a veritable spring in her step. She'd left the office early with every intention of doing her Christmas shopping, but then she'd popped into DKNY and Nicole Farhi on Bond Street and her agenda was shifting.

Two days to Christmas. Rachel almost felt a wave of dread at the imminence of the holiday season. There was no desk to hide behind at home. Four days of him and her mother. Just the three of them and the Christmas edition of the *Radio Times*. Time to be nice. Time to try. Besides, she thought as she admired her reflection in the changing room mirror, how could he possibly resist her? Next stop Agent Provocateur. Then a trip to the off-licence. Sex, satin and champagne—the trusted marriage repair kit. The season of goodwill was underway.

chapter 8

The Ford family had barely eaten a few mouthfuls of turkey before drifting towards the inevitable annual debate on when-and-where-Lizzie-might-find-a-nice-man-to-settle-down-with—a discussion in which she was not expected to take any real part—and then her mother decided to raise the stakes.

'So, darling...rumour has it you were sent flowers this week.'

Rumour has it? How on earth had her mother found out?

'Just a bunch.'

'Really...?' Annie paused for effect and looked round the table at her captive audience. 'Clare said they were quite special.'

Clare. Great. It was fantastic that she was always willing to make polite conversation with her mother, but there were unwritten rules about divulging actual news.

'He's just a friend.' Despite Lizzie's attempt to keep her focus on her roast potatoes, she could feel her brother, sister-in-law, niece and nephew staring.

'Gran...?'

Lizzie still found it very weird when Jess and Josh called her mum 'Gran'...it sounded so...so...set and blow-dry.

'Yes, poppet?'

Poppet? For goodness' sake. Jess had had the same name for all nine years of her life. Next her mother would be stashing crumpled Kleenex up her sleeve and wearing mauve.

'You don't usually send flowers to just friends, do you?' Jessica shot Lizzie a look to indicate that she knew exactly what she was doing. Jonathan silently cast a sympathetic glance at his sister. Ford grillings were legendary, and it seemed that Jessica had honed the craft at a ridiculously early age.

'Flowers, flowers...' Josh had become a four-year-old parrot.

Lizzie gulped down her wine and wished she could be invisible. Just for an hour or two.

'No, you don't, darling...'

Annie might have been talking to Jessica but she was staring at Lizzie, and a smile slowly spread across her face as she sensed the discomfort of her second-born child. Lizzie decided to bombard them with information in the hope that they would retreat for analysis.

'I met him at the City FM Christmas shindig and we've been on one proper date. He's gone skiing for two weeks, during which time I hope he won't go off me. He works in advertising. He's a copywriter, which basically means that he comes up with slogans. I forgot to ask him what his parents do, where he was at school, his inside leg measurement or his net annual income.'

Lizzie beamed at her mother, who usually wanted far more detail than she could offer. Annie would have been happiest if any prospective sons-in-law filled out a five-page questionnaire...not that Matt was a prospective son-in-law yet in Lizzie's eyes. In her mother's eyes, when your daughter was thirty-two every male was a prospective son-in-law.

'There's no need to be so defensive, darling....' Her sister-in-law and her mother exchanged knowing glances.

Who was being defensive? Lizzie had thought she was being funny. Clearly not.

'What's his name?'

Trust Alex to pick up on the crucial information she'd omitted. A natural at everything, and one of those mothers who could flit effortlessly between Play-Doh and Prada and still manage to fit in trips to the gym, Alex had a flat stomach which suggested that Jess and Josh had gestated in her handbag rather than her womb. Lizzie added interrogation to her mental checklist of Alex's talents and filed it in her insecurity folder.

'Matt...Matt Baker.'

'And how old is he?'

It sounded like the final question from Alex, so Lizzie accepted it graciously.

'I haven't asked for his birth certificate yet...' Lizzie smiled wryly '...but my sort of age.' Although, actually, he might be a well-preserved fifty-year-old for all she really knew. But then again he wouldn't have known about the Transformers advert if he was.

Lizzie reassured everyone round the table that it was very early days yet, but conceded that she did like him—obviously omitting to mention intercourse, or Clare's cynicism that he would be in the arms of a chalet girl by now—and the conversation was allowed to move on. Lizzie drank a silent toast to Matt, somewhere up a mountain, and, much as she loved her family, wished she was there with him.

December the twenty-fifth when you are unhappily married with no children, with no close family with children, and with parents who have decided to go and spend the holiday season with your brother and his wife in America is possibly the worst day of the year. Not even the prospect of a skiing holiday next week was helping. Because that was in five days' time, and right now every hour seemed to last three weeks.

Presents had been exchanged over breakfast. Hers: handcrafted silver necklace, voucher for evening spa at the Sanctuary, new coffee table book of Mario Testino portraits—her favourite photographer—and annual subscription to *Vanity Fair*. His: another navy blue jumper—classically expensive and at least one size too big, he could change it—Jamie Oliver's latest cookbook—her favourite chef—and *Breakfast at Tiffany's* on DVD—her favourite film.

They'd spent the rest of the morning preparing lunch—including the new Jamie Oliver approach to Brussels sprouts. He'd tried to be interested in her news, and she'd been more attentive than at any other time over the last six months, but the atmosphere was strained. Laughing a little too hard and too early at each other's jokes. Recalling a little too eagerly anecdotes that proved they'd once had a healthy relationship. Somewhere along the line things had changed. Now they were virtual strangers with a shared archive of memories. Not enough to sustain what they didn't have now.

Today would probably have been a good time for an honest chat. For a start they were in the same place at the same time, and both conscious, but he didn't want to provoke a showdown in front of her mother and so he'd been dutiful and gone through the motions surprisingly effectively. But it was hell. Actually, it was hell with the mute button pressed. No flaming cauldrons. No screams. Instead completely quiet, except for the gentle purring noise coming from his mother-in-law dozing in the armchair by the fire and the occasional rustle of a page being turned.

Satan had this suffering bit down to a tee. Here he was with plenty of time to think, to hypothesise, but no suitable time to talk. And what about Lizzie? Could it work even if he had lied? It seemed an impossible situation. The plot of the book he was reading seemed far more feasible, even though it involved a race of people from a parallel galaxy. He hauled himself from the sofa and decided to make a start on the washing up. The roasting tray would be a welcome distraction.

Happy Fucking Christmas. Rachel was irritated and her pride was well and truly dented. It had been the perfect moment. Candlelight, champagne, and yet he wasn't in the mood. Wasn't in the mood? Now he was in the bath 'relaxing', and he'd even locked the door.

She'd spent a fortune. She'd been in full seduction mode—

balconette bra, stockings, suspenders and a practically transparent negligée hiding under her bathrobe—but, nothing. And she'd thrown away the receipt.

Now she wasn't even sure if she was feeling humiliated, furious or just plain frustrated. She'd imagined an evening like they'd used to have. Limbs and clothes everywhere, frantic excitement, collapsing in a sweaty heap at the end only to shower and start all over again. It didn't make sense. He'd always wanted her. Tonight she'd been ready. And when she decided something was going to happen, it fucking did.

Glaring at nothing in particular, Rachel flung her head back onto the pillow sulkily before swinging herself back into the upright position and finding her slippers. She needed a vodka, a big one, or she was going to lose her temper. Ho Bloody Ho. But if her Christmas spirit had to come from a bottle, then so be it. No one was going to piss on her parade. Not today.

'Your throw.'

'Hmm?'

Lizzie was miles away.

'Your throw.'

So far away that a four-year-old was having to remind her how to play a non-tactical throw-a-dice-and-get-your-coloured-piece-to-the-other-end board game.

'Right. Sorry, Joshie...' Lizzie rolled the dice. 'Four.'

He counted her playing piece along the board.

'One, two, three, four.'

Lizzie had landed on a square with writing. Josh looked beseechingly at his older, wiser sister.

'Read it, Jess.'

'You have missed your train. Go back to the ticket office.'

Josh squealed with delight at his aunt's misfortune. Lizzie moved the piece back almost to the beginning and smiled wanly. She didn't care if she lost. She didn't even care that her mother was cheating. She'd been drinking for over seven hours and now she just wanted to be somewhere else. Somewhere snowy, at altitude. A certain chalet, perhaps...

* * *

'Right, then, I'm going to watch the rest of the film in bed. At least that way your heavy breathing isn't going to ruin all the tension...'

Matt grunted sleepily before rolling over slightly to face the cushions. His breathing sounded laboured, and he was desperate to open his eyes, but knew his plan was on the verge of working. His wife bent down and kissed him on the cheek. The fumes from her all-day drinking session curled the edge of his nostrils.

'Night. See you up there.'

He waited until he'd heard her climb the stairs, check on her mother and switch the telly on, before turning over and propping himself up on his elbow. As he rummaged on the floor for his book and made himself comfortable he allowed himself to wonder how Lizzie's day had been. He was far too young to have screwed up.

chapter 9

The phone rang from somewhere underneath the papers strewn across her desk. Carefully, so as not to disturb her morning's work which, despite its haphazard appearance, was in fact organised into piles that only she could understand, Lizzie extricated the receiver just before the call-minder service kicked in.

'Hello?'

'Lizzie, it's me. I know it's pathetic but I really miss you. Mum's driving me mad.'

It was Clare, stir-crazy, shouting just a little bit, live and direct from the maternal home—a chocolate box farmhouse in a small village just outside Wendover.

'I'll be home in a couple of days. So enjoy having the place to yourself and listening to all your crap CDs before my return!'

'Two days...' Lizzie was on automatic pilot and still concentrating on the letter she had been in the middle of answering when the phone rang. 'Right, OK...' Now focusing on the voice in her ear, she snapped back to the present just in time to take an active part in the conversation that Clare had already started without her. 'What day is today anyway?'

'Sunday...all day. Honestly, you're obviously deep in "Ask Lizzie" land. I don't want to interrupt the master at work, but I am—and I can't say this too loudly for fear of being over-heard by one of her ornaments—bored, bored, bored. You know how much I love my mother, but there are only so many times you can have the same conversation and pretend that it's all news to you without wanting to hit someone...'

Lizzie laughed. Clare made her laugh.

'I can't believe I'm only forty-eight minutes away from Marylebone. It's like a different era out here. I'm beginning to find this whole relaxing thing quite stressful, and if my mother suggests I read another one of her Aga sagas I think I'll scream. There aren't even any proper shops for me to wander round. I can't feel guilty about spending too much money because there is absolutely nothing to buy. I'm starting to say damn and blast. I've found myself poring over catalogues and have even considered ordering a shirt from one of them even though I know it will be disgusting.'

'Hang in there. I'm working away at this end, so it's not like you're missing a great party atmosphere. Putney is deserted. I think about ninety per cent of our neighbours are *chez* parents in the country or skiing. I went to Sainsbury's the other day and there wasn't even a queue at the checkout.'

'Unbelievable...' Scarily, Clare felt, Lizzie's stories were just about as exciting as her mother's. She'd have to organise a girlie night out on the town when she got back before they slid into middle age without even noticing. Next they'd be comparing de-tergents instead of dates. It didn't bear thinking about.

'Any calls?'

'Nope. None for you at all. Sorry.'

'Any for you...?'

Lizzie hesitated. Surely she couldn't be so bored that she wanted to know how many times her mother and Jonathan had called over the last week. She was almost ashamed to admit that it ran into double figures.

'Well, a few.'

Clare sighed. Lizzie was being deliberately obtuse. It might be tactless, but she was going to have to ask anyway.

'So you haven't heard from you-know-who?'

Lizzie smiled at Clare's attempt at tact and diplomacy. She didn't know why substituting his name with the 'you-know-who' thing was supposed to make her think about 'who-he-was' any less. And, thanks to Clare, her mother now knew there was a 'someone-of-interest' who 'might-have-called' too.

'Matt?' As if she was waiting to hear from a selection of recent sexual conquests... 'Nope. He's still skiing.'

Clare knew that much. She also knew that there was an effective telecommunications system which operated throughout Europe, both on mountains and in valleys. Surely he could have found a five-minute window between steins of lager? But she decided to be upbeat for now. 'Right. When's he back?'

'Sixth or seventh I think...'

Clare knew there was no way that Lizzie was capable of being that blasé, but let it pass all the same.

'Oh, and thanks so much for telling Mum about the flowers.'

'Don't be so over-sensitive. Flowers are a good sign as far she's concerned. It gives her hope. She only means well. Strangely enough, she just wants you to be happy.'

'I am happy...' Lizzie made a conscious effort to move the conversation away from her. She had nothing to report. All she'd done was work, food-shop and watch a few classic films on television. 'So how's country life? Been to any gigs at the village hall?'

'Thankfully I've managed to talk her out of all of them. It's at times like this I really wish I had a brother or sister to dilute all this parent-child bollocks. She still thinks I'm fourteen. I mean, it's ridiculous. I have my own business. I employ people...'

Clare suddenly interrupted her own soliloquy of boredom. Lizzie was actually only half listening whilst speed-reading a few letters. She'd resisted the urge to actually type anything into her computer because she knew only too well how irritating it could be to hear other people's keyboards in action when they were supposed to be giving you their undivided attention.

'Look, I'd better go. Mum's just got back from walking the dog and I'll be in trouble if she thinks I've been gassing to you the whole time she's been out as we live together for most of the year. See you on Tuesday... Byeee.'

'Bye.'

So it was Sunday already. Since Boxing Day she'd thrown herself at her postbag and, thanks to a couple of marathon sessions, only had a couple more hours to go. But next week would herald the onslaught of the post-Christmas pre-Valentines blues. January to March was Lizzie's busiest time of year.

She returned her focus to her next letter of the week. In fact it was less of a letter and more of a stream of consciousness. Like many of the people who wrote, this woman had more or less answered her own questions, but Lizzie knew that plenty of her readers would identify with her.

> *Dear Lizzie*
> *My marriage is in dire straits.*

Lizzie had to concentrate hard to override the 'Money for Nothing' chorus which had just surfaced from the recesses of her inbuilt jukebox and smiled to herself idiotically. It was amazing what these letters could trigger. People's lives in crisis and she was humming songs from 1985.

> *I've been married for five years now, but things haven't really been right for the last six months—well, probably more like a year. I know you must get hundreds of people writing to you with this sort of problem, but I read your column this week for the first time and, whilst I'd always thought that agony aunts were for teenagers, manic depressives and people with no friends at all, you do seem to talk a lot of sense. I have friends, but right now I don't know who to turn to. Most of them have no idea how bad things have become, plus there is the added problem of my husband and I sharing friends who would*

feel divided loyalty, and the last thing I want is a series of lectures. So, I thought I'd see what you think I should do. I can always ignore your advice if I don't like it. I don't mean to be rude, but it's a bit like reading your horoscope, I suppose. You only see what you want to see when it suits you.

A bit of background for you: I'm in my thirties, a typical product of the go-get-it-and-while-I'm-at-it-why-can't-I-have-it-all generation, and while I concede that I do work very hard and my career is coming first at the moment, my husband has always understood that side of me (or I thought he did). I am under a lot of pressure at the office, but I do genuinely feel that real success is just around the corner.

My husband's a really nice guy; he's not a cross-dresser, or an S&M aficionado or even a difficult bloke... If only he can just hang in there I feel certain that we can make things work again, and I honestly believe that things will quieten down a bit at work when I get to the next level. The trouble is that he seems to be giving up. I'm beginning to wonder whether he might be thinking about having, or even have started, an affair and I don't think that I could ever forgive him for that. Without being too graphic (although I know these are the details that voyeurs who read these pages are holding out for), we're not exactly sleeping together much these days. I'm exhausted and totally immersed in my work, I'm stressed out, and to be honest having sex is the last thing I feel like at the moment. Luckily, he's usually in bed asleep or out when I get home.

For the last few months I've been burying my head in the sand, just believing that everything will be fine because we did the marriage thing together, but I know he's feeling neglected. He's even stopped bothering to talk to me about things, and seems to be trying to make a point

*by working all hours now as if to compete and prove that
he doesn't need me any more. We used to be really happy.
I just worry that it's too late to do anything about it, so
I'm writing to you. Why...? I don't know. In case you
have a magic wand, I suppose. Anyway, any tips you
have would be very welcome.*

   Name & Address Withheld

Lizzie found herself composing her response before she'd
even finished reading.

Dear Career Girl

   *I'm afraid there's no magic solution to your problem,
but the fact that you're so aware that things aren't right
is a huge help. You've hinted at many of the answers in
your letter, but if it helps to have a total stranger point
them out then here goes...*

   *Being a woman in the twenty-first century is almost im-
possible. There are too many demands on too little time
and this, coupled with the capabilities that many women
now realise that they have and naturally want to utilise,
causes many conflicts of interest. At least when women
were uneducated they would never have dreamed of doing
half the things that they do today—often not only as well
as, but better than their male counterparts. Sorry, guys
who are reading this, but that's how we feel. Ignorance
must have been bliss. Washing yourself, washing clothes,
reading, sewing, cooking, riding and shagging—even if
you had to wear lace collars, petticoats and skirts all the
time—that was it. There was plenty of time for you to
adore and appreciate your husband when he got back
from earning the family income, and lots of uncluttered
head space for you to think about him and his needs
when he wasn't around, in comparison to now when he
is just one more ball to juggle.*

That said, don't forget this is an intimidating age for men. They're adapting as fast as they can, but as we women know only too well they can rarely anticipate our latest demand and need to be nurtured and loved along the way. I know how hard it is to combine success at work with a successful relationship. It is no coincidence that I have no Mr Lizzie to look after or to look after me. But if you have found someone special it is worth putting in the effort. You say that success is just around the corner. Might it still be there if you step back for a fortnight? I know it's hard, but try and retain some perspective. At what cost do you want it?

From where he's standing, there is nothing worse than feeling rejected. We all want to be loved and all need to be needed. Women don't have the monopoly on feeling insecure. He has to believe that he's an important part of your life and that you're still interested in him, or yes, he may well look for someone he feels can be a real soul mate, or even just someone to massage his flagging ego, or some other bits of him that need attention... And, more importantly, however busy you both are, you need to have a part of your life which is yours together. Just because you are married it doesn't mean you can sit back and count the years to your silver wedding anniversary. Communicate. Talk to him. Explain how you are feeling...and, hardest of all, don't be defensive. Admit you are at fault. Take some responsibility. Telling him that you are perfect and that he needs to be more understanding and flexible will not have the desired effect.

Don't wait until it's too late. Make time now, even if it's only a day. (Lunch in Paris, thanks to Eurostar, can't do any harm and won't break the bank either.) We all get sucked into the work whirlpool, but it's only a job and the world will still be rotating on its axis if you take a few hours to sort yourself out. You've taken the first step;

*you've written to me. But it's him you should be talking
to. He may not realise how you're feeling. It may sound
ludicrous, but men specialise in being obtuse.*

*Before you start, though, please do me a favour. Ask
yourself whether you really love him or whether it's just
the thought of failing that you can't deal with. If you do
love him then make sure he knows. If you're trying to save
your marriage because of what other people might think
then, hard as it may be, save yourself a lot of heartache
and call a solicitor.*

*Keep me posted. If you want any more information, or
the name of a good restaurant in Paris, please e-mail me
at asklizzie@outloud.co.uk*

Good luck.

Lizzie typed the last sentence with a flourish before scanning the original letter in and e-mailing them both, along with
her column, to her editor for the next edition. Time for a con-
gratulatory tea and biscuit break.

She was still thinking about the letter as she waited for the
kettle to boil, disappearing momentarily into a cloud of pore-
cleansing steam as it wobbled and rattled its way towards boiling point. Worrying about her readers was an occupational
hazard, and suspected infidelity was a tricky one. As a child
Lizzie had daydreamed of her big white day on afternoons
when she was bored and apparently had nothing else to do. But
the older she got the less she could visualise herself walking
down any aisle that wasn't in a supermarket or a cinema.

Laughably, she was still waiting to be swept off her feet by
an irresistible man who wouldn't let her down, for days and
nights of passion, a relationship of equals and perfect children.
She wanted the happy and successful first marriage that had
eluded her mother. Like many of the children of divorcees, she
had grown up determined to get it right. Matt had been the first
ray of hope in a long time, and while he'd been doing well be-

fore he left, she had secretly been hoping for a slurred Christmas greeting on her answer-phone. There had been nothing.

Lizzie was in pursuit of the perfect cup of tea when the phone rang. She rushed to answer it, only the phone wasn't in its holder on the wall. It was in her study, where she had left it. Damn. Phone calls were the only proof that her life wasn't being lived in a vacuum at the moment, and if 1471 couldn't shed any light on the caller, missing one could lead to hours of speculation as to who'd phoned and why they hadn't left a message. Taking the stairs two at a time, Lizzie legged it down to her study.

She made it just in time. 'Hello? Hello?' Lizzie felt quite light-headed after her burst of activity. Maybe it was time to resurrect 'keep fit'—or, at least add 'get fit' to her rapidly growing list of New Year's Resolutions, but she hated exercising in January. There were always about eight million mince-pie eaters swearing the New Year was all about the New Them. She'd wait until February, when the bulk had given up, having paid a large enough gym subscription to make themselves feel better.

'Hello?'

It was a cautious overture. Whoever it was had obviously been shell-shocked by the frenzy of activity they'd overheard at Lizzie's end. As long as they were shell-shocked and not shell-suited that was fine. The former wasn't life threatening.

'Mum?'

'No need to sound so disappointed, darling.'

'I'm not disappointed. I just thought—well, never mind. How are you...?' Lizzie resisted the urge to add 'today' to the end of the sentence.

'Have you heard from that chap again?'

'I told you; he's skiing.'

'Yes. Of course he is. Silly me.'

God, between them, Clare and her mother were giving her a complex. And she didn't need any help.

'How are you, Mum?'

'Oh, you know. Fine. House seems a bit empty after spending the week with Alex, Jonathan and the kids, but in some ways it's good to be home. How about you?'

Since Lizzie's stepfather had died, she knew how hard her mother found the festive period when for two weeks every year the minutiae that usually filled her every waking hour ground to a halt. Annie liked to pretend that she was the busiest, strongest, all-coping widow London had ever seen, but Lizzie knew that underneath her cardigans there was far more raw emotion than she ever revealed. Lizzie berated herself for not having had the sensitivity to call herself, but if there was one person who could wind her up in under twenty seconds it was her mother.

'I've been working really hard. Clare gets back the day after tomorrow, and I'd really like to be up to date before next week kicks in and I get even busier.'

'You do work very hard, darling. I know that you have to, but do try and make time to have a little fun from time to time. Maybe you and Clare could go out dancing one evening?'

'Mum...'

'I know you think I'm interfering, but I just want the best for you. Look at Jonathan and Alex. So happy. Such a team. Jess and Josh are such lovely children. You don't want to end up on your own.'

'It's not a question of "ending up"...' Her mother was doing it again. 'If the right person comes along then we'll see. But look at Clare. She's much happier since she left Joe. She's gone from strength to strength. Union Jack's is doing really well.'

'Clare's still angry, though. She'll calm down eventually, and then she'll want to meet someone again.'

'I'm not so sure.'

Her mother chose to ignore her. 'It's all nonsense. She's got to let someone into her life again one day...'

'She doesn't have to do anything.' Lizzie knew she was sounding clipped. But in light of the radio silence from the Alps she was feeling more than a little defensive. 'Not everyone feels the need to have their 2.4 children. More and more women find that they are just too busy for all that.'

Annie sighed. 'Darling, having you and Jonathan was the

best thing I ever did. Life doesn't have to stop just because you have children. Without you two, now my life would be empty.'

Lizzie didn't want to talk about this. Of course she'd thought about children, but not unless she'd found the perfect relationship first.

'Mum, you know I love you—very much. But, please. I'm thirty-two. I am quite capable of running my own life. Believe me, if I meet the right man I'm not averse to having a relationship. I'm just not interested in settling for second best.' Lizzie wanted out. This was supposed to be her tea break, not a psychoanalysis session. 'Look, I'd better get on. I'll give you a call later on this evening, OK?'

'Lovely. Great. Just not between eight and ten because I'll be watching that drama.'

Lizzie sighed as, a little emotionally fragile, she returned to the kitchen only to discover that—as she had forgotten that the whole point of a portable phone was that you could walk, talk and even brew at the same time—her tea was unsalvageable: a horrendous combination of 'jumble sale stewed' and 'cooling rapidly'. She threw it away and started again. Life was way too short to drink horrible cups of tea in your own home.

She was just taking a five-minute research break on the sofa with a magazine when the phone rang again. What now?

'This is BT call-minder. You. have. one. new—'

Lizzie cut off the automaton and dialled the number for their message service. It was one of the Laws of Sod. She'd been in solitary for almost forty-eight hours and two people had rung at the same time.

'You. have. one. new. message. message. received. today. at. four. forty. six. peee. emmmm.'

'Hi, Lizzie...it's only me.'

Lizzie could have jumped for joy. It wasn't 'only me'. It was bloody well him.

'Just calling to say hello.'

He sounded drunk. Or was it just a bad line?

'Hope Christmas Day was fun and that you're enjoying the whole festive over-eating, over-drinking season. No doubt you're out partying hard...or watching lots of extra-long festive episodes of soap operas...or both. Well, I'd better get going. There's no point me just waffling into a machine for hours. Happy New Year for Thursday night from the mountains. See you soon.'

Life was so unfair. It was Sunday afternoon. Surely he should be slaloming down a mountain black run, or whatever you do on skiing holidays? Yet he calls. Just like that. Rationale started to creep in. At least he'd rung. Lizzie listened to the message several times before wondering what exactly she was listening for and starting to question her sanity. Satisfied that she had committed it to memory, she deleted it before Clare found it—and transcribed it for her mother.

Mood improved, Lizzie hummed to herself as she returned to her study. She loved this first bit of relationships. The excitement of attraction and not knowing that he clipped his toenails into the bath and left them there. The time when everything was endearing, fun and never too much trouble.

Although she would never admit it to Clare or to her mother, after years of slating women for doing it, Lizzie too had started to imagine every man she met as the potential father of her children. Looking at Alex and Jonathan, she did occasionally have twinges of verdant-edged envy. And she definitely wasn't interested in the freeze-your-eggs, find-a-sperm-donor approach to reproduction. Unlike Clare, who'd become a right old feminist since her divorce, Lizzie did want to try and create a family unit, and she reckoned she had four years left to find a playmate and a father for her children before investing in a couple of cats and embracing the whole spinster lifestyle—reading glasses, amber necklace, meal for one, cut flowers, padded slippers *et al*.

But one brief message and her subconscious was cluttered with images of her and Matt sitting in thick white bathrobes at sunny breakfast tables reading papers and sipping orange juice as their charming, wide-eyed, intelligent, clean and practically silent pre-school children, complete with juvenile bowl haircuts and freckles, arrived to join them. Lizzie forced her-

self to stop when she started to picture him wandering around
'their' garden in a cardigan because:

1) She didn't have a garden
2) She hated men wearing cardigans
3) He was skiing
4) They had only seen each other twice...ever.

chapter 10

Making sure that nobody she recognised was in the vicinity, Rachel picked up the latest edition of *Out Loud* magazine and, as she flicked past the various articles, berated herself yet again for posting the sodding letter in the first place. She must have been a whole lot iller than she had felt. Practically certifiable.

Scanning the magazine every Thursday—often sandwiched between the conveniently outsize pages of *Campaign*—had now become a ritual, even though she had no idea how far ahead of herself this 'Ask Lizzie' person worked. She'd only popped out of the office to make the most of the last week of the January sales, yet here she was in Selfridges, a floor away from the nearest designer collections, just checking.

Finally she found the relevant double-page spread. And there she was. Well, it was. Her letter. Letter of the frigging week. Rachel felt instant colour closely followed by instant pallor hitting her cheeks, and her ice cool façade temporarily slipped as she instinctively clutched the magazine to her chest and her body locked. Regaining the use of her limbs several seconds later, she put the magazine back as discreetly as she had picked it up.

After completing a circuit of the department, and lingering a little in Cards to regain her composure, Rachel returned to make her purchase. She toyed with the idea of buying all the copies on the shelf before eschewing the hysterical approach and instead losing it amongst a few other titles in her basket. At the till, blasé was replaced by bashful, and she could barely look the salesgirl in the eye. Pathetic behaviour. No one knew it was her letter or her problem. Yet she left the store convinced that everyone was giving her sidelong glances. Instant paranoia had descended.

'Hold all calls. I don't want to be disturbed for the next ten minutes.'

Kitty looked up guiltily from her frenetic e-mailing and minimised the dialogue box on her screen instinctively. Rachel didn't know why she bothered. She knew Kitty was doing something personal. She never typed that fast when it was work-related. Nevertheless, Kitty did her best to nod industriously at Rachel as she swept past, before returning to organising her social life electronically.

The office door firmly closed, and seated safely at her desk far away from the searching eyes of assistants, Rachel silently read and reread first her letter and then the answer. So they used real letters. A cynic, and well aware of the short-cuts that the media took when necessary, Rachel had often wondered how genuine the problems really were. But there was her feverish letter. In print. For all the world to see. To read. To judge.

Name and Address Withheld. She searched for any clues as to the identity of the author. Objectively, no one could possibly know it was from her. She wasn't sure that she even knew anyone who read *Out Loud*. Everyone she knew seemed to be reading *Vanity Fair*, *Vogue* and *Tattler* on the days when they weren't immersed in the aspirational lifestyle publications of *Wallpaper* and *World of Interiors*.

Lizzie was good. Most of her response was state-the-obvious without being patronising. Paris for lunch wasn't out of the question either. They'd just have to co-ordinate diaries. She wondered if shopping for the new collections while they were out there would be allowed? Probably not.

She'd only just started on the third read-through when there was a knock at her office door. Luckily, in hanging her coat on the back of the door, she'd obscured the glass panel that usually enabled visitors to watch her check her make-up for imperfections before she waved them in. Flinging the magazine on the coffee table, she opened a new document on her screen before responding to the follow-up batch of knocking. What was it with people? No one had a divine right to see her, and since when had appointments been out of date? Rachel sometimes wondered what she paid her PA for. Next time she'd have to be a bit more specific. Do not disturb until the big hand is on the six...

'Come in.' It was more of a bark than a welcome.

'If this is a bad time I'll come back later. I just wanted a quick word.'

Her annoyance was rapidly evaporating because Will was currently standing at the entrance to her office. Boyishly good-looking—hell, he was only about twelve...or was it twenty-five? Now she was on the wrong side of thirty it was becoming increasingly difficult to tell. Still, despite his testosterone-filled, confident and cocksure approach, Rachel had to admit he was bloody good at his job. Unnervingly, as vile as she could be, he never appeared to be intimidated, and she had to admit that their flirtations gave her as much pleasure as anything these days.

Will headed straight for the couch, placing one state-of-the-art trainer on her coffee table as he lit up. Rachel's office was one of the few places you could still smoke on the sixth floor, and he always used it to his advantage. She could sense her plastic-looking-but-genuinely-living office plant collection holding its breath. He held the packet out to her.

'No, thanks.'

'Not still pretending to be a non-smoker, are you?'

'I haven't had one since...' Rachel didn't have to think back very far. 'Well, I haven't had one during the day for over a month.'

'Or a cigarette.' Will tipped his head back as he exhaled and his smoke rose up towards the ceiling in a vertical column. Rachel, as a rule, hated people smoking in her office—especially when they were junior to her and hadn't bothered to ask first—but she decided to wait and see what Will had to say before she started getting testy. She walked round the desk, carefully resting her bottom on the other side.

'So, what can I do for you?'

'Just wanted to run a few more ideas past you for the campaign...'

Rachel's afternoon was rapidly improving. She loved their meetings. Will was brimming with initiative and his enthusiasm was infectious. Rachel pulled her shoulders back and thrust her chest out a little further. Power-flirting was one of her specialist disciplines. She was sure she must be one of the best in the business.

'I've been brainstorming with the rest of the team over lunch and I thought it'd be better to catch you in the office face to face if I could. This way you can tell me what you think and we can get on with it, or regroup and get our thinking caps back on. Just be honest. If you think any of the ideas are crap, just tell me.'

'Believe me, I will.'

'Yeah, well, you're not known for beating round the bush, are you?'

'No.'

'Right.'

From Will's demeanour, Rachel imagined this ideas session had involved a few drinks.

'Do you want a coffee?' Rachel was determined to send Kitty to the Italian place over the road as her penance for letting Will in early and creating a close call. The coffee there was legendary, if you could endure the hapless lecherous flirtation of the staff. It would've been classified as harassment if you didn't actually choose to go in. 'If you're going to hi-jack the next half-hour I might as well also use it to top up my caffeine levels.'

'Sure. A latte would be lovely.'

Rachel popped out to Kitty's desk with her wallet and ordered two posh coffees and a nice bit of cake. To her horror, when she got back Will was reading the problem page, which unfortunately was where *Out Loud* had fallen open, even after its earlier flight from her desk to the coffee table. Rachel ordered herself to play it cool, despite the fact that Will was sitting there in his baggy trousers, youth personified, still tanned from his recent snowboarding trip and definitely smiling at what he was reading. Smiling out loud. A phenomenon which was more commonly known as laughing. And, to Rachel's despair, the source of his amusement appeared to be on the page he was reading. Rachel pretended to join in with his sentiment in the hope that they could move on...swiftly. She took the initiative.

'Some of it's amazing, isn't it? It makes you wonder who writes in to these magazines. I don't know why people bother.'

'I know. I mean, what sort of loser would write to an agony aunt in the first place?'

Rachel silently ordered herself to relax. It was anonymous. That was the whole point. Will, unfortunately, hadn't finished yet.

'Don't people have mates any more? Anyway, I bet the staff writers make up the letters they reply to, to suit their theme of the week.'

Rachel was rattled, but she knew she couldn't let on. She would be the laughing stock of the department if anyone found out.

'Oh, I don't know. I bet some people write all the time.' She feigned being offhand not entirely convincingly. Luckily Will was on a mini-roll, and oblivious to her discomfort.

'Yeah. The same sort of people who enter word search competitions and watch daytime quiz shows, I bet... I mean, look—take this one...'

Will was now on his feet and using some of his excess energy for pacing.

'I mean, perlease...check this out...' Will adopted a silly squeaky voice and read from the open page. '"My husband is a really nice guy, he's not a cross-dresser, or an S&M aficionado or even a difficult bloke...if only he can just hang in there I feel certain that we can make things work again...The trouble is that he seems to be giving up on me and I am beginning to wonder whether he might be thinking about having or even have started an affair..." Of course the bloke's having an affair. She even admits later on that she's practically stopped shagging him—and think about it from his point of view. He's married to someone who reads agony aunt pages and then writes in. Good luck to him. I'd say he was well out of there.'

Rachel was now sitting at her desk, nervously sliding her chair through one hundred and eighty degrees and back again, trying to look entertained by Will's flamboyant display. Having her letter read aloud to her as if it had been written by a congenital idiot, by a guy who probably still had wet dreams, was not what she had planned for the afternoon. Will perched on the desk right in front of her, and as he scanned the rest of the page he continued his commentary.

'This woman needs to get out there and get herself a life. To be fair, though, the reply's not a lot better. I mean, to write.... "I'm afraid there is no magic solution to your problem..." Get away! You don't need to be a fully qualified aunt of agony to work that one out, do you?'

Suddenly Rachel had had enough. Will's behaviour was making her realise how young he really was. His earlier charm was rapidly dissipating. She resisted the urge to be too defensive of the anonymous author, although she could feel her ears going red under her hair at the indignity of it all.

'What you really can't see from the photo is that this Lizzie woman is seriously fit. I wouldn't mind telling her my problems. She's that blonde one with the phone-in on City FM. Hot property, by all accounts. About your sort of age...'

He gave Rachel a suggestive glance and she met his gaze halfway. She had to hand it to him; the boy had a nerve. His meaningful look delivered safely, and with the desired flustering effect, he consciously increased the distance between them and returned to the sofa, still talking. 'She's one of those older women with sex appeal that we're all supposed to be mad for at the moment. I hope *Loaded* or *Maxim* stump up lots of cash for her to take her kit off. I bet she could solve a lot of problems with that body. Thinking about it, I bet you could too. Maybe you should think about becoming an agony aunt?'

Rachel snatched the magazine and then—having isolated the compliments from his last few sentences and mentally stashed them away for later—hurled it at him in only partially mock disgust.

'You, William, are a pathetic male. When you stop living a life with the complexity of a twelve-year-old's you'll realise that everyone has problems and that life is not just about getting as much great sex as you can.'

'It's not...?' Will affected incredulity followed by a hint of disappointment. In fact he looked so convincing that Rachel found herself laughing. She was laughing so hard that she suddenly felt she might be on the verge of crying. Lowering herself onto the sofa next to Will, she crossed her legs to signal that their meeting was now back in session.

Predictably, Will's suggestions were novel, although Rachel was quick to point out areas that needed refining. All part of her vital strategy to keep Will's confidence in check and straight from the latest '101 Ways to Keep Control and the Upper Hand' manual.

After he'd left she sat back on her sofa and imagined the rewards flooding in. She could almost visualise her winning table at the awards dinner. Success was so close that she could smell it. It was predominantly masculine with a hint of fabric softener and essence of Malboro Lights—well, at least that was the musky trail that Will had left in his wake. And he was a vital part of the campaign team, whether she decided to tell him or not.

chapter 11

Lizzie rolled out of bed for the second time in seven hours. Matt had surprised her with an early lunch, only the food element had fallen by the wayside as their sexual appetites had overtaken their feeding instincts. She whistled to herself as she climbed into the shower. Working at home had definite advantages.

Matt was back and seeing Lizzie again. He wasn't sure how it had happened. No, that was bollocks; he knew exactly how it had happened. He'd missed her. He'd called with every best intention of mentioning the wife, wedding thing, but then Lizzie had asked him round for dinner and before he'd had a chance to say anything... So it was her fault? No, Matt knew better than to try and argue that one. But there'd been no improvement at home. The only thing she'd had for him when he'd got back was a credit card bill. So now, suddenly, in his 'for richer for poorer' capacity she expected him to subsidise her designer wardrobe. It wasn't as if she needed more clothes than her frankly huge salary could provide, and when he'd jokingly suggested she joined Shopaholics Anonymous she'd had

a massive sense of humour meltdown. When he'd less flip-
pantly accused her of using him she'd flown into a rage; she'd
screamed, she'd shouted, she'd almost cried, but she hadn't actually denied it.

He had to leave. He didn't want a wife and a mistress. He
just wanted one woman. Unfortunately not the one he was married to.

He was beginning to feel like the victim of a huge conspiracy. He'd wanted his wedding day to be the happiest of his
life—every groom said it was and he'd believed them, but on
reflection he didn't think they could all have been genuine. And
now there was Lizzie. He'd never been as himself with anyone as he was when they were together. Only she had no idea
who he really was.

Lizzie gave herself a quick blast of cold water in an attempt
to frighten her cellulite into going away and to try and focus
her wandering mind. Matt worked long hours, and often at
weekends, and that coupled with Lizzie's two evenings at the
station, one day at *Out Loud* and total overload of letters,
e-mails and faxes meant that they really had to make time to
be together. But those moments more than compensated for the
time they were apart. Just knowing he was out there was
enough.

Lizzie balked at her latest pulp fiction cliché and turned the
mixer tap to freezing, gasping for breath before turning the dial
back in the red direction. She had punished herself enough. So
what if she'd formerly been the leading protagonist of the
you're-better-off-on-your-own-because-the-only-person-you-
can-count-on-in-life-is-yourself movement? Now she was beginning to wonder whether it was because she hadn't met the
right person.

Matt was the soul mate that she hadn't thought existed outside the scripts of Nora Ephron. It was relaxed and real and
she didn't feel the need to rush things along or make demands
because something was there that she hadn't had before. She
was operating on another plane and, it seemed, fitting more life
into less time.

Clare was now demanding an introduction. Lizzie hadn't exactly been hiding him away, but their long and erratic hours made it difficult to organise a mutually convenient time for a drink. Plus, Lizzie was only too aware that Clare had a generous helping on her own emotional plate. It was almost exactly two years since she'd discovered that Joe was cheating—not the sort of anniversary a young, single-again thirty-something wanted to trumpet, and definitely not the most tactful time for Lizzie to introduce her to Mr New Love Interest. In a no-time-like-the-present flourish Lizzie decided to organise a night out. She'd been doing a lot of working and seeing Matt and not enough being there for her best friend. Towelling herself dry, she decided to rectify the situation right away.

The number rang for ages before it was answered.

'Union Jack's.'

The phone must have been somewhere between the cutlery drawer and the dishwasher. The hubbub of busy restaurant, a total contrast to the morgue atmosphere that Lizzie had got used to working in at home. Lizzie suddenly wished she hadn't called, but hanging up now would just have been juvenile. She dug out her most important voice. 'Clare Williamson, please.'

'One minute.' The phone answerer put the receiver down next to the cappuccino machine. Lizzie's ears had been filled with the sound of coffee grinding and milk frothing—which didn't sound unlike milk being strangled—for a little too long before the phone was picked up.

'Clare Williamson.'

'Hi. Only me!'

'Liz. Hi. Sorry—not a great time. Are you at home?'

'Yup.'

'Everything OK?

'Yup.'

'Can you call me a bit later...?'

'Yup.'

'Say...at about, um...three-thirty?'

'Sure.'

Lizzie liked to vary her single syllable responses.

'Great.'

It was a quick-fire phone call, and by 3:33 p.m. Lizzie hadn't done much except rationalise that Clare being busy didn't mean that she didn't love her any less and called her back. This time Clare answered herself, sounding a lot calmer if a little monosyllabic. To compensate, Lizzie injected a little more energy than normal into her speaking voice in the hope that some of the excess might rub off on Clare.

'Ms Williamson, this is your very own social secretary speaking. Sorry to have bothered you in the middle of everything. I always forget that the times of day when everyone else has time to talk are when you are at your busiest.'

'God, Lizzie, you're going have to be a bit less chirpy. I don't think I can cope with your new euphoric attitude to life and love much longer.'

Ouch. Lizzie detected a raw nerve and resumed her less playful former self. The excess energy ploy had backfired. Probably also not a good time to tell Clare that Matt had called round for a quickie at lunchtime. This was supposed to be about cheering Clare up.

'Precisely what I was calling about, actually. Thought it was high time you and I had a flat outing to drink champagne in glamorous places while setting the world to rights—and to remind you how much better off you are without that two-timing double-crossing shit of an ex-husband of yours.'

Clare laughed despite herself. This time of year was always hard for her, and Lizzie was a good mate. Her tone softened. 'Thanks, Liz, that would be lovely. We haven't had a good night out on the town together in ages. Let me just look at the roster.'

There was a slight pause while Clare located the relevant sheet of paper. 'Blimey. This week's far too hectic... How about next Tuesday...?'

'I'll be in the studio, answering calls and playing CDs.'

'Ah, yes, of course...' She must be distracted. Mind you, Lizzie had called her in the midst of the lunchtime rush earlier. Apparently they could be just as self-centred as each other. 'Actually, how about Monday?'

'Perfect. Leave it to me.'

Lizzie stopped herself from ringing Matt to see if he was free then. Not only was it less than two hours since she'd seen him last, but she didn't want Clare to feel that she'd sabotaged the girlie night she had just promised her. Instead Lizzie channelled some of her nervous energy into tackling the next pile of letters and blasted herself into action with a classical piano concerto on CD at full volume.

Moments later she was typing furiously, captured by the pace and the rhythm of the piece, her hands racing across the keyboard in subconscious imitation of a great composer at work. As the tempo increased, so did her productivity. Soon she was totally immersed in a world of heartache, confession and premature ejaculation.

chapter 12

'So, when am I going to meet him, then?'

'Who...? Matt?'

'No, Robinson Crusoe, Ronald McDonald... Of course Mr Matt. Mr Wonderful. Mr Smile on Your Face. Mr Good News. You haven't looked this radiant for years. He's taken ten years off you...'

'Ten years...?' Clare had such a way with words. Lizzie hadn't thought she looked that different from her twenty-two-year-old incarnation anyway. She stared into her glass, hoping for a glimpse of her reflection. Unbelievable to think she'd now reached an age where you could take away ten years and she'd still be an adult. Lizzie took an extra-large sip to harden her resolve. Maybe it was time to upgrade to anti-ageing eye cream after all. And to think that she had dismissed it as pure sales pitch when they had tried to sell her some at the Clarins counter the other day.

'Well, maybe not ten years...but certainly two.'

That was much more like it. Lizzie raised her glass to no one in particular in celebration of her relative youth.

'You haven't looked this happy since you were with Rob.'

Lizzie grimaced. Rob was a long time ago. He'd been totally the wrong person for her, even if she'd managed to pretend that he was perfect for nearly six months. His idea of
romance was insisting on scaring the life out of her by whisk-
ing her all over Great Britain on his motorcycle at weekends.
'That wasn't happy; that was windburn!'

They both laughed. Rob had even bought her a full set of
leathers and a helmet. A total contrast to the perfectly faded
jeans and huggable blue jumper that he'd been wearing to the
dinner party where they'd met. There'd been no hint that he
was a motorcycle nut. No greasy nail beds, no Harley David-
son accessories, not a Moto Guzzi key fob in sight.

'Well, at least he was about twenty years younger than...
what was he called...?'

Lizzie laughed at the collection of totally unsuitable skele-
tons hanging in her closet.

'Lawrence...and he was only fourteen years older than me,'
Lizzie added a little defensively. So she had been going
through her find-a-less-dysfunctional-than-my-own-biologi-
cal-father-figure-and-then-sleep-with-him crisis? He hadn't
exactly been Tom Selleck to look at either. A pity, Lizzie
mused. A pity also that Clare seemed to have a clearer recollection of Lizzie's exes than she had, and appeared to take such
delight in listing them after a few drinks. She appeared to be
on a roll.

'So when do I get to meet Lover Boy? Why don't you get
him to join us for a quick glass of champagne?'

Lizzie stalled. It would be preferable to them meeting sober
at the flat first thing one morning when Clare would predictably ask far too many questions in the not traditionally wel-
coming style of a Gestapo officer. But Clare could be a bit of
a loose canon when she was under the influence. Matt didn't
need to know about Rob, Lawrence, or indeed any of the others. 'He might not be free...'

'And then again... Honestly, Liz, you are the end sometimes.'

Clare raised her right eyebrow at Lizzie. She was going to
have to do better than that if she wanted to keep him under

wraps. Lizzie knew that attempting to dodge the inevitable was pointless. Once Clare had made up her mind, it was only a matter of time before she got what she wanted.

'Give him a call. If he's in the vicinity he might like to pop in. I mean, you haven't seen each other for—what?—two, no, more like three days now... Poor love...'

Lizzie rummaged in her bag. 'Damn. I didn't bring my phone.'

'Here, use mine...and don't even pretend that you can't remember his number. It must be etched in your memory by now.'

Lizzie had to climb lots of stairs before she was close enough to ground level to get a signal. He answered straight away. Why, when you wouldn't mind getting an answer-phone, does it never happen?

'Matt?'

'Hi, Liz.'

'Is now a good time?'

'Well, it depends on how you look at it. It's not a great time in that it's after nine and I'm still in the office, desperately trying to focus on my computer screen so I can type up a few proposals for an 8:00 a.m. meeting tomorrow, but it's a fantastic time in that I'm dying to be distracted. Everything OK with you? Aren't you and Clare supposed to be slagging off men together right now?'

'We are—we were—well...not all men... Anyway, we were just chatting and we—well, Clare—well, we thought it'd be much more fun to slag off men if we had at least one representative popping in for a quick drink to add more fuel to our fire. I mean it's all very well saying that all men are bastards hypothetically...but you can't beat a real-life example.'

Matt was totally silent. Not a laugh, nothing...and Lizzie had thought that this was one of her more mildly amusing moments. She carried on regardless.

'Hey, I'm only kidding. Look, we're at the Atlantic Bar and Clare would really like to meet you, so I thought I'd give you a call to see if you fancied a quick drink with us before we move on to our next venue.'

More silence. Lizzie wondered if the signal had gone. Maybe she'd been chatting away to herself for the last few minutes? She moved the phone away from her ear. Just far enough to be able to see the screen but not too far just in case Matt was there and about to say something. All the bars were illuminated defiantly. They were still connected.

'Hello? Hello? Matt? Are you still there?'

It wasn't that Matt didn't want to meet Clare. He just wanted to make the right impression. In which case, he supposed it was far better to be introduced in a busy bar over a drink than in their flat in his boxers. Besides, he loved seeing Lizzie when she'd had a couple. Alcohol softened her potentially hard professional edges. 'Hello? Hello? Yes, I'm here.'

'Can you hear me?'

' I can now. You were breaking up a bit earlier.' It wasn't altogether true. But blaming technology was a wonderfully useful device at times.

'So? Don't worry if you can't, but I'd better get back to Clare before she passes out on the table or orders us something vintagely expensive.'

'OK, I'll pop in for a quick glass of something. But don't let me stay long. I've got to come back here...and I don't want to be accused of hijacking your evening or spoiling your fun.'

'Great...' Perfect. 'We're at a table in the corner just to the... um...' Lizzie waggled a wrist for just long enough to ascertain which one was left and which was right. She had patently imbibed more champagne than she had realised, and the first thing to go was her sense of direction. '...left...to the left of the bar—looking gorgeous, of course. Don't be long. It would probably be to your advantage if you turned up while I can still focus.'

Lizzie hurried back to the table via the powder, eyeliner and lipgloss room to tell Clare to brace herself. More excited than apprehensive, Lizzie felt sure she would approve.

Matt strolled in, doing his utmost to keep his nerve. Granted, it would be a cruel coincidence if someone spotted him, but this place was sufficiently exclusive and expensive for her and her agency cronies to consider it one of their haunts. To his relief he spotted Lizzie and Clare almost immediately and, picking the chair with its back to the room, kissed both women hello. It looked innocent enough. He was unlikely to be having an affair with two women sitting at the same table.

Lizzie was positively smouldering. But, as he kept reminding himself, he'd got her under false pretences. On the sly. And he was stolen goods. For once this wasn't an appropriate time for a flash of honesty. Tonight was about Clare. He knew how close they were, and thanks to Lizzie's candour he also knew her husband had cheated on her. Clare's stare was friendly but steely. He was well aware that his perception might be tainted with a touch of paranoia in light of his own marital status, but right now he was under assessment, with a verbal dissection sure to ensue as soon as he upped and left.

'So, have you two put the world to rights yet? Would a man-free Britain be a better place?'

Clare watched Matt and Lizzie exchange an affectionate grin and took a big sip of her drink. To think it had been her suggestion that he came along. Still, at least she knew that he wasn't a figment of Lizzie's fertile imagination. He seemed real enough. Quite boyish. A nice smile. And, from the way he kept looking across to Lizzie, obviously smitten. She decided to break up the little gazeathon which seemed to be in full swing opposite her before she turned green and prickly.

'So, Matt, a copywriter...'

He was quick to give Clare his undivided attention, and gave Lizzie's hand an affectionate squeeze under the table. 'For my sins. I gather Union Jack's is your second home. We'll have to come along one evening. Lizzie says it's fantastic and I've never been.' Matt was much happier keeping the conversation away from his personal life.

After a perfectly polite adult we-don't-know-each-other-very-well-but-are-making-a-concerted-effort conversation about the restaurant, they moved on to the equally formal topic of house prices in Notting Hill which, according to the papers that morning, were now more expensive than parts of neighbouring Kensington. Matt should have seen the next series of questions coming.

'So, where's your place, Matt? I assume you don't actually live in the office between trips to Putney?'

'Chiswick. Well, more like Turnham Green, really. Do you know it?'

Clare shook her head.

'It's a lovely part of the world. One of London's best-kept secrets. Somehow it's managed to retain a villagey feel—there's still a local butcher, fishmonger, a flower stall by the station, that sort of thing. On the downside you can't move on Saturdays for designer couples with designer babies in three-wheeled all-terrain buggies, but the pros outweigh the cons.'

'So you like it, then?' Clare had gone for sarcasm. The lowest form of wit, maybe, but the most appropriate, she felt, in light of the eulogy to the W4 idyll that had just poured out of Matt's mouth.

Matt smiled wryly to acknowledge the rosy picture he'd just painted of an urban village. An oxymoron—unless, apparently, you lived in Turnham Green or the Central Perk neighbourhood, of course.

'Do you own or rent?'

'Own. It's the best investment I think I've ever made... Not difficult, though, considering I am the sort of bloke who struggles to save more than a couple of pounds. You two rent, don't you?' Matt knew the answer, but Lizzie was too pissed to pull him up on it, and he figured it was safer to keep the conversation to familiar, well-trodden, non-controversial subjects.

'Yup. We know we're throwing our money away, don't we, Liz?' Alcohol seemed to have dissolved Lizzie's subtlety, and she nodded without taking her eyes off Matt, but at least she was still listening—which, Clare supposed, was something. 'The thing is we're both slightly allergic to the idea of putting down permanent roots in one place... We're both the product of one disappointment too many, I think.'

The current disappointment drained his glass and quickly refilled it. He wished he'd come clean before meeting Clare. Now he was simply lying to one more person, and he had a sneaking suspicion that she wouldn't be able to see his side of things; he wasn't sure that he could blame her.

Lizzie joined in.

'I think we just like to kid ourselves that we're free spirits...you know, that we could hypothetically walk out of the door tomorrow and become diving instructors in Australia if the mood took us. The fact that we've barely had time for a holiday in the last couple of years is neither here nor there. We know it's illogical...'

Free spirit...yeah right. Only spelt s.c.a.r.e.d.o.f.c.o.m.m.i.t.m.e.n.t.o.f. l.o.s.i.n.g.c.o.n.t.r.o.l.a.n.d.b.e.i.n.g.h.u.r.t. And then of course there was her genuine mortgage phobia. Owing someone in excess of £200,000 was just something her junior savers account hadn't prepared her for.

'I know our rent would more than cover equivalent mortgage repayments...'

Lizzie's mental arithmetic had always been her weakest link, and she hesitated for a moment while she checked with the less pissed part of her brain that she was still making sense.

'But we've just found that renting has worked better for us. And—this always sounds ridiculous—but we really haven't had the time to look for somewhere.'

Clare nodded sagely. 'We'd have to take the girls' approach and suss out all the alternatives before deciding. And it's not like you can get a receipt and take a flat back if you don't like it. Plus, I can't bear to think that there is always the chance that it will be worth less in five years' time...'

'Highly unlikely in London. But your place is lovely. I can see why you're both happy to stay there for now.'

Lizzie was pleased that Clare and Matt were ostensibly chatting away, even if they had picked a rather grown-up subject. The combined presence of her lover and best friend was causing her to feel quite sentimental about life.

'So, Matt, when do I get to come back to Chiswick to play?'

It was an innocent enough question.

'It's time I got to check out your CD collection, the number of bottles in your bathroom, any embarrassing photos of you in school uniform or with exes squirrelled away or lurking on old pinboards...'

Lizzie was quite curious in some ways, but then again she liked the fact that he was happy to come to hers. As he put it, all he needed was a clean pair of boxers and a toothbrush, whereas she needed a small suitcase of cleansing, toning, moisturising and scented lotions and potions, plus a selection of clothes and shoes for the following day. It was a valid point.

Matt tried to change the subject. He didn't know if he was imagining things, but he was sure he could feel a frost rolling in from Clare's end of the table.

Lizzie had now drunk approaching a whole bottle of champagne on her own, and wasn't about to let this go. She wanted to see him in his own place. She'd put money on it being very tastefully kitted out, with a huge television, several remote controls and as many channels—and adverts—as money could buy. Making sure she'd caught Matt's eye, she leant across to Clare and announced in a stage whisper, 'I don't think he wants me to go round there. To be completely honest, I think he's keeping me a secret from his wife.'

It was meant to be a joke. You know the sort of comment. Light-hearted, offhand, flippant, and Lizzie even winked at Matt as she delivered it. Only he was no longer smiling. Her world ground to a juddering halt as her heart climbed into her mouth.

Clare seized the moment to tactfully disappear to the loo and Lizzie wished that she'd taken her with her. For some reason it was taking her a few moments to comprehend what was happening, although it would have been quite clear to the average five-year-old. Her tear ducts obviously worked faster than her brain. They were full to the brim, and tears were now spilling onto her cheeks. To Lizzie's horror she could see that his eyes were moist too, but compassion was rapidly being replaced with a cocktail of self-preservation, anger and the humiliation of Clare being there to witness the whole thing. More fodder for the Williamson vitriol on married men.

'You're not, are you? Are you?'

Lizzie tried to keep her voice steady and calm. After all, they were paying customers in the West End, not punters at the Queen Vic, plus Lizzie needed to hold on to her self-respect even if she suspected that it was only going to be a matter of seconds before maximum strength humiliation kicked in. Lizzie had only clung to the notion that Matt might have been winding her up for as long as it took to say it out loud. His face said it all. No one was that good an actor.

'God, Liz. I should have told you the evening we met, but for some reason I couldn't. I kept meaning to, and then somehow we seemed more important that it did. The truth is, yes, I am married, but I haven't been a part of my relationship for nearly a year. I admit it was easier to stay at first. But I've got to leave. I am going to leave. I promise...'

Matt could hear his voice getting higher and higher pitched. He took a deep breath before continuing at a more masculine, less hysterical level.

'I don't think I'd ever be able to forgive myself if I've fucked up our chances. I've never met anyone like you before...'

He stole a glance. She was just staring at the table. As if looking him in the eye might cause her to suddenly turn to stone.

'Believe me, every time I meant to tell you something cropped up or the moment passed. Only now—and I wouldn't blame you, because I'm not liking myself at all right now—in fact you probably hate me—and...' Matt shook his head. 'How did it all become so complicated? Liz? Lizzie? Please look at me...'

Lizzie looked up, her eyes glassy. This was all his fault. He cupped her crestfallen face in his hands. She was too traumatised to move away.

'Lizzie, we've got something so special. We both know that. I know this is a huge shock for you...'

Lizzie shook her head. He really had no idea.

'But really it's just a technicality. My marriage has been over for months. And I promise I'll leave. I know that it's one of the oldest clichés, even from the King of Cliché himself, but this is me and you we're talking about, and if you feel for me even half of what I feel for you, you'll know that I mean what I'm saying. It wasn't a calculated deception, I swear.'

However often she dabbed at her eyes the water just kept

on dripping down her cheeks. Lizzie had no idea how she felt. She knew she probably should have been screaming or shouting, or at the very least throwing her drink at him, but she couldn't say, do or feel anything. Paralysed from the brain down. She was in total shock.

'God, Clare will hate me after what she's been through.' Matt was thinking aloud. A mistake. 'I'd love to take you back to your flat, run you a bath, make you a cup of tea and try to explain...'

'But your wife wouldn't like it? Oh, please, Matt. I'm not that stupid.' Lizzie shook her head as the truth slowly sank in. 'But maybe I am? And to think I thought you were different— special, even.' Her voice petered out. She was more or less talking to herself.

'I am. I will be. I'll show you. I promise....' Matt looked into Lizzie's eyes but her gaze was empty, as if he could look straight through her. 'I'm so very sorry. This wasn't how I wanted to tell you, and I did want to tell you. And now I've ruined your evening. If it's any consolation I think I've just ruined my life.' Matt tried to smile. It didn't work. 'Liz, I want to be with you. I know it's early days, but I'm completely in love with you. You're such a special person.'

On any other occasion Lizzie would have been cartwheeling at the use of the L word so early on—and not in an in-bed-together situation—but she wasn't sure how she was going to deal with this one. She closed her eyes for a split second and willed it all to be a terrible nightmare, but when she opened them again she was still there and so was he. She believed him. And, while she didn't want to become the founder member of Doormats Anonymous, she knew that she wanted to give him a chance to explain. But Lizzie knew what Clare would say— plus, it was hardly right that an agony aunt should be sleeping with someone else's husband. Lizzie groaned. Aloud or in her head? Judging from the look on Matt's face it had definitely been out loud.

'I'll call you tomorrow...' Matt leant across and, trembling, kissed her cheek tenderly before getting to his feet. He could sense Clare hovering at the bar and could feel the daggers aligning themselves with their target.

Maintaining his composure until he reached a suitably dark alleyway, he finally allowed his face to crumple as his eyes filled with tears of his own, their presence giving him a fittingly distorted view of everything. He'd thought he'd be relieved that it was all out in the open. Instead he felt frustratingly powerless. Consumed by a soul-searching ache that painkillers have never been developed to treat. Matt stopped at an off-licence on his way back to the office. He didn't think he could face the rest of his life—well, certainly not the remainder of the evening—sober.

Clare embraced her best friend, who was currently teetering on the brink of total adversity. Safe in the knowledge that she no longer had to cope alone, Lizzie dissolved into Clare's shoulder.

'Come on...there, there... Go on...have a good cry...'

'He's married.'

'I gathered. The shit.' Clare was livid.

'He said that it's been over for months. But I had no idea. I feel so stupid.' Lizzie's voice was cracked.

'I know, sweetie. You weren't to know. I can't believe he even tried the "I'll leave her" line. What an insult to your intelligence...'

Typically, Clare wasn't trying to be objective. In her world men were guilty until proven innocent, and certainly not entitled to a fair trial. And Mr Matt had just sent himself to the electric chair.

'Everyone knows that's the oldest line in the book. If you look hard enough it's probably even in the Bible, in one of the Old Testament stories—just been lost in the translation over the years or surreptitiously removed by a male editor.'

'But I should have known...'

Lizzie was still sobbing. She knew that she really wasn't handling this at all well. Still, everyone had to fall apart sometimes.

'I really thought we had something so special...' There was

a moment's gap while Lizzie's innate positivity did its best to push to the surface. 'Maybe it will all work out. He said he loved me.'

Uncharitable as it sounded, Clare hoped that Lizzie wasn't dribbling onto her new 'dry clean only' top. 'Liz, don't be so bloody ridiculous. He lied to you about having a wife, so why the fuck shouldn't he lie about leaving her too?'

'I'd like a chance to hear what he's got to say. I just want to talk to him.'

'But his wife might answer the phone.' Clare instantly regretted her vituperative jibe. Lizzie was back to square one and it was her fault. Clare managed a more softly-softly approach and opted for the say less, hug more option until they'd got a cab home.

Lizzie was slumped on the sofa, staring, an untouched G&T tightly gripped in her hand. Clare sat down next to her and raised her glass. 'A toast. Because all men are bastards and controlled by their dicks...'

Lizzie remained motionless. Clare willed her to lift her glass. Just a little. She'd even settle for a lifting of the corners— make that just one corner—of her mouth. But there was no activity from the shell of a person next to her. Not a twitch of a muscle. It was going to be a long night.

Clare took a sip and waited. She was halfway through an article in the *Radio Times* before Lizzie started speaking. Her gaze was now fixed on a point way ahead in the distance, a good few miles on the other side of the wall.

'I know you'll think this is ridiculous. But what if what he said was true? What if his marriage is a sham? If he is going to leave? What then?'

'Liz, if you hadn't made your silly joke earlier you can bet that you'd still be none the wiser. I'm sorry. Really I am. I know how disappointed you must be. I know you were excited and happy and...'

Lizzie's face crumpled again as she recalled just how happy she'd been only hours earlier.

'But I'm afraid that's it. It's got to be over. Where's your pride? You're worth far more than he's bargained for. Either he's lying, and his marriage is fine, or he's so weak that he can't act on his feelings and do the decent thing—in which case you don't want him anyway...'

Lizzie nodded in an attempt to convince herself. Of course Clare was right. But it didn't make it any easier.

'If it's any consolation, his wife will be feeling worse than you are when he tells her. *If* he tells her, that is. Married men should have to have wedding rings tattooed onto their third fingers by law.'

'He's probably never worn a ring. Lots of men don't these days. Some men just don't like wearing jewellery.'

'Some men just don't like being faithful. It's the thrill of the chase. It's knowing that they're not playing by the rules.'

'But Matt's not like that. He's different.' A lone tear rolled down Lizzie's cheek. Neither Julia Roberts nor Meg Ryan could have produced a more poignant one.

Clare was becoming increasingly exasperated at Lizzie's apparent inability to see the facts. Of course he wasn't different. 'Liz, go and get some sleep. I bet this will all look different in daylight.'

Lizzie didn't so much fall asleep as pass out in between prolonged periods of snivelling into her fortuitously absorbent pillow.

When she finally woke, the morning after the night before, for a split second she felt happy—but then she remembered. She should have realised something was up. Things had been going too well. January was traditionally the worst month of the year for morale, men and money. Now it was living up to its reputation. She wished she could just hibernate for a couple of months and re-emerge when time had done its healing thing. She didn't see why she had to be awake throughout the process.

Feelings aside, she knew she had to put a stop to it. She was supposed to help people with their problems, not cause more, and if she turned a blind eye she'd be endorsing a situation that she knew couldn't work. She had to bury her impetuous nature and think about how seeing more of him could jeopardise the real world around her. The one she had to live in every day. And if he'd lied so convincingly about something as big as this, logically how could she believe a word he said?

If she kept seeing him—well, that would make her a mistress. Unofficially she was one already. Certainly not something she had ever aspired to be. She didn't want to put herself in the same bracket as those red-taloned women you saw on trashy documentaries, eulogising about the joys of being wined and dined, flown all over the world and bought expensive jewellery without having to tidy up. Lizzie wanted to come first. Lizzie wanted real love. Love with washing and ironing and cooking and maybe even children. Warts and all.

She had no idea what time it was when the phone broke into her reverie. Her curtains were still drawn and it sounded as if it was pouring with rain outside. Marvellous. Gloomy weather had arrived to cement her depression. Couldn't just one thing go her way?

She thought about just leaving it ringing, but couldn't—just in case whoever it was didn't leave a message, which would be even worse than the phone not having rung at all.

'Hello?' It was listless, a traditional courtesy greeting but with no feeling.

There was silence at the other end.

'Hello?'

This time she was greeted by an equally small, flat voice.

'Liz? It's me. I'm so so very, very sorry.'

Damn cordless phones. There wasn't even anything to strangle herself with if things got worse.

Lizzie knew that she should have refused to speak to him, but she was pleased that he had called. Or at least at the moment she thought she was.

'Liz...are you still there?'

'Yup. What time is it?'

'Eleven-fifteen...are you still in bed?'

Lizzie stretched out under the duvet to prove to herself that she was still a complete human being and not just a head on the pillow before springing back into the foetal position.

'Mmm. Didn't seem to be much point in getting up today.'

Lizzie knew she shouldn't have said that. It exposed her. It told him she cared. But she did and, hey, it couldn't get any worse than last night. In for a penny, in for a pound. If he was going to break her heart he might as well be allowed to stamp on it good and hard a few more times before leaving her to recover.

'I should've told you that very first night in the taxi, but I really wanted to see you again. I was selfish. I was scared. Please, meet me for lunch. I've been going over everything again and again in my head. I'd rehearsed telling you about a hundred times but then last night I was caught off guard and none of it really came out right.'

Lizzie felt oddly calm listening to his voice. She wished it could be yesterday morning again, but things had changed irrevocably, hadn't they? All these hypothetical questions and only answers she didn't want to hear. It was just no good.

'Matt, I'm sorry, but I don't think lunch is a good idea. It's got to be over. For lots of reasons.'

Clare would have patted her on the back, but Lizzie didn't feel relieved, or that she had the upper hand. She just felt very sad. She sank another millimetre into her pillow even though she'd thought she was as low as she could go already.

'Lizzie, I know you have to say that for your pride, for your self-esteem... I've treated you appallingly, and I know you'll need time to deal with this, but I hope that eventually you might be able to forgive me...'

There was a pause. Matt was waiting for Lizzie to say something. Anything. But she couldn't get the words out. In the absence of any input, Matt decided to continue. If she wasn't going to meet him for lunch this might be the only chance he got to say it. On balance he knew that he deserved everything he was getting, and more.

'You must've had letters from people like me in the past. Men who get stuck in a loveless marriage because it's easier to stay there than to rock the boat. I know that doesn't make me look very good, and I know I should have just left. She's changed. She's no longer the person I vowed to love and to honour and I am going to leave. I know you and I haven't been seeing each other for long, but I really believe we're worth fighting for. When I didn't tell you at the outset it was because somehow I just couldn't, even though I wanted to. I didn't want to risk what we had, what we could have... I'm just asking for another chance. I hope in time I'll be able to convince you to forgive me.'

His speech had all the hallmarks of a classic romantic tragedy. She desperately wanted to believe him, but the more she thought about him being married to a person, to a real live woman with a name, a personality and a body, who shared half his bed and half his wardrobe, the harder it became. She wanted to know if they still slept together. If they did, was it good? Did she go skiing too? She wanted to know, and then she didn't. Maybe she was only one of several mistresses—a veritable wifelet. He was right; she had read about this scenario so many times. She had dealt with it during phone-ins and she knew that it was a situation that could only end in tears. She might not have worn them on her sleeve, or rammed them down the throats of her readers, but she had morals and principles.

Matt was waiting for an answer.

He would have got one, only Lizzie couldn't speak. She couldn't risk the pain rising up and escaping noisily while he was listening. So much for control.

Meanwhile she was going through the whole spectrum of emotions. Upset. Angry. With him. With herself for not sensing anything earlier. Disappointed. Disbelieving. Exhausted. As far as a response went, all she could manage was a suppressed wail-cum-snort followed by a deeply unpleasant sniff.

'Mmmmhmmm.'

It was pathetic. Lizzie wished she could be stronger; she would have loved to be brusque at this moment—offhand, even. But she couldn't manage it.

'Listen, Liz. I can't bear to hear you so upset.' What on earth had he done? The woman he loved in tears. His fault.

'I'm fine...' A pause for a big blink and a deep breath to try and convince herself that she was indeed fine.

'Sure you are. If you're fine, the Pope's Jewish.'

'Don't worry about me. I'll bounce back.' Lizzie was sure that she would. Eventually. Probably some time after she'd bounced into a couple of bottles.

'Look, you don't have to handle this all by yourself. Please meet me. Just for lunch. No funny business. Just a chat. We'll go somewhere quiet, I promise.'

'Not today.' No way could Lizzie contemplate lunch on a day when she had to go through the whole studio thing later and actually sit in a room with other human beings.

'Tomorrow?'

'OK...'

'Great. I'll call you in the morning with a plan. Thanks, Liz. I love you.'

Lizzie felt oddly comforted. She only hoped Clare would be out. She couldn't possibly tell the woman who believed all mistresses should be burnt at the stake that she'd agreed to lunch. But surely one of the perks of getting older was the prerogative to make her own mistakes?

chapter 13

Unbefuckinglievable. Who on earth would pay fifty pounds to go running, in winter, in a public park, in London, in their lunch hour, with someone fitter, therefore preventing the walking-most-of-the-way tactic? Yet that was what Gareth, personal trainer to the stars, had just suggested. His client list might resemble the contents page of *Hello!* magazine, but surely you could buy a flat stomach in the twenty-first century without having to sacrifice your knee joints and self-respect in the process?

It took Rachel a full hour of careful preening to look this good when she left the house every morning, and she wasn't about to risk it all with hours of the day remaining. Will might have blagged her the introductory assessment, but that was as far as this particular whim was going. Yet, despite the ludicrous turn her day had taken only moments ago, Rachel was in high spirits.

The campaign was finally snowballing and she could almost see her name in lights—well, she could when she removed her designer shades. Her latest present to herself was just in time to shield her from those winter rays, late enough to already be this summer's hottest shape, but early enough to say 'original' as all the high street copycats were still a good month away. They were currently on the top of her head, assuming the role of designer halo-cum-alice-band.

All was still quiet on the personal front, but at least Valentine's Day was round the corner and for the first time in years she'd decided to arrange a night out. She still hadn't confessed to anyone that she'd consulted an agony aunt. In all honesty she'd probably be amazed for the rest of her life that she'd not only written a letter but sent it in to a magazine. The only upshot was her new e-mail buddy. Dear Lizzie had become a useful sounding board and a fresh breath of non-agency, non-advertising air. Their electronic note-passing did a good job of reminding her to make an effort on the days when it felt as if her personal life was slipping through her fingers. Better still, Lizzie had no agenda. She wasn't angling for promotion or taking sides; she was a bona fide bullshit-free zone. If this was just Lizzie doing her job, she was amazingly good at it.

Rachel was indulging in a quick game of Solitaire on her computer when the whirlwind of energy and creativity that was making her life a whole lot more bearable at the moment burst through the door.

'Morning, Rach.'

Will bounced on to her sofa and slurped at the froth on his cappuccino while waiting for a suitable break in her concentration. Fortunately his most recent attempt to give up smoking still seemed to be in full swing, and Rachel was spared a lingering blue cloud of smoke in her office. Through the strategic positioning of office furniture Rachel had ensured that no one else could see her computer screen, so Will was currently unaware that the delay was due to a pressing tactical decision: should she move the King of Spades to the presently empty column or deal more cards and see whether the King of Hearts or King of Diamonds might still be in the pack? What she really needed was a red king.

'I'll be with you in a second.'

She'd perfected pretending to be engrossed in her work when people came into her office and had stopped feeling guilty about what some people might consider to be wasting time. Advertising might never have returned to the excesses of the eighties but it was still keeping its end up, and she didn't have to be sitting at her desk typing all day to be working hard. While the legwork was done by her talented and incredibly enthusiastic team, Rachel had time to do the whole lunch, drinking club, award ceremony bit. She'd found she could troubleshoot problems just as effectively whether she was in her office or on Bond Street.

Will was becoming increasingly impatient and more than a little fidgety—not unrelated to the fact that he didn't have a cigarette in his hand to play with. Once he'd scooped the residual froth out of his paper cup and eaten it from his finger he watched Rachel. He felt slightly guilty about distracting her, but he did have some exciting news.

'Sorry to disturb you...'

'No, no, it's fine. That's what I'm here for. Go ahead.'

She finally looked up. Will was beaming.

'We've got her...'

Rachel wondered whether there was another quick move she could do. The Ace of Clubs must be under there somewhere. She suddenly realised that Will had already stopped talking. Damn. She minimised the game on her screen, stood up assertively and walked over to the couch to join him.

'Sorry—you were saying?'

'We've got her. She's said yes to being filmed and—wait for this—she's even given us permission to use the archive which, even if I say so myself, is bloody miraculous but makes our lives a hell of a lot easier.'

'Her...?'

Rachel struggled with her short-term memory. In the absence of any recollection she feigned coolness. She didn't want to portray a level of excitement that outweighed the level of his achievement and therefore make herself look stupid.

Will wished that Rachel would just swallow her pride and give him the credit he deserved. Communicating positive feedback wasn't her forte. A couple of weeks ago she'd made him feel like young creative of the moment, yet today—nothing.

Not a glimmer of recognition. She was just so up and down these days. Women. Exasperation and frustration crept into his tone.

'Indigo Jackson. As per our meeting last week. It was touch and go. Her agent wasn't sure at first, but a bit of intensive schmoozing later and she's up for it.'

Will was annoyed. What was the point in him putting his life on hold night after night if Rachel wasn't even paying attention?

Rachel tried and failed to put a human interest story to the name. Who the hell was Indigo Jackson? She sounded like something off a rock chick's paint colour chart. But Will was looking a little pissed off at her less than euphoric reaction to his morning's work. She'd just have to trust him on this one. In Will's eyes Indigo was obviously worth a champagne toast at the very least.

'Great. Fab to have her on board.'

Great? Will thought it was more like fucking amazing. He had just secured an exclusive with the widow of a no longer living legend who had killed himself in search of the perfect high, so depriving future generations of his lyrics and innovative melodies, to talk about the pressures her husband had felt and his regrets at getting in too deep, and all Rachel could manage was 'great'. It was irritating him enough to instantly make his nicotine patch redundant. If ever there was a time he had wanted a cigarette or three it was now.

He wondered what would happen if he got Elvis out of his coffin and on board to talk about his final years... A 'well done', perhaps? A 'good work Will'? He knew the client and the senior partners at the agency were thrilled with the way things were shaping up. Rachel was soaking up all the compliments at the moment, and he knew she could gush with the best of them when she wanted to. What did he have to do to impress her?

'Really, Will, that's great. If you could e-mail me a few cuts and a biog on her when you get back to your desk that would be perfect. Now, who else are we still waiting on?'

Rachel knew that it was thanks to Will, his persuasive charm and his tireless ambition, that they now had several generations of football players, a well-known TV actress and a handful of ageing rock stars signed up to talk about how and why they had beaten their habits, and now this Indigo woman. If Will said she was good news then she was sure she was. Erudite and gifted, he'd cut some powerful montages of archive footage and present-day soundbites to some perfectly chosen and memorable phrases of music, and he'd ensured that she now had the appropriate CDs in her collection and the odd factoid at her fingertips to wow clients with in meetings.

Last week he'd discovered that the guy who'd been tipped as the next baron of the information superhighway, and a sure entry into next year's Rich List, had marvellously—from their point of view—lost five years of his life to heroin addiction but against all the odds had fought back from rock bottom. Human interest tales of rags to riches never failed to sell, and Rachel was in the process of signing him an exclusive with a Sunday tabloid to tie in with the launch of the campaign.

'All we need now is a supermodel and a member of the Royal family—or, more realistically, someone who has shagged a member of the Royal family—who's dabbled in drugs in the past and I think our wish list will be complete.'

Will was encouraged to see Rachel at least had the decency to smile as she asked the impossible. He knew his brief only too well, but she wasn't the one on the phone talking to agents and sending faxes all day. The fashion world was a fiercely closed shop, and trying to get any of their own to dish the dirt on the more sordid aspects of the industry was proving impossible. There were plenty of rumours but nothing concrete to go on. Sure, they'd rooted out a disaffected few, but they just sounded bitter and you suspected that, had their careers gone better, they wouldn't have been remotely interested in taking part. Besides, as far as Rachel was concerned it was either an A-list name or no name at all.

'I know it's tough. But a model would be great. An exposé on the so-called glamour. Everyone knows it's going on.'

'"Everyone" might do, but no one's telling me anything.'

Will tried not to lose his cool. Rachel sensed she was dancing close to the edge.

'I appreciate the effort. I know it's not easy out there—just keep going. You never know who might say yes if you don't try...'

But, Will thought to himself, I know who's going to say no.

'I'm getting a really good vibe about this. You're doing great. You should be very proud of yourself.'

'Thanks.' Now she'd paid him a direct compliment Will had no idea what to do with it. 'I'd better get back to the phone. I'll e-mail you that biog later this afternoon.'

'No problem.' Rachel couldn't remember exactly which biog, but she was confident she'd learn lots from Will's impeccable research when it did arrive. Violet, Indigo—whoever she was—would certainly seem a lot more familiar when she'd read a potted history. Sometimes she missed her days at Will's level. Frenetic, sparky, all-consuming and totally invigorating. So what if the pay had never even been enough to cover alcohol, let alone anything less frivolous? There'd been genuine camaraderie lower down the pecking order. The higher you got, the more the pecking became stabbing, and you became more and more paranoid as you had to watch your back as your increased salary became harder to justify when things weren't going award-winningly.

Rachel owed Will big time. His Midas touch meant they'd be more than fulfilling their brief and reaching out to the age group who were most influenced by the 'glamour' of the drug culture without patronising them. Maybe it was time for a team night out to boost morale.

Rachel wanted this to be a great campaign on every level. Watch out Richard Branson, Ms Nice Guy, queen of motivational leadership, was just waiting in the wings—and she didn't see why she had to wear a sweatshirt or grow a beard in order to be approachable. With this success she would be unstoppable—plus, with a bit of time and the right preparation, she was sure Mr Rachel wouldn't be able to resist her. It was going to be a fantastic year; she could feel it.

Rachel celebrated Will's departure from her office by finishing off her game of Solitaire with unprecedented speed and focus. As she watched the victory cascade of cards through to the end she made an executive decision to pop out. Her head swimming with profile articles and acceptance speeches, she knew that an hour in the shops would work the playfulness out of her system—plus there was already a whole 'next-season' thing happening in the retail world. Her new positivity about life was about to be reflected in her wardrobe, and maybe she'd even pick up a little something for Will while she was out. They had Indigo Jackson. See, she had been listening. Rachel found herself smiling. Will made her feel good about herself. He could help her all the way to the top.

chapter 14

It might have been less than twenty-four hours since they'd spoken, but Lizzie had eaten lasagne two meals running, polished off an entire packet of Angel Delight and done more staring into space than Patrick Moore. From the moment she'd opened her eyes early on Wednesday morning frustratingly she'd been wide awake, and so, at a time of day usually reserved for families getting up to go on cheap package holidays, she'd washed, dressed and headed to her study.

She hadn't logged on since Saturday, and decided to make a start by going through her inbox in an attempt to break herself in gently. Reading messages didn't involve mental agility and proved a useful way of tricking her mind into concentrating on something other than the time, the phone, and the possible outcomes of her currently disastrous personal life. There were twenty-three new items for her to read. Once she'd deleted the junk messages trying to sell her tights, flights and promising her lots of luck and money if only she forwarded it to three girls, six boys and a partridge in a pear tree, she'd whittled it down to fifteen.

Three were from the woman formerly known as Name and

Address Withheld. She and Rachel might have struck up a slightly unorthodox correspondence, but Lizzie found their almost daily asides a useful stress-reliever. It wasn't about professional advice any more, it was—for want of a better word—a friendship. If you could be friends with someone you had never met or spoken to out loud. It was like passing notes. Quick time-outs from their lives. And, in terms of ambitious women trying to make the system work for them, they had a lot in common. The last one had been sent at 22:12 yesterday evening. She really did work late.

Everything OK? You're probably just snowed under—believe me I know the feeling—but I've had nothing from you in three days, and now it's February—don't understand where this year is going. Ever hectic at this end. Before you nag, rang Eurostar—well, got secretary to ring Eurostar—yesterday, which is a step in right direction. So get thinking of those romantic restaurants.
R x

Lizzie hit 'reply'. It was great having a pen-friend who only knew what you'd selected to tell her about yourself. Faceless sounding boards were the way forward. A bit like confession, only not quite as spiritual. Perfect for your average non-practising, half-Jewish agnostic.

R
Worry not. I'm still here. Feeling slightly sorry for myself as my newish relationship (had been looking quite positive) seems to have taken a turn for the worse. Guess I shouldn't be surprised, but failed to see this one coming. Still, enough of the whingeing—we agony aunts have to develop thick skins and stress-free personal lives and carry on regardless. Hope your cam-

paign is coming together well. Can't wait to see the ads. When do they start?
L x

Lizzie steered clear of the specifics of her personal crisis. This was work—well, sort of—and she was paid to solve problems, not share them. She pressed 'send'. It was still only 06:36.

By nine, Lizzie had answered all her e-mailed letters, printed off hard copies for the files and was just starting on a bit of snail mail whilst tossing a few column ideas around at the back of her mind. Despite herself she was feeling a bit chirpier. Her concern was becoming increasingly detached from her reality, as if she was hoping that the having a wife revelation might have been a terrible nightmare brought on by a late-night cheeseburger before bed.

09:17. A message pinged into her inbox. Note-passing was officially underway.

Sorry to hear you've had shitty couple of days, but good to know that you're not immune to the odd personal crisis. Makes the rest of us feel less like failures. Look at it as research. Now you know what the rest of us go through. Fucking impressed (and frankly a bit intimidated) to see you awake and working at 06:36. What's the secret? I'm still waiting for my second coffee to kick in.

Work hectic. No danger of a completed ad hitting the cinema, a billboard or the TV for quite a while yet. Own personal crisis still unfolding. No need for you to put your professional hat on, but getting it out of my system always helps. Seem to be growing further apart by the hour. Becoming convinced he's having an affair. I know there are some people out there who spend their whole marriages forgiving and forgetting, but I couldn't deal with that. An open marriage to me is about as attractive an option as base jumping. So I'm not quite the modern woman that I think I am, but there's plenty of personal baggage that goes with it and you don't need more than a couple of spare brain cells to work out it's all related.

I was only twelve, but I can still remember the day my mum found out that my dad had been having an affair. They stayed together (for better, for worse, for me, etc. etc.) until he died, but she's never really got over the betrayal and I've always promised myself that I would never let history repeat itself. At least we haven't got any children to worry about, but my biggest fear is that now I think I might have actually driven him away. And the million-dollar question is: could I ever forgive him? Answers on a postcard. Suppose I'd better get on with my day.

R x

Children. What if Matt had children? What if he was someone's dad as well as someone's husband? Lizzie added it to her mental list of questions—none of them light and fluffy—which she was saving for lunchtime and clicked on 'reply'.

Sorry to hear things aren't running as smoothly as you'd hoped. My advice—personal and professional—is to stop putting it off and start talking to him. Stop worrying about failing. If you really love him and want to make things work then you need to tell him to his face. If it's a case of mixed messages, harsh as it may seem, you are both to blame—and if making your marriage work is the most important thing to you both, then you'll be able to weather this storm. Think of the long-term bigger picture and throw guilt and pride out of the window. Only you two know what you've had in the past, whether you can get it back, and whether it is

worth fighting for. Hold that head up and go for it. Fingers Crossed. Happy Wednesday!
L x

She got a response right away.

L
Don't mince those words! Thanks, though. Right, as always.
R x

Clare popped her head round the door at 10:28 with a mug of tea and a saucer piled high with chocolate biscuits. In her eyes dire emotional situations called for emergency rations, and yesterday Clare had compassionately filled the cupboards with all Lizzie's favourite foods. She needn't have worried. Lizzie's appetite was usually the last thing to go. Although Clare had failed to notice that the one packet was lasting an eternity—more than half a day was a lifetime in biscuit terms—it was not a good sign.

'Sleep out of fashion these days?' Clare was doing her best not to mention anything that might provoke tears. To be frank it didn't leave her with many subjects to choose from.

'Just woke up really early and thought I'd make the most of the morning, seeing as I did nothing yesterday except stare into space and watch black and white films. Sometimes I think life would be simpler if it was in black and white...' She was off on a whimsical train of thought. It seemed, though, that Clare wasn't interested in anything but the most direct and practical this morning.

'Oh, and doing your show last night wasn't work, was it? Honestly, Liz, sometimes you're your own worst enemy. You put more pressure on yourself than anyone else ever will.'

True, Lizzie had pulled herself together for her radio show, but actually focusing on something other than herself had been a relief.

'Maybe... Thanks for the tea.'

'No problem. Look, I'm heading off in a minute—I've got a few things to do before the lunch rush. If I were you I'd let the answer-phone screen your calls. After all, you don't want any nasty surprises.'

Lizzie smiled weakly. 'I've got nothing to say to him. On-wards and upwards, hey?'

It was fighting talk with no fight. Lizzie wished Clare would hurry up and go before Matt called to finalise their arrange-ments. She'd decided not to mention it just in case Clare de-cided to lock her in the airing cupboard to prevent her from going. She could always tell her that Matt had dropped in unannounced and dragged her out if she needed to talk to her about it later. Still, fight or no fight, Clare was pleased with the apparent change in Lizzie's attitude.

'That's my girl. I know it's hard, Liz, but it's the only way.'

'Mmm.' Lizzie was pretending to be deeply absorbed by a letter from her postbag. It felt very wrong to be deceiving the closest thing she had to a sister, but maybe he wouldn't even call and then she wouldn't be lying to Clare anyway and could probably get off on a technicality. Lizzie was suddenly aware of the fact that Clare was now just standing in the doorway, staring at her.

'Clare?'

'Yes, Liz.'

'Please stop feeling sorry for me. I don't think I can bear it.'

'Don't be daft. Just thinking how brave you're being. I know it's been tough for you...'

Been tough? Clare really had no idea what she was going through, did she? A mere day and a half into her crisis, it was getting tougher every hour. Lizzie didn't have the energy to have a whole conversation right now, so nodded in a 'thank-you-now-piss-off-with-your-tea-and-sympathy-so-I-can-get-on-with-agonising-over-what-to-do-next' manner. The mes-sage wasn't conveyed. Lizzie obviously had a bit of work to do on her meaningful nods. Clare was still chatting.

'Listen, I was thinking—one of the girls at work does Reiki massages. She's fully qualified and everything. Why don't I see if she could pop over and give you one here? My treat. I'm sure we can spare her for a couple of hours this afternoon.'

'Thanks, but...' Lizzie didn't quite know how to put this without sounding ungrateful and spoilt, but the last thing she wanted was someone dropping in this afternoon. She had to nip Clare's latest scheme in the bud or run the real risk of being found out. 'How well do you know me?'

'Very well?'

Clare was tentative. She wasn't sure what the right answer was. Lizzie obviously had one in mind, and she didn't want to get it wrong when she was patently teetering on an emotional tightrope this morning.

To Clare's relief Lizzie nodded. 'Yes. Sometimes better than I know myself...in which case you should know what I think of alternative therapies...' It was meant to be sarcastic bordering on the amusing but out loud it just sounded rude. 'Reiki...whatever next? Shovelly... Trowelly... Spadey...? Clare, you of all people shouldn't be taken in by this Eastern channelling of energy, I'll lay my hands on you for forty quid bollocks.'

Clare decided to overlook Lizzie's lack of gratitude in light of everything going on.

'So I take it that I shouldn't send her over?'

'No, thanks. I appreciate the concern but I'll be fine. I'd rather you bought me forty pounds' worth of white toast and chocolate spread than a massage.' Lizzie smiled to demonstrate to Clare that she appreciated the gesture even if everything that came out of her mouth was acid-coated at the moment. It was the best she could do.

Clare swallowed her slightly dented pride and administered a maternal peck to the top of Lizzie's head. Clare knew she'd probably burst into tears the minute the front door closed behind her, and irritatingly all she could do was make sure Lizzie knew that she was there for her. 'Look after yourself. You know where I am if you need me...and ten out of ten for washing your hair this morning. No wonder you're feeling more human today. Lots of love.'

Lizzie heard the front door close and gave it ten minutes before she took the saucer of biscuits back to the tin for recycling. Just because she was confused and depressed didn't mean she wanted to be fat too.

Eerily the phone rang only seconds later as if Matt had sensed Clare's recent departure. True to his word he'd booked lunch somewhere quiet in Richmond, and was coming to collect her *en route*.

They were quiet in the taxi. It was as if they were saving heavy conversation for the table and small talk at this point would somehow have been hypocritical. Lizzie checked her bag and was relieved to discover that she'd had the foresight to bring her sunglasses. It wasn't exactly sunny, but it wasn't raining either, and she was sure that they'd prove useful when leaving the restaurant.

Meeting up to talk to Matt had appealed to the drama queen in her. Now, at their table tucked away in the corner, she was wondering whether this had been such a good idea. Matt looked tired. His eyes were dull, his face haggard and drawn. His skin was—well, grey. He reached across the table and took Lizzie's hands in his.

'I am so sorry. You've really got no idea how sorry. I'd do anything to turn back the clock and to have told you at the beginning. That was the original plan.'

But, Lizzie wondered, if he had told her, would she still have gone out with him? It was a tough one. Probably not. But then she'd never have known what she was missing. Part of her could understand why he'd found it so hard to bring it up but, she reminded herself sternly, he'd tricked her, he'd lied, and that was unacceptable however flatteringly you tried to pitch it.

'When did it all get so complicated?' Her voice trembled as she started to speak and she swallowed in an attempt to steady it. 'I wish I was a child again, when the most stressful thing about life was whether it was hair-wash night or not.'

Matt smiled. Lizzie was incredible. Trying to retain her sense of humour when he had given her every reason to trade it in for a machete. She looked pale and resigned, but underneath the shadows she was still Lizzie. 'Thanks so much for agreeing to meet. I just wanted a chance to set the record straight. To tell you how I feel. To try and explain. I had the best intentions...'

The blood was visibly draining from Lizzie's face, and if her eyes had been any wider they would have met in the middle. She snatched her hand back and ran it through her hair distractedly. Matt was confused. He hadn't really said anything yet. Suddenly she leapt to her feet, a pseudo but instant smile now plastered across her face. Matt turned to follow her gaze.

Small world alert. Friends on the horizon. Lousy timing. One beautiful young Elizabeth Hurley body double and an older well-dressed woman with something familiar about her.

'Darling! It is—you see...' She turned to her companion. 'What a coincidence. I thought it was you, but Alex was trying to tell me that you'd be hard at work, not lunching in Surrey. But I just knew. Is that a new jumper? Very nice. The colour really suits you.'

Lizzie glared at her mother as she advanced towards her. This was definitely not a moment for her to grab the scruff of her daughter's neck and inspect the label. Lizzie leant forward and gave her a kiss. It seemed to be enough to distract her.

'Working hard?' Did Alex look mischievous or was Lizzie just feeling ridiculously guilty? Had she whipped her hand away in time?

'Mum, Alex...what a surprise!'

Matt breathed in. Lizzie's mother. And the legendary Alex. He'd heard plenty about her. And, surprisingly, on first appearances she did live up to her reputation. Her physique didn't suggest that she'd ever been anywhere near an obstetrician. Matt didn't really know where to look. He had no idea how much they did or didn't know. He was going to have to follow Lizzie's lead.

'Working lunch?' Annie Ford was almost rubbing her hands together with the excitement of the moment.

'Something like that. Are you two having lunch here too?' Lizzie prayed very hard that they were running late for a very important appointment. They had to be going. They just had to.

'No...unfortunately not.'

Relief flooded Lizzie's system. In her opinion there was absolutely nothing unfortunate about it all.

'We came in for a morning coffee and were just on our way out when I thought I saw you walk past.'

'Annie we've got to get going. I'm supposed to fetch Josh in ten minutes and we've got to get the car from the multistorey. I don't want to be late. He'll think he's been abandoned.'

Lizzie could have kissed her sister-in-law. Regrettably, though, her mother didn't seem to be going anywhere. She now seemed to be staring at Matt, just waiting for an introduction. Lizzie was going to make it a quick one.

'Sorry—how rude of me...' Lizzie turned to Matt almost apologetically.

'This is David. He works at the advertising agency that runs the City FM account.'

Lizzie glared at Matt/David. He beamed back at her, any surprise or confusion carefully camouflaged. Lizzie shouldn't have underestimated him. After all, she kept forgetting he was practically a professional liar.

'Lovely to meet you, David.'

'And you...' Matt left a gap for her to fill.

'Annie—Annie Ford. Lizzie's mother.'

'No, surely not. You couldn't possibly be. You simply don't look old enough.'

Lizzie balked, glad she had just invented his persona. She couldn't have anyone she was supposed to be in love with saying things that cheesy in public. But, judging by the rapturous expression on Annie's face, it appeared to be working.

Luckily there were no more chairs at their definite table for two, and her grandson was demanding vehicular attention, or Lizzie felt sure that her mother at the very least would have sat down to join them. But, with Alex now practically rattling her car keys under Annie's nose, 'David' was spared an interview. As Lizzie watched them walk into the street she waved, silently waiting until they had turned the corner just in case her mother's bat-like hearing was in extra-sensory pick-up mode. Matt was the first to speak.

'Sorry, Liz, I had no idea your mum lived in Richmond.'

'She doesn't. She must be on day-release from Hampstead. Do you think they suspected anything? I bet Alex knew what was going on; she just had that glint in her eye.'

'Knew what? What is there to know? Surely you haven't mentioned a mystery David from the agency before today?'

'No, course not. But you don't know my family. They're not going to a let a little thing like a different name get in the way. Shit. This could even get back to Clare now. It's not going to take a lot of imagination on her part to work out what's going on.' For the moment Lizzie's mind was overcrowded with every possible nightmarish eventuality.

'Just for the record, they seemed very nice. You're right about Alex. Gorgeous. A little too groomed for me, but I can see what you mean.'

This was all too weird. She shouldn't have come. Yet Matt had handled it all so well and now, inspired by his stealth, she could feel herself weakening. Lizzie took a deep breath and told herself not to be so pathetic. There was a silence at the table while they gathered their thoughts, recently scattered by their surprise visitors. Matt was the first to recover.

'But, Liz, look—getting back to why we're here... You see, the thing—'

'Matt.' Lizzie interrupted him before he started to make sense. 'This can't work. You're married. You've got a wife. For all I know you've got children too.'

'No. Liz. No children. And a wife in name, yes, but we don't do anything together any more.'

Anything? Lizzie wanted to ask when they'd last had sex. She wanted to know, and then she didn't. You see. How could she have ever entertained—even fleetingly—the idea that this could all work out. No children, though. That was a relief. At least he wasn't a 'Daddy' as well as a 'Darling'.

'But you're somebody else's husband and I assume your wife doesn't know about us.' Lizzie looked directly at Matt. He looked back blankly. She had her answer. 'For all you know she's just waiting for a chance to try and work things out with you. For all I know you still sleep with her every night.'

'Of course not. Do you really believe I'd do that?'

Right now Lizzie wasn't sure what she believed. Matt gripped Lizzie's hand tightly between his palms as he searched for the right thing to say next. Lizzie started speaking first.

'I never had you down as the devious type...until Monday.' She couldn't compete with someone she didn't know. And she wasn't interested in competing, full stop. She deserved to be somebody's one and only.

'I'll tell her. I'll leave.' Matt heard his voice. It sounded hollow. He wished he'd been honest from the start. He knew how it looked now. It was up to him to prove his worth, yet every time he set himself a challenge he seemed to fail miserably. It was time to get tough. To get a grip.

So he hadn't told her yet. Interesting, Lizzie thought. A definite case of has cake, will eat it too if given the chance. Clare was being proved right yet again.

'If you hadn't met me you'd still be with her, wouldn't you? What am I saying? You're still with her now. What I mean is that you wouldn't have left, wouldn't be leaving...whatever...'

There was a long pause.

'Probably not.' Matt sighed. 'I suppose I was resigned to my fate—thought that half a marriage was better than none. But then I met you and knew we should never have even got married. There were a couple of years when all our friends tied the knot and we just followed suit. It was never a case of not being able to live without each other. More like being used to living with each other. Romantic stuff.'

'Come off it. You can live without anyone if you have to. You don't go into any relationship expecting your partner to take responsibility for your happiness. You're still the same person.'

'You know what I mean, Liz. Sure, I was fond of her—yes, I even loved her. And I went into our marriage believing it was for ever. I don't think you can do it any other way. But she's changed. She cares about her job, about having enough money, the right clothes, about what other people think, but she doesn't care about me...not really...only what I can provide. I admit, I tried to make it work. I wanted us to sort things out. I was determined. I'm not a quitter. I know relationships aren't always easy. My parents are only still together because they've worked bloody hard at their marriage in the past, but she's never listened. She could never see things from my point of view or maybe she just didn't want to. You know me much better than she does right now.'

'I thought I knew you.'

'You do know me. We're both suffering. Why? Because we should be together. But now I'm scared that I've blown it all before we've really even had a chance to get started.' Matt felt his throat constrict. Tears scratched at his eyes.

Lizzie watched him struggling to control his emotions. Did she only want him because she knew that she couldn't have him? If only it was that simple. No, she actually believed that she really did love him. Damn. This was much harder than she'd thought it would be.

'What if your wife loves you but is just too proud to admit it?' Lizzie thought back to her earlier e-mail exchange with Rachel. 'I've had letters in the past from people like that.'

'Well, if she loves me she's got a funny way of showing it. Come on, Liz, you must've seen and heard this all before, and from lots of different perspectives.'

'I don't want to be responsible for breaking up your marriage. If it's over then leave. If it's not over then stay. Don't do any of this on a whim. If you decide to move on it's got to be because it's the right thing for you, and you should do it whether I'm around or not.'

'What are you saying?' An edge of panic crept into his voice.

'Matt, you know how hard this is for me. But we're not the only two people involved. I'm trying to think about how I would feel if I was your wife. No one said marriages maintained themselves, and you know I'd love for us to gallop off into the sunset together, but this is real life. You have a career. I have a career. You have a wife. I've got principles.'

'I've got principles too. I'm not trying to trade my wife in

for a younger model...this is all wrong...I just want us to be together, Liz. Please...'

Lizzie thought she'd said a whole host of sensible things
quite coherently and maturely and felt she deserved some sort
of major recognition for having managed not to cry. Now Matt
had beaten her to it. Silent tears were running down his cheeks.
Sometimes she wished she'd trained herself to be totally un-
emotional. Her life would have been easier if she'd learned to
worry less about other people and their feelings and just concentrated on looking after herself. Lizzie wanted desperately
to reach out to him. To help. So she did. Her tone softened.

'Hey, Matt.'

He looked up, relieved to hear that the controlled, more
abrasive edge to her voice had gone.

'Listen. This is so hard for me, on so many levels. You know
how much I care about you. I can't sleep. I can't eat. I can't
bear it. But I can't do the whole mistress thing either.'

'I know, I know.'

'Everywhere I've looked for the last thirty-six hours there's
been something about "the other woman". Magazine covers
are the worst—"My life as a mistress..." "Why three is better
than two..." "Being a mistress ruined my life..." You know the
type. I know they're probably always there and I'm just noticing them more now, but I'm innocent. I was unsuspecting—
naïve, maybe—yet I feel like a social outcast. I can't live this
way. I feel battered and bruised inside and out. It's not fair.'

'I'm sorry. I know I've been selfish but I really believed we
could work.'

So did I, thought Putney's latest pariah. So did I.

They barely ate. They talked about everything and anything
except the things that really mattered.

As the taxi pulled up outside Lizzie's flat, Matt reached for
Lizzie and smothered her with a hug. He wasn't sure what happened next but he didn't want to let go.

Lizzie heard herself speaking before she could stop herself.
'Why don't you come in for coffee?'

Matt pulled back, surprised, but his hesitation was only momentary. He paid the taxi driver without a second thought and

followed an equally stunned Lizzie up the path. What on earth did she think she was doing? She didn't even remember wrestling with the idea. It was as if her heart had bypassed her brain.

It was the first time that Lizzie had had sex in the full knowledge that she was a mistress—and she didn't intend for it to become a habit.

Sometimes the best intentions are laid to rest.

chapter 15

Death to all things pink, red and heart-shaped. It was just another Tuesday in Lizzie's world, but to rest of the human race it appeared to be much, much more. It was Valentine's Day—although, observing the reddish tint that had descended over London during the last seven days, one would be forgiven for thinking that it was Valentine's Week. Who on earth had picked mid-February as the moment when you're supposed to declare your undying love? Not only is it one of the coldest, bleakest months of the year, but everyone is a little too dull in complexion, a couple of pounds heavier—for comfort and warmth—and still paying for the indulgences of Christmas on their credit cards.

As far as Lizzie was concerned it had always been a day for greetings card manufacturers and restaurant owners, who could charge the earth for one night only, but now it seemed that nothing was immune from the hearts-and-flowers marketing approach. Even the opticians in Putney were attempting to lure in new customers for eye tests with their catchy slogan 'Don't get hooked up with the wrong girl this Valentine's!'

Smug marrieds said that they didn't need a special day to

tell each other how they felt. The rest of the world waited for
the postman, pretending that they didn't care, and then rang or
wrote to Lizzie in the evening. Good, then, that this year her
studio night fell on the day when those people not at a table
for two needed some common sense and a bit of perspective.

Lizzie was looking forward to being able to lend a hand.
She'd already faxed her playlist to Ben. Soppy Phyllis Nelson
'Move Closer' soul numbers were out. George Michael
wouldn't be whispering carelessly or indeed at all on City FM
tonight. Instead Prince was waiting in the wings, ready to tell
London that they needed another lover like they needed a hole
in their heads, Aretha Franklin would be demanding 'Respect',
the Soup Dragons reminding listeners at home and in their cars
that being 'Free' was no bad thing. 'I Will Survive' was on
standby. While Lizzie thought it was over-used, she knew that
it was an anthem of the sisterhood and that most women over
the age of twenty-five had turned, pointed and waggled their
fingers at each other during the chorus somewhere, some time.

But tonight wasn't an 'I hate men' evening. While they
might rarely admit to tuning in to a problem phone-in, the most
recent ratings breakdown revealed that over forty per cent of
Lizzie's listeners had a penis, and there'd be plenty of guys
who'd be just as gutted by their lack of postal attention.

Over at Union Jack's, red was the colour and romance was
the game. At a price, of course. Five courses, if you were being
pedantic. And Clare was packing them in to the rafters. Can-
dles had been bought in bulk for instant atmosphere, and to top
it all Clare had demanded some last-minute research, leaving
Lizzie to trawl the internet for romantic quotes to write on the
bottom of the menu and chalk up on the specials blackboards
around the restaurant—an at times nauseating task. Thanks to
Lizzie, Clare was now in possession of wise words from everyone from Mae West to Miss Piggy.

Time had flown and frustratingly, in the real world, Lizzie
was now running late. She'd been ignoring the new messages
sing-songing their way into her inbox, postponing them for
later. Only later had just run out. Her cab had arrived a good
ten minutes ago and was idling impatiently across the road.

Lizzie highlighted the new arrivals and pressed 'print'. That way she could glance through them in the car before she got to the studio, just in case there was anything she really should know about before going on air. While the printer rattled into life Lizzie rushed upstairs to grab her jacket. At least she didn't have to do the whole getting ready, wash and blow-dry thing. One of the best things about being a radio presenter was not having to choose the right colours and the right neckline. She could have sat in the studio in a hessian sack if she'd found one to fit.

She stuffed the printouts into her bag as she dashed back to her study and logged off. In a whirlwind of papers, files, keys and scarves—well, one scarf, but it seemed to be getting in the way of everything—she finally made it into the taxi. She checked her watch. Shit. How could it possibly be 7:00 p.m. when it had been five-thirty-five for ages? She was supposed to be at the studio now for the production meeting. She jiggled her knee impatiently in the back just as, as if to spite her, the cab swung round the corner, instantly joining a traffic jam. Lizzie puffed audibly. The driver, until now blissfully mono-syllabic, to her horror took it as a sign that she wanted to chat.

'It's terrible, isn't it? Traffic in London is just getting worse and worse. Sure, sometimes you feel like punching the lights out of the van driver that has just cut in front of you, but it wouldn't do any good—and besides, you always get there eventually.'

'Mmm.' Lizzie didn't want the driver to think she was in-terested in talking about urban congestion in any sort of de-tail.

'I mean, you can't help thinking that one day London will literally grind to a halt. And if they keep selling new cars with-out taking away the old ones it's going to happen sooner rather than later. Total gridlock... Anyway—Jesus, mate, call that driving? Sorry, love...but, God, sometimes you wonder where these people learnt to drive...I mean, look at that...'

'I know.' Lizzie wasn't quite sure what she was endorsing and she didn't really care. She needed to collect her thoughts, or at least have time for a couple of thoughts of her own before her show started.

The driver wound down his window and leant out, beckoning madly. A freezing gust of air swirled into the back seat. If Lizzie breathed out she was sure her breath would be visible but she didn't dare tell him to close it.

'Go on, love. Go on. You could get a bleedin' Range Rover through that gap.'

Slowly but surely the driver—unfortunately female—of the Range Rover—not bleeding as far as Lizzie could see—edged through the totally adequate space for her car and the traffic started moving again, slowly. He wound up the window and Lizzie removed her hands from under her armpits, where they were keeping warm.

'I know I shouldn't say anything, and I'm not saying all women are bad drivers or anything, but you do see it more and more these days. W.I.B.C.S.—that's what I call it...'

'W.I.B.C.S.?' Lizzie really didn't want to start a conversation, but she was sort of curious.

'Women in Big Cars Syndrome. Their husbands should buy them superminis.'

Lizzie mentally buttoned her lip. It was either that or time for one of her lectures on the joys of womanhood. And he was a cab driver. Opinions set in stone. She only hoped that was the end of that little discourse. She could only keep her feminist gene latent for so long.

'So I take it you're in a hurry, then?'

'Yup. Have to be at the studios by seven-forty-five at the absolute latest.' Allowing her to race through, shout her apologies to the rest of the team and be in her chair with five minutes to go. He tactfully didn't bring up waiting time at this juncture, and Lizzie was grateful for this smallest of mercies. She was sure that City FM didn't pay through the nose for 'executive cars'—basically vaccumed and waxed mini-cabs—so that their drivers could lecture the presenters on their punctuality, or indeed anything else.

'I'll get you there as fast as I can, my darling.'

The cab lurched off the main road and swung into a network

of side streets. Lizzie called Ben to blame the traffic and let him know that God willing she'd be in the studio long before the opening jingle, but had a quick word with Phil, her sound engineer, behind his back, about the first track and the feasibility of doing her opening link on her mobile just in case.

The alternative route seemed to be working. Lizzie located the already slightly dog-eared messages in her bag and started reading, holding the pages up just in case the driver was in any doubt that she was working and not to be disturbed.

Lizzie scanned them. One from Rachel, one from Susan Sharples, her editor at *Out Loud*, reminding her that her column was due to be on her desk by Thursday, a joke—in the loosest sense of the word—forwarded to the whole team by one of the girls at City FM, the punchline buried in amongst meaningless lists of who the message had been forwarded to, by and from, and one from Matt.

Lizzie smiled. So he might not have remembered to send her a card in a pink envelope, but at least she had heard from him on the fourteenth. She was sure that Valentine's was the last thing that he wanted to celebrate. She decided to save his message for last and turned to Rachel's instead.

L

Just a quickie. You'd be proud. I'm making an effort and it's not work-related. Just nipped home pre Valentine's-dinner-date-with-my-husband-haircut and have managed to beg, borrow and schmooze a table at that new place on the river by Tower Bridge. According to all the glossies and colour supplements it's the place to be seen. Hope all's well with you. Catch up soon. Must dash. Steve won't wait for me, scissors poised, all afternoon!

R x

Lizzie smiled. Trust Rachel to book a meal, and book it in style. Image was everything in her world. Lizzie hoped that they had a good evening.

She settled back in her seat to read the one she'd been saving for last. At a glance it wasn't exactly heart-shaped—still, a message was a message, and she was the other woman...what did she expect? Furtive wasn't likely to be ostentatious. Although trust her to be the sort of mistress who wasn't showered with Tiffany boxes at every opportunity.

> Dearest Lizzie
> Only me. Just to say Happy V. Day—not that I'm sure St Valentine would approve of our current status... According to my sources, he is the patron saint of young couples and happy marriages...oh, and of love, lovers and love lotteries, which is, I guess, where we come in. I know you think today is all a gimmick, but anybody who likes romantic comedies would be devastated not to receive at least one amorous missive on today of all days...

Lizzie couldn't help but smile. He could read her like a book. She might not have known him for long, but Matt already knew her very well.

> Just wanted you to know I was thinking of you, that I love you, and I promise I'll sort this mess out just as soon as I can. I hope that one day you'll be able to forgive me for putting us through this.
> Lots of love, and speak to you soon, Matt xxxxx
> PS Do not, I repeat do not, hit the reply button. I'm sending this one from her home terminal as she's popped out.

The warm feeling vanished. Great. So he was e-mailing from the marital home—all set, it seemed, to spend the evening with his missus. At least Lizzie's scarlet woman status fitted into the mid-Feb colour scheme, but what a nightmare for his wife: a bombshell about to hit as soon as it wasn't the fourteenth or national love week, or whatever they were in at the moment.

Maybe she wouldn't care. Maybe his wife was seeing someone else too. Lizzie could only hope. She almost wished he hadn't bothered with an e-mail. Thanks to him, her rational streak seemed to have temporarily deserted her. There was probably stuff to be positive about—the fact that he had sent her a note had to count for something—but what she really wanted was a second opinion, or in actual fact Clare's. But if she asked her it was highly likely that she'd be shot at point-blank range, probably using the silencer that Clare kept in her handbag for certifiable flatmates at times like this. She pushed her thoughts to the back of her mind. Right now she had to prepare for the airwaves.

According to the green luminous digital numbers of the in-car clock, it was already 19.28, but thanks to their creative route, and with a little bit of luck and a few green traffic lights, she was going to be there on time. Lizzie opened her folder and, using the rings to punch holes in the pages, added her e-mails to the back of the file. As she shuffled the pages something caught her eye. She froze.

A gasp escaped. A gasp that sounded remarkably like 'fuck'. But this was one of the few moments that truly merited that sort of language—even from a woman. Unfortunately the noise had attracted the driver, who perked up at the prospect of more chat.

'Everything all right, love? Should be there any minute. Told you I'd get you there on time. You can trust Tony. I know these roads like the back of my hand.'

Lizzie didn't hear him.

It couldn't be. Her heart hammered in her chest. She stared. She checked. She double-checked. She triple-checked.

At first she thought she was just being technically moronic—it wouldn't have been the first time. But, no. There at the top of the printouts:

To: Lizzie Ford asklizzie@outloud.co.uk
From: rachelb@msn.co.uk

Identical to the header on the message from Matt.

The realisations came in waves. They hit her one at a time but in quick succession. In no time the barrage had become a tide. Lizzie could feel herself drowning.

Rachel was the wife neglecting her husband.

Matt was the husband that Rachel was so terrified of losing.

Rachel was the wife that Matt said he no longer loved.

Matt was the husband that Rachel had suspected of having an affair.

Rachel was married to Matt.

Matt was sleeping with Lizzie.

Somehow Lizzie got through her show. As she went from the last caller to the last song on automatic pilot, Lizzie wondered sado-masochistically what they were up to. By the time she left the studios she'd been torturing herself for at least an hour with thoughts of their moonlit stroll along the Thames. After an enormous comfort blanket of a takeaway—even though she'd learned in a slightly wider incarnation of herself a few years earlier that Chinese food after 11:00 p.m. was waistline suicide— Lizzie checked the messages again. The addresses were the same as they'd been four hours ago. The same. Period.

In bed, Lizzie read and re-read the words as she wrestled with her duvet. It was an impossible situation. Even Houdini would have been sweating at the challenge of getting out of this in one piece. Finally, at 3:43 a.m., she made a mental list of options; it was the middle of the night which explained why some of them were less plausible than others.

Option A - Invite Rachel and Matt over for dinner and tell them face to face.

Option B - Change name. Move to Australia. Join religious order.

Option C - Tell Matt the truth.

But Rachel had contacted her in confidence initially. Betraying her trust—totally unprofessional. Plus, if anyone found out, she could end up losing her job at the magazine. Unless she swore Matt to secrecy. But could she trust him? She thought yes, but then again he had been married and not told her, so maybe no.

Option D - Tell Rachel the truth.

But how? And just because Matt had misbehaved that didn't mean she had to follow suit. Playing dirty was not her style...and for all she knew Rachel was a karate black belt, mentally unstable, or knew a hit man.

Option E - Ask Clare what to do.

But probably not live to see the light of day once Clare found out she'd continued seeing Matt behind her back.

Option F - Write letters to Matt, Rachel and Clare explaining everything before choosing Option B.
Option G - Run away with Matt. Let dust and tabloid outrage settle before writing a book on subject, selling film rights and returning to do chat show circuit in five years' time. But alienate friends and family in process.

There was no way out. She'd screwed up on every level. Her transgression was professional, personal and simply unbelievably unlucky. Lizzie felt sure that she would have been more likely to win the lottery than for this to have happened. If only she'd bought a ticket.

There was always Option H—The Pretty Woman plan. Disappear to LA under assumed identity, become hooker on Hollywood Boulevard and hope a Richard Gere character scooped her into his sports car, giving her lots of money to spend, falling in love with her and providing a penthouse for them to live happily ever after in.

What was it with her romantic core? It only caused trouble.

Deep down Lizzie knew that there was really only one option. She had to tell Matt it was over and get him and Rachel back together. For his sake, for Rachel, for Clare and for her career. That way there was a real chance that they could all be happy— well, happy enough—and Lizzie might get to keep her job and at least some vestige of her sanity.

It was starting to get light as Lizzie slipped into a fitful sleep, her subconscious content to let her rest, now safe in the knowledge that she knew what she had to do even if she had no real idea how she was going to go about it.

Lizzie had woken up with every intention of calling Matt to tell him it was over, but by ten-thirty she'd decided it would be more civilised to meet up for a chat. Plus that way she could see his face just to make sure that this all really did add up. But, as good as her advice got, she was never going to repair their marriage while she continued to provide the problem. At least she'd never met Rachel. Only a small mercy, perhaps, but something to hold onto all the same.

Lizzie fabricated a magazine meeting in Soho before suggesting they grab a coffee together. By three-fifteen she was in situ, Option F looking more attractive by the second. Matt breezed in while Lizzie was leafing through an abandoned tabloid at a table by the window.

'Tall, skinny, wet latte to stay.' Lizzie listened to him place his order and looked down at her more rudimentary cappuccino. She hadn't quite got to grips with coffee jargon yet.

He drummed his fingers on the counter impatiently while waiting the few seconds for his drink. He couldn't wait to see Lizzie's face when he gave her his news. He would've been whistling if it wouldn't have made him sound like a builder. He was at her side in moments and playfully kissed her hello.

Lizzie was trying to combine small talk with pseudo-off-hand-but-detailed questioning. Her combined lack of sleep and lunch started to take their toll, and the caffeine seemed to be going straight to her bloodstream, causing an almost out of body experience. Matt for some inexplicable and almost irritating reason was overly chirpy. Maybe it was good that she was finding him annoying. Maybe the bubble had burst. She only hoped that his good mood had nothing to do with last night. Childishly she decided to test him.

'Thanks for your e-mail. So, did you have a nice evening?'

'Well, if you take away the fact that I'd obviously rather have been with you, it could have been worse, I suppose. We went out. She took me to that new place near Tower Bridge...'

So he could discern between fact and fiction. Lizzie was relieved.

'The food wasn't bad, but the atmosphere was pretty strained at first. I felt a bit of a fraud, to be honest. All I've been thinking about recently is how to get out of there, and I could tell she was making a huge effort. We don't normally eat together at home, let alone go out...but it all got easier during the second bottle of wine...'

'Oh.'

It was in the running for the smallest noise that Lizzie had ever made.

'...huge effort...all got easier...' They were the words that lingered for a few extra seconds before vanishing into the ether to be reunited with their counterparts. While she knew that she was supposed to be getting Matt and Rachel back together, Lizzie hadn't really considered how she might feel if they did end up being happy.

'Easier. Not fun. Well, not like we have fun. I suppose it was just better than I thought it would be. I thought it was going to be a hideous evening and it was quite bearable—but then I guess we have got years of old stories to fall back on...'

It came out wrong. He could see Lizzie's face had fallen. He seemed to be stuck in a cul-de-sac of inarticulacy. It was incredibly frustrating.

'Listen...what I mean—what I'm trying to say is—she was excited about going to this new restaurant. She always likes to check out the latest places before everyone else, and fortunately the food was a lot less bland than the conversation. I can't even remember the last time we ate out on our own together. She's on a bit of a roll at work, which is great—it's all she's ever wanted—and wanted to talk all about it. Anyway, I don't want to talk about her. How are you doing? How was your show last night?'

Matt gave Lizzie his best winning smile. He'd show her. It would all work out in the end.

'Maybe you're making a mistake? Maybe you should give it another go?'

OK, so his smile was only in the bronze medal position at the moment. He'd have to try harder.

'Look, I care about her, like I'd care about a sister if I had one, but I'm in love with you.'

'So you keep saying.'

'Listen, I spoke to a solicitor yesterday.' This wasn't how he'd envisaged telling her.

Lizzie paused momentarily as her heart skipped a beat. Maybe she was too late.

'And?' she dared herself to ask.

'Well, if I leave her for you I'll probably get stung in the settlement...but what does that matter? I probably deserve some of it. I mean, it had all gone wrong long before I met you. Fact. But I, the self-appointed captain of the inertia team, was still there, and let's face it I'm the one who's failed to mention you so far. I just can't seem to find the right moment. It feels like she's always in the office, shopping, out for a drink or asleep. And it's not like I can send her a text message about all of this. I'm not the sort of guy who's just going to leave a note on the kitchen table either. But I am genuine, Lizzie.'

Lizzie was panicking. If she was to stand any chance of getting him and Rachel back together this was not the time for him to get honest.

'But you don't have to tell anyone you've met someone. Can't you just cite irreconcilable differences, irrevocable breakdown, general growing apartness?'

'Sod that, Liz. I'm sick and tired of all this deceit. If I'm leaving her for you, I don't care who knows.'

'No, Matt. I don't want to be the reason. Can't you see...?'

No, if he was being honest, he couldn't. Not unless he'd missed something crucial along the way. He'd thought she'd be thrilled, maybe a little bowled over, but definitely not this hesitant.

'Look, you have to decide if being without her is what you really want. It's early days for us, and I think you probably need some time on your own first before we go any further. I mean, you can't just go seamlessly from her to me.'

Matt was feeling very uncomfortable. He didn't understand when this conversation had careered off the rails. He couldn't see why things were any different today. Maybe he should have bought her a heart-shaped present or something. Sometimes he really didn't get women at all. They weren't from Venus. More like a whole different galaxy. He'd thought Lizzie was different. She *was* different. Only today she was in a very peculiar mood.

'Come on, Liz, don't be all funny with me. It'll all sort itself out, you'll see. I can't tell you how relieved I am that it's all going to be over soon. It's been doing my head in. Imagine how nice it will be to just be able to spend some normal time together. Just watching videos curled up on the sofa at home, reading the papers in bed on a Sunday morning. Normal time. Not all this emotional freefall. A bit of fun.'

Lizzie had to admit it would definitely have been something to look forward to if the situation could have been different. Instead she focused on the reason she was sipping coffee in W1, dressed in a suit, having hot-footed it there from a totally spurious meeting.

'I saw from your e-mail address last night that your wife's called Rachel.'

It was a total change of tack. Matt wasn't sure what came next, or indeed what the point of the question was. He'd always made sure that he hadn't used her name around Lizzie because it did personalise things, and he didn't really want to have to think about her all the time or indeed any of the time that he and Lizzie spent together.

'That's right.'

'What does she do?'

'I'm sure I've told you before. She's in advertising.'

Matt was concerned. Maybe this whole deception thing had finally got to Lizzie. He was amazed at how well she'd managed to handle it so far, but now she was asking lots of strange questions—apparently apropos of nothing—about his dinner with his wife. It was probably only natural in a competitive female sort of way. He was only a man. What did he know?

He humoured her. Seeing Lizzie in this slightly confused state of mind made him want to take care of her even more. The question and answer round seemed to have come to an end, and Matt hadn't seen Lizzie for over a week and hadn't slept with her for nearly two. He leant across and kissed her, and then immediately recoiled. When he was with Lizzie it was easy to forget to be furtive.

As the tube rattled through central London, Lizzie knew she should have said no. But Clare was at work and things really couldn't get any worse. But unknown to him this was the grande finale. Something for her to remember him by. She knew now what she had to do.

chapter 16

Clare was worried. Something wasn't quite right with Lizzie. In fact, thinking about it, it was precisely the reverse. After barely a couple of weeks of moping and generally dodging anything except work and their video collection, it appeared she'd decided to take a deep breath and move on. Yet Clare sensed all was not well in Lizziedom.

However many times she told herself not to be silly, Clare was disappointed that Lizzie hadn't felt she could open up to her after everything they'd been through together. Instead she'd erected an invisible wall, and it hurt every time Clare ran into it. She'd been careful not to crowd her, to give her enough of her precious space, and done her utmost not to interfere, but they were best friends for God's sake. If Lizzie was suffering then so was Clare.

Bruised ego and over-sensitivity aside, she had to admit that objectively Lizzie was doing OK. But Clare was beginning to resent the fact that her job almost always prevented her from physically being there for Lizzie. What if Lizzie needed a spontaneous heart-to-heart at the kettle? Or over a cup of tea and toasted muffin? She was an expert in outwardly keeping it together in a crisis. The sort of person that Clare would happily have followed into the trenches. But no one was invincible. Maybe this time she'd fallen apart and Clare had been too busy at the restaurant to notice.

By the middle of the afternoon Clare had wound herself up enough to organise someone to cover for her. This morning Lizzie had announced she was having a quiet evening in and Clare was going home to join her. Nostalgic for a girls' night in, she stopped off at the florist, followed by the off-licence for wine and ice-cream. She was back in the best-friend business.

To Clare's relief the front door wasn't double-locked. On the tube she'd had visions of Lizzie trading in the remote control for a night out, leaving her to wallow in calories and concern on her own.

'Hey, babe, I'm home.'

Clare popped her head round the door to Lizzie's study, only to find it empty. More like deserted. The computer was off and there was no tell-tale half-started cup of tepid tea on the desk. She wasn't prostrate on the sofa upstairs either.

'Liz—Liz...'

She increased her volume.

'Lizzie?'

Surely she wasn't in bed? It was only five-thirty—a little late for an afternoon nap and very early for even the earliest of nights. Maybe she'd developed one of her migraines? Clare felt guilty. She should have been taking more notice. For all she knew this was the time of day when Lizzie was mid-nervous breakdown.

Clare flicked the kettle switch and was just making a cup of tea to take upstairs in her new role as Florence Nightingale when Lizzie appeared at her side in a white waffle bathrobe and slippers, looking a little dishevelled but not altogether pale and pathetic. Maybe she had a fever? Clare was no nurse, but Lizzie looked a little flushed and very tired. Poor girl. She really was suffering.

'You're home...'

A good sign, Clare thought. Lizzie was clearly still capable of stating the obvious.

'Is everything OK?' Lizzie sounded concerned and, if Clare was being over-analytical, a little confused. Maybe she'd been drinking?

'God, yes, fine. Sorry, I didn't mean to wake you. It's just well...I was thinking about things this afternoon and I've decided that I haven't been looking after you properly.'

'I thought you were working late tonight?'

'I was, but I got someone in to cover for me. I thought I'd come home early and we could spend the evening together. I'm just sorry that I've been so busy recently. You've been having a crisis and I've been at work.'

Clare walked over and gave Lizzie a hug. It was like hugging a tree trunk—a thin tree trunk—more of a sapling, in actual fact—resplendent in white waffle but wooden, that was the point. However she tried to dress it up, the fact was that Lizzie didn't hug her back. At all. Clare was determined not to take it personally. After all, they had years of friendship behind them. She wasn't going to get hung up about one flipping hug. Maybe she was the one having the nervous breakdown and Lizzie was fine.

'You shouldn't have got up. Go back up to bed. I'll bring you a cup of tea in a minute. I thought we could do duvets on the sofa and get a pizza delivered if you feel up to it. I've bought ice-cream.'

All of a sudden Lizzie looked paler and greyer. Maybe the pizza wasn't such a good idea.

'Or we can just chat, or...whatever you like. You choose. You really haven't been yourself lately.'

'No, I'm fine. It's fine. It's been a weird few weeks. Pizza would be lovely...'

Lizzie felt terrible. Clare was going for mate-of-the-year, yet any second now she'd discover that her best friend had been lying to her and, while Lizzie had tried to convince herself that she hadn't actually lied *per se*, because Clare hadn't asked her a direct question about what was happening, now, standing a few feet from her best buddy, she was feeling very small and very dishonest indeed. She only hoped that Matt had been listening from the landing and seen fit to hide himself somewhere. Although, thinking about it, there definitely wasn't any space in her wardrobe, or under her bed, and the laundry basket would only have just about been big enough to provide a suitable hideaway for Paddington Bear.

'Great. Now, why don't you go and rest? I'll come and wake you when I've finished faffing down here and we can argue over toppings. I'll even let you have pineapple on half of it if you want.' It was an overwhelming gesture of love and compromise. Clare hated pineapple.

'Really, no—I'm fine down here. It's nice to see you...' Lizzie spotted the gerberas in the sink. 'Oh, Clare, you've bought me flowers. You shouldn't have...' Lizzie wished she hadn't. She was feeling more guilt-ridden by the second. 'How are things at work?'

Lizzie perched on the sofa and sipped at her mug of tea. Clare totally ignored her question.

'Well, at least let me go and get your duvet so you can snuggle up down here.'

'No, no. Don't worry. I'm fine.'

'It's no trouble at all. It'll take me ten seconds.'

'Really, I'm fine,' Lizzie snapped.

And when Clare got over the initial shock she was suspicious. She changed tack and put her sympathy to one side. It hadn't got her anywhere so far.

'Elizabeth Ford, there's no need to bite my head off. Listen, you're a grown-up, and you pay good money to live here, and no one—certainly not me—is going to bring you your duvet or force you to go back to bed if you don't want to. But I know you well enough to know that something's up. And, while I can't make you tell me anything, I think I deserve a little bit of honesty. I'm worried. You've got a lot on your plate and I'm only trying to help, but if you'd rather battle on by yourself then that's fine.'

The way Clare spat the last sentence out, Lizzie knew that it wasn't fine at all.

Now she'd pissed Clare off and soon Matt wasn't going to

be too fond of her either. The master plan was backfiring. Tears sprang to her eyes. Clare's expression instantly softened.

'Sorry. I didn't mean to shout.'

'No, it's fine. Sorry. I haven't been altogether up front with you recently. I didn't think I needed to tell you because I thought it wouldn't be necessary, I thought I could deal with everything on my own, but obviously I can't.' Lizzie wiped her tears on her sleeve.

Clare felt herself tense with concern. Her hunch had been vindicated. There was something going on.

'Tell me what?'

'The reason I don't want you to go upstairs is because there's someone up there.'

'Upstairs...'

Suddenly she understood. Clare was slightly taken aback, but if Lizzie needed to have sex to get over her recent setback then who was she to stand in her way? As she got used to the idea her mood transformed. The jammy so and so. She should have guessed—the rebound reaction was certainly well tried and tested. Clare wondered what he was like. She giggled as she tried to picture the current occupant of Lizzie's bed. It all made sense now. Did Lizzie honestly think she was so judgmental? If anything she was a little envious. Sometimes she wished she could be a little less uptight about the whole meaningless sex thing. But the last time she'd had a one-night stand was last century. Intimacy scared her. It could only upset the even keel which had taken her over a year to establish. Clare Williamson had become a self-protection guru.

'Good on you, Liz. Well—who is he and where did you find him?'

Clare smiled encouragingly at Lizzie, who couldn't have been looking any more grave if she'd tried. It was only sex, for heaven's sake, not nuclear war. And this was the sort of excitement that Clare was only too happy to enjoy vicariously.

'Actually, you know him already.'

Clare racked her brains for eligible young and not so young men. Then she moved onto the not so eligible category. It couldn't be Colin from downstairs. He was definitely one hundred per cent gay. She stared at Lizzie, hoping for something in her expression to give her a clue. But as Lizzie refused to meet her gaze Clare's concern turned to anger. Anger was shortly followed by fury. The changes of mood seemed beyond her control. Before she knew it she was shouting. Loudly.

'It's him, isn't it? You're still fucking Matt.'

Lizzie recoiled at the undiluted aggression now coming from Clare. And only a minute ago she'd been standing there claiming that she wanted to help.

'How could you, Liz? He's married. He's got a wife. After everything I've been through. All the tears I cried on your shoulder. I can't believe you...and to think that I came home early because I was worried about you... Jesus, Liz. What the fuck are you playing at?'

Lizzie didn't think she'd ever seen Clare so furious and upset all at once. Instinctively she tried to calm things down.

'I'm sorry, Clare...'

'Well, obviously not that fucking sorry. I can't believe you. How the fuck did you get to be an agony aunt in the first place? You don't give a shit about anybody but yourself.'

'I wanted to tell you, but... Look...it's over now. I should've listened to you earlier. You were right; it can never work out...'

Lizzie wondered if Clare was actually listening. Her eyes were dancing with rage and disappointment.

'Really, this afternoon was the last time. I know I've been stupid, but I can't help it. I love him and I suppose I was hoping for a miracle.'

'Screw up your life. See if I fucking care.'

Clare couldn't listen any more. Everything was muted by the sound of blood rushing furiously in her ears. She stormed past Lizzie, up the stairs and into her room. Her door slammed. Lizzie wanted to follow her, but first she had to usher Matt out of the war zone.

He was dressed and sitting on her bed quietly. From his shell-shocked and timid demeanour Lizzie imagined he'd heard every syllable.

'Oops.' It was English understatement at its most masterful.

Lizzie sat down next to him. She was shaking. 'I think I'm going to throw up.'

'I'd better go.'

Lizzie couldn't look him in the eye. Instead she spoke directly to his shoulder. 'I don't think this is going to work any more. Go back to Rachel. Give it your best shot. Maybe there's still a chance. You don't need all this extra hassle...and neither do I.'

Matt looked at Lizzie incredulously. 'You're upset. You don't know what you're saying.'

'I do know. I just should have said it a lot earlier.'

'But you just told Clare that you loved me.'

'God, I was stupid to see you again once I knew... Anyway if you were eavesdropping properly you'll also know that I told her that this afternoon was the last time.'

'I'll call you tomorrow.'

'Don't bother.'

'I'll call you tomorrow.' Matt gave Lizzie a kiss and then did a good job of getting the hell out of the flat.

The front lock had barely clicked shut when Lizzie knocked on Clare's door. There was no answer. But Lizzie knew she was in there. She just started talking.

'Clare. Please. Let me explain. I couldn't tell you because I knew how you'd react. I wanted to. I can't bear it when we fight.'

'Well, you should have thought about that before you opted to be the other woman.'

Clare's voice was cold and controlled. On balance, Lizzie thought she preferred the hysterical shouting and swearing stage.

'It's complicated. More complicated than you know. I know I've got to end it. I have ended it. But it's like we can't keep away from each other. I know it doesn't make sense, and it's been hell trying to deal with it all by myself.'

'It hasn't been great being the one who's left out either, believe me.'

'I'm so sorry, Clare. Please, let's get that pizza. Let's talk.'

'You've left it a bit late, don't you think? If you want time on your own, you've got it. As much as you bloody well like. Get him to invent a business trip. Then you two can shag all day, every day and run around the flat with no clothes on while his wife sits at home. Don't worry. I realise there isn't room in your love triangle for anyone else...'

Clare finally opened the door to her room and to Lizzie's horror she could see that she had been crying. Worse still, she had packed a bag.

'If I hadn't come home early today you wouldn't have told me, would you? No, of course you wouldn't. Why not? Because you knew how I would take it. Badly. You of all people. You know how gutted I was when I found out that Joe had been unfaithful. I know you were lured in unsuspectingly at the beginning, and I was here for you, but for the last few weeks you've been totally selfish. You've hurt me, you'll hurt his wife, you'll hurt him, you'll hurt yourself. It's a no-win situation for a mistress...'

Mistress. The word resounded for a second as Clare paused for breath mid-tirade. Labels, in Lizzie's opinion, were for clothes. And this was the ultimate in unfashionable brands.

'Do you know what hurts the most?'

Clare paused for a split second. Lizzie waited. She didn't trust herself to speak. Whatever she said at this point was bound to be wrong.

'That you knew all that. You knew exactly what you were doing and yet you still carried on. Day after day after day. Look, I know I'm probably overreacting, but I need some time to calm down and I can't do it here. I'm going home. You blew me away with this one. I'm sorry, Liz, but I'm really disappointed in you.'

Frozen to the spot, she listened to Clare walking down the stairs, her feet heavy with disgust. The door slammed. Lizzie was alone. All alone. In every sense of the word. She slumped to the floor and sobbed.

chapter 17

When the doorbell rang eleven days after that fateful Wednesday Lizzie was in full tracksuit-bottomed despair and currently running the experiment on her hair that she had so often wondered about. Apparently if you left it for long enough it sort of washed itself. She was still waiting. And when Lizzie saw Matt standing forlornly on the doorstep she wished she hadn't let herself go quite so much. Then again, she knew she had to send him away, however hard it felt. She'd managed to ignore the faceless phone messages and e-mails, but this was much harder. Matt followed her up the stairs in silence, and as they sat down opposite each other in the sitting room he was the first to speak.

'How are you?'

She looked terrible. She knew she did. But she also knew that she had to be strong. Matt was worried.

'Fine.'

'I wish I was...'

Lizzie was doing a very good impression of a bloodhound. Her nose was indulging itself in the faintest trace of the familiar aftershave that had followed him up the stairs. Drawing on every milligram of will-power, she resisted the now almost compulsive urge she had to bound over to the chair and dissolve into his chest. Her head was aching with the effort.

'I love you, Lizzie. I can't stop thinking about you. Even more now than before.' It was true. Matt felt as if he was wading knee-deep through mud on a daily basis. He'd never felt like this before. His self-diagnosis: lovesick with a hint of self-loathing. Prognosis: apparently terminal. He didn't know what to do. He was running on instinct.

Lizzie was torn. In all her years of unfulfilled dating—and there had been many—the only people who'd been this keen on her had been the ones that she wasn't really interested in at all. Perhaps she had stumbled unsuspectingly into the plot of a Shakespearean tale of unrequited love, a West End musical, or even an opera. She'd seen it all before. Boy meets girl, circumstances—convention, religion, family feud, skin colour, class—dictate that they can't be together, so they agonise to close friends, children and wild animals of the forest, before moping—and singing—for about an hour and then, after the interval, just when they think they can't cope any more, something happens.

Heartache had always been big business. But there was no happy ending in sight. Not in Putney. Not today.

'You only think you love me. We both know it's the thing you can't have that you always want the most.'

'I don't understand. What's changed?' Here he was, finally face to face with Lizzie, and she remained as steely as she'd been when he'd seen her last. She couldn't really mean it, but he didn't know how to prove it. And the only person in the world that he could confide in was sitting opposite him, her arms firmly folded.

'Me...' Even at this intensely painful time Lizzie could see the funny side of this statement. A few more chocolate biscuits and a velour tracksuit and Waynetta Slob would have a serious rival vying for her place on the three-piece suite. 'Matt, you tricked me. I've never been interested in being the other woman. Ever. I want to be the only woman. The one. The one you can't live without. The one you have to tear yourself away from in the morning and the one you want to come home to at night. I can't deal with being plan B, the one in reserve, second best.'

'Liz, it was an accident—'

Matt interrupted himself. He'd done it again. As soon as his mouth had closed behind the third syllable he'd known it was a mistake. He started again. Second time lucky.

'What I mean is that I wasn't looking for you. I didn't want to start a double life. But then we met and I knew. I don't want you both. I just want you.'

Lizzie wanted to fling her arms around him and tell him it would all work out, but this was not the time for her to suffer a moment of weakness. She'd indulged in one of those and look where it had got her. She went on the offensive.

'Why do men do it? Apart from the ego thing, of course, and the fact that most men can be flattered into bed if the woman is pretty enough. Make that keen enough. The fact that your wife was trusting in you while you were in bed with me makes me feel like shit. And no one gave me a choice until it was too late.'

'Believe me, Liz, I've suffered too.'

'Sure you have. Must be really tough having to remember who it is you're shagging.'

Matt shook his head. He could see where she was coming from, but it wasn't like that at all. He also knew that trying to tell her when she was in this sort of mood would be futile.

'I'm trying to work a way out of this mess.'

'You're only saying that because now I'm telling you I'm no longer an option. Frankly, you might as well stay with Rachel. You've probably gone and put me on some sort of pedestal by now, and I'm probably no better than her in lots of ways. I'm just the forbidden fruit...'

'You're much better.'

Lizzie was playing her role to perfection. A bit of her wished she wasn't being quite so convincing, although it was good to know that she could remain articulate in the face of a crisis. Usually she came up with her best lines when she was relating events to a third party, a good couple of hours after the confrontation had finished.

'Don't kid yourself. Believe me, underneath my exciting mistress veneer I'm just the same. I have bad breath in the morning and armpit stubble. I can just choose to be at my moodiest when you're at home or in the office. Mistresses aren't nicer or better than wives, you just see them less. The whole concept is based on fantasy and it's flawed.'

'I thought we were worth fighting for. I thought things were going really well... I love you, Lizzie. I know you love me too. I want us to work, and so do you. I can feel it.'

The words just hung in the air. He didn't want to leave. She sat back in her chair and began an intense study of her cuticles. Well, that was how it appeared. She was actually concentrating on not crying. No wonder people ignored their principles when it suited them. Doing the right thing was the hardest thing she'd ever had to do. The tension was unbearable. It was minutes before Matt broke the deadlock. His voice was calmer again.

'You're just saying that it's over, Liz, you don't mean it.'

Lizzie took a deep breath.

'I do mean it. We had fun. You were going through a bad patch, but it doesn't matter how you dress it up—you're married to and living with someone else. Someone that's not me. I just think you owe it to yourself and to Rachel to give it your best shot. You can't just walk away. Believe it or not, I'm the easy option.'

Matt's body was now hunched in defeat. 'Is this what you really want?'

Her heart was shouting *No. No. No. No. No.* Lizzie ignored it. It didn't deserve a fair hearing. So far it had only got her into trouble. 'Look, we had great sex. We had a laugh. But we've only known each other for a few months. It was just a fling. An affair.'

'An affair to remember?' Matt couldn't resist finishing off the 1957 film title. He did it automatically and with no enthusiasm.

Lizzie's heart felt as if it was breaking, but she knew that this was damage limitation. She forced herself to think of the repercussions of another moment of weakness. She couldn't lock herself away with Matt for ever. She had to get up every morning and face the world.

Lizzie was silent as Matt finally got to his feet, numb in defeat. This wasn't how he'd envisaged the end of this afternoon at all. In his version there was more smiling—laughter, even—promises, a future, kissing—yes, lots of kissing. He could feel himself shaking as he leant over and kissed her tenderly, breathing in slowly for a fix of her smell. She was motionless.

'Take care, Lizzie...' Just saying her name out loud made him want to cry. 'I'm only leaving now because you're telling me to, and because, most importantly, I want you to be happy, not because I want to go. And later, if you think you've made a mistake, you know where to find me. I knew it wouldn't be easy, but I really believed we could get through this together. You are the best thing that ever happened to me. Maybe I just don't deserve you.'

He turned and walked to the door. His eyes were wet with tears that Lizzie couldn't see. He didn't know where he was going. His feet were on automatic pilot. He was no longer aware of his surroundings.

It was the worst moment of Lizzie's life. What on earth did she want? An Academy Award? A Joan of Arc statuette for services to martyrdom? What if he had been it? What if he was 'the one'? She knew that it was an old-fashioned concept, but deep down she was just an old-fashioned girl.

chapter  18

Mornings became afternoons and afternoons became evenings. The only consolation was she knew she wasn't alone in her suffering. She only had to watch *EastEnders* to know that what she was going through would've been ten times worse if she'd lived in Albert Square.

She shouldn't have been so surprised—after all, she'd gone from born-again-virgin to mistress and back again in under three months. But why hadn't she learned from previous mistakes? She'd known from an early age not to take things out of the oven without wearing oven gloves, she'd discovered to her cost that tapered trousers were never flattering, bitter experience had taught not to drink beer after champagne or wine, and yet she still hadn't worked out how to avoid heartache.

All this time on her own wasn't helping. In the age of communication Clare was single-handedly resisting all Lizzie's attempts to get in touch. Worse still, she'd been back to the flat, collected more stuff and hadn't even left a note. Lizzie had apologised repeatedly, and couldn't manage another morsel of humble pie, but in Clare's eyes she'd betrayed the sisterhood and purgatory wasn't over yet. But if Clare was stubbornly determined to take the side of a woman she'd never even met, let alone lived with, Lizzie knew she was better off on her own. Clare would calm down eventually. Her high horse always ran out of steam before the final fence.

February became March and April beckoned with the promise of warmer, longer days, and as a slim woman oozing vitality and toned thighs jogged past Lizzie she knew it was time for the next phase. New me. New trainers. New attitude. Time to get fit for life. Or at least buy all the gear.

Lizzie's daily run ritual was on its fourth consecutive day and she was already feeling a lot better. Her heart and liver were enjoying her overture to normality, and once again there was colour in her cheeks. Quite a lot of colour. They were currently deep crimson as her capillaries did their best to radiate as much heat as they could before her body overheated. As with everything, Lizzie had thrown herself into this running lark one hundred and ten per cent and right now her body was trying to keep up with her mental ambition. Once Lizzie concentrated on breathing, not tripping over and retaining at least a shred of finesse she had no energy or mental space left for worry. Running had become her therapy. Sanity was round the corner. Plus, while she might end up terminally single, at least she might have the legs of Anna Kournikova for company.

She turned the corner into Oxford Road, her arms still pumping like pistons while her legs, now heavy with exertion, forced themselves along behind her. Her heart was pounding and a moustache of sweat had not altogether alluringly graced her top lip. She could taste the salt and was anticipating the welcome surge of her power shower when Colin pulled up alongside her in his red convertible.

Timing was everything.

'Hey, is that Liz Ford or Liz Colgan?' If you're in a hurry I can offer you a lift home.'

It could only be one hundred metres to her front door, yet if he hadn't been so obviously mocking her Lizzie would've been tempted. Instead she reduced her already snail-like pace to a sort of bouncing around on the spot movement while stretching her arms across her body, pretending to be warming down.

'What on earth has driven you to exercising outdoors? Why do you think they invented the running machine? It's much less painful if you can watch MTV at the same time!'

Colin was a confirmed gym-user, although Lizzie suspected that his frequent visits also included a generous helping of tight arse and perfect pec spotting. Thankfully he didn't ask her how far she'd run. She knew it was a pitiful distance, but it was definitely an improvement on nothing, and judging by the pounding in her chest it was quite sufficient exercise for her out-of-shape heart. He revved up and parallel parked with incredible speed and accuracy before leaping out and opening the gate for Lizzie, who had used her last ounce of competitive spirit to get there before him and was currently bent over in the leapfrog position, desperately trying to get enough air to her lungs to prevent herself from passing out.

Colin, it seemed, wanted a chat. For once Lizzie was not at her speed-talking best.

'What have you guys been up to? I haven't set eyes on either of you for ages, let alone managed a conversation.'

'Fine...' *Breathe in...and out...* 'I'm fine...' *And again...* 'Been through a bit of a rough patch... But...' Breathe... 'Seem to be pulling through.'

Lizzie was proud of herself. A week ago she would have been in tears at this point. Any grimaces now were attributable to her calf muscles currently smarting rather painfully as she allowed herself to stiffen up.

'Fancy a quick cup of tea?'

He didn't actually say...and a gossip...but it was implied. Tea without talk for Colin would be as alien a concept as a holiday without sunshine—although Lizzie was sure that his year-round healthy skin tone was sustained with the help of fake tan and solarium minutes.

'Or maybe something colder. Cranberry? Elderflower?' Lizzie smiled. Most men wouldn't know an elderflower if it came up and punched them in the face. Meanwhile Colin was mentally running through his cordial collection, trying to tempt Lizzie into his flat. 'Lime...Ribena?'

He was standing at the top of the stairs that led down to his front door, awaiting her decision. Lizzie looked down at her running top, which was now attractively a darker shade of red under her arms and breasts and completely stuck to her back. She wiped the sweat from her temples into her hairline. Jane Fonda must have had her pores somewhere else. Even in her feel-the-burn heyday you never really saw her sweat. A little glow, attractive breathlessness and maybe even a few droplets glistening on her cheeks and chest. But then Lizzie clung to the belief that if you weren't totally dishevelled at the end of a run then you hadn't been working hard enough.

'Might nip upstairs for a quick shower first. Don't think you'd want me sweating all over your furniture in my current state.'

Was that relief on Colin's face? Lizzie thought it was.

'OK. Just pop down when you're done.'

As Lizzie showered she was thankful that she'd run into a familiar face. For starters she'd be tempted to put on some of her smarter clothes, and secondly Colin always made her laugh. Usually at some outrageous and highly improbable tale of sexual conquest which made Lizzie feel totally heterosexually inadequate but quite impressed all the same.

For once she had a story to tell, but instinct told her to leave it. It hadn't exactly been one of her proudest relationship moments, and continuing to see him after she'd discovered that he was married meant that she'd sort of shot herself in the foot as far as getting any sympathy was concerned. She reached for her exfoliator and scrubbed hard. Twenty-first century self-flagellation at its best.

'Well, well, well.' If Colin was a witch he would have been cackling. 'You have been busy. Who'd have thought the agony aunt upstairs would've got herself embroiled in a love triangle...?'

A long burst of laughter. From Colin, not Lizzie. She hadn't meant to tell him, yet she'd found herself confessing before she'd even finished her first drink.

'It's no wonder you're out running, trying to sweat the guilt out of your system. Well done for coming home so soon. I think I'd have been tempted to do a Forrest Gump.' His eyes radiated mischief and the sort of joy that can only be derived from someone else's misfortune.

Lizzie poured herself another coffee and wondered whether, even in light of her recent burst of activity, consuming a third biscuit would just be plain greedy. This confessional stuff was making her very hungry, and at least if she was eating she might not incriminate herself any further. She hadn't told him the bit about knowing who Matt's wife was yet, but it had been a relief to get the rest of it off her chest, and for a few minutes it didn't seem like such a big deal at all.

'So, tell me—was he gorgeous?' Colin wanted details.

'Well, I'm not sure that he'd be your type, but, yes...' Lizzie sighed. 'He was definitely mine...except for the having a wife bit.' Sometimes the whole episode almost sounded surreal. It almost felt as if she was talking about someone else's life.

Colin roared with laughter. 'Oh, well, no one said love was perfect, darling...' Spotting a flicker of sadness in Lizzie's eyes, he toned it down. 'Poor you. You should've come down and cried on my shoulder weeks ago. I've had my heart broken more times than most.' And he was off. Colin could regale you with stories of doomed relationships for as long as you had and, listening to him, Lizzie felt positively pedestrian.

Lizzie didn't know whether she could attribute it to the biscuits, human company, Colin's cat redressing her recent affection deficit, or his candid tales of love-gone-wrong, but she was feeling loads better. Back in her own flat, she made a decision to analyse less and do more. Self-pity was so last season. Determined to make some changes, Lizzie called Clare's mobile. Clare obviously wasn't paying attention, or was expecting someone else to call, because she answered it straight away.

'Hello?'

'Clare?' Lizzie could barely contain her excitement. 'It's me—Liz. How are you?'

'Knackered. Totally shagged. Lunchtime was mad today. We had a private party in and they've only just gone.'

It was all great. Clare was being civil. They were almost having a normal conversation. Maybe the time and healing thing had finally happened. 'Packed on a Sunday—that's great for business.'

'Suppose so. What do you want, anyway?'

OK, so maybe it had all been too good to be true. 'Just thought I'd say hi. Remind you that I miss you and want you to come home. The usual.'

'Oh. Right. You sound quite perky. Everything OK?'

'Fine. I've just been for a run, and I suppose I'm chuffed that you a) answered the phone when you knew it was me and b) didn't hang up straight away. Please come home and forgive me.' Lizzie was burbling.

Clare soon halted her improving mood in its tracks. 'Not that simple, Liz.'

'Why not? I know I was wrong...but I can only apologise so many times before it gets boring.'

'I know you're sorry, and I'm glad you are, but so you should be...'

Lizzie could feel herself bristling. She'd made a mistake, a big one, but surely she'd paid the price. It must be time to move on now.

'Look, I know you think I'm trying to be difficult, and I know it looks like I've overreacted, but it must've triggered off a whole lot of emotion that I had suppressed over the last two years. Stuff that I have to deal with. I used to think you were pretty much perfect. And then—well, you let me down. I know it sounds extreme, and I'm sure if Joe hadn't done what he did then this wouldn't be happening. But he did and it is. I just need time.'

Oh, no, this was worse...emotional stuff...the old letting me and letting yourself down line. Guaranteed since school to make Lizzie feel utterly terrible.

'Can't we just put it behind us now? Move on.'

Lizzie could sort of see where Clare was coming from, but she wasn't asking her to have her babies, just to share a flat with her.

'Can't you see, Liz? I just need some time to deal with this my way.'

But she'd had loads of time. Right, this was it. Lizzie was going to have to take a chance and try and restore some perspective to the situation.

'You're not going to like this, but I do think you're overreacting...'

Lizzie held her breath, braced herself, and waited for Clare to explode. She didn't. Lizzie continued with some trepidation. But she had to say it. She couldn't just sit back and let Clare contemplate her navel for months and months while she started talking to herself every morning.

'You're my best friend. And I'm sorry I'm not perfect. Believe me, it would be far easier if I was. But people make mistakes every day. I made a mistake. I'm sorry I let you down—but, believe me, I let myself down even more. And I miss you.'

'I'm thinking about it Liz. But at the moment I'm sort of house-sitting for a friend near work. I'll pay my rent—don't worry, I won't leave you in the lurch. But maybe it's time for a change. Maybe it's time we didn't live in each other's pockets any more.'

'Oh. Well.' Lizzie felt sick as the latest plot twist in *Her Life—The Soap Opera* was revealed. She didn't want to be alone permanently. 'Give it some more time and then see how you feel. There's no need to decide anything now...' Lizzie was doing her best to hide her disappointment. 'In the meantime how about dinner some time? I'll cook.'

'Maybe...that would be nice...I'll call you.'

Would she? Lizzie wondered.

Lizzie could feel her frustration and disappointment transforming into anger. Maybe she'd be better off just getting on with everything on her own. Maybe Clare was right. Maybe this had all been a blessing in disguise.

chapter 19

Dear Lizzie

Two simple words. But two words that seemed to take him to the edge of a precipice that he couldn't quite bring himself to look over. And just because he'd started it didn't mean he had to finish. He thought he knew what he wanted to say and then, on reflection, it was always the same: too distant, too clingy, too clichéd, too desperate. Just too...too bloody difficult.

Matt doodled on the bottom half of the page as he waited for it to get late enough for him leave the office. He was at one of life's crossroads, only he seemed to have arrived there in a fuel crisis and every time he made a move in one direction something pulled him back. He loved Rachel like he loved *Star Wars* and Mars bars, but he was in love with Lizzie. But if she said that she didn't love him, that she didn't want him, then he had to deal with that.

He scrunched up his latest attempt at a letter and slam-dunked it into the wastepaper bin, where it started a second layer of paper balls. He was fed up with pretending he didn't care. He cared more than he could bear to admit to himself.

Because if it mattered then he had a lot to lose. If he tried to make things work with Rachel he wasn't being true to himself. If he went for Lizzie he might only be left with memories of them both. He leant forward and rested his forehead on the desk.

His head ached.

Life has more dimensions if you have oestrogen...
Lizzie was deep in this week's column.

Women agonise over details that men haven't even noticed and, while you can argue that it makes life more fulfilling, unfortunately it often makes things more complicated. The solution is simple enough. Teach yourself to sit back and enjoy the moment before it passes you by altogether. Stop beating yourself up. Whatever it is can wait until tomorrow.

Judging by the contents of my in-tray, you all want to know how to shake up your sex lives. You're tired, you're bored, and, most amusingly of all—from where I'm standing, at least—you all think I have the answers. But my relationship-saving tactic for today is a turn-off of the television variety. Ditch that remote. For starters, men by their own admission can only do one thing at a time. Secondly, take off your watch. How can you possibly be totally absorbed in the moment if you know exactly how many minutes there are to go until the ten o'clock news?

Sex isn't something to fill the gap between the regional weather and The West Wing. *It's not best slotted into the half-hour before you go to sleep, or squeezed into your schedule before you shower in the morning. Enjoy, cherish, immerse and then lose yourself in the moment. We've all been found guilty in the past. Yes, we've all taken advantage of our ability to multi-skill and planned something else while on the job. Reminded ourselves to buy risotto rice when we are next in the supermarket, to pick up the jacket that has been languishing at the dry cleaners for weeks, to ask the man you are currently straddling whether he'd like to book tickets for the theatre, or whether he might be interested in accompanying you to the new*

*exhibition at the Tate Modern which you have just read about
in last week's Sunday supplement.*

*But when you are kissing your man you should be a million
miles away from your shopping list. Remember that first time?
Those teenage kissing marathons? When the world stood still
until you had finished? Granted, the only other potentially
pressing concerns were probably homework and curfews—
both of which were better off forgotten. But as you get older
achieving good sex is all about focusing your mind. If you are
a man there is no other way. In order to be victorious on the
pitch, on the sofa or under the duvet you need to be concentrating one hundred per cent on the job in hand, in utero, etc.
etc....*

Lizzie was back on track. It was 7:00 p.m. and still sunny.
The clocks had changed. Even the air in Putney was smelling
sweeter. Summer was round corner and her self-esteem was
on its way back from its spring break.

A couple of glasses of Chilean Chardonnay over lunch in
the uncharacteristically warm April sunshine and Rachel was
feeling quite sentimental about life. A cocktail of alcohol and
UV rays was all it took. Everything seemed to be coming together. Saint Will of Battersea was working his magic, plus she
was finally getting Matthew back where he belonged. Only
now did she realise how much she'd missed her anchor, and
his reluctance had made him all the more desirable. This time
she'd appreciate the people around her. She smiled to herself.
Lizzie Ford was a lifesaver.

Rachel leant back in her chair and re-read the e-mail on her
screen. She hovered above the 'send' icon before letting her
mouse give it the go-ahead. It was a bit more gushing than she
usually felt comfortable with, but daytime drinking had definitely softened her edges.

Dear Lizzie
Haven't heard from you in ages. Needless to say
you've been busy helping people round the clock, but
this isn't business—instead, hopefully, it's a bit of plea-

sure, and no less than you deserve. I want to invite you round for dinner. Before you say no, I promise I'm not a psycho-stalker. I'd just really appreciate the chance to say thank you in person for all your advice and support.

Everything you suggested seems to have worked, and you really helped me to understand how my husband's mind was working when I hadn't got a clue. Oh, God, reading this back again, this is so not me. Gush, gush, gush. If anyone I work with saw this they'd think I was suffering from an overdose of *Oprah*. But I bet you don't get lots of thank-yous.

Anyway, I would really like Matthew to meet the woman who has given us another chance at being happy. I can clear most evenings next week—just let me know when would be good for you.

Look forward to hearing from you soon.

Yours, Rachel x

Lizzie was in her inbox and her heart was pounding in her chest as it concentrated on pumping all her blood to her temples in a hopeless attempt to blur her vision and prevent her from reading the message in front of her. Pulse thumping, she read the e-mail again. Just to make sure.

And then she woke up...

No, she was awake already. Awake, dressed and breathing. Why couldn't it all have been a dream instead of a living nightmare? How could Lizzie contemplate dinner in Turnham Green? Yet how she could turn Rachel down without emigrating or befalling a tragic accident and losing her memory?

In the absence of an answer Lizzie employed pure ostrich tactics and ignored the invitation. When, bored with waiting, Rachel started e-mailing suggested dates, Lizzie side-stepped each and every one, concocting a spurious cocktail of last-minute work engagements. After several days of procrastination, having drafted several versions of varying apology and in the absence of Clare's spectacular sounding board properties, Lizzie finally got the balance right.

> Rachel
> Apologies for the delay in getting back to you but I've been rushed off my feet at this end.

Efficient, but not brusque enough to arouse suspicion. Lizzie knew she could do this convincingly.

> Thanks for your kind invitation for dinner. I'm very flattered, but for many reasons I think it would be best to take a raincheck. General busyness aside, the magazine does have a policy which strongly discourages me from meeting my readers in person on a social basis. I'm really glad that things are going well for you and Matthew. It's all part of the service.
> Yours, Lizzie

She read it back. Perfect. What a relief for her readers and listeners that she was better at her job than she was at managing her own life.

Never underestimate the power of a grateful career woman. Lizzie was at home, answering yet more letters, when her editor at *Out Loud* called the same afternoon.

'Darling. How's my favourite columnist doing?'

Lizzie was concerned. Susan never rang her at home. She didn't see the point. After all, that was—she believed—what having e-mail and a PA was all about. Lizzie sensed an impossible deadline on the horizon.

'Fine, thanks.'

'Listen, I won't keep you from your work. I'm sure you're up to your armpits in dreary heartache, as usual, and far be it from me to get in the way of you helping people who can't help themselves.'

Despite all the spin to the contrary, churned out by the press office, compassion for the general public was not something that oozed from her editor.

'How can I help?'

'Well, I've just had a conversation with the most charming woman. It's restored my faith in our readers. She wasn't a fuck-wit at all...'

Lizzie smirked as Susan flouted every convention of political correctness.

'She's got just the reader profile we want. Anyway, she's so pleased with you and your advice that she wants to invite you round for dinner.'

'Really?'

Lizzie's stomach lurched. She'd been outplayed.

'Yes—and by the sound of her I think it'll be quite a decent dinner at that. She says that she's already asked you by e-mail but that you're being all professional about mixing business with pleasure.'

If only Susan knew quite how unprofessional she'd been. Lizzie mumbled something about confidentiality clauses and anonymity but was soon interrupted.

'Anyway, I was just calling to say that there's no reason why you shouldn't go. It's not like you get lots of perks in this job, is it? You know I'm always impressed by your professional attitude, but for God's sake lighten up. Take some of your own advice and be cool, chill out, whatever... Where was I? Oh, yes—this woman...what was she called...I wrote it on a Post-it here somewhere... Jesus... Why is it you can never find these things when you want them? I am practically drowning in paper. God knows why I have the only PA in the country who is allergic to filing... You wouldn't believe how messy my desk is... Got it... Yes, this woman... Rachel, I think my writing says...yes, Rachel...seems genuine and charming and—well, normal in a you and I, PLU sort of way.'

Lizzie flinched involuntarily. She hated all these 'in' acronyms. Especially when they meant 'People Like Us'. If it was a time-saving thing, it didn't take much longer to say all three words, but more importantly it was the smug middle class inference that really got to her. Them and Us. Fine if you were a Shark or a Jet, a Greaser or a Soc, or even a Capulet or a Montague. Not fine if you ran a magazine and lived in Notting Hill. Plus Lizzie resented the fact that Susan thought that she and Lizzie were in the same bracket.

'Look, she only wants a chance to say thank you, and it's not like she's offering you a suitcase full of used twenty-pound notes or a stolen Cartier wristwatch, is it?'

Lizzie couldn't help but laugh at this latest analogy. She liked Susan. She might at times be a veritable caricature of herself, but at least she was consistently eccentric and her heart was usually in the right sort of place.

'No...I suppose not. Thanks.'

Lizzie thought she should at least try and sound grateful.

'Anyway, in case you've been turning down dinner invitations by the handful, this particular fan is called Rachel Baker and I promised her that you'd be in touch soon. I've got her work number here.'

'OK. I've got a pen...'

Lizzie went along with the charade of writing it down, even though it was part of the autosignature at the bottom of every e-mail that Rachel had sent her. How on earth was she going to get out of this one now?

'One more thing, Liz...'

'Yup?'

'Well, I was sort of thinking—if this woman is as nice as she sounds on the phone maybe we should be thinking about running a feature on the two of you. She told me earlier that she'd never imagined she'd ever consult an agony aunt. An article might encourage more people like her to write in.'

More people. Looking at the postal debris creatively piled around her study, Lizzie didn't feel that she was short of letters. As for an article—no way was she going to advocate that all members of the West London Love Triangle be featured on one double-page spread.

'I don't think Rachel would be interested. Dinner's one thing, but I don't think she's told anyone that she wrote to me so I can't see her baring all. In some ways she's quite a private person.'

'Well, maybe we could just use her first name and use a model for the shoot? We could even try for an interview with the husband instead...'

Lizzie refused to be rattled. She couldn't be bothered to argue this one out now. It wasn't happening, but she didn't feel the need to antagonise Susan by being quite so apparently difficult right now this minute.

'Thanks for calling with that. I'd better get on, or you won't have next week's column by the end of tomorrow.'

'Marvellous. I loved "Life has more dimensions if you have oestrogen". Genius. But I guess that's what we pay you for. Keep up the good work. Maybe I'll run into you in the office soon? I always seem to be in meetings when you're here. Maybe it's time we had a lunch?'

'That would be great.'

'Excellent. Give Bridget a call. My expanding waistline is testament to the fact that she is better at booking restaurants and co-ordinating lunches than she is at filing. Speak to you soon. Bye.'

'Bye.'

Lizzie had been cornered. As she was discovering to her dismay, Rachel had the determination and focus to succeed in every area of her life provided she put her mind to it.

A flurry of e-mails ensued, and it seemed she'd agreed to a date in about three weeks' time. She still had a few more weekends to dream up excuses, but it seemed that yet again fate wasn't on her side. She must have really fucked up in a previous life. Surely it was someone else's turn now?

chapter 20

Rachel applied a second coat of lipstick. It was only another magazine launch, but if things went according to plan she would finally get to meet the elusive Lizzie Ford.

She marvelled at Lizzie's modesty. Modesty was a quality that she aspired to add to her repertoire one day. People always had more admiration for people who kept their trumpets hidden enigmatically from view, but Rachel always found herself blowing hers after a few drinks. She could try and dress it up as reaction to a deep-seated insecurity, but she knew that if she was being honest she was just a bit of a show-off. She couldn't bear other people taking the credit for her achievements, and just batting her eyelashes and saying 'it was nothing really' seemed like a bit of a waste of time. Why be demure when you could be direct? She was her own life coach, marketing manager and spin doctor rolled into one.

Rachel made her way to the bar and perched on a stool with the launch issue of *Blue*. If Lizzie didn't show up tonight then she'd persuade Matt to take her out for dinner after a few free cocktails. It was a no-lose situation.

* * *

Matt listened to his voicemail message one more time and sighed at no one in particular as Rachel's excited tones radiated from his speakerphone. There it was again—a quickfire delivery of directions and instructions. There didn't appear to be a 'no' option and, as he hadn't been sitting at his desk when she'd called, now he'd have to go.

He rummaged in his bottom drawer for his sparkling wit. As he gulped down a couple of mouthfuls of vodka with a mouthwash chaser he could feel his body waking up. He turned the volume up on his computer and forced himself to jig about to a couple of dance anthems at his desk. Wednesday night. Party time. He was ready.

Lizzie could tell the party was already in full swing before the lift doors opened on the sixth floor of the Kensington Roof Gardens. The oasis of calm had been transformed, at undoubtedly vast expense, for the launch of *Blue*, and if she was to believe the call she'd received a few days ago from her very excitable agent, Robyn Summers, they wanted to sign her up when her contract at *Out Loud* expired.

Going to suss out the opposition all seemed a bit cloak and dagger to Lizzie, and she was sure that Susan Sharples wouldn't have been thrilled to find her on the guest list of this particular party, but after a firm arm-twist from Robyn, who could obviously sense a greater percentage hitting her coffers, she had promised to make an appearance and check them out.

Lizzie was under no illusions about her negotiating skills. In a world of sharks and charlatans she was a serious loyalty case and had never been very good at the cut and thrust of playing hard to get or selling herself to the highest bidder—a failing of hers both in and outside of the business arena. She'd learnt the hard way in her first few relationships, but when it came to her professional life she was relieved to have the pecuniary Robyn Summers at hand. The bigger Lizzie's deal, the more Donna Karan Robyn could have in her wardrobe, and there was no harm in doing a bit of window-shopping and nowhere better to start than Kensington.

If Lizzie had been blindfolded and dropped into the party by helicopter she reckoned she'd have been able to guess the magazine title in a matter of seconds. Blue was the theme—right down to the garish cocktails that were being mixed. She took her complimentary launch pack and made a beeline for the nearest barman.

She hadn't taken more than a couple of sips from her outsize blue glass of wine when a beautiful dark-haired woman swept up to her and embraced her like a long-lost friend. Her mind went into free fall as it tried to link voice and face. She was normally quite good with the latter, and she was almost certain that she had never set eyes on this woman before.

'Lizzie? It is you, isn't it? Rumour has it they're trying to lure you in—and who can blame them? It seems that transfer deals are no longer limited to footballers. Astrologers, editors and agony aunts are all fair game these days...'

Lizzie smiled sheepishly in the hope that someone nearby might enlighten her as to who this woman actually was. But no one else at the bar had even looked up, and there was no tell-tale name badge to give Lizzie a clue in her moment of need. She racked her brains. But the face in front of her really didn't ring any bells. Not even a little tiny one at the back somewhere.

'A colleague at my agency has been running *Blue*'s campaign. It looks fabulous, doesn't it?'

The woman gestured towards six enormous stylised floor-to-ceiling flats which displayed the current, now subliminally familiar, poster campaign, and Lizzie racked her brain for the name of the editor of this new title. It couldn't have been more than an hour since Robyn had reminded Lizzie to introduce herself...and it was important. So important that she'd scribbled it on her hand—a terribly unsophisticated habit that she'd continued from school—but she must have washed it off before she left home. The surname and first name started with the same letter... Melissa Matthews? Yes, that sounded right. But something told Lizzie that this wasn't her. Even in media terms she was being over-familiar. Lizzie concentrated on not looking as bewildered as she felt. Instead she focused on taking all this in her stride.

'Projected sales are good. The whole team at the agency have pulled together to give it a new feel. Quite a tall order in such a crowded marketplace, I think you'll agree, but it looks like all of us at CDH are having a good year. Thought any more about whether you might want to sign up with *Blue* when your current contract expires?'

'Us'. 'CDH'. 'Agency'. This woman had to be Rachel. Without even thinking about what she was doing, Lizzie stole a glance at her left hand, and sure enough a platinum wedding band and matching diamond engagement ring winked back at her. Despite all the e-mails they'd never spoken, and fortunately for Lizzie no one, not even Susan Sharples at her most effervescent, had given Rachel her home number.

'Sorry, Lizzie. You've got no idea who I am, have you? And why should you? You don't see pictures of me plastered on the back of buses. I'm Rachel. And I can't tell you how great it is to finally meet you. I owe you. A prawn?'

Rachel had located a plate of Thai prawns—thankfully non-blue, normal-coloured—arranged radially around a sweet chilli dip, and Lizzie was relieved at the distraction. She helped herself to a couple and generously covered them in chilli seeds. She hoped their potency might take her mind off the fact that all she seemed to be able to think about at this precise moment was Rachel and Matt in bed together. Her recovery process, until ten minutes ago practically complete, had just suffered a monumental setback.

'Are you still on course for our dinner? I'm half expecting you to cancel again. I know what it's like. What with my hectic schedule and your workload it's useless. But you might even get to meet Matthew tonight. He's supposed to be trying to join me here later on. All part of my strategy—or should I say your strategy?—to make him feel more included in my life.' Rachel was exuding energy and positivity.

'Oh, right. Good idea.' Lizzie, conversely, was in decline. Just for a split second she wished that she hadn't been quite so helpful. Her gaze was currently resting on Rachel's enormous diamond solitaire as she wondered how Matt had proposed. She tore her eyes away and concentrated on the woman she was speaking to. Rachel was dressed immaculately and stylishly in black, from her head to her Choo encased toes. Designer black. You could just tell. There wasn't a Top Shop accessory on her person—or indeed, Lizzie suspected, in her life.

Lizzie smiled broadly in an attempt to conceal the nervous glance she was just casting over Rachel's shoulder in the direction of the entrance. Running into Matt without months of preparation—or psychotherapy—was not an option. She had to put him behind her, and seeing him again would be bound to set her back a good week or three. Time to invent a migraine.

Rachel, however, wasn't even giving Lizzie a chance to mention the fictitious headache which was on the verge of 'ruining' her evening.

'You know, I always used to think that agony aunts were a total con. I thought they just stated the obvious with little real compassion for the people that were asking for their help. I was convinced that they were all laughing at their readers behind their backs. I'm sure some do. But you really seem to understand the people involved. A new breed of aunt. Thanks to you, I think my marriage has a real chance. You were right. It was tough at first, but hopefully in a couple of weeks we'll have returned to the honeymoon period...not bad considering we both have a tendency to work late.'

Lizzie nearly choked on the remains of her prawn. She had to get out of there and fast. Just standing opposite her was too much. Immaculately groomed. Dark. Short. Petite, even. But feisty and scarily self-possessed. Almost hyper. Exhausting, in fact. And married...to him. But there was something about her that Lizzie could relate to. She was ambitious and had a passion for life that was infectious even if everything did seem to revolve around herself.

'So how's things with you? Did you manage to sort out that bloke who was mucking you around? He must have been mad. How can someone like you have been left on the shelf? It just doesn't make sense.'

On the shelf. Hmm. Rachel needed to work on her tact. But

Lizzie was thrown. She wasn't used to people asking her how she was feeling. Maybe Rachel wasn't as self-centred as she'd just thought. It was only a shame that the question had made her think about its asker's husband. It still seemed ludicrous that the one person Lizzie had met in recent years who she'd thought might be able to make her happy was already married to this not unattractive and not horned woman in front of her. How she would have loved to be able to hate Rachel. But, as it happened, it wasn't that easy.

'I just pick the wrong ones, I guess. That bloke was sent packing. Could do better...the traditional story.'

Shit. The perfect opportunity to mention her headache and she'd completely forgotten.

'Must be difficult for you to find time for yourself in amongst everyone else's problem-ridden lives...'

'It—'

Lizzie had been about to answer Rachel but, a new breath taken in an inaudible gasp that would have impressed all but the most advanced ventriloquists, her soliloquy continued.

'I know what I do is totally different, but finding time for myself in the average day is hard work. Aside from the odd leg wax and haircut I seem to be continuously on the go...'

Lizzie nodded empathetically and took another sip of her drink before starting to plot an escape route.

Matt was exhausted. Work was hectic, even if he wasn't really achieving anything, and this kick-starting his marriage thing was really taking it out of him. Rachel seemed to have got what she wanted, and one out of two wasn't too bad. Probably better than being all alone. Probably.

The pull of home and the call of the sofa were only getting stronger in inverse proportion to his proximity to Turnham Green. Even the gym was looking like an attractive alternative. Going to your own work party was enough of an effort without having to make small talk with all your wife's cronies. Most of them never seemed interested in talking to him at all. No doubt that young, cocky Will bloke would be hanging around, making him feel as if he was part of the past-it posse.

He breathed in and tied his navy jumper round his waist in a token attempt to hide his rapidly increasing one-lunch-with-a-client-too-many waistline. He didn't want to further decrease his credibility by entering this party as part of the pushing-forty-with-a-paunch crew.

As he searched the sea of blue for a familiar face he couldn't help but wonder how many millions of pounds had been wasted on creative away days, reader research and focus groups before they had decided on the title. Rachel didn't stand out, or rather she wasn't standing on a table, and therefore he was highly unlikely to be able to pick out her diminutive frame from the entrance. It was, he mused, the only small thing about her. He elbowed his way towards the bar. He always felt happier—well, more detached from the reality of his life—with a drink in his hand.

He heard Rachel before he spotted her. She was talking animatedly to someone, and that someone was female which certainly made a pleasant change. Or did it? His jaw dropped. It couldn't be. It was. Rachel was talking to someone with a very familiar back. A shiver of paralysis ran down his spine. Maybe he'd been set up? He was sure he'd seen it in a movie once. A revenge of the sisterhood type thing. But he was sure that Lizzie wasn't like that. Rachel, maybe, but not Lizzie. He felt the now familiar surge of disappointment at the status quo. Maybe it wasn't too late. But not now. Not here.

He turned and started to head back the way he'd come. But she'd spotted him, made eye contact, and was now waving and beckoning. Lizzie still had her back to him. Trapped.

Her voice came sailing over the crowd. 'Matthew! Over here, darling. There's someone I'd like you to meet.'

It wasn't a request. It was an order, and not one that he was allowed to ignore.

Lizzie's heart nearly stopped at the mention of his name. The 'darling' just added insult to the multiple injury she was currently suffering in her pericardium. She leant lightly against a conveniently adjacent pillar for physical support. Her body thermostat had lost control. She was cold—frozen, in fact—

with the exception of her neck which must have been crimson it was burning up so rapidly.

What could she possibly have done to deserve this? Until recently she'd lived by the rules that western society dictated were the norm. She'd worked hard at school. She'd kept her room fairly tidy. She was one of the few people who still gave up her seat on the tube for old people and mothers with young children. She didn't smoke. She didn't do drugs. She always washed her hands after going to the toilet. She hadn't poked fun at disabled people since she was under ten and didn't know any better, and she had almost always told the truth.

Granted, she'd fallen head over heels in love with a married man—but she wasn't the first and she wouldn't be the last. It was as if her name had been drawn out of a hat on some higher plane as part of some sick, twisted after-dinner game. Someone up there was picking on her. But someone might at least have had the decency to give her advance warning if it really was have-a-go-at-Lizzie year so that she could have emotionally sandbagged herself to dampen the blows a little.

Matt walked over, willing the person his wife was talking to to be Lizzie's body double. His own body was apparently insisting on putting one foot in front of the other instead of running in the opposite direction. Lizzie was doing her utmost to look relaxed, but there was already so much just-below-the-surface tension between the two of them that he was surprised Rachel hadn't picked up on it. This was one occasion when he was glad that she was so self-centred.

The effect of Lizzie's presence on him was electric. Every hair in every follicle on his body was now standing to attention. Every muscle twitched. But if she didn't want him he had to move on. Matt had given himself this lecture countless times over the last few weeks. There was nothing to be gained by him moping. Just because he was an ever-hopeful—make that hope*less*—romantic he couldn't wallow in brat-pack happy-ending fantasies any longer. He had to toughen up. Love was a four-letter word, after all. For years he'd refused to believe it. Now he was starting to empathise with the bitterness of so many of his peers.

'Hello, darling. Thanks for coming.'

Rachel kissed him lightly on the lips. He barely kissed her back, aware of Lizzie's eyes fixed on him. Rachel didn't notice; she was too excited. This was her moment—as usual.

'There's someone here I'm dying for you to meet. Lizzie Ford—this is my husband Matthew. Matthew, this is Lizzie— she's the agony aunt at *Out Loud* and she has that phone-in on...'

'City FM.'

Matt was staring at Lizzie as he finished Rachel's sentence for her and reached out to shake her hand. It was a ridiculous moment and almost seemed to be taking place in slow motion. Lizzie's hand was ice-cold. He smiled at her to try and relax them both. He really needed a stiff drink; the lager in his glass was nowhere near alcoholic enough. As the two protagonists struggled to come to terms with their evenings Rachel provided a babbling soundtrack over the top: a welcome distraction.

'Yes, that's right...' She sounded like a mother talking to a four-year-old child. All that was missing was a patronising 'well done'. 'How do you know?'

'Oh, I've worked on a couple of the campaigns.'

'So you two have met before, then?'

'Not really,' Lizzie answered confidently, if a little too quickly.

'I think we were in a meeting room together once,' Matt added.

Well, it's a small world, isn't it? Matthew—I had no idea you worked on that campaign.'

'I did tell you.'

'Oh, you know what I can be like. Totally preoccupied.'

Rachel was showing off in front of Lizzie and trying to make sure that she came across as the trouser wearing, controlling member of the marital team. Lizzie wasn't impressed. She knew she had a vested interest, but Rachel's display of powerful woman was wasted on her.

Matt nodded in agreement with Rachel's last statement,

which had been more honest than usual. He knew only too well. He turned the questioning on his wife.

'So, how do you know Lizzie?' He was genuinely interested.

Lizzie wanted the floor to swallow her up—and the sooner the better. From where she was standing there seemed to be no way out. Clusters of partygoers blocked her exit route on all sides.

'Remember the day I was ill just before Christmas and you bought me some magazines...?'

Matt nodded.

'Well, I was just flicking through *Out Loud* and I started reading Lizzie's pages...' Rachel, overcome with the moment and the cocktails, was about to confess. Hell, why not? She had nothing to lose. 'You won't believe this, and I still sometimes think that I must have dreamt it, but I wrote to her.'

Matt's jaw had slackened in disbelief. Rachel noticed and felt that further justification was required.

'I know it was totally out of character. I must have been really, really ill.'

Lizzie had an unaskable question. She wanted to know whether Matt had bought the magazine for Rachel before or after they'd slept together. Either way, it appeared that Matt had inadvertently introduced Rachel to Lizzie. Matt, meanwhile, was still trying to deal with the fact that his wife and his mistress were pen pals. Lizzie hadn't bargained for the fact that Rachel would tell Matt that she'd consulted an agony aunt. It hadn't even occurred to her. Apparently her plan wasn't foolproof—more like hare-brained.

'You did what?'

Matt looked bewildered, dismayed—or was that angry? Yes angry...but Lizzie could see the hurt in his eyes too. How on earth had she convinced herself that getting everything back to 'normal' would be easy?

'I wrote to her. She's good. And after the first exchange of letters we sort of became e-mail buddies. But I'd never met her—until about twenty minutes ago, that is. I keep inviting her round for dinner because I want you to meet her, but she's never free. One commitment after another. A bit like me, really. I don't think we should take it personally...'

Rachel laughed, self-satisfied by her own wit and failing to note the grim expression on her husband's face.

'What with her radio show, her column and all her other responsibilities it's a wonder she has any time for herself at all.'

Matt had now substituted stonyfaced with confused, and kept running his hand through his hair distractedly. He'd have loved to call a 'time out'. To ask Lizzie to run through the finer points of the situation with him. But it wasn't going to be feasible for them to glean two seconds, let alone two minutes together. He stared at the two women.

Lizzie gave Matt what she hoped was a reassuring look before deciding that it might be best if she took the conversation into her own hands. At least that way she could change the subject, or at the very least move them along before one of them made an irrevocable blunder.

'So, Matt—Matthew...um...are you working on any interesting projects? Any more slogans I should prepare to be brainwashed by?'

Matt could feel Rachel watching him, willing him to be the fantastic husband she had undoubtedly told Lizzie he was.

'Well...'

'How did you know he does slogans?'

Lizzie was regretting ever speaking. It had taken less than ten seconds to insert her foot firmly into her mouth. Her cheeks were now puce under her foundation, but thanks to Lancôme she was probably about to get away with it. She could be quite a good liar if she had to be, provided her blushes didn't give her away, and make-up and alcohol were proving to be the perfect accomplices.

'He's a copywriter, isn't he? I think you told me in one of your e-mails.' Inspired. Well recovered under pressure.

'Oh, yes, probably.' Rachel seemed almost apologetic.

'I have this weird selective memory. I always remember what people do for a living and what pets they have.' Lizzie knew she was spouting drivel, but it seemed to have done the trick.

It would've been sensible to quit while she was ahead. To make her excuses and leave. But the combination of Rachel's chatty disposition, Matt's proximity and the genuinely bizarre nature of the evening encouraged her to stay a little longer.

They progressed gingerly. Lizzie asked polite questions about Rachel's job and the campaign while Matt stared at her. Lizzie then transferred her interest to Matt and asked lots of questions that she already knew the answers to. Rachel rolled her eyes impatiently every time he used one of his trademark corny one-liners that Lizzie had come to love.

At the first opportunity he had to escape Matt obligingly offered to go to the bar for refills and left Lizzie chatting just a little too amicably with his wife. He had quite a few important questions. Like at which point exactly had Lizzie known that he and Rachel were married? He suspected that he already knew the answer. What a fucking mess. He downed a blue vodka shot at the bar before returning to the ever-so-cosy conversation armed with the next round of drinks.

He dutifully handed his wife her usual G & T and presented Lizzie with a vodka and blue cranberry.

'I thought you might like one of these.'

'What is it?'

'Vodka and cranberry...with a hint of something blue, of course. I think they said it was blackcurrant...'

Rachel wasn't impressed. 'Why couldn't you have just got her another glass of wine instead of going for the glorified Ribena option?' She turned to Lizzie to apologise for Matt. Lizzie could have punched her.

'Sorry. Hope you like it. He never has been very good at following orders.' She threw back her head and laughed conspiratorially before raising her eyes to heaven. 'Cheers, anyway.' She raised her glass.

It was the final straw. Lizzie couldn't bear the way Rachel was treating him—and besides, cranberries reminded her of the Christmas party. She sipped her drink and turned to thank him.

'How lovely. One of my favourites. Thanks, Matt.'

He almost blushed.

'You might remember jobs and pets. I never forget what a girl likes to drink.'

They both laughed. For a split second it was as if Rachel wasn't there. Only she was. Staring. Silent. Her eyes were cold, her mouth tightly closed, a horizontal line on her otherwise beautiful face. Matt looked shocked as he realised the implications of his comment. Rachel stared at Lizzie, then at Matt, then at Lizzie again. She looked as confused as a cat watching tennis on television.

Relaxed by the alcohol, Lizzie decided that Rachel deserved some sort of explanation. She was feeling so guilty that her hormones simply took over, and it didn't look as if Matt was going to say anything.

'Rachel, I can explain...' Could she? Lizzie wished she felt as confident as she had just sounded. 'I *have* met Matt before. We had a drink together at the City FM Christmas party. I just didn't put two and two together when he arrived this evening and you introduced us. He must have looked different back then. More hair, more weight...something...'

'Oh.' What the hell was going on? Lizzie was trying far too hard and Matthew had just begun a detailed study of his shoes. 'So when did you realise that you knew each other?'

'To be honest I thought he looked vaguely familiar when he first came over, but I wasn't quite sure where I'd seen him before. You know how it is...I meet so many people in the course of my job. Then as we were chatting I gradually realised, and the drink thing sealed it for me. We ended up debating the popularity of cranberry juice at the party but we'd both had a skinful and that was...' There was a pause while Lizzie counted the months on her fingers. 'Well, nearly five months ago.' Was it really? Lizzie had surprised herself.

Matt joined in. Not a moment too soon in Lizzie's opinion.

'Chill out, Rach. I dread to think how many men have bought you drinks at office parties and you don't see me getting my knickers in a twist. So Lizzie didn't remember me at first. Can't say I blame her. I'm hardly Mr Memorable, am I?'

Chill out? God, it annoyed her when he tried to do 'street'.

At his age it just seemed so try-hard. She had a few questions, but he could wait.

They returned, somewhat stiltedly, to their small talk.

Lizzie was relieved that Matt's self-deprecation seemed to have pacified Rachel. It looked as if they'd got away with it and, heart pounding, Lizzie decided that it was time to excuse herself. She conspicuously checked her watch.

'Look, I'd better get on. I've still got to try and track down Melissa and introduce myself before I leave. Rachel, it's been great to finally meet you.' She leant towards Rachel and kissed her on the cheek. Very media. But a handshake seemed inappropriate somehow. Rachel didn't pull away. The conversation ended more or less as it had begun, if a little less effusively.

'So, see you for dinner in a few weeks, then?'

'Sure. That'd be great. I'll e-mail you nearer the time.' As if. She'd start thinking of her next excuse just as soon as she got home.

'Any special requests? Anything you don't eat?'

'I think I pretty much eat everything—usually all at the same time...'

Matt was suffering with *déjà-vu*.

'Bye, Matt. Nice to meet you...again. Sorry I didn't recognise you at first, it just took a bit of time to place that face... Mr Memorable. I'll remember next time. Good luck with everything.'

Instinctively she leant forward and kissed his...cheek. Bonus point for Ms Ford. Luckily Matt had helped by moving his cheek into the casual acquaintance position. Lizzie was really flustered and, again, it was all her own doing. She could feel Rachel watching her. Matt took over. He was remarkably calm. No mean feat considering that he'd had more surprises to deal with than Lizzie this evening.

'Thanks...and you. Maybe we'll run into each other at City some time. Next time just make sure you remember where you've seen me before.' Matt smiled at her mischievously. He was incorrigible.

Inwardly Lizzie breathed a sigh of relief, silently promising the goddess of gym membership that from this day forward she'd be a good girl, exercise regularly and drink two litres of still water every day if she could just leave now, her reputation intact.

But Rachel wasn't about to let her husband have the last word.

'Oh, and Lizzie...?'

'Yes?'

'You know... Um...this is going to sound daft after all I've said...um...but I'd appreciate it if you didn't tell too many people...well, anyone really...about how we know each other. It's just that—well, you know—people might not understand.'

Rachel thought back to an effusive Will, strutting around her office, mocking Lizzie's letters page. He was one of the people that she never wanted to find out.

'No problem. Confidentiality is my career.'

'Great. Thanks.' Rachel gave Lizzie a mildly irritating insincere media wink as she was gratefully swallowed up by the rapidly expanding crowd.

Lizzie marched to the loos as assertively as she could and had barely locked the cubicle door behind her before the tears started. She wasn't sure why she was crying. Guilt? Relief? Unrequited love? Once the pent-up emotion had been released, she pulled herself together quickly, splashed some cold water onto her burning cheeks, took a deep breath, re-applied some eyeliner and prepared to re-enter the fray in search of Melissa Matthews.

She would've preferred to head straight for the sanctuary of her sofa, but the spirit of Robyn Summers was nudging her into action. It probably wasn't a bad thing. It would only look odd if she left this early.

As she applied a self-protective coat of lipgloss, Lizzie wondered if she and Matt had got away with it. She didn't have to wait long for an answer. Rachel burst through the door which, at the receiving end of her fury, smacked loudly into the wall, and marched straight up to Lizzie, only just stopping short of pinning her up against the wallpaper. A lone hand-washer left hurriedly, without bothering to dry or thinking to stay and watch. The difference in Rachel couldn't have been any greater. She'd gone from charming to civil to psycho in minutes.

The goddess of gym membership had obviously run a check on Elizabeth Ford of 56 Oxford Road only to discover that she'd previously promised regular attendance and higher intake levels of non-alcoholic and decaffeinated fluids in return for a favour, only to rescind on her side of the bargain once she was out of harm's way.

'What the fuck do you think you've been playing at?'

It looked as if a lucky escape was no longer on the cards. Lizzie was terrified. An instant headache thumped into her temples and a surge of nausea swept up from her stomach like a giant tsunami. She didn't bother mentioning it to Rachel. She sensed that she wasn't in a sympathetic mood.

'Ah...umm...'

It was a pathetic display of inarticulacy from someone who was supposed to do communication for a living, but she didn't know where to start. Rachel was only too happy to take over. Lizzie braced herself.

'Why the hell didn't you and Matthew tell me that you knew each other when I first introduced you?'

That one was relatively easy. She just had to go over what she'd told her earlier. She employed the tried and tested repeat-the-question-to-give-yourself-a-little-bit-more-time-before-answering tactic, to calm herself down and regain her composure. She was sure it was still around here somewhere.

'Why didn't I tell you that Matt and I had met before? Well, um... As I said out there, it took me a few minutes to realise that he was the same guy I'd met at the Christmas party. I didn't recognise him at first. And it was all out of context. I was expecting to meet your husband. I didn't expect your husband to be someone I'd ever met before. We only spent that one evening together, and the party was nearly five months ago.'

'OK, so you pass the memory test. But don't patronise me. Something's going on here and I think it's only fair that you tell me what it is.'

Lizzie re-adopted the mute approach and shrugged her

shoulders, as if confused. Unfortunately it only seemed to augment Rachel's irritation.

'Listen, I'm not an idiot. Something was going on out there. I've just asked Matt for an explanation and he told me to "simmer down". *Simmer down*, I tell you. I'm not a fucking pan. And this from a word-man. No wonder he's still small fry. I expected more from him, and I certainly expected a lot more from you. You two have done a lot more than just meet before, haven't you? You conniving bitch. Not so fucking saintly after all, are you? You must think I'm stupid.'

Rachel was going out on a limb. It was only a hunch at this stage, but the eyes had it. She was bloody well going to be proved right, and if there was one occasion in her life that Rachel had wished she was wrong, it was right now. Molten hysteria bubbled in her ears.

Lizzie thanked the powers that be that she was British and that no one in Kensington was allowed to carry a gun to parties. Had she been in America she feared that she would currently be sliding down the designer-papered walls of the Ladies' leaving a dark red trail of her own blood behind her. Rachel was certainly angry enough.

They say that you never know how you will react to a crisis until you are knee-deep in one. Curiously, Lizzie's brain seemed to have closed down. Before it did, though, it had chosen to flag up its most relevant saying from deep in its recesses. The archivist had obviously been busy. 'Hell hath no fury like a woman scorned' was currently playing on a loop in Lizzie's head.

Lizzie could well believe it, but right now she needed to be paying attention. Hell also hath no fury like a woman who isn't being listened to in the heat of the moment. It might have been a less well-known epithet but it was just as true and, faced with Rachel Baker on the brink of eruption, Lizzie went into automatic pacifying mode. She'd never really understood why two people couldn't just sit down and talk things through. The trouble being that if you tried to quieten down someone who liked a good old shout you were in danger of making things worse than they had been at the outset. From her current display Lizzie suspected that Rachel was a shouter. Still, it was worth a try.

'Listen, Rachel. I'm sorry you're so upset, and I'm sorry if it's my fault, but I think there's been a misunderstanding.' Too many sorrys, perhaps? Too late now.

'Please, calm down and I'll try and explain. It's not as bad as you think.' Unfortunately in order for Lizzie the Pacifier to be successful she had also become Lizzie the Liar. *Not as bad as you think.* Who was she trying to kid? It couldn't get much worse.

Rachel folded her arms. 'Go on, then.'

The truth beckoned, and it wasn't going to sound any better in ten minutes' time when her current flight of fancy fell flat on its face. Lizzie blinked hard and took a deep breath before punching her next few sentences out as fast as she could.

'Look—it's been over for a long time, and I didn't know he was married at the time we met. And I certainly didn't know he was married to you. I know it all sounds a little too convenient, but I can explain.' It was all true, even if Lizzie had to admit it did sound pathetic out loud. She waited to see what happened next. She was never doing this again. No orgasm was worth what she was going through right now.

'What's the extent of the "it" we're talking about here?'

Lizzie was floored. What she really needed to do was confer with Matt quickly, just to get their stories straight, but Rachel obviously wasn't going anywhere until she had more information.

'Look, Rachel, as I said earlier, Matt and I have met before. Several times. Well, we've more than met. It all sounds so calculated now, but believe me nothing could have been planned any worse. It's true...' Lizzie looked crestfallen '...we had a brief liaison.' In this situation Lizzie didn't feel the need to be one hundred per cent honest about the duration or the intensity of their three-month relationship. 'But it's been over for a long time. I made a mistake. He made a mistake. I'm so sorry. If it's any consolation—and I doubt it is—my life will never be the same again. I hate myself for what's happened. I only hope that there'll come a time when you'll be able to see things from my point of view and forgive me.' Lizzie knew it was a tall order, but right now she had nothing left to lose.

Rachel was quiet—too quiet, for too many seconds. Lizzie was praying that someone would interrupt them. There must be a few hundred people drinking out there. One of them must have a bladder that needed emptying. The suspense was too much to bear. Lizzie was almost relieved when Rachel started to scream and shout.

'Too right your life will never be the same again,' Rachel exploded. Lizzie couldn't blame her, but it didn't stop her from promptly bursting into tears. It made no difference to Rachel, who had apparently stockpiled a battery of expletives, threats, rhetorical questions and insults during Lizzie's last speech.

Rachel couldn't believe it. Less than two hours earlier she'd been applying lipstick. Now she was involved in a showdown with her guest of honour in the ladies' loo. It was too unbelievably downmarket for words. Not the sort of thing she did. But she couldn't help herself; she had to finish her off. No one was going to break her marriage up.

'How can you hold your head up high and have the audacity to call yourself an agony aunt? How can you believe that you're helping people when you're probably causing as many problems as you solve? Did you really think you'd be able to get away with this? Did you?'

Lizzie shook her head, thankful for the veil of tears that now meant she couldn't see Rachel clearly. The blurred version was scary enough.

'Where was your precious "code of ethics" when you were humping my husband?'

Lizzie grimaced. Rachel made it sound like a cheap porn flick. Or, worse still, *Carry on Copywriter*. Lizzie was sure she could hear the 'uck-uck-uck' laugh of Sid James, sinisterly ricocheting off the inside off her skull.

Rachel was only just warming up. Nothing that Clare had said to her had prepared Lizzie for this level of hurt. Her feelings of guilt were only making the pain more acute.

'I can't believe it. You fucking bitch. After everything I've told you. I confided in you. I opened up to you. I trusted you. There I am, worrying that my husband was having an affair, and it was you all along. To think that you get paid to advise people for a living when you can't even organise your own life properly! It's fucking ridiculous. Do you really think you deserve to get paid for screwing your readers' husbands?'

Rachel, in Lizzie's very humble opinion, was managing to make her sound a lot worse than she was. It wasn't as if she made a habit of this. Plus, she kept reminding herself, as soon as she had known that Matt was married to Rachel she'd done the right thing. The trouble was, now she could see what Clare had meant. It shouldn't have mattered who Matt's wife was. She should have ended it after that night at the Atlantic. Not that it would have changed the way Rachel saw any of this at the moment. Sex was sex. Sex with someone else's husband was an affair. Even if Lizzie didn't know about the husband bit? Somehow it seemed a bit childish to bring it up again. She was in The Wrong, with a capital T and a capital W.

Rachel was still ranting, and now turned as if to address a crowd. Thankfully for Lizzie it was an imaginary one.

'Ask Lizzie?' Rachel scoffed. 'What a joke. Why fucking bother? She lives her own life by a very different set of rules.'

Lizzie resisted the urge to retaliate. She figured it was probably better for Rachel to get it all out. At least she hadn't confessed that she'd loved Matt, that he'd loved her, and that she'd made the ultimate sacrifice to save Rachel's marriage. She didn't think Rachel would appreciate her generosity of spirit at this juncture. 'I know how it looks—'

'You have no idea how it looks. You'll live to regret this, I can assure you. You're a two-faced, lying hypocrite and I'm sure all the other people who pin their hopes on you, who write in, who call up and who e-mail you, would love to know what you're really like. And who was that charming woman I spoke to the other day? Susan? Yes, I'm sure Susan would love to know what you've been up to. I can see the front page of the tabloids now... "Agony aunt beds husband of heartbroken woman who writes in for advice because she suspects her husband is having an affair..." You haven't just let me down, you've let yourself down—and all the people you offer hope to. I had come to regard you as a friend—and I'm sure I'm not the first.'

'I'm so sorry.' It was all Lizzie could manage. And she was. Very, very sorry.

Rachel was pacing. Something about her movements was reminiscent of a caged animal. 'It's so humiliating. To think that I was pouring out my personal problems to you while you were probably still warm from your sex sessions with my husband.'

Sex sessions? Now, hang on. Lizzie was sure that she had never had a 'sex session' in her life. Interesting, too, that Rachel was humiliated rather than heartbroken. Lizzie was beginning to wonder whether Rachel wasn't enjoying the drama of the whole situation just a little too much. But she stopped herself. She was the one who had been sleeping with someone else's husband. Rachel was entitled to be livid. She was sure she'd do her crying later, behind a closed door somewhere, when the shock wore off.

'I suggest you start at the beginning. I seem to have my dates all mixed up. Just remind me. When exactly did you sleep with my husband?'

Lizzie wished she would stop saying 'my husband'. It sounded a lot worse than just 'Matt', and despite her height advantage she was feeling smaller and smaller. In her own mind she had practically reached Mrs Pepperpot dimensions. She only hoped that Matt was using this time to get a taxi to the airport. She would much rather have had a chance to explain all this to him.

Lizzie took a deep breath. 'I first met Matt at the City FM Christmas party last year. We got chatting. That was all. I didn't know he was married. He didn't tell me. I didn't ask. Nothing happened...that night anyway. We met up a couple of days later and then, what with him going skiing and everything, it all took off. At that point I hadn't had your letter, and even if I had I wouldn't have known that you two were linked in any way.'

Lizzie shook her head. 'By the time I discovered that he was married, and married to you, I was in up to my neck—and, believe me, I did everything in my power to make things better again. I thought we could all move on and put it behind us. I should have known better. I wish that none of this had happened. I just want my old stress-free life back.'

Lizzie's voice sounded hollow. She was drained. It all sounded unconvincing now. Rachel had every reason to feel angry and hurt. Lizzie knew that. But she couldn't ignore the fact that she'd fallen in love with Matt, and what made it even worse was that she honestly had believed that he'd been in love with her too. But did she wish that she'd never met him? Even now that was a tricky one.

Rachel was finding the line between fury, hysteria and tears incredibly fine. There was nothing she hated more than to be a made a fool of, and yet in a peculiar and irrational way, despite herself, she was jealous of Lizzie. Rachel knew her own control freak tendencies only too well, and it was true she did like to have the power to pull the strings, but Matt was hers. She'd always believed that he was hers unconditionally, and that as bad as things got he loved her enough to stand by her. She'd thought that even at her worst she'd made him happy. Apparently not. And instead of finding a clone replacement he'd gone for the archetypal leggy blonde. Jesus. She wasn't about to give up on him. She might have been betrayed by the two people she'd trusted above all others, but she wasn't about to let either of them get off lightly. No one fucked up Rachel Baker's perfect life plan without asking first.

Lizzie sensed Rachel's distress and, oblivious to the depth of her anger, allowed her professional persona to take over for a second. 'Look, Matt and I weren't together when things between you two started picking up. He'd obviously hit rock bottom when we met and he used me. I was an unwitting accomplice. But you two are back on track now. You told me that yourself.'

Lizzie knew that this would offer little consolation to a woman who'd been paranoid about infidelity since her childhood, but she had to try everything. It was her turn to be selfish. She could see the tabloids now. They'd have a field-day.

And her job was all she had left. Lizzie swore to herself that she would never have sex again, ever, if she got out of this party alive. She'd always wanted to travel. Maybe this was the perfect time for her to buy a herd of sheep, embrace a nomadic lifestyle and go and find herself—or better still lose herself—on the mountainsides of Peru.

Rachel had finally come to the end of this phase of her attack, and she wasn't quite sure what to do next. She needed some time to plan her next move and she had to get out of the Ladies'. 'This isn't over yet. Once I've got the sordid details out of that low-life of a man I was once proud to call my husband, I'll decide what to do next. I don't need him. I don't need you. I don't need anyone.' Rachel gathered her last ounce of composure and stormed out of the toilets and out of the launch.

Lizzie really had to hand it to Rachel. It was quite an exit. She bundled herself into the nearest stall where she could at least lock a door and lick her wounds in semi-private while trying to compose herself sufficiently to re-enter the arena. She shuddered as she recapped the last hour. She only hoped that their exchange hadn't been audible in the main party area.

Lizzie remained in hiding until she'd heard a few flushes and a corresponding number of hand-washing and drying noises before making the unilateral decision that she couldn't spend the rest of the evening in hiding.

She'd almost convinced herself that the crowd were going to part before her like the Red Sea as everyone stopped to catch a glimpse of tomorrow's news headlines, but to Lizzie's relief the DJs were now in full swing and she made it to the exit unscathed and unhindered, her publicity smile plastered somewhat unconvincingly across her face.

Melissa Matthews would just have to wait.

Lizzie barely breathed on her taxi ride home, much to the annoyance of her cab driver who was trying to get as much information and advice as possible out of his semi-celebrity passenger. She stuck with the gruff lip-biting approach all the way to SW15, before giving the bloke a generous tip and flashing him her best I'm-having-the-worst-day-of-my-life-but-know-I-can't-afford-to-be-moody smile, hoping that he wouldn't tell all his future passengers that Lizzie Ford was 'a right moody cow—all compassion on the radio, but very rude when I drove her home'. She knew never to underestimate the power of a black cabbie—so much more than just a ride home, and worth their weight in leather interiors and word-of-mouth publicity.

Back in the empty flat, she grabbed a couple of bottles from the drinks cabinet and made it to her bedroom before breaking down uncontrollably. Every time she closed her eyes she could see career-ending newspaper headlines projected onto the inside of her eyelids. How could she have risked everything she had worked so hard for, for a man? And, even more of a concern, why, right now, when her world was hanging in the balance, the Sword of Damocles swinging gently above her head, was she wondering if he was OK?

She had to speak to someone—but her mother would need the whole back story, Colin would be too flippant, He would be at home with Her, and the only other person she really wanted to talk to wasn't really speaking to her. She dialled Clare's mobile anyway, and when it clicked on to answerphone—as she had known it would—she left the most pathetic message she'd ever left before hanging up and wallowing in a new wave of self-pity which rolled in over the duvet as she sobbed herself to sleep.

For the second time in six months her life had fallen apart. Only this time there was no saving grace. Rachel was determined for revenge and there was only Lizzie's job left to take. And Lizzie had just handed her the perfect story on a plate.

chapter 21

Clare listened to Lizzie's message once more in the cab before dialling the flat again. There was still no answer. It didn't make sense. Lizzie had to be there. Maybe she'd unplugged the phone? Clare smiled to herself. Lizzie was about as likely to have unplugged the phone as she was to eat an apple if there was a biscuit in the house. If you wanted to torture her all you had to do was prevent her from answering a ringing phone. But the mystery remained unsolved. Where was she now?

Clare wished she was a bit more up to date. From what she could make out from Lizzie's almost unintelligibly slurred message, she thought she was going to lose everything. Clare wasn't sure how literally to take it. There could be a pinch of drama queen in there, but as a rule she'd never been that good an actress—and even allowing for the distortion of her mobile phone Lizzie sounded terrible.

As angry, bitter and disappointed as Clare had been when the whole Matt saga had unfolded, Lizzie was her best friend in the whole world, and at the end of the day she did want Lizzie to be happy—just preferably not at the expense of an innocent party. But maybe she should've done more sitting and listening. She'd been meaning to call for a couple of weeks, but work and pride just kept getting in the way. Clare was sure that if she couldn't quite forgive she would learn to forget. Friends like Lizzie were hard to find, and in a less than perfect world maybe Clare had expected too much.

Lizzie wasn't to blame because her own husband had failed to keep it in his trousers, but she still found it hard to distance herself from the hurt she'd felt when Joe had cheated. She'd loved him with every molecule, and had happily been planning their soft-focus future when he'd stopped her life in its tracks, and, while she'd rebuilt her self-worth, it would always be something that she'd take personally. When your partner slept with someone else there was no other way to take it.

It was 11.25 p.m. when Clare finally let herself in. All the lights were on, but there was no sign of life. On closer inspection, the pile of clothes on Lizzie's bed was person-shaped. Still dressed, she had assumed the crumpled heap position, face down, her duvet half-on, half-on the floor, her mascara half on her eyes, half on her cheeks. An empty bottle of gin was at her side, adjacent to an empty bottle of tonic. Clare looked down affectionately at her best friend. Even at rock bottom she hadn't been able to swig neat alcohol. She had, though, it appeared, stopped short of a slice of lemon and a glass.

Clare undressed her totally comatose flatmate and put her in the recovery position before going to get a few cushions from the sofa and setting up a nursing station at the end of the bed. She had no idea that things had reached the drinking-in-your-bedroom-until-you-pass-out stage. She checked Lizzie's CD player. Just as she'd thought. Travis were *in situ*. She must have been up to her waist in heartache as she'd lost consciousness.

Lizzie woke up to find herself naked and someone asleep on the floor at the end of her bed. She didn't remember even getting into bed. Using her arms, she hauled herself to the edge of the bed and let her head hang down. She just stared at the sleeping face for a few seconds as the blood rushed to her brain, and put her arm out to touch her just in case she was hallucinating. It was Clare. Asleep. In her room. In their flat. A series of tears relubricated the rivers of eye make-up that had dried overnight. Clare was home. Lizzie almost managed a smile before her body reminded her why it had seen fit to rouse her from her coma a few minutes earlier. She stumbled to the bathroom where she was violently and repeatedly sick. Her nurse slept on.

chapter 22

According to her watch it had just gone 8:00 a.m. but for a split second when Clare woke up she had no idea where she was. Sitting up, she reeled as the beams of daylight highlighted the picture of devastation all around her. The air in the room was probably forty per cent proof, but after breathing gin and goodness knows what else all over them Lizzie had obviously gone in search of fresh air. As Clare subjected her lungs to another intake of stale, stuffy room, with just a hint of ethanol, and observed the clothing debris draped over every available chair and bedknob, she could understand why.

'Coming up after the break, we talk to women who just can't say no....'
'...the trouble with the children in the area is that they have no respect for anyone but themselves...'
'...just add the rest of the ingredients and stir gently...'
'A new survey published this morning reveals that Britain now has the highest divorce rate in Europe. We ask: is divorce too easy? Should we work harder at our marriages? Or is staying together for better or for worse an outdated concept?'

'Who's on line four? Angela, good morning to you. Where are you calling from?'

Clare stood in the doorway to the sitting room. Lizzie, clad in tracksuit bottoms and favourite hooded sweatshirt, was perched on the sofa. Her hood was on. She was hiding. Blinkered from the rest of the world, she had failed to notice Clare watching her. Lizzie was almost a woman possessed, doggedly flicking from channel to channel, following the morning's stories as they unfolded. She'd obviously been up early and out already as the day's papers were strewn all around her and a now empty bottle of chocolate milk had been discarded on the coffee table. Clare wasn't at all sure what she was looking for. She needed to do some catching up—and fast.

Clare went to make tea before returning to the newsroom. This time she announced her arrival, and as she sat down Lizzie relinquished the remote control, grabbing hold of Clare instead and hugging her.

'Thank you so much for coming over. I've missed you so much. I know I've been stupid. Naïve. Selfish. Whatever. I didn't mean for all this to happen.'

'Hey, it's OK.'

Clare felt awful for having left Lizzie to stew for so long. She'd always had a dogmatically stubborn streak. In that respect she was an archetypal Taurus.

She held Lizzie close.

'Everything will be fine.'

Lizzie shook her head numbly. Her eyes lacked their usual vitality. Her body language was negative. She slumped back into the sofa. Tired, drawn and dejected.

'I'm not so sure. I think I've really blown it this time.'

Lizzie recounted the evening to Clare, who did her best to keep positive until she had all the information at her disposal. In a nutshell it sounded as if Lizzie had innocently gone to meet someone about a job, bumped into someone else and pretty much succeeded in losing her career in the process.

'And so you bought all the papers because you thought they might be running a story on you this morning?'

'Yes.'

Clare raised an eyebrow at Lizzie.

'Look, you didn't see Rachel last night. She wants my blood and she's the sort of woman who gets exactly what she wants.'

'I felt like that once. And I hate to say it but it doesn't get a lot easier.'

'Thanks, I feel heaps better now.' Lizzie tried to give her a wry smile, but she suspected it looked more like trapped wind. 'Look, I hope you don't mind me saying this, and I know I'm biased, but I've thought about this a lot and I honestly think your situation with Joe was completely different. It's just that when I saw Rachel and Matt together they didn't look that happy. And I don't think she really loves him. Not the right way. Not as much as he deserves.'

'Liz. Please. You have no idea what goes on between those two behind closed doors. For all you know they had a row about toothpaste lids that morning. Just because they weren't all over each other doesn't mean that their marriage is back on the rocks. I know you don't want to think about it but they could be having great sex right now.'

Lizzie felt shaky. She knew Clare had to be honest, that was what friends were for and all that stuff, but maybe just not quite this blunt. Lizzie refused to be drawn by Clare's logic. She didn't know Matt—or Rachel, for that matter. Common sense was one thing, but it didn't apply to every situation. Otherwise everyone would always know what to do and what to expect.

'But you haven't met Rachel. She's totally focused. I admit I thought she was great at first—but by the end of the night she was intimidating me. I just think Matt needs something more.'

'Something more...like you, perhaps? Don't forget, you lied to him too. Matt had no idea that you knew about their marital problems from her point of view. He didn't know you and Rachel were pen friends and I'm sure you're not the only one feeling lousy right now. Being lied to hurts...you learnt that from him in February.'

Lizzie wasn't really listening. She knew Clare had a point, but she didn't want to face up to yet more of her failings. All she really wanted was a bit of sympathy and someone to tell her that everything would work out. Suddenly she was exhausted and shivering. She pottered off to the kitchen in search of painkillers and carbohydrate.

'Poor guy.' She had meant to think it. Unfortunately it slipped out and Clare was right behind her to catch it.

'Hmm. Look, Liz, I don't want to be brutal but right now we can assume that Matt is at home, with Rachel. The one thing we can be sure of is that he's not here consoling you. Now, I know that you need to justify your relationship with Matt to yourself and to me, and you keep telling me that their marriage was as good as over when you started seeing each other, but—as you of all people should know—that "married in name only" line is a pretty standard pick-up line for an adulterer. I'm just surprised you fell for it.'

'I know all that—but, Clare, you know that feeling you get when someone cares about you? We were both so happy in each other's company. It was—well, looking back, it couldn't have been, but for a few weeks everything seemed perfect.'

'Because he was lying to you...'

Clare was bowled over by the feelings that Lizzie still had for Matt. Only now did she realise how deeply Lizzie had come to care for him over the last few months. But she'd been brave, she'd done the right thing in ending it, and now she had to stand by her decision and move on. Boy, Lizzie knew how to pick them. She was obviously still in love with Matt. Yet again she seemed to have chosen to invest her emotions in someone who, when the crunch came, didn't choose to love her back.

'Listen, Liz, hard as it may seem, you really need to try and forget all about Matt. Stop being a true heart-following romantic just for a minute or two. Right now you need to concentrate on keeping your job and your credibility.'

'But how?'

Clare had to admit to herself that at this precise moment she wasn't sure, but she refused to admit defeat so early on in the day. There must be some options available to Lizzie even if she hadn't worked out what they were yet. It was all about being rational—although, even in the sober light of day, Clare had to admit that there was currently more drama in Lizzie's life than there had been on television since Christmas. She followed her back to the sofa with a fresh mug of tea and a sponge finger—the nearest thing she could find to breakfast in the cupboard. 'Just give me a second. I'm thinking. You're the person who does advice for a living. And to be honest I'm a bit behind and slightly confused about who knew what about who when.'

Nearly an hour later Clare was up to speed on Lizzie and Matt, Matt and Rachel, Rachel and Lizzie, and Rachel, Lizzie and Matt. It was a truly three-dimensional love triangle. A sort of Rubik's Cube conundrum for the twenty-first century. And Clare had to admit, if only to herself at this stage, it didn't look good. There might not be anything in the papers this morning, but it was likely to take a couple of days for Rachel to sort out a reporter, a paper, contacts and enough photos to fill a double-page spread. Somehow they had to try and keep one step ahead, although unless Rachel had woken up in a totally different frame of mind Clare wasn't sure what they could do.

Only time would tell whether Lizzie's career could weather this storm, and while there seemed little point in Lizzie drawing anyone's attention to her indiscretion on the off-chance that Rachel changed her mind, conversely it would be better if she got to Susan before Rachel did. In the interim Clare was adamant that she just had to carry on as normal, which didn't mean sitting around in front of the television in a tracksuit at 11:00 a.m., waiting for her world to end or for Pauline to leave *EastEnders*. It was difficult to say which one was more likely to happen first.

Clare collapsed onto the sofa after one of her biggest pep talks ever and for a few minutes the old I-can-do-anything Lizzie was back. She even fetched herself a pint of water from the kitchen in an attempt to start today again. But slowly, visibly, the energy and enthusiasm drained away. At a loss as to what to do next, Clare adopted the I-won't-take-no-for-an-answer bossy matronly approach, finally forcing Lizzie to have a bath and change her clothes. She was determined to get her off the sofa and away from the television for at least an hour before she cooked her some lunch.

Lizzie was woken by a bell. Instinctively, she reached out with her arm to silence an invisible alarm clock while her brain took a couple more seconds to register the noise and ascertain its source. She'd been totally unconscious. Out cold. As she attempted to make it into the upright position without passing out she saw a note from Clare on the floor. She concentrated on focusing on the words which were currently skating across the page as her blood did its best to redistribute itself throughout her body following its concentration at her stomach, where it had been shopping for post-lunch nutrients.

Popped to chemist to stock up on tissues and ibuprofen. Back in a few minutes. C x

Maybe she'd forgotten her keys. Lizzie went through the motions of looking at her watch. She could see both hands, but she was still too groggy to be able to interpret them.

She stumbled to the entryphone and peered at the screen. Adrenaline surged through her veins as, frozen, she just stared at her arch enemy. Rachel was looking straight at her. A few seconds later the bell rang again. It was a long, impatient answer-me-now blast. Rachel only gave it a few seconds before she started shouting.

'I know you're up there, Lizzie...'

Totally illogically Lizzie squatted down below screen level. Out of sight? Well, if Rachel could see through doors and up stairs it was. If not, the walls were probably doing quite a good job all by themselves. It wasn't a two-way camera. Honestly. Sometimes she wondered about herself. She was the sort of person who ducked inside a car when you drove through a low tunnel.

Lizzie willed Clare to arrive back now. Why on earth had she left her at home alone? She didn't need a chemist, she needed a bloody alchemist. But Lizzie knew she couldn't hide from Rachel. It wasn't worth it.

'I suggest you let me in now...unless, of course, you'd rather I came back a little bit later with a reporter and a photographer?'

Lizzie took solace from the fact that, on analysis of that last threat, Rachel hadn't already been to the papers. Her relief was fleeting. Concerned that the rest of Putney would convene on her doorstep for the next instalment if she didn't open the door, and worried that Colin might be at home and only too eager to witness the next instalment of her new soap opera existence first hand, Lizzie went downstairs to let Rachel in.

As she reached the front door she realised to her horror that she was wearing an old gym sweatshirt of Matt's, and hurriedly ripped it off and flung it into her study. A narrow escape. She was now having a bit of a thin T-shirt nipple moment, and wanton hussy was the last look she wanted to portray today. She folded her arms defensively across her chest at breast height and hoped for the best.

Rachel swept up the stairs, casting her judgmental gaze over the flat and, Lizzie felt sure, her attire. Her home might have benefited from a good dust and a vacuum, but it was far from a den of iniquity or somewhere that a 'sex session' would ever have occurred. For a start there was no pile carpet. Rachel was power-dressed to the hilt and had entered the flat wielding her mobile phone, obviously ready for battle. Lizzie felt as shabby as she looked.

Rachel refused to sit down, nor did she seem interested in a coffee, a tea, an orange juice, a glass of water or anything else that Lizzie tried to offer her. The flat was now silent aside from the tense clicking of Rachel's heels on the varnished floorboards as she paced up and down the sitting room. Lizzie watched her turn on her heel a couple more times and clutched a cushion to her chest for warmth, for comfort, for protection and for decency. Rachel was now staring straight ahead of her, apparently focused. Finally she spoke.

'Listen...'

Lizzie couldn't have been listening any harder.

'I haven't got all day, but I just wanted to give you one more chance to explain to me what exactly has been going on before I tell you what I propose that we do about all of this.'

'...that we do about all of this...' Lizzie didn't like the way that sounded. There was something quite sinister about Rachel today. She was cold and way too calm. Lizzie couldn't have been any more scared had Vinnie Jones been standing in front of her cracking his knuckles.

'And don't even think about lying to me. Matthew has told me everything and I suggest you do the same.'

Lizzie sighed. Despite her trepidation, she was almost getting bored with going over it. Each time she came across as a less nice person. Still, telling Rachel a little bit more of the truth wasn't going to make things any worse, and suggesting that she was fed up with recounting the events wasn't going to go down well.

Rachel started listening calmly, but by the time Clare arrived back about ten minutes later she was ranting and raving again. Clare was alarmed at the confrontation taking place in their sitting room, but despite her kind, breezy and conciliatory offer of tea and biscuits she was completely ignored by Rachel. As Clare listened to her lay into Lizzie it was almost as if she was enjoying herself, as if she'd only come over to hammer the first nail into the career coffin of Lizzie Ford. Her concern for her husband and her marriage was nowhere to be seen. Clare soon tired of pretending to be invisible in the corner and eventually just joined in. Rachel looked surprised at her interjection, but she let her finish her introduction at least.

'Rachel, I'm Clare—Lizzie's flatmate.'

Lizzie noted that she hadn't said 'ex' or 'former'. She silently prayed that this meant she was coming home.

Clare proffered a hand for Rachel to shake, but either she didn't see it—unlikely, as it was attached to her arm and pointing directly at her—or she chose to dismiss it as part of her 'I am beyond reproach' attitude to this meeting. Clare was becoming increasingly irritated. Just because your husband had slept with someone else, it didn't mean that you were entitled to eschew years of training on the manners front.

'I know this really is none of my business...'

Rachel looked as if she were about to step in to confirm this but Clare didn't give her a chance.

'...but I really think we can sit down and work out a compromise of some sort. I appreciate you must be furious, hurt, and looking for revenge, but, tempting as it is, I'd just ask you not to do anything rash until you've had a chance to calm down a bit first.'

Clare Williamson, restaurateur, mediator and general good-egg was in action. Lizzie watched in awe. Full to the brim with admiration and grateful that at least one of them was feeling erudite today and queuing up to put Clare's six-week absence from the flat behind them.

'Would you now? Well, I don't know what the fuck Lizzie's told you about all of this, or whether she's fed you the same patchwork of fact and lies that she's peddled to both me and to my husband, but it's bullshit...'

OK, so Clare wasn't the most effective mediator in South West London, but at least she was trying.

Lizzie was fuming. Rachel was bent on making her sound a hell of a lot more devious and calculating than she had ever intended to be. This was her reward for jumping through hoop after hoop, for trying to do the right thing. If only Matt hadn't bought Rachel a bloody copy of *Out Loud* magazine, then Rachel wouldn't have written in, Lizzie could have waited for Matt to leave his nameless, faceless wife and maybe, just maybe, they could have lived happily ever after. So it was his fault.

Her relief at shifting the blame only lasted a couple of milliseconds. That scenario was no good either. Waiting in the wings wasn't her style, and she should have known that Matt was married. How on earth would such an ostensibly nice guy have got to his mid-thirties and still be available? When she should have smelt trouble from fifty paces, her optimism and naïveté had combined to lead her a merry dance. Lizzie knew that men got the getting married urge when they hit thirty. She read letters from them and their commitment-phobic girl-friends every day.

Rachel was now laying into Clare, who'd succeeded in temporarily diverting the attention away from Lizzie. Big mistake. If anyone had an ability to bear grudges it was Clare. Rachel might be about to meet her match. Lizzie hoped so. She felt like a Plasticine spectator at *Celebrity Deathmatch*. She had a ringside seat. This was the wives-who'd-been-let-down-by-their-husbands bout.

'But I suggest that you....you....'

'Clare.' This woman was exasperating. Unwittingly she had driven Clare to put her hand on her hip, and Clare was now shifting her weight from one foot to the other. Lone Ranger eat your heart out. As her aggression boiled in the pit of her stomach she swaggered from side to side and waited for the next wave of Rachel's attitude problem. Main Street had come to Putney.

'I suggest that you...Clare—' she practically spat the name out '—that you keep your opinions to yourself and keep out of it—unless, of course, you've been screwing Matthew too...'

Oh, to have had a pistol. There was no need for Rachel to be so deeply unpleasant. She'd been arguing Rachel's case to Lizzie all morning and this was all the thanks she got. Clare excused herself before she started shouting back. She was determined to keep the moral upper hand. However, she was careful not to retreat any further than the kitchen, where she would still be in total earshot range.

Lizzie grimly observed the exchange from her corner of the sofa. Round One to Rachel. The focus reverted to her.

'I'd like you to think hard about what you've done. And then have a think about this. Either you give up agony aunting by the end of the month, or I'm going to your bosses and the papers. Needless to say, Matthew is off-limits. If I find out you've been in touch with him, I'm not waiting another minute.'

Lizzie nodded. This was her first ultimatum. She wasn't sure what the proper procedure was when you were being threatened. But, well brought up as she had been, she was sure that this was one occasion when you didn't say thank you. She decided that silence was probably the most sophisticated approach. It was also the easiest option when you were trying your hardest not to burst into tears or throw up.

'I'll see myself out.'

Lizzie—impressively, she thought—had managed to keep her composure in front of Rachel, but as soon as she had gone there was absolutely no point in being brave any more. Clare watched aghast as Lizzie knocked back a couple of ibuprofen with a Tia Maria chaser. Their drinks cabinet definitely needed restocking. It was high time she moved back in. Clare removed the bottle from Lizzie and gave her a glass of mineral water instead. Lizzie barely seemed to register the change.

'What am I going to do?' Her voice cracked. 'I suppose I'd better give Susan a call.'

'Don't do anything yet. Rachel said the end of the month, and luckily for you this storm broke at the start of one.' Clare was desperately trying to keep positive. No mean feat, given what she had to work with. 'Listen, June doesn't start for about three weeks, and I don't think you're in a fit state to do anything right now. Let alone make any decisions about anything important.'

'But I can't just bury my head in the sand.'

'I didn't say anything about burying heads anywhere. I just think you need to give yourself some time to think through all your options rather than making a knee-jerk decision that you might regret later.' Clare was buying time. She wasn't sure what for yet, but whatever it was she was going to need more than ten minutes. Lizzie didn't even protest and Clare decided to capitalise on her uncharacteristic submission. 'I suggest you phone Ben now. I'm sure they don't want you sobbing live on air for three hours tonight. It won't be good for the listeners' morale.'

Lizzie flinched visibly. Clare knew how much she loved her work, and the thought of them having to get a stand-in always triggered her insecurity circuit and made her worry in case they didn't want her back.

'Listen, Liz, I'm only suggesting this week. I just think you need some downtime. You are allowed to be ill, you know.'

Lizzie nodded. But Clare hadn't finished yet. 'Then do your-

self a favour, clear the decks and call Susan too. I'm sure
they've got enough from you to be getting on with. If not,
they'll have to get cover.' And, she felt like adding, they might
need to get a new person in at the end of the month. Clare didn't
like to appear defeatist but she wasn't exactly bursting with alternatives at the moment. 'Right now you need some time to
get a bit of perspective. I know it seems that your world's ending, but I can tell you that you'll be OK whatever happens. You
are Lizzie Ford. Just remember that. And just in case you forget I'm going to dispatch you to the one place where you will
get more TLC, home-cooked dinners and general pampering
than anywhere else I know...' Plus, Clare thought, there was
the added bonus that Lizzie wouldn't have enough time on her
own to even contemplate doing anything stupid. Lizzie hadn't
even looked up. 'Yes, I'm booking you into the Mrs Ford
clinic. Not Betty, but Annie. I'll give her a call...or do you want
to?'

'But she doesn't know about any of this. She'll be furious
with me for not telling her earlier and then she'll worry. Non-
stop. You know what she's like.' There was a slight edge of
panic to Lizzie's voice.

'It's her job to worry. She'd hate to think you were going
through a crisis without her. Mothers love to be needed...and
I'll come and visit. You're only going to be in Hampstead, for
God's sake. It's not like I'm suggesting you leave the civilised
world behind.' Not yet, Clare added to herself.

Lizzie shrugged her shoulders. She had no energy to protest.
Plus there was the added bonus that Rachel didn't know where
her mother lived, so she wouldn't have to live in fear of the
doorbell and telephone threats. She only hoped that her mother
wouldn't be too judgmental. Of course she could just not tell
her the whole truth, but lying seemed to have got her into
enough trouble already.

Clare could sense she was on the brink of victory. One of
her plans was going through uncontested. It had to be a first.
She resisted the sudden childish urge she had to the punch the
air victoriously.

'Listen, I'd have loved to take the week off and look after

you myself, but I've already written today off and they do need me there this weekend. I can't help but feel that the change will do you good, and away from all your work at least you'll have time to think. Meanwhile I'll move my stuff back in. It'll be just like it was before, and I promise I'll come and fetch you a week on Saturday.'

'That's...' There was a momentary pause while Lizzie counted them out on her fingers. 'Nine days...'

'Not very long at all, then.' Clare was determined to get her to go. She needed time to think too, and Lizzie festering at home all day was only going to hinder her progress.

'But I suppose if it all gets too much I can just get a cab back here earlier...'

'Of course. I'm suggesting you stay at your mother's for a bit, not that you go into exile.'

Lizzie smiled for the first time that day. Clare was right, as usual. Thank God someone had taken charge. When Clare said it, it all sounded so simple. Take a week off. Go home. Think. Sleep. Put it all in perspective. She'd missed this. Clare hadn't even been back for a day and already it felt better. Much calmer. More balanced. Who needed Feng Shui when you had Clare? And besides, they already had a water feature in Lizzie.

'Thank you.' It was all Lizzie could manage. Right now, between the waves of narcolepsy that were trying to persuade her to assume the hibernation position, her mind was cluttered with deadlines, headlines, threats and alternative life plans.

With Clare practically dialling for her, Lizzie rang Susan, Robyn and Ben and told them she needed a few days off. She didn't need to act. She sounded and felt appalling. They all told her to rest up and take her time getting better. Even Ben, who only had precisely five and a half hours to get a replacement or talk to the head of department about rescheduling her slot. Obviously Lizzie was not as indispensable as she'd thought. In her current state Lizzie couldn't even work out whether this was a good or a bad thing.

'Will you ring her? Please?' Exhausted by all her phoning, Lizzie was back to being *girlus patheticus* on the sofa.

'She's your mum.'

'But you know what she can be like. She'll be a paragon of concern if you call and just cross with me for not saying anything earlier if I do it. Besides, I'd rather tell her face to face than have to go over it all again on the phone...and it's always easier to be perfectly lovely to a mother when she's not your own.'

'What drivel, Liz. You're being pathetic and you know it.'

Lizzie reluctantly took the proffered handset from Clare and then promptly gave it back. 'Please. I just don't know where to start. Anyway, sending me to stay with her was your idea not mine.'

And so Clare rang Annie.

Annie Ford didn't come to the flat very often. Lizzie hadn't given her mother a key to try and discourage spontaneous visits and general snooping, but when she did visit she certainly made the most of it. In anticipation Clare had embarked on a mammoth fold-and-put-away-athon and wiped all the surfaces down. Thanks to her industry Annie's self-guided tour-cum-nose-around-and-run-a-finger-along-the-shelves wasn't going to take very long.

Clare went down to answer the door. Lizzie was currently staring into her wardrobe and wondering what to pack. What did you take into the emotional and professional wilderness? She didn't seem to have a white floaty kaftan number anywhere, even though she could have sworn she'd bought something similar from Oasis a couple of years ago in the whole Moroccan boho look that had never really been designed for her. Oh, well. It was going to have to be jeans. She was going to have to do her retreat in denim. But then she spotted her white waffle dressing gown, perfect for a crisis, and threw it into her bag to join the mounting collection of items that each had their individual merits but didn't really go with each other. A comfort blanket of a T-shirt went in next.

'I got here as soon as I could. We always play Bridge on Thursday afternoons and I couldn't let the girls down. You know how it is.'

Clare wasn't sure that she did know how it was. She wasn't an afficionado herself, but as far as she could remember Bridge was a card game and Lizzie was a daughter. But, to be fair, she supposed it wasn't a life or death situation—and maybe when she got to Annie's age and lived on her own she'd be set in her ways too. She liked her regular appointments. She needed to feel needed. Luckily for Annie, needy was Lizzie's new middle name.

'How is she?' Annie was worried. Clare had given her very little information over the phone.

'She's been better. She just needs a bit of TLC, an alcohol-free environment and some time to think.'

'What on earth has happened? And why do I always feel that I'm the last person to know? We used to be so close, you know, we were best friends...'

Clare smiled. Somehow she doubted it. Closer than most, yes, but best friends...? Annie had always liked to think that despite the dysfunction all around her she had raised the perfect family.

'Now she never tells me anything... Is it a man thing or a work thing? And what about her show tonight? Oh, God, she hasn't been sacked, has she?'

Clare shook her head. 'Of course not. She's fantastic at her job; you know that.'

Annie at least had the decency to look apologetic. 'Of course. Of course I do. But she can't just let everyone down at the last minute.'

'Don't worry, the station are getting cover for her. She's really in no fit state...'

Annie tut-tutted. No wonder Lizzie had a complex about getting a stand-in.

'Look, I'll let her fill you in. She's very upset, though, so please go easy on her.'

'Of course.'

Despite Annie's reassurance to the contrary, Clare knew that she would employ her entire repertoire of extortion tactics as soon as she was on her own with Lizzie.

Lizzie had pulled herself together for her mother. She was

incredibly pale, and there wasn't enough Optrex in the world to make her eyes sparkle, but she was doing her very best and Clare was proud of her.

'Hi, Mum.' As Annie hugged Lizzie the familiar scents of Imperial Leather and Chanel N° 5 washed over her, and Lizzie felt herself relax. She hated to admit it but it was a relief to know that she was going to be looked after for the next few days. She was only too ready to opt out of being a grown-up for a while.

'Hello, darling. You've gone and got yourself into a right pickle again, haven't you?'

Lizzie's projected idyll of the next few days shattered. Pickle. She was a single woman in her thirties with a huge fucking crisis on her hands. She was not, however, in, next to, or remotely close to...a pickle. Maybe Hampstead was a spectacularly bad idea. She stole a glance at Clare, who was struggling to control the corners of her mouth which were definitely upturned in light of the whole pickle moment.

Annie stroked her daughter's hair. 'You've always been a one. Jonathan was so easy. Look at him now. Lovely wife, wonderful children, and you—well, you've done fantastically well at work, but you've never really managed to settle. You need some stability. But you probably get it from your father. He was difficult to live with. Always wanted everything on his own terms...'

Lizzie could feel herself prickling. All she wanted was a bit of innocuous everything-will-be-all-right-if-you-just-eat-this-biscuit-and-drink-this-cup-of-tea. But then she realised she'd picked the wrong mother for that.

'Has this whole thing got anything to do with that chap who sent you flowers at Christmas time? Or that dishy guy from the agency Alex and I caught you having lunch with in Richmond?'

Trust her mother, now in her sixties, to still have a photographic memory.

Clare's eyebrows shot skywards. She didn't know anything about man number two. Lizzie decided to clear it up straight away. No more secrets.

'It has everything to do with him. It was the same guy.'

'But he had a different...' Annie spoke slowly and then stopped herself triumphantly when she worked it out for herself. 'Ahhh...I see...'

She wasn't exactly Agatha Christie. A name-change was hardly the most cunning of disguises, but it had done the trick. Masterful.

A quick glance across to Clare and Lizzie was thrilled to note that on this occasion she looked relieved rather than disapproving. They were definitely making progress. Annie, encouraged by her moment of detection, hadn't finished yet. Her opinions were always valued—well, she'd always thought so.

'You're still looking for the one, aren't you? I blame those books you used to read as a child. You know—the ones about doctors and nurses and true love.'

'Mum. Stop it. Sorry I can't be more like good old Jonathan and Alex. And I'm sorry I remind you of Dad. I know how much of a disappointment I must be for you. No husband, no children, and a career where I get to say masturbate and orgasm on the radio...'

Annie looked decidedly unflustered. If Lizzie was going to try and provoke a reaction she was going to have to try a lot harder than that.

'Anyway, just for your information, this time I thought I had met the perfect man. It wasn't my fault that he was married and didn't tell me. Besides, it's not like you and Dad got it fantastically right, is it? You of all people should know about the realities of relationships.'

Her mother paused for a moment before replying. Just long enough to make a point. To let her daughter know that the invisible mark had been overstepped. Lizzie knew her last comment had been a bit underhand, but she didn't need her mother making her feel useless. She'd managed to do that all by herself.

'Mum, it's not as simple as it first appears. I promise I'll fill you in with as much detail as you want when we get home. Even I can't believe how complicated it's all become.'

Clare nodded supportively and beamed at Annie, hoping to melt her approach just a fraction.

'OK, darling, I'm only trying to help. You know how much I love you.'

Sometimes, Lizzie thought to herself. Sometimes.

'Let's get going. Why don't we get an Indian takeaway tonight and you can fill me in? I think I've even got some of that beer in bottles that you like.'

Lizzie didn't like to ruin the moment by asking her how old they were. Annie had a well-intentioned habit of filling her cupboards with things that Lizzie had once mentioned that she 'quite liked' and had been buying Hob Nobs religiously since the day Lizzie had once stated a preference for them when she was at university. She took a bottle of red wine from the rack in the kitchen and stuffed it into her bag. Just in case.

Clare piled Lizzie's bags into the car and promised to bring anything she'd forgotten when she popped in to visit. Her mother just stopped short of fastening her seat belt for her. Talk about undermining her sense of self. For the second time in ten minutes Lizzie wondered how on earth Clare had talked her into this.

Clare waved them off before returning to the flat, and would have rolled her sleeves up if she hadn't been wearing a T-shirt. She had a plan of sorts. Well, at least a starting point. She went into Lizzie's study and turned on the computer.

chapter 23

'Won't be a minute, mate.'

Matt wrestled with his keys before flinging the front door open and legging it up to the bedroom in search of his trainers. Tennis after work. Who was he kidding? He hadn't watched a game since Boris Becker had won his first Wimbledon and he hadn't wielded a racket for at least five years. He'd just have to wing it and pray his body remembered what hand-eye co-ordination was all about.

But tonight wasn't about skill. According to reliable sources, James was soon going to have a spare room. Ritualistic humiliation on an astro-turf court was a small price to pay for an exit route. Matt was hatching a long-overdue plan. Whatever happened next, things had to change.

Now, standing in the bedroom—their bedroom—in the unfamiliar and soulless early-evening silence, he felt a momentary pang of something. Hunger? He consulted his watch. Probably. He loved this house, but in the last few months it had ceased to feel like home.

Since last night Rachel had been treating him worse than ever. He couldn't blame her for that. But amazingly, despite the subsequent showdown, she still wasn't listening. He'd apologised, then tried to explain, told her the truth. She said she wasn't interested in what she dismissed as his opinion and that it would all be fine in a few months. She refused to get the message. Said that he deserved to suffer. But as usual she was missing the point. He'd been suffering for months. Rachel wasn't the only injured party. This wasn't just about her.

Over the past few weeks he'd spent countless hours trying to see things from Lizzie's point of view. At best he'd been a naïve, indecisive, two-timing, dithering male. At worst he'd been devious and calculating. It was time for him to take control. He should have done this months ago.

A sliver of hope was enough to power him for now. He'd sent Lizzie flowers to pave the way, but he hadn't called. After everything she'd been through it was time to show her that he meant what he'd said. Actions speaking louder than words and all that jazz. He didn't want to imitate the perennial Nick Hornby anti-hero, the too nice boy who got it wrong or left it too late; he wanted the happy ending. He wanted emotional completeness. And right now he wanted his left Nike... He glimpsed a lace protruding from under a pile of clothes by the window and, rummaging to the bottom, found the missing trainer.

He hoped James was feeling compassionate.

Maybe Lizzie had been right. Maybe Rachel wasn't the perfect wife that Clare had presumed her to be. Anyway, she couldn't just sit around—and Lizzie was currently in as fit a state to help herself as your average suicide bomber. It was time for Clare to take matters into her own hands. Not in some mad vigilante sawn-off-shotgun-drive-by-shooting manner but in the old-fashioned way, by talking.

Her detective work had paid off. She'd located all Rachel's contact numbers from the autosignature at the bottom of her e-mails, but there was one immediate psychological hurdle. From the lengthy disclaimer that preceded every message sent by Rachel Clare now knew that she worked at CDH. Not high on her list of places to swing by, the D being for Dexter—Joe

Dexter—chief love rat and ex-husband—the latter, a piece of life's baggage collection which still sounded like something she was far too young to have. But if Clare wanted to see Rachel she'd have to go back to a building filled with ghosts from a previous life. She'd definitely hated him then, but if she was honest she was mellowing in her approach. However, forgiveness *in absentia* was one thing. Face to face was another.

She dug out her best black trouser suit for the occasion and at 4:30 p.m. on Friday afternoon she swept into the eerily familiar reception area. She was hoping to catch Rachel off her guard, but first she had to get the full attention of the receptionist.

'Clare Dexter...my God it is you. How the devil are you? Long time no see.'

A familiar voice, still steeped with plum. Clare wheeled. Ed Wallace. One of Joe's better-looking, more genuine friends.

'Ed? God. A blast from the past. I didn't know you worked here.'

A blast from the past? Had she really said that? Aloud? Next she'd be adding 'jolly good wheeze' to her vernacular. She must be nervous if she was allowing her Enid Blyton back-catalogue of well-loved idioms to run riot. She was seriously in danger of being fifty years out of date—quite an achievement when you were only thirty-three years old.

'I don't. I think Joe would quite like to get me on board, but until he makes me an offer I can't refuse I'm just visiting.'

'That makes two of us. I've just popped in to see Rachel Baker.' Please don't ask me what about. *Please don't ask me what about.* Clare was saved from having to fabricate a reason for her meeting. Ed didn't seem at all interested in why she was in the building.

'So what are you up to these days? You're looking gorgeous. Black really suits you. Very sophisticated.'

Ed had always been a smoothie. Who didn't look good in black? But a compliment never went amiss.

'I'm still doing the restaurant thing.'

'Fantastic. That place worked out, did it? Great... Whereabouts was it again? Sorry—you know what I'm like...memory not my forte. Sometimes I struggle to remember where I live at the end of the day. Please don't take it personally.'

'I won't. It's in Notting Hill.'

'You trendy young thing.'

'Not so young and not so trendy these days, I'm afraid.'

'What's it called again? God, I'm hopeless. Good job I've never got married. I'd probably have trouble remembering her name.'

'Why do you think so many couples call each other darling?'

'Ha! Good point. I'd never thought about it like that.'

'Anyway, it's called Union Jack's.'

'I think I've heard of it...'

'Probably from me...'

'No. No. Oh, ye of little faith... Just give me a minute. British food with a twist and the odd celebbo hanging out there?'

Clare smiled and nodded. The power of celebrity never ceased to amaze her. Why was it that if people had been on television or in a magazine they were instantly more interesting?

'That's the one.'

'So what on earth brings you to CDH on a Friday evening? Hot date?' For some reason Clare blushed. Nothing could be further from the truth. 'Does JD know you're here?'

JD was what Joe had been called at college. Ed had endured three years at London University with him and so had earned the right to call him by his initials.

'Of course not.'

'Such a shame, you know.'

'Ed...'

'I know, I know—none of my business. I just thought that you two... I mean, he'll never...'

'This is your first official warning, Mr Wallace.'

'Got it.'

'It's a long time ago now. In two months we'll have been divorced for two years.'

'Is it really? Unbelievable.'

A silence. Awkward? Reflective? Just a natural break? It was hard to tell.

Clare had always liked Ed. He was just one of the many casualties of her divorce, when people who had been 'their' friends had all regrouped into the 'mine and yours' camps post decree nisi. A shame. Ed could always be counted on to be hugely entertaining. Usually at his own expense.

'So, have you got to dash off right now or have you got time for a quick beer for old times' sake? I've got to be at some hideous leaving party later, but I don't have to leave for an hour or so.'

Clare looked at her watch. 4:35. She could spare half an hour. 'That would be lovely.' She really meant it. Ed Wallace was good for the soul. And a sip of Dutch, French, Australian or even Russian courage wouldn't go amiss.

After the standard What are you up to? and Where are you living? lines of questioning, and tongues loosened by an inter-beer round of vodka and tonic, they moved onto mutual acquaintances. Luckily Ed, like most blokes she knew, was only too happy to volunteer all the information he had on everyone she asked about.

Fortunately, Clare mused, men have never really grasped the tactics necessary for a good gossip. Ed hadn't saved up any ammunition to exchange for more confidential info from Clare later. But thanks to his candour Clare now knew that Joe was still not in a serious relationship and strangely she was pleased. To bolster her ego further, in an equally only-makes-sense-if-you're-female way, Ed harped on a bit more about the fact that everyone had thought that Joe would never find anyone as special as Clare again—although he couldn't be sure whether anyone had bothered to tell Joe that was what they'd thought at the time, or just tacitly bought him a few beers to help him deal with putting it all behind him.

Ed grilled Clare about her love life and Clare did her utmost to make it sound a little less than non-existent. She knew that any information would be relayed to Joe and so adopted the enigmatic smile, less is more approach, disclosing nothing, which Ed fortunately and predictably took to mean everything.

Ed lapped it all up as Clare ordered another round and started
to make her excuses. Five-fifteen. She couldn't afford to miss
Rachel.

Ed, it seemed, had another twenty questions.

'So you're here to see Charlie's Angel. Business or pleasure? I didn't realise you knew her.'

Clare had no idea what Ed was on about. Charlie's Angel?
Maybe he didn't need another drink.

Ed obviously spotted Clare's confused expression. 'You did
say you were seeing Rachel Baker back there, didn't you? Or
am I imagining it all?'

'Yes...I've got a meeting with her...'

Clare racked the creative banks of her brain to try and come
up with a professional reason for having an appointment with
her at all.

'She called me about organising a do at the restaurant. I
don't think she knows that I'm Joe's ex-wife. I'm sure he'll be
over the moon if she proposes CDH have a party there.'

Clare decided to quit while she was ahead on the tall story
front. Ed didn't seem to think there was anything amiss, which
was a relief. It suddenly occurred to her vodka-sullied mind
that Ed's seemingly bizarre 'Charlie's Angel' reference was in
some way connected to Rachel. But how had Rachel become
associated with the trio of seventies sirens? Maybe she had a
secret penchant for tight jumpsuits, blonde layers or lipgloss?

'When you said Charlie's Angel...you meant Rachel, didn't
you?'

'Yup. Sorry. I didn't stop to think that an in-house nickname
would mean diddly-squat to you. I used to work with her before she joined CDH. Rachel has always been known as Charlie's Angel—or just Angel throughout her department.

'Oh...'

Clare thanked her lucky stars that she had nothing to do with
the sort of industry where you had cliquey nicknames for people you worked with. The sort of industry where people still
said things like diddly-squat... But on reflection that was probably just Ed.

'So how did the Angel get her nickname?'

Clare just had to ask. She just had to know if it was the jump-suit thing.

'Filthy coke habit.'

Clare nearly slid off her bar stool.

Ed was so matter-of-fact about it. Maybe she had misheard? Obviously she had 'shocked' written across her forehead.

Ed laughed.

'Good to see that you're just as innocent as you always were.'

Clare made a rapid recovery and punched Ed playfully.

'Listen, I'm not that naïve. I'm just a bit surprised, that's all. Isn't she masterminding the anti-drugs campaign at the moment?'

Ed smiled at Clare's well-intentioned concern.

'She is—yes. I suppose it's a little ironic, but then there aren't too many people in the industry—and even fewer at her level—who haven't dabbled once or twice. No one can afford to be judgmental, and to be honest no one really cares as long as the job gets done well or, better still, they get an award and some international recognition. From what I hear she's got everything under control, and as long as she can handle it no one in the industry is going to bat an eyelid. Unless you are, in fact, an undercover tabloid hack and not a restaurateur at all, Rachel has nothing to worry about...'

Clare laughed. She could do this innocent, carefree, take-everything-in-your-stride thing when she had to. But her mind had lurched into overdrive. It appeared there were no saints in this little love triangle. The question was, How to play it? What if Ed's knowledge was just hearsay? Alternatively, Ed might just have earned himself 'hero of the month' status in Putney. Clare hated to admit it, but she was obviously a bit squarer than she had thought. The only coke habit she had was the diet variety...even if she was partial to a few rocks of ice with it.

'She's quite a character. She seems to get away with letting young, talented, good-looking men do most of her work for her. Or, what I should say, if I am being politically correct, is that she puts a good team together. She lives and loves the high life.'

'Don't you all?'

'Well, I suppose there might be a small element of truth in that...'

'Oh, come off it, Ed. Advertising is one big piss up. Launches, awards, lunches, team-building drinks. Don't forget I was a Grosvenor House widow once...'

'It's quietened down in the last couple of years.'

'Of course it has.' Clare gave Ed her best and-of-course-I-was-born-yesterday look. He smiled to acknowledge it as he continued.

'But all credit to her she's made the system work for her. Rachel plays the game better than anyone I know. Watch this space. She's going all the way to the top.'

Ed picked up his glass and drank to Rachel's success. Clare used the break in conversation to look at her watch as pointedly as she could without actually rolling up her sleeve and bringing her wrist up to her nose. She feigned shock at the time, even though she didn't have an appointment *per se*.

'Shit—sorry, Ed, but I'm going have to shoot off. Thank you so much. Fantastic to see you.'

She leant over and gave him a kiss. He beamed at her.

'Hey, no problem. It was only a drink.'

Oh, but it wasn't. 'Seriously, it was great to see you.'

Ed Wallace's ego was responding well to its massage. He was beaming.

'We should do it again. Maybe go the whole hog and do dinner too?'

'Definitely. Why don't you come over to Union Jack's and I'll give you the five-star treatment? On me, of course.'

Clare had better watch herself. At the delighted expression on Ed's face she suddenly panicked that in the excitement of the moment she might have been sending out the wrong vibes. She didn't want Ed telling Joe that she'd gone and flung herself at him.

'Deal.'

'What's your number? Just in case the hanging-around-an-ad-agency-lobby trick doesn't work twice.'

Ed laughed.

They programmed each others numbers into their mobiles in true twenty-first century style and promised to call each other. Gone were the days of scribbling deliberately unintelligible phone numbers on scraps of paper and pretending you'd lost them should the other party track you down. But Clare promised herself that she *would* give Ed a call. He'd earned a dinner, even if he would never know why.

chapter 24

At 5:58 Clare entered Rachel Baker's corner office for their second introduction in twenty-eight hours and closed the door behind her for maximum dramatic effect.

'Rachel.'

'Clare.' If she was surprised to see her, it didn't show. She glanced towards the desk where Kitty sat, ostensibly to protect her from flatmates of husband's mistresses just marching in unannounced, and rapped on the window of her door. Startled, Kitty looked up for long enough to see her boss mouth 'glasses' at her.

Clare didn't wait to be offered a seat and sat down on the sofa. Beneath her carefully applied mask of make-up Rachel looked tired. The effect, Clare was sure, of an incredibly long week. Rachel perched on the edge of her desk. The last thing she needed was a do-gooder of a flatmate getting in her way. Where was Kitty with those glasses? She really needed a drink.

'I don't remember inviting you to my office?'

'I invited myself.'

'And to what do I owe this unexpected pleasure?'

Every one of Rachel's words was intended to make Clare

feel as unwelcome as possible. She was glad that she'd decided on her thickest skin under her suit. From the minute she had locked the front door she had known this was going to be a tough one. She decided to take the more softly-softly approach and at least see how far that got her.

'Look, Rachel. You can guess why I'm here. Lizzie is so desperately sorry. She never meant for any of this to happen. By the time Matt told her that he was married she was already up to her eyeballs. She had no idea that you had anything to do with him until much later on, at which point she did everything in her power to get you two back together at the expense of her own happiness.'

'My heart bleeds.' How could she be expected to feel anything other than contempt for someone who couldn't even fight their own battles?

'Believe me, Rachel, Lizzie is very sorry.'

'I don't see her cluttering up my office, begging for my forgiveness. Look, I appreciate your concern but I'm busy. I've got deadlines to meet. Lizzie should've thought about the consequences before she started sleeping with my husband.' Boy, she needed a drink. Thank God for artificial stimulants. She owed her career to nicotine, coke, Diet Coke, espresso and Red Bull.

Thankfully Kitty had finally located a couple of clean glasses and was now waving them at Rachel through the door. Why she couldn't just knock and enter with them like a normal PA, she had no idea. It felt as if everyone was conspiring against her to make her week as difficult as possible. Grumpily, Rachel waved Kitty in.

'Here you go. Wasn't sure what sort you wanted, so I just brought tumblers. Harvey says you can drink anything out of this sort.'

'Thanks.'

Rachel didn't give a flying fuck what Harvey thought, but this was not the time to tell her PA to ditch her boyfriend and find someone with a proper name and a job that didn't involve computer programs. Kitty was now hovering by the door, shifting her weight almost imperceptibly from foot to foot. She'd either just wet herself or she wanted to go home. It was, according to the clock on her computer, 6:06. Rachel wished she would just bloody go.

'Um...if it's all right with you, I think I'll head off now. Have a good weekend. I'll be in early Monday, so if you need anything typed up or filed before your ten o'clock just leave it for me and it shall be done.' Kitty made it sound like a favour instead of it being what she was paid to do.

'Thanks.'

Kitty closed the door behind her and only stopped at her desk for a couple of seconds to pick up her bag and turn her computer off before practically sprinting out of the semi-deserted office. Rachel wasted no time in reaching into her most coveted piece of office furniture and liberating a bottle of white wine which had been chilling all afternoon. Her lunchtime intake had worn off a while ago. Rachel offered a glass to Clare out of courtesy—very generous, she thought, given the circumstances. To her surprise Clare accepted. Obviously Clare was a little bit less uptight than Rachel had thought.

Confidence bolstered by a couple of sips, Clare stepped it up a gear. 'For the record, Lizzie has no idea that I'm here and she'd be mortified if she found out. She knows she's done wrong, and she's confused. She can't see any way forward. I just wanted to talk to you—career woman to career woman. I know how you must be feeling.'

'The fuck you do. You can't have the first idea. To know that your husband has been having an affair is devastating enough, without discovering that the person he was seeing was someone that you knew and trusted. Someone, I might just add, who in her professional capacity was supposed to be helping me.'

Rachel was no less aggressive in her response, but at least sitting down with a glass in her hand she had stopped shouting.

'Just give me a minute and listen to what I've got to say. We've got more in common than you think. I've been married.'

Rachel softened a little at Clare's use of the past tense. 'What happened?' Despite herself, Rachel was curious. She'd never have guessed that Clare had been married. She had single-woman-in-her-thirties written all over her.

'He was in advertising too. He worked all hours and had an affair with a colleague less than six months after we got back from our honeymoon. I was setting up a restaurant business at the time and was totally wrapped up in what I was doing—only I thought he was right behind me, not running about behind my back. I only found out when a friend of mine showed me a picture in one of our trades. The photo was actually meant to show off the interior of a new gastrodome, but they'd taken it on the night of an agency party and there was my husband in glorious Technicolor, draped around her...'

Up until now Clare had managed to be fairly matter-of-fact, but a hint of emotion entered her voice as she started to think about the details. The feelings that she'd buried for the last two years were starting to defrost. Their marriage had become a statistic. If only he hadn't done it, they might even have had a child by now.

'I know having your arm round someone is hardly grounds for divorce, but there was something about the way that she was looking at him. I got suspicious. After two days of telling myself to calm down I confronted him and he confessed. He told me it had all been a mistake and even tried to make me feel better by telling me that they'd only spent one night together. But I've never believed that you can sleep with someone "by accident" full stop...'

She paused for dramatic effect.

'...let alone four times in one night.'

Clare smiled resignedly despite herself. It was tragic. Tragically funny. Rachel, she was pleased to see, was looking totally shocked. Everything was going according to plan.

'What did you do?'

'What choice did I have? I threw him out. He begged to come home and I told him to fuck off. It was over. I was devastated. I loved him...'

Unsure of what to say next, Rachel poured more wine. She had to admit that she was impressed at Clare's cut-throat attitude. He cheated, therefore he was ejected. Maybe she was turning into a softie in her old age. Clare was still in full flow. Rachel interrupted her self-questioning. She was genuinely interested in what Clare had to say.

'I never thought I'd recover...but I did. I have. I don't even hate him any more. I suppose I'm just sad it ended the way it did. I always believed that you got married and that was it. He ruined my fantasy of marriage and my Martha Stewart outlook on life.'

Clare stole a glance and was relieved to see that Rachel couldn't have looked any more sympathetic.

'Did you ever find out who he had the affair with?'

'Yes. It gets worse. I couldn't tell from the picture in the magazine, but I later discovered that I'd met her before. She was at our wedding.' Clare smiled again. She couldn't help it. Objectively, in retrospect, despite her high hopes her marriage had been a complete farce. And if she couldn't see the funny side at this point she would most certainly have cried.

'Well, it sounds like you were very pragmatic about it all.'

'Believe me, I was much less sorted at the time. Looking back on it, there are times when I think I might have shot myself in the foot. I was so proud. I told myself that I could never forgive him. Yet there are still mornings when I wake up wondering if I did the right thing. Life's not perfect. I'm not perfect. So why should I have expected him to be? I sometimes wonder if we should have worked through it, or at least tried to. My anger was all-consuming. I wasn't capable of thinking straight. Now I know lots of people whose marriages have survived an affair. Sure, it takes time, but there's usually two sides to every story—and while everyone's always quick to judge your relationship, only the two people at the heart of it know what they have had or could have again.'

'Do you still see your ex?'

'Never. I decided to cut all ties at the time. I was too hurt. All he seemed to care about was his work, and even when he was begging to come back it was only in between meetings. I know you advertising people have some crazy deadlines to meet, but it's all about priorities and I felt I was coming second to his job. And to think that he'd made time to shag some other girl when we hadn't even been married a year... I suppose now it might be different, but my life's hectic enough without meeting ex-husbands for a drink from time to time. No, looking back on it, it was probably a lucky escape, a blessing in disguise...'

Rachel wondered who Clare was convincing. Her or herself.

'I guess I've become a bit of a fatalist. If we'd been meant to be together I think it would have worked out. He's climbed his way to the top, and I haven't been there getting in his way. I run a successful business. If you remove the emotions from the equation you could say that it was the best thing for both of us.'

Clare was delighted when Rachel came over to join her on the sofa. This was much more promising than the locking of horns which had appeared inevitable when she'd first arrived. Rachel sat back, resting her head on the cushions. They there were, united in Chablis. One divorced. One debating what to do next. It was Rachel's turn to share.

'It's interesting. I know what you mean, but I think I know what your husband was going through too. I love my job. I love the people. I love the challenges. Between you and me this campaign I'm working on is going really well. I don't know whether...she—' Rachel couldn't bear to use Lizzie's name at the moment '—told you, but it's the new national anti-drugs campaign. It launches next week and it's going to be huge. This could be my meal ticket to the top.'

There was a momentary pause while Rachel admired the view from the heights to which she hoped to climb.

'What's your surname, Clare? If your ex is still in advertising, you never know I might know him. The industry is a small world.'

'Oh, I think you'll know him...'

He was probably strutting around an enormous office a few floors up. Clare was looking forward to Rachel's reaction to this piece of news. The build-up had gone perfectly. 'My surname is Williamson, but that's my maiden name; I took it back after the divorce. My married name was Dexter. My husband was—'

'Joe?' Rachel interrupted her straight away.

Clare nodded.

Rachel's face was a picture of disbelief and admiration. 'I don't believe it.'

Clare could tell that Rachel was impressed, even if she was doing her best to disguise it. Joe had been a great catch. She felt her credibility with Rachel had just leapt up a few hundred points. A small consolation for the pain he'd put her through, but it was something. His betrayal still hurt her more than she liked to admit even to herself. Why else would she have flown off the handle and treated Lizzie that way? Thinking about it now, she realised she couldn't blame the woman he'd slept with—just as Rachel couldn't blame Lizzie, if she thought about it. It was convenient for a wife not to have to blame her own husband for an affair but it wasn't fair. And it wasn't real. Clare owed Lizzie a little more understanding. Blind fury had left quite a trail of destruction in its wake.

Rachel's mood had done an about-turn, and the new Rachel was almost dancing round her office, pointing out framed pictures of tables at awards dinners. Clare feigned blasé and declined Rachel's repeated invitations to come and peer at pictures of Joe in black tie, even though part of her was dying to have a look. Fat? Thin? Hair? No hair? Clare's image of him was frozen in time, and nearly two years out of date.

'Joe Dexter. I can't believe it.'

It must be about the fifth time she'd said it.

His name still provoked a reflex reaction in her central nervous system. She could picture herself at the altar, taking Joseph Arthur Dexter to be her lawful wedded husband. Even now she could feel the hurt and anger as she remembered the humiliation she'd felt when she accused him and he confessed to his infidelity. Clare had thought she'd feel vindicated but instead she had been devastated.

'I'm amazed. Joe was married? Our Joe Dexter?'

No, Clare felt like saying. My Joe Dexter.

'He must have fallen for you in a big way. He's always been a bit of a player. He still is. But it's worked for him. Only thirty-seven and already a partner in one of London's biggest agencies.'

Rachel was beside herself. She wondered how many people on her floor knew that he had been married. What a scoop. Boy, did she have some gossip for Monday morning. She was itching to tell someone. She might just have to call Will in a minute. She couldn't help herself. Joe was a terminal playboy...and a divorcé after an affair with a colleague. She wondered who the 'four times a night' girl had been.

'You're well out of there, Clare. I'm sure I don't need to tell you that everyone loves Joe, but I can't imagine anything worse than being married to him. I suppose, if you think about it, advertising is a touchy-feely industry run by lots of beautiful people, so you shouldn't be surprised when temptation wins. But, having said all that, it's funny—I never thought Matt would be the unfaithful type.'

'Funnily enough I didn't have Joe down as a love rat when I bought the big white dress. I don't know that there is a type either. Everyone loves to be loved and needs to be needed. In my experience men don't like having to compete with your career on a daily basis, but sometimes I think people hang on for the wrong reasons.'

There was nothing more that she could do. So far Rachel had listened. Clare had bitten her tongue on several occasions and hopefully the crucial seeds had been sown.

'Look, I'd better be off. I know how busy you are. But, please, take stock before you set out to ruin Lizzie's life. You won't want to hear this, but in some ways you and Lizzie are very similar. You're both ambitious. You're both in the ascendant of your careers. She couldn't be any sorrier for what's happened. Just bear in mind that revenge might make you feel better in the short term but, painful as it may seem now, it takes two to have an affair.'

It had all been going like clockwork, right up until the last seven words had left her mouth. Now Clare could feel the office temperature changing around her.

'Are you saying that this was my fault?' Rachel's tone was ultra-defensive.

'Of course not. I'm just saying that Lizzie isn't the only one to blame. I know for a fact that if Matt had told her he was married when they first met Lizzie wouldn't have seen him again, and she certainly wouldn't have slept with him. She'd never have deliberately subjected anyone to what you've been through. I suppose you could count yourself lucky that Matt picked Lizzie to have an affair with. At least she sent him back home when she realised what was going on.'

Rachel could feel her hackles rising. Who the hell did Clare think she was? They'd only met once before and now, after a little heart to heart, she seemed to think she'd earned the right to stand in her office and tell her that she should be grateful that Matt had picked Lizzie to sleep with.

'Lizzie should have thought about her career before she started screwing around with a married man. She's supposed to help people with their problems, not go out there and generate more. Someone has to expose her hypocritical behaviour. She's not the person people think she is.'

The woman had a nerve. If Ed was to be believed, Lizzie didn't have the exclusive on hypocritical behaviour. Clare decided to do a very un-Clare thing and gamble. She had nothing to lose and, more to the point, Lizzie presently had little to keep.

'I think you might want to reconsider.'

'Really?' Rachel doubted it. Frankly, she was getting bored. Clare could take her holier-than-thou am-dram attitude and just piss off as far as she was concerned. 'Look, if you must persist with your campaign to clear Lizzie's name, I suggest you liaise with Kitty on Monday and make an appointment to see me—like everyone else has to round here.'

'I'd slow down if I were you...' Rachel's increasingly hostile mood was only going to make her part more fun. 'After all, it appears that you're no angel either...'

Clare said the word 'angel' very slowly.

She didn't know if it was just her imagination, but she thought she saw Rachel sit up a little straighter. Her expression didn't change. She was an impressively cool customer.

But there was no way that Clare was going to let her wheedle her way out of this one. 'I'm sure that your clients would be very interested to hear about your cocaine habit. Thought you'd road-test a few of the products, did you? I'd hazard a guess that your fast track to the top would be over if wind of this got to a national newspaper. Not quite the publicity the campaign was hoping for, I imagine.'

Rachel felt as if she had been turned inside out. Surely blackmail was only administered under the cover of night? And it wasn't even dark yet. But despite the defensive surge of instinctive anger she knew she was in trouble. She could feel the shakes spreading down her arms. Nothing must go wrong with the campaign now. This was to be her greatest moment.

Clare had everything crossed. Beneath her calm, collected veneer her heart was racing. She knew that she had no concrete evidence. But her confidence was boosted by Rachel's current expression. Three gold bars...kerrrrrching...Clare had hit the jackpot.

The blood drained from Rachel's face. Distractedly she rubbed her nose. It was a timely affectation. Finally she broke her own silence. Her tone had changed and now there was a thinly disguised element of fear in her voice. Yet, true to her character, she started on the offensive. This time Clare was ready. Her armoury fully stocked, her weapons loaded.

'You can't just make allegations like this.'

'And why not, exactly? How the hell you have the nerve to accuse Lizzie of double standards I have no idea. Delusions of defamation? I suggest you drop all your plans to go to the papers if you want to keep your golden reputation in the industry. I don't care if everybody in this building is high as a kite most of the time; you're the only one running a campaign telling everyone to live their lives without regret, to say no to drugs, encouraging clean living—'

Rachel interrupted.

'Who told you?'

'Like I'm just going to tell you! Look, I might not be an expert at all this double-crossing stuff, but no one reveals their sources...'

'You're blackmailing me.'

'I'd rather see it as more of a bargain that needs to be struck. If you promise to leave Lizzie to her career then I'll leave you to yours. Simple as that.'

'But it's completely different. Lizzie had an affair with my husband. Our marriage may never be the same again.'

'Don't kid yourself. If it hadn't been Lizzie it would probably have been someone else.'

'But, Clare, you of all people know what I'm going through. We've both suffered because of our partners' infidelity.'

'Don't try and pull sisterhood rank on me. You're no victim, Rachel, except perhaps of your desire to climb the corporate ladder two rungs at a time. Leaking your story would make me feel a whole lot better about you pulling Lizzie's life apart. Revenge might not be politically correct these days, but I have to say I'm finding the prospect of the eye for an eye philosophy quite satisfying, not to mention effective...'

Rachel was now slumped in her chair, chewing anxiously on a cuticle. Clare, conversely, was suddenly on a roll.

'At least now you know how Lizzie must be feeling. Everything you've worked so hard for hanging in the balance. How dare you be so sanctimonious about what's right and what's wrong? Sorry, angel. Your halo seems to have slipped.'

Clare was surprised at how easy she was finding this. There must have been some gangster in her genealogy somewhere back along the line—although disappointingly she didn't seem to be able to crack her knuckles. She decided to quit while she was so obviously ahead. Even in defeat, Rachel was quite scary. Besides, she wasn't sure what to do next. It wasn't as if she'd rehearsed an ending.

'I'd better get going. I won't be telling Lizzie about any of this, so you're going to have to contact her yourself—and I'd suggest sooner rather than later. I assume that your deadline no longer applies?'

Rachel kicked her desk as Clare swept out of her office. She couldn't even be gracious in defeat.

Clare resisted the urge to break into a skip as she hit the pavement outside. She'd sat through a lot of gangland films in her time and she'd never ever seen a gangster skip. They didn't even smile. She concentrated on looking mean and moody as she walked down the stairs to the tube station.

chapter 25

The weekend hadn't been a success. Matt had been out for most of Saturday, and he'd just sat and stared at the television yesterday. Still, at least he was at home with her—which was something. He probably just needed time, but she was already getting bored of waiting for him to bounce back. And to think she'd even turned down brunch with Will in Soho. Maybe if she'd met him and then pottered round Covent Garden in the afternoon, instead of spending it avoiding the ironing basket, football on the television and her monosyllabic husband, she would've been feeling a little less highly strung today. Marvellous. Just another Manic fucking Monday. Without the fucking, of course.

Clare fetched Lizzie early. She'd only been in Hampstead for five days, but—taking their last phone call as a yardstick—any longer might have done her more harm than good. And besides, Clare couldn't wait to have her back. Her new-found double life as a private investigator had made both her step and her mood more buoyant than they had been in years. 'Normal' behaviour was going to be tough. Clare had never been very good at secrets or surprises. Furthermore, she'd have to react convincingly if and when the news broke. It was a challenge that she hoped she could live up to.

Lizzie was glad to be back. Once you hit your thirties there is only so much mothering you can endure before you need a serious dose of own space. The maternal home might be over twice the size of their flat, but it had seemed impossible to find even a cubic foot of her own on any of the three floors. She'd felt like a rare and unpredictable specimen under observation. *Daughterinastateus.*

Even the phone hadn't provided life-support. Her mother had scrutinised every call, incoming and outgoing. If Lizzie wanted a cup of tea she wanted to know why; if she didn't want one she wanted to know why not. She might still be a little un-sure of what to do next, but if she wasn't allowed to make some of her everyday decisions without justification her sanity was in jeopardy. She knew her mum only meant well, and she'd bit-ten her tongue more often than it had managed to escape, but if she'd stayed any longer the charge of adultery was in dan-ger of paling into insignificance alongside matricide.

Besides, Lizzie still had over two weeks to go till the end of the month, and if she didn't get Susan a column by the end of tomorrow or turn up at City FM on Thursday evening she might manage to end her career all by herself. She knew she was sounding a little melodramatic. But that was the way she was feeling—and, she felt, with good reason.

Clare had spring-cleaned. 56 Oxford Road was bursting with cut flowers and smelt gorgeous. As Clare whipped up a storm in the kitchen Lizzie went to confront her inbox. She felt sure that a quick peek before dinner might halt the dread that was starting to envelop her. As the smells of Clare's culinary endeavours wafted down the stairs Lizzie realised how glad she was to have her back. While she couldn't have hacked ten more minutes at her mother's, she didn't want to be all alone any more. She was just logging on when Clare summoned her for supper.

Clare was fidgeting. Since Friday night she'd been saddled with a surfeit of energy, and if Lizzie hadn't been quite so preoccupied with trying to organise the rest of her life then Clare was sure that she'd have noticed that her once serene flatmate looked like a break-dancer in a disco being forced to go cold turkey. She wondered when Rachel would be in touch. She still couldn't quite believe what had happened.

'This is delicious, Clare. Thanks.'

'Pleasure.' Clare clutched the seat of her chair with both hands to stop herself jiggling around. She'd already inhaled her portion. At least with her mouth full she hadn't been tempted to say anything.

'Listen, thanks for everything. You were right to send me to Mum's. And thanks for coming to get me this afternoon. I can't tell you how good it feels to have you home.'

Clare had never been very good at taking compliments. It wasn't that she didn't want or need them; she just didn't know what to do with them when they arrived and invariably ended up deflecting them rather awkwardly. She changed the subject.

'So, have you got a long night ahead of you?'

Lizzie had her mouth full.

'Mhmm.' There was a momentary pause while she chewed and swallowed. 'I need to get a column in by noon tomorrow. I jotted some stuff down at Mum's, but I need to fine-tune it and add a bit more. I thought I might take it in myself and see if I can arrange a time with Bridget to have lunch with Susan. I'd rather talk to her about things face to face and not in her glass-fronted office if I can avoid it.'

'Have you decided what you're going to say?'

'Pretty much. I think the truth would be a good place to start. Susan's always been good to me, and I think I owe it to her to be straight. God knows how she'll react. I'm clutching on to the admittedly rather vain hope that she might think it's funny... Still, I'd rather get in there now in case Rachel flips out again. I'd rather she heard my version first.'

Clare was panicking slightly. What was the point of everything she'd done if Lizzie was going to go and talk to Susan before Rachel had withdrawn her ultimatum? But practically what could she do about it? Lizzie was hardly going to be thrilled to think that Clare had been snooping round her inbox, delivering threats behind her back. She knew that if their positions were reversed she'd be livid. What if Rachel told Lizzie what Clare had done? Her good mood was starting to recede.

'I wouldn't rush anything, Liz. You've still got a bit of time.'

'I know, but I just can't leave it all till the last minute. As hard as it is, I got myself into this mess and it's up to me to get myself out of it. And if I don't sort it out soon I'll only spend every other moment hypothesising about every possible eventuality. You know what I'm like.'

Lizzie sounded calmer than she felt. But she knew she was right. Fed and watered, she returned to her study and, slightly subdued, started sifting through her e-mails. There were a few from readers, and a surprising number of get well messages from people at work, but her moment of belonging was short-lived. Lizzie's improving mood dissipated abruptly when she discovered a new e-mail from rachel.b@CDH.co.uk sent yesterday.

For a few moments she just stared at the information on her screen. The hairs on the back of her neck were now standing to attention. There was nothing to help Lizzie ascertain what the content was likely to be. The subject had been left blank. What if Rachel had sent her a lethal virus to wipe her hard drive? Paranoid? Well, maybe just a little. To open or not to open? That was the question.

'Clare!'

It was an instinctive cry for help, and not a particularly loud one. Lizzie waited a few minutes and shouted this time. Nothing. Either Rachel had sent a virus that had got to Clare first or, more rationally, Clare was washing up with the radio on and couldn't hear her. Anyway, what could Clare do? At the age of thirty-two Lizzie had forfeited the right to be rescued. Right. Dread coursing through her veins, she took a deep breath, closed her eyes and double-clicked.

She opened one eye and then the other before reading the message as fast as she could—and then reading it again, syllable by syllable.

Lizzie
Having had the weekend to cool down, I have decided not to go to the papers if you promise to stay away from Matthew. Despite your recent behaviour, I do believe that you have a gift with people. However, should I discover that you have contacted my husband I will not hesitate in systematically destroying everything you have worked for.
Yours, Rachel Baker

A subsistence lifestyle in South America was on hold. A veritable U-turn. Lizzie was instantly circumspect. Perhaps this was a trap—some sort of twist in Rachel's smear campaign? Lizzie must have missed something. Compassion and forgiveness were not traits she associated with any spurned wife, and certainly not with Rachel Baker. Even this apparent gesture of goodwill left Rachel holding all the cards. What if Lizzie ran into Matt at work? Or he contacted her?

Lizzie called Clare again...and again...and again. Eventually she came. Running. Breathless.

'What is it? Are you OK?'

'Look at this.'

'Look at this? *Look at this?* God, Liz, at the very least I was expecting you to have been impaled on your letter-opener. Jesus. Don't do that again. What's wrong with getting off your arse and coming to find me?'

'Sorry...' Lizzie pointed at her monitor. 'I just had to show you this, and I didn't want to take my eyes off the screen just in case something happened and it wasn't here any more. I didn't want you to think I was hallucinating or anything.'

Clare read the e-mail from Rachel while Lizzie looked on anxiously. And as she skimmed over the text for a second time she had to concede that actually Rachel had been quite clever. Clare could see why a nice-as-pie note would've been out of place. Lizzie was even suspicious of this acerbic one.

'Good news, Liz. Sounds like she's had a change of heart.' Clare did her best to mix surprise with rationale.

'She's definitely up to something. Something that I'm obviously too dense to work out by myself.'

'It does seem a little odd, I agree. But it's hardly a chatty little let's-be-friends note, is it?' Clare stopped herself. She was on the verge of giving something away. She shrugged her shoulders. 'Look, Liz, I haven't got a clue what goes on in her head, but if I were you I'd just go with it. It's good news. At least you don't have to look for a new job.'

'But she's toying with me. What if I run into Matt at work and she finds out? Does that count? I can't control what he does, and I don't want to live my life on a knife-edge. I think I'd honestly rather work in a bar and not feel threatened.'

Clare loved Lizzie, but right now she could happily have slapped her. Talk about ungrateful. Here it was, a second chance on a plate, and she was talking about pulling pints for a living. 'Don't be stupid, Liz. You love your job and...you're bloody good at it. If I were you I wouldn't ask too many questions.'

'Well, that's where we differ, then. I've done enough treading on eggshells over the last few months to last me a lifetime. I don't want to be stitched up a few months down the line when I least expect it because she's still pulling the strings. I'd better give her a call. At least if I talk to her I can gauge how she sounds. I mean, anyone could have written this from her desk.'

'Anyone? Don't be so bloody ridiculous. I doubt she's told too many people. Honestly, do you have a conspiracy theory for everything?'

'Apparently so.'

'You're mad. Who else could have written that message? Who else knows anything about your ultimatum?'

Lizzie had to agree that Clare was making sense. As usual.

It made less sense at 1:30 a.m. when Lizzie finished her column. And less sense still at four-fifteen, when Lizzie was still trying to find a comfortable enough position to go to sleep in. By nine-thirty Lizzie was pacing up and down the sitting room with the phone in her hand. By nine-forty Clare had talked her out of calling. At ten-seventeen Clare had left the house and the line was ringing.

'Good morning—CDH. How can I help you?'

'Rachel Baker, please.'

'Just one moment, please. Who should I say is calling?'

'Lizzie Ford.'

'Thank you.'

'Hello...'

Lizzie was fired up and didn't want to waste a moment.

'Hello, Rachel, it's Lizzie. Listen—'

'...this is Rachel Baker's phone. I'm sorry I can't take your call at the moment. I'm either on the other line or away from my desk. If you leave your name and number after the tone I'll get back to you as soon as I can. Alternatively dial 455 now, to speak to Kitty my secretary. Thank you.' *Beeeeeep.*

Shit. Voicemail. Should she leave a message? So far she hadn't said a word. Her overriding urge was to hang up, but she forced herself to go through with it. Eventually Lizzie found a voice. It wasn't her normal one, but it would just have to make do for now.

'Rachel. It's Lizzie Ford on Wednesday morning. I'll try you later. Thanks.'

Thanks? *Thanks?* For what, exactly? For being married to a man that Lizzie had loved so much it hurt? For threatening to end her career and causing her to have a five-day stomach upset? For the outbreak of acne that had recently graced her shoulders...in her thirties? Yes, 'thanks' was patently what it was all about, and pretty much the opposite of what she'd really wanted to say.

Now what? Lizzie hung around for about an hour before calling back. This time the 'hello' was really Rachel's voice.

'Rachel, it's Lizzie.' Time to be brave. She stood up straight. 'Have you got a minute for a quick word?'

'Sure. Hang on a second....'

Lizzie heard her get up and the click of a door. She was baffled. Rachel's tone was—well, it wasn't exactly friendly, but it was certainly civil.

'Did you get my e-mail?'

'Yes. Thanks. It's why I'm calling, actually.'

Nothing from Rachel.

Lizzie continued. 'What are you up to?'

'What do you mean?' Rachel said it in as charitable a spirit as she could muster.

'It just seems a bit of U-turn, I suppose. How do I know you won't change your mind again? And probably when I least expect it.'

'Look—' Far too snappy. Rachel took a deep breath and started again, a little more softly. She just couldn't help it. Being all there-there didn't come naturally to her. 'I've done a lot of thinking. I'm not saying that you weren't at fault, but I suppose that, while I hate to admit it, if things had been great between us Matthew wouldn't have been wandering the streets looking for someone else to sleep with...'

God, Rachel had a way with words. *Wandering the streets.* Thanks to her, Lizzie currently felt worth all of fifty pence. So much for love and romance, thunderbolts and mutual attraction. Lizzie thought back to her time with Matt to remind herself that she wasn't actually an easy lay for unhappy men. Rachel, on the other hand, was still going strong.

'In a way I suppose I know that I should be relieved that he picked you to shag...'

Shag. Never a nice verb.

'...rather than some brainless bimbo who wouldn't have sent him home again.'

Was Rachel being nice or not? Overall, Lizzie suspected that she was, and she hadn't mentioned tabloid newspapers once— which was a definite turn-up for the books. Plus, there was almost a compliment in there. At least she didn't perceive Lizzie as a brainless bimbo, which had to count for something.

'Listen. You're good at your job. Everyone makes mistakes, and I suppose I thought that maybe you deserved another chance.' Rachel was doing everything she could to sound as if she meant it. She was still irritated that she wasn't going to be able to finish Lizzie off, but thanks to her interfering flatmate the stakes were just too high.

'Thanks.' Lizzie was doing it again. Rachel was insulting

her and she was saying thank you. Years of minding her p's
and q's at school had taken their toll. She'd been brainwashed
by the manners police.

'Just stay away from Matt. I really think we have a chance
at making things work together.'

'Of course.' The words stuck in Lizzie's throat. She knew
it was the least that she could and should do. And, unsurpris-
ingly, she'd lost all interest in having recreational sex. Especially when it involved shagging men who were wandering the
streets.

'Look, I've got to go'

'Right.'

'Bye.'

'Bye.' Civil, but strained. Lizzie was confused. Rachel's
new approach was disconcerting to say the least.

The flat was quiet. As Lizzie returned the phone to its
charger, the clock on the video saw fit to remind her that in the
real world it was 11:45 and counting.

Hot and sweaty, she delivered her column to Susan's office
with only seconds to spare, before stopping at Bridget's desk
to book herself in for a lunch with her editor. Next stop, City
FM. It was a tactical move. Time to re-kindle her enthusiasm
with the team—just in case they were starting to think that she
was on the verge of self-important celebrity disdain for the production process. How better to win them over than taking them
out for a coffee-and-cake-fuelled production meeting the day
before their next show? If work was all she had for now, Lizzie
was going to make damn sure she enjoyed it.

chapter 26

'Great show tonight.'

'Thanks. You were right. I couldn't have just given it all up overnight.'

'I still don't know how you do it. I couldn't think of any-thing remotely positive to say to most of the people that ring in...but I guess that's why I run a restaurant and not a helpline. I think I'd want to give most of them a slap and tell them to stop whining about everything. No one said life was a fucking fairytale.'

Lizzie helped herself to a bit more food while Clare finished her familiar rant. On a post-show high, and full to the brim with euphoria but nothing of any calorific value, she'd made the mistake of ordering a takeaway and was currently working her way through a second plateful. Clare had managed to resist the first round, but now had a large slab of peshwari naan in her hand which was making Lizzie feel a lot better about her own gluttony. With Clare keeping her company the whole feeding frenzy seemed a little bit less like a binge.

'I'm starting to feel like myself again.'

'Well, you've certainly got your appetite back... Agony aunts are supposed to be rotund and motherly, aren't they?"

'Not in their early thirties...'

Clare got an impressively clear view of half-chewed lamb pasanda and sag aloo as Lizzie forgot her manners and combined talking with shovelling another forkful of colourful food into her mouth. She was mid-feeding frenzy and not going to let a little thing like aesthetics get in her way.

'Well, for some totally unfair and inexplicable metabolic reason you seem to get away with eating this late at night. I only have to look at a biscuit after 10:00 p.m. and I might as well apply it directly to my abdominal area.'

'I do prefer it when you're here to look after me when I get home. I can't believe it's only just over a week since you packed me off to Mum's; it feels like ages since Rachel was standing here reading me her version of the Riot Act...'

Clare nodded. It had been quite a week. She decided to ignore Lizzie's lack of table—well, sofa—manners, and the graphic washing machine window display of mastication, and began leafing through one of last Sunday's newspaper supplements which had taken up residence on the sofa. She didn't look up when Lizzie started speaking. From the sound of it, the coast wasn't quite clear yet.

'It's funny, though. While the whole showdown scenario was horrific, now that Rachel knows I feel like a huge weight has been lifted. For the first time this year I'm no longer part of some intricate web of deceit—not that I knew what I was getting myself into at the start. One minute I was dating Matt and the next minute, boom, in trouble up to my earlobes and no failsafe escape route.'

Lizzie poured more red wine into Clare's empty glass and to her delight could see that her friend was succumbing rapidly to the powers of Chilean Merlot. She deserved it. Clare needed to relax. The washing was done, the ironing basket was empty, and today there were more beautiful flowers on the kitchen table. She'd been making a huge effort and it hadn't gone unnoticed.

Lizzie had a confession to make. In light of the last few

months of her life she had decided to live a secret-free existence—as far as Clare was concerned, at any rate. 'I spoke to Rachel yesterday.'

Everything stopped. Clare's mouthful stuck in her throat and she gulped at her wine. Her stomach knotted in anticipation. 'Did you call her?'

Lizzie nodded. 'Yup.'

Clare shook her head. She hadn't meant to but the Merlot must have loosened the joints in her neck.

'I know—I know you told me not to, but I had to after that e-mail. It didn't really make sense to me. It still doesn't.'

'What did she say?'

Clare was genuinely interested. Lizzie didn't seem to be cross with her, so Rachel had obviously been discreet. Clare focused on every word that Lizzie said in the hope that she would remember it later for further analysis. She hated the effect alcohol had on her memory when she was trying to concentrate.

'Oh, something about her accepting a minuscule amount of responsibility for driving Matt into someone else's arms, hence my reprieve. The trouble is I'm not sure that I trust her. I mean, what if she changes her mind again?'

'Maybe she's just calmed down a bit?' Clare started to relax again. She knew it wasn't in Rachel's interest to mention her to Lizzie, but it had been a worry.

'Maybe...'

Lizzie didn't sound convinced.

'Anyway, I've arranged to see Susan. She owes me a lunch and my contract's nearly up. The more I think about it, the more I think I might just hand in my notice. Even if Rachel's feeling charitable at the moment, the scandal's bound to catch up with me sooner or later, and to be honest I don't think I'm the right sort of person to deal with that sort of notoriety. I'm not interested in being a tabloid headline, or a Trivial Pursuit answer of the future. Maybe this is a chance for me to try something new?'

Lizzie was trying to sound as optimistic as she could. Every time she said it to herself it sounded like a better idea. Far more attractive than living on a knife-edge. She wanted to try and retain some element of control.

Clare was shocked. Not least because it actually sounded as if Lizzie had really thought about this. 'Don't do anything rash, Liz. Look at how much has changed over the last week. Now the ultimatum has been lifted there's no hurry.'

'I had nothing else to think about when I was at home. I could probably move into another area of writing or broadcasting...I don't want to leave the industry altogether...but at the moment part of this second chance thing is linked to me never seeing Matt again. Obviously in the light of everything that's happened I'm not about to give him a call.' She had been so close in the last couple of days. So close. 'But what if he gets in touch with me? Just say...'

Clare was horrified. Lizzie could tell. But at least she was being honest now, and not just saying what she knew Clare wanted to hear.

'I'm just saying, what if...? You know...hypothetically speaking.'

'What? Change your career in case Matt deigns to give you a call some time?' Clare snapped. She knew she shouldn't but she couldn't help it.

'Thanks. I knew I could count on your support...'

Clare had promised herself that she'd try and be more understanding, yet here she was once again dismissing Lizzie's point of view out of hand.

'I know you think I'm being ridiculous, but humour me. What if...? Well, hypothetically just say—I know it probably won't happen...but if it did...' Lizzie was sputtering as she tried to find a way to keep Clare on side. She took a deep breath and just went for it. 'OK. Just say that he leaves Rachel of his own accord and then looks me up when I've got my life just about back on an even keel, and this whole scandal is still just waiting to be wheeled out and ruin everything. Think how much more bitter she'd be then, if he'd actually left her for me.'

'Hello...? Hello...?' Clare was pretending to knock on Lizzie's forehead. 'Hello? Is that Lizzie Ford? Where are your pink slippers? You're sounding a bit like the late Barbara Cartland... Right, no more schmaltzy romantic comedies for you. From now on you watch the *Alien* movies, Westerns and that's it. Honestly. What if he leaves Rachel? He's hardly been round here checking you're OK so far... And, conniving as she is, we can assume that she hasn't tied him up and left him for dead in a cellar somewhere. Where is he? With her. Where he should be.'

Clare's good resolutions deserted her for pastures new. She couldn't believe how sentimental Lizzie was being, after everything he'd put her through.

If she was totally honest, Lizzie was disappointed and surprised that she hadn't heard from Matt since the Kensington showdown. If he really did care about her as much as he'd said he did, it didn't seem to make sense. Lizzie didn't like to admit that his failure to get in touch might in any way be related to her own frankly dishonest behaviour. To the fact that on that same evening that Rachel's world had been upended he'd discovered that Lizzie had been corresponding with his wife for some time. The fact that in some ways he'd probably left feeling as betrayed and confused as Rachel had. Lizzie wished she'd managed to find a moment to explain everything to him. But if he thought back to the times they'd had together as often as she did, surely he'd know that what they'd had was very special.

To Lizzie's dismay it looked as if Clare was revving up for more.

'Matt's a no-win situation. Think back over the last couple of months. On a scale of one to ten, where one is miserable and ten is ecstatic, how would you rate them? Honestly—overall—not including any moments when you were in bed together.'

She was getting the message. Lizzie hesitated for a moment as she recalled the extent of the low moments.

'The worst time in your adult life?'

'Definitely.'

'I rest my case. Put him behind you.'

Lizzie nodded.

'I know you don't believe me; I can see it in your eyes...'

Lizzie blushed. As far as her emotions went, a mistress of disguise she was not.

'Believe it or not, I only want the best for you—but if you must persist with the whole happily-ever-after, bratpack ending thing please do yourself a favour and find someone who doesn't have a wife. Even if you leave your job now and take up waitressing do you really think Rachel would forget to go to the papers if you started sleeping with Matt again? Matt, incidentally, being the man who you haven't heard from in weeks... And besides, can't you see? If you start waiting tables for a living then she's won...'

Lizzie seemed to have temporarily mislaid her in-built self-preservation gene. Clare couldn't see a solution where they could live happily ever after and, from an objective standpoint, she couldn't help believing that, if it came to a choice, Lizzie's career was far more important than a few months or even a few more years with Matt. If that made her hard and insensitive—well, maybe she was.

'And maybe there's more to Rachel's U-turn than meets the eye.' As soon as she heard the words spill out of her mouth Clare regretted it. Lizzie was terrier-like in her inability to let things go, and from the glint in her best friend's eye she knew she was about to wish she hadn't had that last glass of wine. Lizzie was on her case at once.

'Clare Williamson. Spit it out.'

'I just said maybe... Maybe she and Matt are getting on so well now that she doesn't mind if you keep your job or not.'

'Yeah, right.'

Clare had to admit it was a fairly far-fetched theory, but it was the only one that had sprung to mind in the heat of the moment. She decided to feign total ignorance. 'How would I know anything?'

'God knows. But you can't just sit there and go all Jessica Fletcher on me and expect me to buy it. When do you ever say "more to it than meets the eye"?'

'I've just started.'

'Clare...'

That was it. One unit of alcohol too many coupled with a

general level of pride in what she had achieved on Lizzie's be-half and it all came flooding out.

Lizzie just sat there, her mouth not quite open and not quite closed, as she tried to digest the latest chapter in her very own love triangle.

'But, listen, I'm only telling you all this so you don't make a career decision that you come to regret.'

Clare still wasn't quite sure how her confession had come about and was deep in self-justification mode. Lizzie was oblivious to her protracted flannelling. Mentally she was miles away. Her Putney-based persona remained mute for a moment. When she did regain the power of speech her sentences were short and sporadic.

'Cocaine. I don't believe it. No wonder Matt thought she was moody.'

'Hey, Liz. This mustn't become public knowledge. I struck a deal, remember...'

Lizzie wasn't really listening. All this discussion of Rachel's darker side had led her subconscious to progress naturally to her husband. She wondered if Matt knew. There was absolutely no way she could tell him, but maybe someone else could. But who? Or maybe Clare really was right. Maybe it was time to move on.

Clare was now panicking fully at her indiscretion. 'You can't tell anyone. Do you understand?'

'Yup.'

'I mean it, Liz. I know you. Look at me. N-o-b-o-d-y.'

'But what if Matt doesn't know?'

'You see. I know you. You mustn't tell a soul. No one. *Personne. Nadie. Niemant.* Not even in confidence. Anyway, for all you know they freebase together.'

'Thanks for that.'

'Well, you don't know that they don't.'

Lizzie ignored Clare. She didn't want to think of Matt and Rachel flinging themselves at each other or swinging from the ceiling rose during ardent coke-fuelled nights of passion. 'Hardly Little Miss Squeaky Clean, is she? And to think she had the balls to try and lecture me on ethics and moral codes. What a bloody cheek.'

'Listen, Liz, I don't think you've earned the right to gloat. You were sleeping with her husband while you were giving her advice on how to save her marriage, remember?'

'Mmm.'

It was true. But gloating was much more fun.

'Look, I only did what I had to. I didn't want you to lose everything because of one mistake, but don't even think for a minute that you're off the hook as far as sleeping with a man that you knew was married goes.'

'I know. I know...'

Lizzie's mind was still struggling to come to terms with all the information. As she recapped the latest developments, the significance of what Clare had done while she'd been loafing about, picking her feet and watching *Countdown* under house arrest in Hampstead, hit her.

'Well, I suppose I should be thanking you. Even if you were interfering behind my back.' Lizzie beamed at Clare to demonstrate that she was just joking on this occasion. She didn't want to run the risk of any misunderstandings. 'There I was feeling sorry for myself, and you were masterminding my future... What can I say?'

Lizzie was visibly moved. All the effort made her feel very special. Not something she'd felt for quite some time.

Clare smiled and drained her glass to wash down the newly formed lump in her throat. She was enjoying the appreciation and relishing the feel-good moment of having done a good deed. On reflection, and finally out of the proverbial woods, it had been worth every angst-filled moment. Despite the panic of the last few minutes, it looked as if everything might just work out after all.

'Would Miss Marple care for some more wine?' Lizzie smiled at Clare as she filled her glass and emptied the bottle.

chapter 27

Getting the bus had seemed such a great idea at the time. A chance to take in the bit of London that she was usually underground for—the romantic's alternative to the claustrophobic, energy-sapping hot filth of the tube. But now the bus was practically stationary on Oxford Street, and time marched on irreverently as Lizzie stared powerlessly from the top deck. People strode past and disappeared into distant crowds while the double-decker crept along a paving stone at a time. She was trapped.

There was always the get-off-and-run-the-last-half-mile option, but her impractical shoes coupled with a generally nonexistent level of fitness would guarantee a totally dishevelled arrival—if indeed she made it at all. Plus, from past experience, she knew that the second her foot hit the pavement the bus would accelerate into the distance, coating her with a black puff of pure carbon monoxide from its petticoat of dirt. So she sat tight and watched the second hand on her watch complete another circuit of the dial. Just on the off-chance that she might have persuaded herself that perhaps her watch had gained ten minutes since she'd left Putney, the Selfridges clock, just to her left and at top deck eye-level, struck one. She was now officially late.

Perhaps getting the tube from Bond Street to Green Park would be quicker? Or hailing a cab? She doubted it. Rupert Street wasn't far. Maybe a brisk fifteen-minute walk would be the best option. Fifteen minutes late was better than a coronary and a no-show. Anyway, fifteen minutes late was the norm for some people. She was just going to have to learn to go with the flow a little bit more. Susan was never on time anyway.

Despite her attempts at rationale, Lizzie could feel her pulse increasing. She gathered her things together and decided to break for the pavement.

Just as she got to her feet the bus lurched forward as it finally but assertively ground through the lower gears, and, having managed to regain her composure with the help of a fortuitously placed handrail, Lizzie opted to see how far they got before she made a decision.

As they finally rumbled into Regent Street she could almost see the finish line. She bent her knees slightly to help with the whole stop-start balance thing and willed the bus to speed up just a little bit for the final leg of her journey.

Against all the odds, Lizzie's life had returned to a surprisingly high level of normality, and she'd thrown herself at her work with the enthusiasm and energy known only to those who have been given a reprieve. She added adultery to her list of specialist subjects, and as she read the contents of her postbag slowly came to realise that maybe she'd elevated Matt to pedestal level without him really having earned it. However great they had been together, it had always been a lie.

At the back of her mind she was still worried that Rachel had the upper hand. As far as Lizzie could see there was nothing to stop her leaking her story and twisting the truth to a few hack journalists at a later date, once her campaign was over. Lizzie couldn't help feeling that maybe it was time to move into a different sphere of writing or broadcasting altogether, so she'd decided to seek advice from the woman who had been largely responsible for her present niche—Susan Sharples. She was the one who'd seen her potential as a new breed of agony aunt and Lizzie respected her vision. Plus, Lizzie hoped, she wasn't the sort of woman that you could shock easily. Bus permitting, she was on her way to Café Fish to confess all.

Lizzie finally gave up on London transport outside Hamleys and half-walked, half-jogged the final leg, arriving fashionably late at 1:17 p.m. Sophistication had deserted her. She might have looked quite smart when she'd left the house, all blow-dried and perfumed, but now her look was more distressed. Well, just stressed. Her cheeks had taken on the deep crimson hue that always characterised any exercise that Lizzie endured for more than a minute, and were now a beautiful contrast to the pale blue of her cardigan. And while the cashmere was doing wonders to soften her appearance it was failing miserably in its promise to be cool in summer.

Either way, Lizzie wished that she'd opted to wear a little top underneath. She didn't think the crowd at the restaurant were ready for her slightly sweaty M&S bra lunchtime look. She flapped her arms a couple of times in an attempt to let convection take place and assist her under-arm protection—currently working on overtime and about to take issue with its union about having to work through its lunch-hour—before firmly pulling the push door while the welcome committee of waiters looked on in amusement.

If you'd looked closely, you would have observed her already rosy cheeks growing a little redder.

She puffed her name at the *maître d'*.

'Ford, Lizzie. Table for two. Probably booked in the name of Sharples.'

He ran his perfectly manicured finger up and down the reservations list. Lizzie had seen their booking long before he found it, but knew better than to point it out to him. Besides, this was valuable getting-her-breath-back time. As he finally found her name Lizzie felt she had to apologise.

'Sorry I'm a bit late.'

He ignored her, and in so doing instilled the confidence of a twelve-year-old in his slightly flustered client, before turning on his well-polished heel and leading Lizzie to a booth where Susan was waiting, killing time—and a few brain cells—with a mobile phone call. It was the first time that Susan had beaten Lizzie to a venue, ever.

Susan, characteristically unfazed by anything, said her goodbyes and stood to greet Lizzie. After an exchange of mwah-mwah air kisses Lizzie was pleased to be sitting down. Her shins were now smarting from the jog in her slight heels— which, Lizzie had decided before leaving home, were more appropriate for their meeting than boots or trainers.

'Lizzie. Darling. Are you OK? You look very, um, flushed.' Susan turned to the waiter now hovering behind Lizzie to take the jacket that she'd just bundled up on the seat next to her and addressed him with some urgency. 'A bottle of still mineral water, please. Two glasses. Ice and lemon.' Her tone was a verbal click of her fingers and as she ordered she nodded towards Lizzie to indicate the priority treatment she felt they deserved. Lizzie unrolled her jacket and shook it out apologetically as she handed it to him. His duties complete, he vanished at once in search of water.

'I'm fine. I was just running a bit late and thought I'd jog the last few metres.'

Susan looked at her in disbelief. Jogging was something that she only did in the presence of her personal trainer, and certainly not in kitten heels. 'Well, let's get the ordering out of the way and then we can get down to gossip.'

Lizzie wasn't going to let her down on that front; she was sure of it.

They studied the menu, their silence only punctuated by the occasional self-absorbed mutter as they sounded out their options and tried to decide whether their palates would prefer buttered skate or seared scallops. They had successfully whittled the menu down to a couple of dishes, when a tall, dark French waiter joined them brandishing a little blackboard. His role: to throw their almost-made choices into disarray.

'Good alfternoon, ladies. May I draw your attention to zer specials of tooday?'

Without looking at each other, Lizzie and Susan both sat up

a little straighter to give the *monsieur* their undivided attention.

'We haf for you a deleecious deesh of wild sea bass. Gently pan-fried with a delicate sawce of the mushroom and spinach, served with a bake of potato, cheese and shallot.'

Lizzie and Susan were both salivating, although from the amount of hair flicking and direct eye contact going on opposite Lizzie it appeared that Susan was as taken with the waiter as she was at the prospect of sea bass. He must be almost half her age.

'Or, if you fancy something cold...'

Did he look at Lizzie then, or was she just feeling self-conscious? Thanks to the recently poured mineral water she had actually stopped sweating now.

'...today we have a dressed lobster with a salad of mixed herb leafes and a light limon dressing.'

'I think I'm just going to have to go for the wild sea bass.' Susan lingered just a little too long over the 'wild', and almost created a small breeze in the W1 area with the rapid fluttering of her eyelashes. Lizzie had to sip her water to prevent a snigger escaping. Susan was shameless...and a thoroughly entertaining lunch companion. Waiter aside, however, Lizzie had to admit that it did sound good—even if she was sure there was no such thing as tame sea bass and the 'wild' was probably pure marketing.

'I'll have the same, please.'

'He was rather nice,' Susan whispered just a little too loudly to be discreet. 'I love this place. Full of young red-blooded Frenchmen. In my prime I was always a sucker for a bit of a foreign accent...beats the Croydon twang hands-down every time!'

Lizzie had never seen the attraction of surly Gallic men—nor their Croydon counterparts—but laughed and nodded conspiratorially with her editor, whom she imagined had once been a bit of a man-eater. Luckily for the young waiter, it seemed she had moved on to fish. Susan took the initiative.

'So how *are* you, Lizzie? We haven't had a proper chat in ages...'

By 'proper chat' she meant a good gossip. Lizzie could feel a new wave of totally non-exercise-related heat sweeping across the surface of her skin underneath her cardigan.

'Still happy at *Out Loud*?'

'Oh, very. You know I love my job.'

'Well, you're very good at it, and the readers love you, so we love you too.'

'Thanks. How's circulation?'

'Levelled off a bit in the last couple of months, but overall still increasing. No mean feat when you look at the new titles out there now.'

'That's good...' Lizzie wasn't really listening. She was actually rehearsing her next sentence in her head. And there was only a slight pause before she decided that the sooner she got her hidden agenda off her chest, the sooner she could relax and actually enjoy the complimentary croutons and fish pãté. She took a sip of water and cleared her throat before continuing. 'Actually, Susan, I wanted to ask your advice about something.'

'Really?' Susan leant forward, her chin practically resting on Lizzie's side of the table with the anticipation of a potentially juicy titbit. 'Personal or professional?'

'Professional...although it was my personal life that got me into this mess in the first place.'

Susan remained motionless, determined not to miss a syllable.

'Well...' Lizzie took a deep breath '...I wanted to talk to you about my options. About the possibility of me moving away from the agony aunting side of things and maybe doing something a little less emotional—something a little less hands-on with people.'

Susan leant back against the wall of the booth, her brow furrowed. Concern and confusion tinged her usually radiant complexion. 'Why make the break?' Her tone was perplexed. 'People love you; you're a real natural. And why now, just when you've got your broadcast career up and running? It doesn't make any business sense. From what I hear, The *Agony and the Ecstasy* is outstripping all its rivals.'

'I know. I know it all sounds strange. It's just that... well...people might not love me quite so much if a certain bit of gossip gets to them.'

'Tell Auntie Susan...I promise I'll be honest. I bet it's not as bad as you think. It never is.'

Lizzie looked at her fork before making a potted confession at break-neck speed, finishing with Rachel's ultimatum at the *Blue* launch. Tempting as it was to include Clare's revelation, Lizzie knew better than to tell Susan. It would have been as discreet as projecting the information onto the side of the House of Commons. When she finally looked up, expecting disapproval from her editor at the very least, Susan was beaming at her, apparently unruffled. If anything, she looked amused.

'I wondered when you were going to tell me...'

Lizzie stared at her lunch companion. Rachel had promised she wasn't going to say anything. She knew it had been too good to be true. Unless, of course, Clare had been interfering again. Secretly she was becoming a little bit annoyed at Clare's repeated intervention on her behalf. She knew she was being ungrateful, but she had to learn to deal with her own fuck-ups.

'When did she tell you?' Lizzie carefully left the 'she' non-specific, so she could work out for herself whether it was 'she' Clare, or 'she' Rachel.

'You're not going to like this, but I overheard your little spat at the *Blue* launch.'

'At the *Blue* launch...?' Lizzie's heart nearly stopped dead mid-beat. 'You were at the... What? You weren't...? God...'

It took a couple of goes for Lizzie to regain her composure. Susan waited patiently for Lizzie to put an intelligible question together.

'What were you doing there?'

'I could ask you the same question.'

Lizzie could feel herself blushing again. Her capillaries were working on overtime. 'Well...I...well...Robyn...she told me to go. Apparently the editor...um...what was her name? Oh, anyway, well, the editor...'

'Melissa Matthews?'

'Yes, that's it. Melissa Matthews...' Lizzie was concentrating so hard that she failed to acknowledge the fact that Susan seemed to know exactly who Melissa Matthews was '...was interested in meeting me. As it happened I never got to meet her anyway.'

Susan was smiling. 'It isn't the first time Melissa's wanted something that I already had.'

Lizzie looked at her boss quizzically.

'Well, she thinks you're fantastic—perfect for *Blue*, just what they need, etc., etc., and then, of course, there is the as yet unavenged fact that I went and married the man she'd always lusted after.'

'I didn't know you'd been married.' Lizzie had always seen Susan as the archetypal vixen. Self-assured, hard to get, but worth the wait. The woman men always looked back on and reminisced about as the one that got away.

'Oh, it didn't last very long and I was quite young. I'm not sure that I really loved him, you know. Everyone else did, but once the thrill of the chase was over and we'd got back from our honeymoon in the British Virgin Islands he was actually quite dull—'

Lizzie interrupted her. 'I take it that you don't have to be a British Virgin when you arrive there?'

Susan laughed. 'I'd never have been allowed off the plane! I'd never thought about it like that before...'

Lizzie was full of misplaced admiration for Susan. She wasn't exactly a guru of how to live your life—unless, of course, you were aiming to live it as selfishly as possible. But in terms of anecdotes and far-flung stories she was excellent value. Guaranteed to have been there, done that, bought and given away the T-shirt long before anyone else had even heard of it.

'Anyway, where was I? Yes, so you see Melissa and I go back a long way. She's heading up the team at *Blue* and invited me along partly to thank me for all the tips I've given her over the years and largely, I'm sure, to gloat a little and show off at its launch. We've managed to flout convention and keep it very much a friendly rivalry.'

'Did she ever get married?'

'Oh, yes, she got her man in the end...' Her eyes were shining. 'Shame he turned out to prefer men after all the effort she put in. We should have known. He'd always had suspiciously good taste in clothes—oh, and in women, of course...' Susan couldn't stop a smile from spreading across her face.

Lizzie was amazed. Susan had been at the launch. And if she and Melissa were friends then she probably knew that Melissa had been talking to Robyn about contracts. But how on earth had she overheard her and Rachel? And if she'd been listening in how many others had been close enough to the Ladies' to be privy to the whole thing?

'No wonder you didn't want to meet that Rachel woman for dinner. It was that same one who rang me a couple of weeks earlier, wasn't it?'

Lizzie nodded. She wasn't coming out of this very well. Unless, of course, her objective was to tell her boss as many lies as possible—in which case she must be on the leader board for Deceitful Employee of the Year.

'She sounded quite a character. Feisty. Who'd have thought it? My very own *Ask Lizzie* a mistress.'

Lizzie looked devastated. Susan didn't even look cross.

'So where were you? Did you hear everything?' Lizzie just had to know.

'I'm afraid so.' Susan at least had the decency to look sheepish at this point. 'I hate to admit it. It's so uncouth, and dreadfully seedy, but I was in the toilets the whole time. Behind a locked door...in a stall... It would have been pretty difficult not to listen. I would have left, but there didn't seem to be an appropriate moment so I thought I'd be better off staying put.'

Lizzie's head slipped into her hands. At least Susan hadn't decided to make a break for the basins. She wasn't sure she'd have been able to cope with her presence if she'd known about it.

'I'm surprised you didn't just post me my P45 the next morning.'

'To be honest, I'm actually a little bit disappointed that you haven't come to see me sooner about it all. I'm hardly going to sack you because you fell in love with the wrong man. It's not like I'm perfect, is it, darling?'

'But he was...sorry, I should say, he *is*...married to someone who had written to me asking for advice.'

'But I bet he wasn't wearing a label saying "married man" when you met him, was he? They never do. Bloody unfair, if you ask me.'

Lizzie pulled herself into the upright position as she realised Susan was on her side. 'So you're not cross, then?'

'Cross? What for?'

'Well, I could bring the magazine into disrepute if this gets out.'

Susan laughed again. Lizzie wasn't sure how she felt about the fact that she was providing her editor with such an entertaining lunch break.

'I very much doubt it. Just think Marje Proops. She was a mistress for years, and after the news broke everyone still valued her advice. Plus, a few column inches in a few choice publications might get us a few more readers. I employed you as an agony aunt, not as a saint. You're human. Don't underestimate how important that is to your readers. Some employees have to go on courses to gain qualifications, just see your training on this occasion as a little bit more hands-on!'

Lizzie couldn't help but feel that Susan was being a little bit flippant about the whole thing. Fancy dismissing her affair as vocational. The bottom line was that it wasn't funny. Well, not that funny. Well, OK, quite funny if one of the people involved wasn't you. But Lizzie seemed to have temporarily misplaced her sense of humour. She was sure she'd had it there earlier.

'But Rachel has threatened to end my career if I so much as speak to Matt again...'

'Calm down, will you?' Susan shook her head disapprovingly. 'You really are very uptight about all of this, aren't you? Maybe I'll get Bridget to give you a massage later on—she's a fully qualified aromatherapist, you know—or maybe you should try doing a bit of yoga...it's done wonders for my quality of life. Pilates is another one. It's just amazing how the way you breathe can change your posture and your outlook. It really toned me up, you know. But if you want to see definition that Ashtanga power yoga is what you need. It's the business. Just look at Madonna.'

There wasn't a fad that Susan hadn't embraced like a long-lost relative.

'I'm fine.' Lizzie tried her best to act cool.

'Now, where was I? Ah yes...you being a mistress...'

Lizzie flinched inwardly. She still couldn't quite deal with 'mistress' being used as an adjective to describe her. It made her sound so calculating. As if she'd deliberately gone out there in search of a married man, determined to ride roughshod over some unsuspecting little wife, her actions dictated by her raw and potent sexual magnetism. The stereotype was all-prevailing and totally detached from the reality of what had happened.

'Well— 1) He didn't tell you he was married when you first met him. 2) You're not with him any more. You tried to do the right thing when plenty of people would have been less considerate and much more selfish. 3) You genuinely fell for him. It's not like you deliberately set out to sabotage her marriage. Your readers—and the same will apply to your listeners, I'm sure—would rather take advice from someone human but flawed than some sanctimonious do-gooder who wouldn't know great sex or physical attraction if it got into bed next to them.'

'I suppose so.' Lizzie was feeling much better already. She wished now that she'd told Susan weeks ago. It might have saved her a few sleepless nights.

'I know so. First-hand experience is always the most educational... Maybe we should make this a bit of a feature...'

'Susan...' Lizzie knew what was coming next. Susan had a very commercial handle on everything. 'I don't want to become the "me and my love triangle" side show, OK?'

'OK. Although, now you come to mention it, it does have a bit of a ring to it.' Susan was just seeing how far she could push her.

'Susan...' Lizzie's voice was loaded with warning tones.

'Come on, now—give me a bit of credit, will you? All I was going to say is, how about you write about all this for the magazine and come clean? You don't have to name any names, but I bet you'd get a lot of sympathy...'

'And a few letter bombs?'

Susan ignored her interjection and carried on regardless. 'That way you pre-empt any future "scoops" by the tabloids, and Rachel is left high and dry and without any ammunition.'

Lizzie could see that Susan had a point. A very good point. Susan was right; she was going to have to learn to lighten up a bit. What was done was done. Time to move on. And if she could use all this to her advantage then what was the harm in that?

'Not a bad idea.' She had to concede that Susan, on this occasion, had made a not entirely unreasonable suggestion.

'Why—I thank you.' Susan dipped her head and took a mock bow before an imaginary crowd. 'I only wish you'd come and spoken to me earlier. I bet you've been worrying yourself silly.'

Lizzie half-shrugged, half-nodded. 'Well, the way I saw it, and the way Rachel had pitched it, I thought I was going to have to give up everything I've worked for—but I was hardly about to come running to you with my job in my hand. I needed some time to think.'

They were momentarily interrupted by the arrival of their wild sea bass, and Lizzie busied herself with water-pouring while Susan flirted shamelessly. She was poised to take her first mouthful when Susan refocused her attention on her.

'So now, of course, what I really want to know, darling— and what I've been dying to ask ever since the launch—is was he worth it? I want all the details. You dark horse, you...'

'Well...' Lizzie put down her knife and fork. It was going to be a long lunch.

chapter 28

'I've got it, I've got it—and guess what? You're on the cover...'
Clare's voice, a crescendo of excitement, swirled up the stairwell.

Lizzie's heart stopped mid-beat before starting again about
three times faster than normal. Cover-girl? No way.

'Prepare for sales to be up this week. Harri has got a pile on
the counter by the till and he's telling absolutely everyone in
there that you only live round the corner...'

Harri was one of life's unsung heroes. His tiny shop was a
neighbourhood cornucopia and thanks to his cash and carry
card and dedicated opening hours they'd survived many potentially ruinous dinner party crises as he'd bailed them out
with emergency supplies of everything from turmeric to tights
to tonic water. Lizzie blushed at the thought of him reading all
the details of her personal crisis. The total strangers didn't
worry her. It was everyone else she had to be able to look in
the eye.

'...saw Colin in there. He sends you a kiss and asked me to
give you this.'

Clare produced a Toblerone from her jacket pocket.

'He said to tell you that they don't make chocolate love triangles but this is as close as he could get...' Clare giggled.

By the sounds of it there was almost a street party atmosphere down at the shop. Lizzie was glad she'd sent Clare instead of going herself when woken early by a bout of publication-date insomnia.

Clare practically pirouetted into the kitchen with her 'hot off the press' copy, and Lizzie, hot on her heels, grabbed it from her. There she was in colour. Glossy A4 colour. Susan had a nerve. She'd never said anything about front covers at lunch; nor when she'd rung to thank Lizzie for the first draft of her article; nor when she'd asked if they could have a new photo done to publish alongside it. No wonder she hadn't biked round an advance copy this week. Shifting print deadlines, my arse. Lizzie looked at the kitchen clock. Too early. She could wait.

She didn't dare say anything out loud for fear of inciting serious allegations of vanity, but Lizzie had to admit that she wasn't looking too bad. She knew that on her way back from the brink of despair, the fleeting appearance of her cheekbones in a photo wasn't supposed to even register, and, granted, the woman on the front didn't really resemble the flannel pyjama girl in the kitchen right now, but Arabella was a marvellous make-up artist. Without spots and bags, and with a lot of blow-drying, she could apparently look the part.

Her mother was always complaining that she didn't have a decent up-to-date photograph of Lizzie. Now everyone who knew her could buy one. The only problem was, she'd sort of been hoping that Rachel and Matt might not see the article, but this whole cover dimension was going to make that pretty impossible. Obviously she hadn't mentioned them by name, and she'd been careful not to identify them by association, but all of a sudden the sense that Susan had made over lunch was deserting her.

'I can't wait to read it, Liz.' Clare was hovering at Lizzie's elbow, keen to reclaim her purchase, impatiently shifting her weight from mule to mule, dying to see the article.

Lizzie, it appeared, wasn't quite ready to hand it back yet.

'Yeah right. I dare say you could have written it yourself.'

If anyone knew the situation inside out it was Clare. Lizzie just hoped that she felt the article was appropriate. Lizzie needed her on side. She was nervous. Her private life was about to hit the public domain and, as confident as Susan had been, Lizzie was sure that she'd underestimated the repercussions. For one thing, she wasn't going to be able to go into a newsagent or a branch of WH Smith for at least eight days without a disguise.

Lizzie stared at the magazine in her hand. And there it was, about two thirds of the way down on the right-hand side, half printed over her shoulder.

MY AGONY AND MY ECSTASY
CONFESSIONS OF AN AGONY AUNT

Lizzie thumbed past countless adverts, scattering a broad selection of flyers and offers on the floor in the process. Finally she found page 154 and started to read. Clare gave up waiting and busied herself with tea and toast duties, annoyed that she hadn't thought to buy two copies or stopped to read it on the way home.

Apparently absorbed by her all too familiar words, Clare watched Lizzie walk over to the table and sit down on automatic pilot. Lizzie could feel the pit of her stomach tighten. Reading it all again was a bit like picking a scab. Impossible to stop once you've started but something she knew she'd end up regretting.

I've always lived my life by the rules—well, by most of them. OK, I might have bought my first alcoholic drink in a pub when I was fifteen, I might have parked across a driveway or on a double yellow line in an emergency, and I might have even smoked a joint or two at university, but I'd never purposely done anything to hurt anybody. I regret to inform you that unwittingly I just have. I hurt three people. Four including me. Badly.

Emotional pain is much worse than any other kind. You can't treat it with sutures, with Savlon or with any of the modern medicine that, fed on a television diet of Casualty *and* ER, *we think we understand. We're not talking de-fib, myocardial infarctions, pulmonary embolisms, lacerations, enlarged livers or any of the other conditions that we are alerted to on our weekly dose of danger. We're talking heartache and heartbreak. Charging up the paddles won't help. There is only one cure known to man. Time.*

We will all recover. No blood was shed. Plenty of tears and a couple of pounds (there had to be one upside), but none of the red sticky stuff. But in order to move on we all need to learn to forgive and not allow ourselves to be consumed by bitter grudges. The parties involved will all have to accept their own imperfections alongside my own.

The biggest lesson I've relearnt this year is one of the oldest. It is, of course, that nobody's perfect. There are times in all our lives when our selective memories see fit to inform us that we are unassailable, above reproach. But no. Not me, not you, not anyone. I'd always thought that I had good judgement, and then I met a man—my own Mr Perfect-for-now. I was ready to stare cynics in the eye and undo their years of research in one fell swoop. I was invincible. I had a ticket to ride on the love train. And then, without any warning, it careered off the rails and crashed. There was definitely a signal problem.

For the first six weeks of our relationship I was totally unaware of one detail. He had a wife. When the truth did finally surface, he told me that he was married in name only. I wanted to believe him, and so for a few weeks I joined the ranks of all those alleged heartless bitches, those red-taloned, calculating, materialistic husband-stealers. But was it all long nails, negligées, turquoise Tiffany boxes and steamy dates in European cities? Was it glamour? Was it excitement? Or was it disappointment, guilt, heartburn, rejection, betrayal and dissatisfaction? I think you're probably beginning to get the picture.

I fell in love with the wrong man, and yet by the time I found out I was in up to my neck. Head over heels. It was new. We were perfect for each other—or so I thought. Workaholics with a shared passion for romantic comedies and my duvet. I should have known better. How many good-looking guys in their mid-thirties come with hand luggage only? Did I smell a rat? Not even the one I was sleeping with...yet my perfect date had become my worst nightmare.

'Tea?' Clare tried to break into Lizzie's consciousness, but the question ricocheted straight back. She might as well have been invisible. Clare cleared her throat noisily. Still nothing. Lizzie skipped forward to the final paragraph; she'd seen enough.

...there'll be wives out there baying for my blood. There'll be mistresses too, desperate to explain the attitude you need to have to make it in life as 'the other woman', but I'm coming clean to you now because I want you to know...and to know from me. Now I just want to be able to move on. I don't want to have unwittingly created a legacy that'll come back to haunt me, and if there's anything to be learnt from all of this I guess it's not to judge a situation, however it might first appear, until you have all the facts. Whatever labels you want to give us, we were just two people caught up in a whirlwind of intensity. There was chemistry, there were promises, there was even love. But there was no winner. Love did not conquer all. Real life got in the way...

There was a deathly silence at the breakfast table. Matt had only popped out to get milk, but the familiar face staring at him from the magazine racks had been hard to miss and even harder to ignore. At first he'd been surprised—angry, even—that Lizzie had sold out, but once the shock had passed it didn't seem that unreasonable. It was perfect spin. After all, she was in the business of talking about problems, and he'd forfeited the right to pass judgement a long time ago.

Having stared at a two-dimensional Lizzie all the way home, he couldn't wait to read all about it. Rachel, on the other hand, seemed to be having a sense of humour failure. He'd patently managed to do the wrong thing—again. But surely if he'd seen the magazine and not said anything he'd have been accused of keeping it from her? Plus, as Matt had just tried to explain, no one would or could know who Lizzie was writing about.

Mistake of the morning number two. Rachel had immediately accused him of taking Lizzie's side over hers. He didn't understand—if anyone came out of all of this badly it was him, the two-timer. But maybe she would see that when she had finished absorbing every syllable. She hadn't made a sound since she'd snatched the magazine from him. She was usually an incredibly speedy reader. He could only presume that she was committing a few key phrases to memory.

He stared through her, waiting for her to finish. He wasn't in love with her, and she knew it. Five years down the line, she was just reluctant to give in, to be 'beaten'. It wasn't about love for her, only a question of lifestyle, of appearances. He hoped she was ready for a new look.

Back at Oxford Road, Clare had read the whole article and was still talking to her—a tacit thumbs-up. Lizzie was relieved. She'd had enough tension to last her a millennium. She pretended to read the rest of the magazine as she waited for the inevitable but it wasn't until nearly eleven that the phone rang for the first time that morning.

'Darling.'

She'd been beginning to worry. The newsagents must have been open for at least four hours by now, and she'd hoped her mother was going to be sympathetic. Confessions *à deux* on the sofa were one thing, but an article that her friends could read was a different ballgame altogether. She just wanted everything back to normal, when the most stressful things involved missing buses and trains, running out of milk, paying credit card bills—that sort of thing.

'Are you OK? Have you seen the article? Of course you have...silly me. What am I saying?'

From the general babble she figured she wasn't about to get

the 'letting me and yourself down' lecture. She felt her spirits lift a little.

'Well, well... My daughter, the mistress...who'd have thought it? You look beautiful on the cover. So beautiful. Don't worry about keeping your copy pristine; I just had to buy a couple of spares. I'll keep one safe for your children. I'm so proud of you.'

If Lizzie wasn't mistaken her mother was sounding quite emotional. She decided not to ruin the moment by pointing out that sleeping with someone else's husband wasn't especially laudable. As for the 'keeping a copy safe for her children' moment, it was best ignored.

'Thanks, Mum. I'm fine.'

'Well done, darling...' Lizzie noted her mother had reverted to full stiff-upper-lip-matter-of-fact mode. She knew only too well that underneath there was a ton of carefully concealed emotion. She had to have inherited it from somewhere. 'Very brave of you. And very poignant. Although I wish you'd come to me about all of this straight away when it first happened, instead of bottling it all up and waiting for Clare to send you home. That's what I'm here for. I don't like to interfere most of the time, but I have lived a life or two myself—and besides, I am your mother.'

'Exactly... I guess I just thought you might not be thrilled.' And, call her conventional, but Lizzie still felt a little uncomfortable discussing her sex life with her mother.

Luckily Annie couldn't reprimand and listen at the same time. She'd already moved on. 'Is everything all right between you and Clare? I didn't realise you two had fallen out in the first place. Honestly, darling, I'd really rather have heard it all from you instead of having to read about the details in an article. You are a funny one. I mean, thank God I got my hands on a copy straight away before someone rang me about it. Could you imagine the embarrassment if I hadn't seen it first?'

'Sorry. It was a very difficult time for me.' Lizzie interrupted her mother. Irritation was beginning to creep in from somewhere.

'I can see that. Well, I think this article can only do you

good...although heaven knows what the Monday Bridge girls will think about all of this...'

It had to feature somewhere. Her life might be in tatters but surely Lizzie should have thought twice before risking Annie's standing in the Hampstead Bridge circles.

'And I didn't know you were going to be on the cover...'

'Neither did I until this morning.'

'This'll be the talk of the village. Goodness knows what they'll all say.'

Lizzie's mother still referred to Hampstead as a village. It was all about perception.

'They'll probably excommunicate you.'

Lizzie couldn't help but smile as she imagined an army of sixty-year-olds refusing her entry to coffee mornings and leaving her to sit alone at a green baize card table in the corner.

'You may well laugh.'

'To be honest, Mum, I doubt that *Out Loud* has a big circulation among the over-sixties...'

A silence.

'Mum...?'

'You wouldn't think so...and it probably doesn't in most places...but over the months I've probably—well, I might have just possibly...'

'Browbeaten the entire female sixty-something population of NW3 into reading the magazine?'

Honestly, Lizzie thought, sometimes Annie was her own worst enemy. Maybe this would teach her—highly unlikely... but just maybe...

'It's only because I care, darling. I know the industry is all about circulation figures, and I must say quite a few of them have become a little bit hooked.'

Marvellous. Lizzie was glad that she'd only just discovered that her mother's friends were becoming addicted to reading her, at times, frank advice. Having a sexagenarian following might just have inhibited her style a fraction. Her street cred was shrinking rapidly.

'I know, Mum. Thanks. So, I haven't let you down?' She had to ask. Her mother was only too aware of the surprising chink of insecurity in her daughter's otherwise self-sufficient armour.

Her tone softened. 'Of course not. It'll take more than a two-timing husband to bring you down in anybody's estimation, you'll see...'

Relief washed over Lizzie. At times like this her family was the business.

'I wonder whether he's seen it yet?'

The million-dollar question.

Matt was sitting on a bench by the station. Rachel had finally gone to work, taking *Out Loud* with her, and so Matt had bought another copy *en route* to the tube. Over an hour later he was still there. There hadn't been a day since that magazine launch that he hadn't wondered how she was. And then the killer blow. In unassuming size eight Arial font. She had loved him. Up to her neck.

He wanted to call. He knew he couldn't. On the face of it things were just the same. He was still married. Still living with Rachel. Not for long, though. He had to move fast. You didn't just fall out of love with people, did you? In Hollywood's celluloid world people didn't—true love always won in the end—but in London?

It appeared that more people read *Out Loud* than Lizzie had previously thought.

The City FM switchboard was flooded for the entire three hours of her show, and only two of the eighteen callers who actually made it on air were baying for her blood. Susan had been right. Infidelity was flavour of the month. Confessions poured in. The stereotype needed tweaking. Mistresses were apparently one a penny and came in all shapes and sizes and from all walks of life. No one, it appeared, was safe from a willing adulterer.

Everyone wanted a piece of her. Robyn was playing the weekend supplements off against each other while juggling re-

quest faxes from several talk shows. Lizzie just waited for her
to call with a short list.

Her postbag swelled to new dimensions and the overwhelming emotion coming through the letters wasn't bitterness, hostility or revenge but relief. A lot knew their mistakes.
Just not what to do about them. They were not alone.

chapter 29

'Look, we can't just go on pretending that everything's OK. I'm leaving...' Matt spoke earnestly to the bathroom mirror as he heard the front door click.

'Matt?' Rachel was confused. The front door wasn't double-locked, but it was very early for him to be back. 'Are you home?'

She'd had a shit day. No one had appreciated her at work, and since Lizzie's article things with Matt were definitely more than strained. She suspected there was no way back from this particular precipice, but she couldn't bring herself to jump either. Total inertia had set in—if you could be treading on eggshells and in a state of inertia all at the same time.

'Up here...' Matt didn't know why he was telling her. It wasn't as if he wanted her to join him in the bathroom. 'I'll be down in a sec...'

Too late. By the time he'd nervously had one last pee he'd heard the bang of the wardrobe door. He took a deep breath as he flushed and felt his lungs fill with perhaps the most important oxygen mixture of his life. He walked into the bedroom. It felt like a moment. A proper, adult fucking scary moment.

His head suddenly pulsed with an emergency supply of adrenaline.

'How was your day? Mine was crap...' She hadn't let him get a syllable to the surface. Rachel, naked from the waist up, was rummaging in her chest of drawers for something comfy. The items discarded in her search for perfect casual attire were strewn on the bed.

'Oh, not bad...' Matt was determined not to get side-tracked. He had to keep himself focused.

'Fucking art directors... Think the whole world needs them when quite frankly they're all shit...' Rachel wasn't listening, just off-loading as she pulled on a T-shirt. Matt noticed that her nipples were clearly visible through the thin fabric. He didn't feel arousal, nor affection. He walked over to her. At the incisiveness of his move Rachel stopped faffing for a few moments. This was it. His chance.

'Rach...' Matt hesitated for a second.

'Yeah...? What? *What?* Come on—out with it.' Rachel felt dread inching along her spine as she sensed the inevitable. A thousand years ago there would have been a sign—an omen, a portent, a river of blood, a comet—something...something more substantial than just a shitty day. Actually, come to think of it, faced with wardrobe ennui that morning she'd picked something new-old to wear, and her trousers hadn't felt as if they'd fitted all day. She should have known something was wrong.

'I'm leaving. It's not working and I can't keep pretending that it is any more.' Relief surged through his veins. He'd done it. Said it. Out loud. He only hoped Rachel had been listening. Her emotional control was tip top.

'Don't be ridiculous. Where are you going to go, for goodness' sake?' Rachel's fear metamorphosed to incredulity. How could he leave her? She was the sort of person who did leaving, not him. His loyalty was one of the things she'd found so incredible when they'd first started dating. He was the ultimate 'for better for worse' candidate.

'James has got a spare room. I've packed a bag and I'm

really going. Tonight. I know you thought I'd never leave, but it's time.'

Rachel felt sick. He'd actually made a proper plan. Atypical behaviour. It wasn't that she hadn't seen this coming—of course she had. But foolishly she'd just hoped it would all blow over.

'You're out of your mind.' Instinctively she went on the offensive.

'What?'

'You're just having a mid-life crisis..'

Why did she always have to try and undermine him? 'Don't try that I-know-what-you're-really-thinking bollocks. I'm fine and there's nothing mid-life about this. Just accept it—we're over. I've been trying to tell you for weeks, but you just won't listen to me.'

'You'll regret this. If you go now there's no second chance. No kissing and making up when your testosterone levels return to normal.'

'I don't want a second chance. We've given it about eight chances already...and it's not what I want or what you want. Admit it. Go on. Fucking admit it. Please, Rach. For Christ's sake. You must live in some perfect dream world. We haven't had a healthy marriage for ages.'

Rachel paused for a moment as she recoiled at the poise of his attack. 'But...you'll never meet someone else like me.'

'Don't you get it, Rach? I don't want to.'

'Is this still about her? I can't believe it. A flash of blonde hair and a longer than average inside leg measurement and you men turn to putty. It's pathetic. She knows more about male inadequacies than you ever will. She's an agony aunt, not an oil heiress. She probably doesn't earn that much either.'

Matt felt his hackles rise. How could he ever have married this in the first place? 'I'm not seeing her.'

'Not now, maybe... But you can't just go and test the water. You leave and that's it.'

Rachel's aggression was building, and Matt resisted the urge to rise to it. He knew she was upset, she'd lost control, but the way she was behaving now was only making it easier for him to go. He had never needed a beer more in his life.

'This isn't me leaving you *for* anyone. I need to sort myself out. I need some time on my own. I think we've reached a point way beyond repair, Rach, and if you were honest with yourself for just a few seconds, instead of pretending to be emotionally battered and bruised, you'd see that. Forget the hard-done-by role-play, this is me you're dealing with. Me— Matt. Don't even try and blame Lizzie for this. "We" had stopped being "us" long before I ever met her. You've changed—we've changed. You're happiest at work, surrounded by adoring young boys, impressed and impressive older men and a bottle or six of wine. All we have left is this place and a not unimpressive joint collection of books, films, CDs, photos and memories.'

He always had been proud of their DVD collection. She was going to enjoy decimating that, just for starters. 'She's not just going to let you walk back into her life, you know.'

This was weird. Funnily enough, they'd never really discussed his feelings for Lizzie. But he knew he owed it to Rachel to be honest this time.

'Not now, perhaps, but maybe one day. But even if it never happens I can't do this any more. You can't be happy. I know you want more—or me to be something more. Face it, we've grown apart...'

Her expression was glazed. Matt had to make sure she was listening. He had to penetrate her self-protective veneer. She had to know he was serious.

'I'm not in love with you any more, Rachel, and if you're completely honest with yourself I don't think you love me either. We've just become a habit. A collective noun on paper but not in practice. Security for each other. It's not enough any more. I want more.'

Message sent...and from the change in Rachel's composure he was sure that this time it had been received.

'But...but...' Rachel's bottom lip was quivering. It had started as a distress signal, but she could already feel her distress mutating to anger. To add insult to injury Matt was making up for his weeks of one grunt or two communication with a veritable stream—make that a swollen river—of emotional claptrap, and apparently he was still going strong.

'Face it, this isn't working. It hasn't been for months—maybe even years. I only want the best for you, and for me...and this isn't it.'

She snapped. 'You calculating son of a bitch. You had this all planned out, didn't you? And I suppose this time I'm supposed to be eternally grateful that you're bothering to tell me first? So that's it, is it? Lizzie fucking wins.'

'This isn't about winning or losing. It's about the rest of my life. I'm not happy. Don't you see? Don't you care?'

'You know how I feel about divorce. I never wanted to be a divorcee.'

'Then maybe you should have treated me a bit more like a husband and a bit less like a doormat.' Matt's voice was soft.

'You bastard, Matthew Baker. And to think I thought you were different. Get out. Go on, go.' Rachel's tone was steely, if eerily controlled. Matt couldn't wait to go. 'What the fuck are you hanging around for? What do you want? A fucking leaving fucking good luck in your new fucking home card? Get *out*.' Rachel was shrieking—and then suddenly she was sobbing.

Matt watched her crumple, and as Rachel wiped the river of mascara from her cheeks he was shocked. He didn't think he'd ever seen her look so vulnerable.

She was the first to speak. 'How did this happen? I know I've been blind...stupid...selfish, even. I know it's not been right between us. But, Matt...I'm scared...I need you...'

Matt was touched by this rare display of human frailty. He crouched down and held her to him. 'It'll be OK...'

'I know, I know.' She was back to being brave, or trying to be. 'I'll be fine. I guess I'm not in love with you either, but it's just—I guess—well, I know you so well. I love having you around.'

'You've got a funny way of showing it...'

Matt went for humour. It seemed to work. Rachel smiled, albeit wanly.

'I do love you, though...'

'Like a brother, maybe...but you're not in love with me. I'll always be very fond of you, Rach, there's a part of me that will always love you too. I don't want us to be bitter...and I don't want you to blame Lizzie.'

'Well, as long as everything's all right for you, then. Don't mind me. I'll try not to fuck up your fairy-tale ending.'

'Rachel...' Matt could feel her tensing again.

She wrestled herself from his grip. 'Look, go if you're going. We can talk about this tomorrow or the next day. Maybe we should meet for dinner next week?'

'Maybe.'

'Right.'

'Right.'

So this was it. Five years reduced to monosyllables. Matt kissed Rachel on the cheek, picked up his bag and left.

'Fuck. Fuck. Fuck. Fuck.' Overwhelmed with frustration, Rachel threw her empty wine glass into the kitchen sink and watched it smash before heading for the drinks cabinet and knocking back a few neat vodkas straight from the bottle.

She welcomed the almost instantaneous feeling of increasing distance from reality as alcoholic warmth seeped through her veins. Instinctively she rummaged in her bag for her mobile and scrolled through the numbers. She found 'Will mob' and pressed 'call'. It might not be Friday, but she needed a lost weekend starting right now.

chapter 30

Lizzie and Clare sat cross-legged on the floor, their backs against the sofa, sorting letters into piles. Faced with a couple of extra postbags, Lizzie had broken house rules and brought her work upstairs. Clare, at home on a rare day off, had soon tired of watching television round her flatmate, who was apparently constantly and increasingly irritatingly tearing open envelopes. According to Lizzie's plan, Clare had adopted the 'if you can't beat 'em join 'em mentality', for which Lizzie was incredibly grateful. The radio was on just loudly enough to inject a little banal Top 40 normality into their day.

Provided they enclosed a return address, all the letters got a reply of some description whether they were published or not. It was the least she could do. If someone had taken the time and the courage to write in, she owed it to them to compose a personal response. Not a photocopied *Dear.......*—insert name with a Biro—*thank-you-for-your-letter* circular signed by an assistant or a computer, but a proper note with, wherever possible, some constructive advice.

In amongst the letters there were always a few red herrings. People who'd sent in chain letters, messages from Jesus, bills that needed paying, soft toys and the occasional shattered round of home-made shortbread for Lizzie to enjoy with a cup of tea and sympathy. Clare, to Lizzie's amusement was just unpacking a hideous miniature cuddly frog from a grateful reader when Lizzie opened an envelope which transformed her mood completely.

> *Dear Lizzie*
>
> *I just had to write in after reading your article. I'm afraid that I'm one of those men who's had an affair, but I suspect unlike some of your readers and listeners, it was the best thing that I ever did.*
>
> *My marriage was effectively over. I'd just been too lazy to do anything about it, and then, when I met the woman I really wanted to spend the rest of my life with, I was still married. Needless to say the woman in question left me when she found out, and now I've finally decided to leave my wife whether or not I get her back because I've realised that I will never have with my wife what, for a few precious weeks, I had with her.*
>
> *She was a mistress. But only because I hadn't been brave enough to make myself a divorcé before she came along.*
>
> *Good luck with everything. I hope that you find the happiness that you deserve.*
>
> *Name & Address Withheld.*

Lizzie turned the piece of paper over in search of clues, and even smelt the sheet before checking the envelope. It was all inconclusive. She read the words again before alerting Clare to her latest wave of insanity.

'Clare. Read this.'

Lizzie handed her the page and watched Clare intently as she read it. Her face remained disconcertingly expressionless throughout.

'My heart bleeds. Well, you can't reply. He hasn't left his

address... Shall I trash it?' Clare was ready to crumple it into a little ball.

'No. *No*...don't you see?' Lizzie wondered whether Clare was being dim on purpose. 'I think it might be from him.'

'From...?' The penny dropped. Clare didn't need to say his name out loud. 'Don't be daft, Liz. Rest assured he doesn't have the monopoly on not having the guts to leave his wife.'

'But it could be...' Lizzie handed Clare the envelope as further proof.

'Yes, it could be...but then again all you have here is a bit of Times New Roman font, not professionally centred, margins all over the place, on a sheet of white A4 printer paper posted in a self-seal white envelope which the author probably pinched from the office stationery cupboard before licking a stamp and walking to the postbox outside his office in time for the—' Clare squinted at the postmark '—five-thirty collection in London W1.'

'Precisely.'

'Which means "precisely" nothing. Liz, the number of workers with access to white paper, a computer and a letterbox in W1 is probably well over half a million.'

'But something about it makes me feel like it might be from him.'

'Look, if you're going to become little Miss Clare Voyant on me I might just have to move out again, which would be a shame, because between you and me it's great to be back. Face it, Liz, why would he bother with the whole anonymous thing? It just doesn't make sense. You're doing so well at the moment. Please be strong about all of this. You don't need him. And, remember, he doesn't deserve you.'

This time Lizzie had to concede that Clare had a point. Still, it didn't mean that she couldn't want it to be from him. That just made her...certifiable?...a romantic?...embarrassingly optimistic...? All of the above.

She was brought down to *terra firma* with a jolt when she picked up the next letter in her pile. Unless she was totally mistaken, it was a handwritten letter from Joe Dexter. His elongated script was as distinctive as the brown ink that he had

always insisted on using. As if she needed any further confirmation it had been franked at CDH. But it wasn't addressed
to Clare.

Gently folding it in half, she slipped it into the back pocket
of her jeans before heading for the bathroom. Resting her back
against the cistern, she skimmed the letter. Her hunch had
been correct.

> *Dear Lizzie*
> *Congratulations on a great front cover and a frank and*
> *interesting article.*

He always had been a smooth operator. Lizzie felt her muscles tense defensively and involuntarily. What on earth could
she do for the great Joe Dexter?

> *I hope you don't mind me writing. I know I'm proba-*
> *bly still* persona non grata, *but I guess reading the arti-*
> *cle made me think—and by some spooky coincidence*
> *Clare recently bumped into Ed Wallace. I don't know if*
> *you remember him—he was one of the ushers? Anyway,*
> *I thought I'd be better off writing to you at work because*
> *I suspect should Clare recognise my handwriting on an*
> *envelope she might just file it, unopened, in the bin, or*
> *flambé it ceremoniously on the hob. Anyway, it's not ad-*
> *vice I need but a favour. I'd really like to talk to Clare.*
> *Just talk to her—to say sorry, maybe to meet up just as*
> *friends if that's possible—but I don't dare call her at the*
> *restaurant. It wouldn't be fair and I'm not trying to give*
> *her a nasty surprise. I've put her through enough but we*
> *both know how stubborn she can be.*

Lizzie smiled despite herself.

> *Anyway, I figured that you were the only person who*
> *might be able to persuade her to call me. She can reach*

*me at the office on my direct line, at home or on my
mobile.*

   Yours, Joe

Scrawled barely legibly beneath his excessively large signature were his contact numbers. He'd always had the most difficult handwriting. He probably should've been a doctor. Lizzie felt sure that without the computer revolution people like Joe would never have made it to the top of their trees. One handwritten memo and they would have been fired or sent to night school.

Lizzie felt guilty. Clare was currently sitting on the sofa sorting out her postbag while she was furtively and conspiratorially reading letters from her ex-husband in their bathroom. She put the letter back in her pocket and remembered to flush the toilet for authenticity's sake, in case Clare was listening out for her return.

Back in the sitting room Lizzie sat down and, without Clare noticing, removed the letter from her pocket and pretended to read it for the first time. Eventually Lizzie felt Clare watching her.

'This one's for you.'

Clare sat back and uncrossed her legs, stretching them out in front of her to allow some of the blood that had been queuing up behind her knee joint to make the journey all the way to her toes. The relief was quite tangible as the blood almost fizzed down the arteries in her shins.

Was this one going to be about a flatmate who was so highly principled that she'd moved out over an affair? Was it about someone who had started working in a restaurant and had put on three stone in as many weeks? Or was it about a woman who was addicted to having sex with waiters in staff toilets? They'd had the latter already this morning. But Lizzie wasn't cracking any jokes this time. Instead she just proffered a folded piece of paper and a slightly apprehensive expression.

Lizzie might have known Clare for more than a decade but she wasn't sure how she was going to take this one. She could recall Clare's total devastation as if it were yesterday, and sure enough Clare stiffened as soon as she saw her ex-husband's distinctive brown script. Lizzie scuttled off to the kitchen to give Clare a little bit of space, but returned a few moments later brandishing two chilled bottles of Fosters Ice and waited for Clare to finish.

Clare instinctively reached out for the drink and took a long swig of the ice-cold lager—unnervingly refreshing and entirely appropriate even at 12:03 p.m.—before she looked up from her letter.

Lizzie stared at her, looking for any tell-tale cracks, but there was nothing. Only six months earlier the sight of Joe's writing would have guaranteed tears of hurt or frustration. Today she was calm.

'He's got a nerve, that man.' Clare was staring at a fixed point on the horizon. Lizzie didn't know how to take her last comment so decided not to take it at all, and instead concentrated on reading a few more letters until Clare returned from wherever it was she had just gone.

It was minutes before Clare started speaking again. Lizzie put her work down and gave her her undivided attention. She didn't want to miss a syllable or an inflection.

'Of course I'll never be able to forgive him.'

'Of course,' Lizzie echoed. She was doing that friendship thing. Just reiterating what was being said without adding anything new. That way she wouldn't have to do any colossal U-turns a few minutes, days, weeks, months down the line.

'But I might just call him.'

'Why not?'

But Clare wasn't listening to Lizzie.

'It's funny...but since I ran into Ed the other week at CDH I've thought about Joe quite a bit. It all seems so long ago, almost another lifetime. I was such a different person. So naïve. So in love. So not aware of who I really was and what I really wanted.'

'Mmm.'

'It's weird, but in a strange way now I see our divorce as the end of my childhood—my coming of age or something. Maybe

I'll give him a call... What do you think? I suppose in a way I'm curious. It wouldn't do us any harm to meet up, would it?'

'As long as you feel that you're ready and it's on your terms I don't see why not. Phone him. Have a chat. And if he doesn't annoy you in the first ten seconds then suggest a drink...'

Clare paused while she reflected on the reality of meeting up with her ex-husband. Lizzie took her silence to represent doubt.

'If it's all too much, and too painful or awkward or difficult, you don't have to meet him more than once. And if you tell me which night you're going I'll arrange to be working at home just in case you decide you need me and want to meet up for a post-drink drink or something.'

'Thanks.'

Lizzie was secretly delighted at Clare's new approach. While she doubted that a romantic reunion would ever be on the cards, the clearing-of-the-air-and-remaining-occasional-friends option would certainly be much better for Clare's liver—which presently had to endure her drinking herself into oblivion on their wedding anniversary, his birthday and other significant dates from their shared past.

'I'm absolutely gobsmacked that he wrote. It's so...so...so...well...un-Joe.'

Lizzie had to agree. 'Maybe it's from an impostor?'

Clare laughed. Lizzie could be so left of field sometimes. 'I think I will give him a call.'

Lizzie leapt to her feet and returned with the handset in seconds.

Clare shook her head. 'Haven't I taught you anything? I'll think I'll give him a call means some time in the next couple of days, not some time in the next ten minutes.'

'Oh. Right. Course.'

'In fact, Liz, I was going to ask you something else.'

'Mmhm?'

'Well...'

If Lizzie wasn't mistaken Clare was almost being coy.

'Well, I was actually thinking about giving Ed a call anyway.'

'Really?'

Clare was doing her best to be offhand. She might have fooled a few people but not Lizzie, not this time.

'Well, he was quite sweet the other week, and he's left me a couple of messages since...'

A couple of messages and Clare hadn't breathed a word. Lizzie was amazed. Clare had missed her vocation. She would have been a great member of the intelligence services. Secrets really were her forte.

'I promised him supper some time and—well, I thought we could have dinner together. I'd always thought he was a bit too posh to be truly desirable, but there was definitely something there the other day...although I'm so out of practice that maybe it was just nerves.'

Lizzie laughed. 'Just get a load of yourself. Justify, justify. Go with the flow and see what happens. Stop worrying.'

'Well, I might.' Clare pretended not to care and busied herself with shuffling an already fairly tidy pile of letters on the floor next to her.

'Go on. Call him. It's about time you had a bit of fun.'

'I might do. Anyway, it's just dinner.'

'Just dinner...look, I'll call him if you like. I owe you about forty-three favours at last count.'

'Don't even think about it. Anyway what would you say? No... Look, now you're making me nervous. I knew I shouldn't have said anything. Honestly, I'll do it myself...'

Lizzie proffered the phone for the second time in several minutes.

'Later. Maybe tomorrow. But you don't think it would be a strange thing to do?'

'What? Phone someone who's left you a few messages and who you promised dinner to? Now, let me see...'

'Don't be so hard on me, Liz. You know—in terms of Ed being an old friend of Joe's and everything.'

'Absolutely not.' Lizzie got to her feet and returned the handset to its base on her way to the kitchen. Clare really was a very cool customer.

chapter  31

'Bugger. Bugger. Bugger.'

Lizzie took the stairs two at a time and wished she could be just a little bit more organised. There was no fresh air in London at all, and the warm sticky humidity was responsible for the grimy film of sweat that had now formed an uncomfortable layer between her linen shirt and her skin as she battled the heat all the way back to Putney to pick up her production file. Grime permeated every pore. She was going to have to change.

She looked at her watch and wondered if she might be able to squeeze a two-minute shower in to the now non-existent time she had before she had to brave the London Underground again. Flinging her paper on the kitchen table, she rubbed her hand on her nose, coating it in newsprint. She'd gripped the *Evening Standard* like a baton since she'd bought it, but hadn't even had the space to open it on the tube so, with the exception of a couple of the larger headlines which she'd managed to pick up over the shoulders of her fellow commuters, she was none the wiser as to what was happening out there. Current affairs would just have to wait.

She was pulling a skirt up over her not entirely dry legs when the doorbell rang. She checked her watch for the fifth time in as many minutes. She was turning into the white rabbit. Four forty-five. Intrigued as to who would ring their doorbell on a Tuesday afternoon, Lizzie half hopped to the entryphone as she attempted to slip her shoes on and button up her shirt over a clean strappy top while maintaining a constant velocity in the general direction of the intercom. She got to the screen without breaking a leg, although she seemed to have managed to start sweating again, but her discomfort was quickly forgotten as to her delight there appeared to be a florist on the doorstep.

She shouted hello before tying her hair up in order to allow convection to start cooling the nape of her neck. Flapping her arms in a chicken-like manner, to encourage air to circulate under her armpits, she arrived on the doorstep to relieve the delivery man of his bouquet. Like most girls, Lizzie didn't believe that you could ever have too many stamens in your house, and even the most ardent feminists and all coping women were reduced to mush on receipt of a large bunch. Clare was a true believer in the uplifting power of the flower, and their flat had been truly petaltastic since she'd moved home.

Maybe they were from Ed? It was about time Clare was hotly pursued by an eligible male, but that would mean Clare had called him within forty-eight hours after all. What a fluke that she'd been home, and what a relief. The trouble with having Colin as a neighbour was that any flowers ever left with him were always arranged in a selection of vases and distributed throughout his flat—just so they could have a drink, of course—before Clare or Lizzie got there. It then somehow seemed petty to gather them all up and take them upstairs, even if they had been theirs in the first place.

Lizzie resisted the urge to kiss the Interflora man when he told her that the flowers were in fact for her. She might have been more tempted if he hadn't had a moustache.

'What a lovely surprise—and what a fantastic bouquet. Mmm.' Lizzie stuck her nose in amongst the heads and breathed deeply. 'They smell gorgeous.'

'Sign here, madam.'

'You can't have too many—that's what I say.' She signed his chitty with a flourish. Her time deadline forgotten in the pollen of the moment, and elated by his delivery, Lizzie chatted at him. She was determined to coax a conversation out of him. What was it with people in London? Would it have killed him to say just a few words? Did you have to pay extra for friendly?

'I can't wait to get them upstairs and see who they're from. I bet they're gasping for a drink. It's so hot today, don't you think?'

The smile on his face was sardonic, to say the least. But Lizzie had done it. He was going to say something. The art of conversation might be rusty but she'd be damned if it was dead yet...not on her doorstep.

'Well, I hope you've got enough vases in there. You girls are very popular.'

Lizzie laughed out loud. She wasn't sure why. He hadn't said anything particularly funny. But she was very over-excited. What a great job he had. Delivering happiness to women all over London.

He turned assertively, silently intimating the end of their exchange. As he ambled towards his van he was muttering so loudly that he was practically talking to himself. Great. He wouldn't talk to his customers but he'd talk to himself. Lizzie refused to let it get to her. After all, she had an enormous bunch of flowers to arrange. As he walked up the path and closed the gate behind him she caught the end of what he was saying.

'Daft cow. "Lovely surprise..." Yeah...good one. Like blimmin' clockwork for the last six weeks. Poor geezer has even stopped bothering to leave a message on the card these days.'

As Lizzie carried the flowers upstairs to the kitchen she went over what she'd just overheard. Last six weeks? Either the heat had got to him or Clare was secretly sleeping with a man with an Interflora account... And Lizzie had thought she'd been buying flowers to cheer her up in her moment—well, moments, make that weeks—of need. Cheapskate!

Lizzie rushed to find the biggest vase they had and carefully fed a few weary stems to their spring-loaded, aggressive American-style swing bin to avail herself of the ideal receptacle. Half hurrying, she filled it from their over-zealous mixer tap, giving herself her second shower of the afternoon. She was well aware that flower arranging would be frowned upon as an excuse for her tardiness at City FM, but by the same token she couldn't just leave them gasping for water on the worktop. She shook in a generous helping of the flower food that had come attached and stirred it vigorously with a knife that was handily lurking amongst the drying up. While she was waiting for the powder to dissolve she unpicked the mini envelope from the brown paper and opened it.

The card was blank.

Lizzie must have turned it over several times before conceding that there really was nothing on it except for the slightly naff print of a rose in the top left-hand corner and the florist's stamp on the reverse. She checked the envelope in case there was another card lurking within. Nothing. She'd been cheated. She toyed with the idea of calling the shop in case the woman with the bubble writing and only rudimentary spelling skills had somehow forgotten to include the vital greeting bit, but she really didn't have time. She could always pop in tomorrow on her way to the station.

Lizzie automatically went to pin the card on the kitchen noticeboard, next to her and Clare's collection of yellowing wedding invites, expired coupons off new cereals and cleaning products, mini-cab numbers, assorted takeaway menus and postcards. As she took a pin from a remote area of the board a whole pile of papers floated towards the floor, dispersing far and wide in their moment of liberation on their journey to the tiles. Lizzie gathered them up as quickly as she could, and was assertively pinning them back while searching for an alternative and less crucial drawing pin from their collection when she caught sight of the writing on the half-hidden card that had accompanied the flowers Matt had sent her after their first night together.

Momentarily distracted from the task in hand, Lizzie indulgently, and a little wistfully, carefully freed it from its position. Over the months it had disappeared under several layers of junk mail. It was a little faded, but otherwise intact. Bar, of course, half a dozen pin holes where layers had been added on top. It was also, Lizzie noted, identical to the blank card in her hand. The same pink rose in the corner and the same florist's address on the back. Could they be?

Lizzie picked up the bouquet and cut through the string holding the flowers together before shoving the stems roughly into the water. In Lizzie's imagination she could almost hear them sigh with relief as they took a long cool drink. Aesthetics could wait. Right now she had a call to make and a meeting to attend. Time was ticking confidently towards an inflexible deadline, and so she took the executive decision not to risk the jackpot of the tube and called a cab before leaving a message on Ben's voicemail. She was on her way. In just a minute.

For once Clare answered her mobile almost immediately. Lizzie was relieved. She needed a good dose of Williamson cynicism and fast.

'Clare. Thank God.' Lizzie was now running so late that she was practically out of breath. It didn't really make sense, but right now very little about the last half an hour did.

Clare sounded concerned at her best friend's agitation. 'Liz? Are you OK? Is something the matter? What are you doing at home? Shouldn't you be at City?'

Lizzie was fine. Except for a serious case of stomach churning which she was sure wasn't fatal, and a bit of a bad hair day which hadn't been helped by London Underground, the humidity, her shower or their mixer tap. All she needed Clare to do was shoot her latest madcap theory down in flames so she could get to work.

'Cab's on its way. Muppet that I am, I flipping well left my file on the kitchen table this morning, didn't I? Running seriously late now.' Lizzie looked at her watch. Yup, they'd all be waiting, slagging off self-important-presenters-who-just-thought-they-could-waltz-in-whenever-they-felt-like-it. She hated being late. 'Listen. I'm sorry to disturb you but something strange has just happened.'

'What?'

'Well, flowers have been delivered for me. At first I thought they might be for you, from Ed or someone, but they weren't. Anyway, there's nothing on the card.'

'No message?'

Clare, it seemed, was being dense—on purpose.

'Exactly.'

'Anonymous flowers?'

'Yes.'

'I wonder who they're from?'

'That makes two of us.'

'Oh, by the way, I'm seeing Ed tonight.'

'Anyway, I sort of had this mad idea— What? Ed?' Lizzie stopped herself for a moment. 'What—really?' Lizzie was temporarily blown off-course by this pseudo-offhand delivery of what at any other less self-centred moment would have been a very juicy bit of gossip. Typical Clare. Just throw in that rather significant detail when Lizzie was barely paying attention. 'Are you going on a date, Miss Williamson?'

'Hardly. Just a bit of dinner.'

'Bit of a busman's holiday for you, then.'

'Well...'

'Did you call him?'

'Of course not...'

Of course not. What was Lizzie thinking?

'I told you before. He called a few times and then he popped into Union Jack's the other day. Said he was passing.'

'Passing Notting Hill...from Fulham?'

'Well...'

'Clare, don't be so naïve. I think you'll find that Mr Wallace has a bit of a thing for you. How exciting. Just what you need.'

'Well... Look, it's probably nothing. Just a bit of dinner.'

'Whatever.' Lizzie was beginning to get annoyed. If Clare just chilled out a fraction she might even her enjoy herself.

Clare was beginning to wish she hadn't said anything now.

She wanted the spotlight switched off, but there was only one way to get Lizzie off the subject and that was to return her good self to the centre of the conversation.

'So—a secret admirer. How exciting for you... Any ideas? Had any over-attentive cab drivers lately?'

'Well—and let me finish before you tell me to get a life— but, well, I was just pinning the card on the noticeboard, as I always do, and in the process a whole lot of stuff fell off... Anyway, underneath I spotted the card from the flowers that Matt sent me in December...and...well...the card's identical and the flowers are from the same florist...' Lizzie was beginning to realise quite how ludicrous this was all sounding now the words had left the confines of her over-active mind. She wished she hadn't rung Clare. This moment wasn't going to help her credibility at all.

'So...?'

Clare the pragmatist was in town. Probably no bad thing as far as Lizzie's sanity went. She really had a vivid imagination.

'They came from the same florist. That's all. It must be our nearest Interflora-affiliated one. They obviously only have one naff card design to choose from. Conspiracy theory over.'

Clare was right—as usual. Lizzie was a little disappointed— as usual.

'Maybe you're suffering with a touch of heatstroke, what with all this rushing around.'

Lizzie was on the verge of conceding defeat and handing herself over to social services when she remembered the cryptically certifiable delivery man. 'But hang on. The guy that delivered them said something about us having flowers delivered once a week..."like clockwork", I think was what he actually said. For the last six weeks.'

'Well...' Clare's telephone manner changed instantly. Hesitancy crept into her usually dogmatic tones. Lizzie detected the transformation at once.

'Well what?'

'Sounds like a load of nonsense to me.' She'd made a good recovery, but something still didn't ring true.

'Clare...?'

'What?'

'Come on. You've gone all defensive on me.'

'Have not.'

'You have.'

'Haven't.'

This wasn't going anywhere. Clare and Lizzie were currently espousing the we-are-seven-and-a-half-years-old approach to discussion. The sort that only ended in hair-pulling, scratching or pinching. Lizzie decided to break the deadlock before it got out of hand.

'I know you, Clare, and I can tell when you're being all funny with me.'

'Well...the thing is... No... I can't... Wait there. I'll come home.'

'For God's sake...just spit it out, will you? I can't hang around. I've got a live radio show starting in under two hours and a production meeting ten minutes ago, and I'm not doing either until you stop playing silly buggers with me.'

Clare took a deep breath. 'You're going to hate this...promise you won't hate me?' Clare was sounding quite anxious. Not something that Lizzie had realised Clare knew how to sound.

'Of course I won't hate you. Well...?'

Clare exhaled audibly before beginning a confession at break-neck speed. 'You'vebeensentflowerseveryweekforthelastsixweeksandI'vebeeninterceptingthemandgivingtheoddbunchtoColinandspreadingtherestroundthehouseinvariousvasesandpretendingthey'refromme.'

'Why on earth...?' But Lizzie already knew. She wasn't sure whether to jump for joy or burst into tears. Her mind was racing and she was struggling to keep up.

'Liz...Liz...? Are you there? I'm so sorry. I thought I was doing a good thing. Only now I'm having to confess it sounds nothing but bitchy and calculating, but that's honestly not what I intended to be at all. You've just had so much on your plate, and you're doing so well again now, I guess I didn't want anything to spoil it...'

Lizzie was speechless. Genuinely speechless.

'I've got the other cards. They're not all blank. If you go to my bedside table and forage in the second drawer down, under all those ripped-out recipes which are still waiting to be put in a file, they should be there.'

Lizzie found them in no time. Five cards. All the same. All from previous bunches. Four with messages. One blank.

'Listen, Lizzie? Liz, honey, are you still there? Look. I'm so sorry. I realise that it wasn't up to me. I mean, who am I to decide whether or not you have flowers?' And then, to herself, 'What did I think I was playing at? Have I completely lost my marbles?'

Lizzie was barely listening. She was just staring at the cards. Enthralled. They were all from Matt. Matt who she didn't think cared any more. Matt who had been ignoring her since the *Blue* launch. Only he hadn't been. There, in front of her, were the sort of messages that she'd been hoping so hard for over the last six weeks.

Can you ever forgive me? Sorry. Love you. Matt
Hope you're coping. Can this have a happy ending? Love Matt
I have some news. Call me at work. Enough Agony. How about some Ecstasy? Love Matt
I'm not giving up. I'm here for you any time you need me, Matt xx

Lizzie was somewhere between euphoria and hysteria. Clare was still on the other end of the phone justifying away. Lizzie was only dimly aware of what she was saying. Something about Rachel going ballistic if she found out that Matt had been in touch. Some more about Lizzie being hurt enough already...and lots about being sorry.

Lizzie had had enough.

'Clare. Shut up.' It didn't even sound aggressive. Lizzie was too pleased with herself to be properly cross. She was, however, a little disappointed at Clare's behaviour.

'Oh, good. You're still talking to me.'

'How could you?' Clare felt silent while Lizzie did her best to sound disapproving even when she felt like cartwheeling across Clare's room. The trouble was, even though she knew she should have been, she wasn't really angry. For once she'd played hard to get—admittedly, not of her own volition—but she had and, while she hated to admit it, it almost felt good.

'I thought we were a team, Clare.'

Clare found her voice again and decided to use it. 'We were. We are. *We are.* I'm so sorry. I don't know what came over me.'

'You were just trying to protect me from myself. I know exactly what you were trying to do. But, Clare, I'm old enough to make my own mistakes. You're my flatmate, not my guardian.'

But despite the frown in her voice Lizzie couldn't drum up any real fury. If she and Matt were meant to be there would come a time when they would look back on this and laugh. Six weeks ago she wouldn't have been ready for this moment, but now her demons had been exorcised and she was. However, she didn't want to be too easy on Clare. This was a very rare reversal of power.

'I know—I know...' Lizzie wondered where Clare was at the moment. By the sound of it she was practically genuflecting. 'I'm sorry. I feel like such a cow. Why don't you give him a call?'

'Nice try, but I'm learning. I'm not going to call him in the next five minutes.'

'Why not?' Clare was surprised at herself. 'It won't do any harm. He's already been waiting for weeks, and if you call now you might still catch him at work. He's obviously mad about you. What on earth did I think I was doing?'

Lizzie noted that Clare must be feeling incredibly guilty to be actively encouraging her to call him. She smiled to herself. 'Look, I'm not rushing into anything. First things first. I need to know what's happened to Rachel.'

'Good girl. I'm proud of you. Listen, I only want the best for you.'

'Thanks. I love him, you know.'

'I know...' Clare was genuinely moved by the strength of Lizzie's feelings. Her principles were melting around her. 'And if Matt really is the one for you then, believe me, I will be skipping up that aisle behind you.'

Lizzie laughed. 'Hey, one step at a time.'

'That's rich, coming from you...'

'Well, maybe I've changed.'

'That'll be the day. Just woe betide Matt if he turns out to be another Joe.'

'Speaking of whom...'

'Yes...?' Clare was stalling.

'Has a call been made?'

'It's only thirty hours since I got the letter.'

'And counting... So? How long, according to your rules, before you are allowed to pick up the phone while maintaining full ice maiden status? Do yourself a favour, Clare, lighten up and don't worry about every eventuality all the time...'

'I'll call him.'

'Promise?'

'Promise.'

'Good...' Lizzie caught a glimpse of Clare's alarm clock. 'Shit. I've really got to go. I'm running seriously late. I hope my cab's outside.'

'Listen, good luck with the show. I'll see you later on, when you get home.'

'If you're back from your hot dinner date.'

'Shut it, Liz. It's just dinner.'

'Course it is. My mistake.'

'Liz...' Clare was feeling quite giggly despite herself. If she wasn't mistaken she was feeling—well, just old-fashioned excitement. '...just once more for the record, I'm sorry.'

'You will be if you've got a stash of love letters in a shoe-box under your bed.'

'None, I promise.'

As the cab fought its way to the studios Lizzie resisted the increasingly strong urge she now had to call Matt. She didn't want to snatch a five-minute call, and she was late enough for her meeting without deliberately delaying herself any further.

There were only a few minutes spare after the production meeting before she was due on air, and as the opening jingles rolled she did her utmost to ignore her hyperactive mind, which was currently insisting on presenting her with a multitude of hypothetical scenarios. She tried to focus on the amended running order in front of her as she wondered whether Matt would be listening tonight, or whether after weeks of dedication he had finally given up on the girl who had failed to acknowledge a single petal?

As the red light flicked on to give Lizzie her final cue, a surge of adrenaline finally emptied her mind of all the unanswerable questions.

chapter  32

'You're listening to City on 99.9 FM, and this is summer in your city. Keep it cool while we get hot.'

The all too familiar pre-recorded growl of Danny Vincent—thankfully the closest he got to her these days—cut to the studio where Lizzie was waiting live and ready for action.

'Hi, I'm Lizzie Ford and you're listening to *The Agony and the Ecstasy* on City FM. It's Tuesday night, it's 8:03, and I'm here with you for the next three hours. So, if something's bothering you at the moment—if you've got an emotional or personal crisis on your hands, or you just want a shoulder or a sounding board—give me a call. The time is now and you know the number. 0990 99 88 77. That's 0 double nine 0. Double nine, double eight, double seven.

'Coming up over the next three hours we'll be taking lots of your calls, playing some top summer tunes and giving you the last clue for our competition. So, if you want to find yourself and a mate jetting off for a weekend to die for in a Hot City, stick with us.

'But first it's time for some music. Coming up, a bit of "Fast Love" from George Michael. Sit back, open a window and a can of something cold, turn this up and enjoy the feeling of summer with *the* city. We'll be going to the phones right after these two...'

Lizzie looked across to her sound engineer, Phil, who effortlessly mixed George up and Lizzie down while giving her a wink. They were off. She now had five minutes and twenty-five seconds of George Michael and four minutes and twenty-one seconds of Stardust in which to study the running order and get the lowdown on her first two callers.

Matt drummed his fingers on the steering wheel in time to the music as he inched forward in the traffic jam. This was precisely why he rarely drove in London any more. Heat seeped into his personal space from every angle, and despite the fact that his car was a roof-free zone there was a total absence of anything remotely fresh about any of the air around him. As he ground to a halt a wave of hotter air cascaded into his lap and a new trickle of sweat melted into his already damp T-shirt.

Forgetting about his lack of roof, Matt sang along enthusiastically, failing to notice the bemused expression of the motorist to his right. George really knew what he was talking about. Infected by the beat, he was soon nodding moronically in time to the music, and as he started dancing in his seat he joined in again. More song lyrics that seemed to have entered his subconscious by osmosis. It never failed to amaze him just quite how extensive his archive was. Forget MP3, he had his own built-in download facility. Matt adopted a suitable falsetto for the Patrice Rushen sample. Maybe he should have sent Lizzie forget-me-nots instead of a mixed bouquet this week.

He had to admit she was sounding good tonight. He'd only ever used to drive into work in emergencies in the past—what with the second mortgage for parking all day, the worry that his car might not even be there when he got back, or that someone might have slashed his roof—but now it was the only way he got to listen to her show on his own and, while he didn't want to come across as some sort of stalker, it was the only contact he had with her these days. Not that it was real contact, of the two-way variety, but at least by listening he could chart her mood, gauge how she was doing—or at least that was what he told himself.

She still hadn't called. Upset? Hmm, yes...but he couldn't blame her. In fact, if he was honest, he actually had a great deal to thank her for. Since he'd moved in with James he'd been feeling a lot more like—well, like he'd remembered he used to feel. That anything was possible, that the world was his, every dream a real possibility. He knew that to the uninitiated it looked bleaker—he'd lost his wife, his home and his love interest—but it didn't feel like that. He was liberated. Free. To do exactly what he wanted to do. His only regret: that he hadn't done it years ago.

He watched the lights change as he crept forward a few metres in total synch with the bumper of the gleaming TVR in front. It was a modern-day tragedy. £45,000 of hand-built performance car forced to do 0-30 in thirty minutes. Matt almost believed that it was crueller than battery farming. Almost.

Before she knew it Ben was counting her down to the next link. Lizzie scribbled a few notes on her next callers in the margin as the last few bars played out. Some tracks were just pure summer, and tonight it was un-Britishly hot—one of the four or five evenings of the year when she wished that she and Clare had a garden for BBQing and al fresco beer-drinking. Lizzie was determined to make the most of the heat before the idiosyncrasies of global warming let everyone down again with a late-June cold snap just when they'd managed to find a flattering pair of shorts.

'Well, that was George Michael and "Fast Love", followed by Stardust and "Music Sounds Better With You". More music coming up in a few minutes—and believe me, we've got some great tracks lined up for you this evening, including classics from the New Radicals, Texas, Lauryn Hill, and some even older tunes that I guarantee you'll enjoy. But first let's take a couple of calls—after all, that's why I'm here. It's 8:12 on a hot, sticky evening, and we've got Sarah on line one. Hello, Sarah. What can I do for you?'

'Hi, Lizzie.' She sounded quite upbeat. Lizzie gave her team a thumbs-up. There was nothing worse than a monosyllabic first caller.

'Hi...'

'Well, the thing is...'

Sometimes Lizzie really had to fight the urge to hurry her callers along. It didn't help that tonight she was feeling more impatient than normal and there was a surfeit of nervous energy currently looking for a channel out of her system. But she had to be a paragon of patience and understanding. The listeners were patient and anxious to hear the full story, and therefore, Lizzie argued, so should the production team be.

'Go on...'

'Well, it's this bloke at work. I got off with him last Friday night. He said he'd fancied me for ages and we went for a few drinks, and—well, you know...'

'Right.'

'Well, we didn't sleep together or anything, but I was really excited and he said some really nice things to me. I played it cool all weekend...'

All weekend... Ben started laughing silently in the corner of the studio and whispered, 'Give the girl a medal,' to Phil. Lizzie shot him a dirty look. She understood exactly where Sarah was coming from.

'...and when I got into work on Monday I sent him an e-mail—just to say thanks, you know, and to suggest that we did it again some time...'

'Mmhm...' Lizzie made sure that Sarah knew she was listening without interrupting her.

'But he completely ignored it. At first I wondered if, you know, maybe it had got lost in a cyber cul-de-sac or something, or that maybe I'd spelt his name wrong or put the dot in the wrong place. I know, I know—I should've known better. Anyway, this morning I found out that he spent most of yesterday dissing me to his mates, telling them that I couldn't keep my hands off him, that I was really desperate, all that sort of stuff. But that's not how it was on Friday at all. *He* made a move on *me*. I just can't bear the thought of everyone talking about me behind my back. I can't believe he's behaving like this. I'm not even gutted any more. I just feel stupid for not seeing through him earlier.'

'Sounds like a case of immature office male to me. How old are you, Sarah?'

'Twenty-six.'

'Right. Well, as hard as this may seem, you've just got to take this in your stride and not let him get to you. From the sound of it he's not worth it, and if you're not visibly reacting to him and his mates then I'll bet he'll soon lose interest in spreading unfounded rumours. By getting angry and defensive I'm afraid it only looks like you have something to hide. If you just get on with everything as normal he'll be the one that ends up looking stupid. Ten out of ten for keeping yourself out of his bed. That would have made you feel a whole lot worse.'

'You're right. Thanks. I just can't believe I was so stupid.'

'You're not the only one out there, Sarah. In fact—straw poll. Hands up here in the studio everyone who's snogged a colleague in the past and it's all ended in awkwardness or tears... Hmm. Let's see...I'd say that's five out of six of us.'

Sarah giggled. 'Thanks, Lizzie. I feel heaps better already.'

'Hey, no worries, Sarah. Better luck next time.'

All was not well in the driver's seat. He didn't like to admit it, but Lizzie was sounding different tonight. Her mood was— well, cheeky, almost, excited, happy. Too happy. Something had changed since last Thursday. She'd been just as good then—funny, even—but this was different. Now she was being almost flirtatious. He slumped in his seat. Fuck. Could she have met somebody else? All the odds were in her favour. Intelligent, beautiful, funny, sexy—very sexy—and available. God, he was stupid to think she would just be around for him for ever.

He took a piece of chewing gum from the supply he kept in his glove compartment and chewed vigorously. He'd kept telling himself that he just wanted her to be happy, and after what he'd put her through it was the very least she deserved, but what about his chance to get things right? To show her he was serious? He was living on his own now. Happy alone. Not just behaving like a typical male and flinging himself from one woman to the next, regardless of name, face or personality. She deserved so much more than he'd given her. She wasn't responding to his overtures of reconciliation, but he really wanted to talk to her.

Frustrated, he spat his gum onto the tarmac before drumming his fingers on the side of the car. He dialled the City FM number into his mobile and held the phone to his ear, but he didn't press 'call'. As the traffic ground to a halt once again, he closed his eyes, rested his head on the headrest and listened. Lizzie's voice soothed and haunted him all at the same time.

'Right. Who's next...?'

Lizzie looked down at her scribbled notes in the margin of the running order.

'Remember, the number to call is 0990 99 88 77, and I'm here for you until eleven tonight. Next I'm going to see what I can do for Robbie on line four... Good evening, Robbie.'

'Hello, Lizzie. All right, sweetheart? Here it is in a nutshell...'

In a nutshell? Was the man a squirrel?

'Ready?'

Lizzie could feel instant dislike creeping into her headphones, but made sure her feelings remained undetectable beneath several layers of professional veneer.

'Ready.'

'Me and me best mate—'

Lizzie winced. She didn't like to think that she was one of those people who pulled grammatical rank, but sometimes the increasingly everyday use of *EastEnders* English grated. She buttoned her lip and resisted the almost overwhelming urge she had to mutter 'my best friend and I' or just 'me and my best friend', and focused on listening sympathetically instead.

'—are in love with the same girl. We met her at the same time and we both fancy her like mad. The trouble is I really want to ask her out again, but I think my mate would go spare.'

Go spare... Another phrase straight out of Walford's mouth. 'Ask her out *again*? So you've tried and failed in the past?'

'Yeah. Well, not exactly failed. We both went out with her— if you know what I'm saying—in our first year at college. He went out with her first, but then I sharked her off him. He was well cross.'

'Right. OK.'

Lizzie wasn't sure that it was right or OK. She was tempted to ask him what he'd done at college that didn't require him to be able to formulate a coherent sentence, but decided to keep her prejudice to herself. Robbie seemed to think he was a bit of a stud. Lizzie's gut instinct told her otherwise. But she knew better than to get personal.

'Does the girl involved know how you both feel?' Lizzie never ceased to be amazed at how people got themselves into these situations. There was a slight pause while Robbie did his best to summon any emotional intelligence he had to the fore. His search engine was going to have trouble finding any.

'Not sure. Not really. We're all still mates and that. We have a few classes together every week. It's just that I really want to be with her. We had some good times, you know. If you know what I mean. Trouble is, she's sort of got a boyfriend at the moment. Nothing serious or nothin', but it makes it all a bit more tricky.'

'I see...' It seemed the girl had managed a lucky escape...unless, of course, she was still working her way through all the undergraduates. Lizzie doubted it. She was sure she could do better than Robbie at any rate. 'Can I ask how old you are, Robbie?'

'Twenty.'

'And your mate?'

'Twenty.'

Mere children. In men's years they were still only in their

early-to-mid-teens, with way too much testosterone for their own good. Lizzie knew she had to take his problem at face value, even if she was certain that he wouldn't know love if it came up and tapped him on the shoulder.

'And the girl?'

Poor love, Lizzie thought to herself. Two hormonally charged students lusting over her and calling up a radio station for maximum embarrassment when she's trying to date someone else. Lizzie hoped she wasn't listening.

'Twenty-one, I think.' True love? Hardly. He didn't even know how old she was, let alone her star sign.

'Have you seen anybody else since the two of you split up?' Deathly silence. 'Robbie?'

'Well...no...not really. I could've shagged untold women if I'd wanted, but trouble is I'm in love with her. I should never have let her go.'

'And can I ask why it ended?'

'Um...well, she said something about me being immature or something...' Lizzie had to swallow hard to remove the smile in her voice '...but that was like a year and a bit ago. Now I know what she wants. Trouble is my mate thinks that he does too. I don't want this to become some sort of competition.'

Oh, yes. Much less immature now, quite obviously. 'Well, Robbie, if she's seeing someone else at the moment and seems to be quite happy with him then I think you and your friend have got your answer. She's not the only girl on the planet, or even on campus, and I think you'll find it's much easier and much more fun to go out with someone that wants to go out with you too. Plus, it isn't just up to you two to decide, as you so generously put it, "who gets her". If this girl was single— and she's obviously not at the moment—ultimately it would be up to her to decide who she wanted to go out with, and assuming that she would even contemplate going back over old ground, if you and your mate don't think that you could cope with one of you being chosen over the other then maybe you should agree that she is off-limits for both of you.'

'But...'

'You'll get over it. You're still young. I'd say get out there and have some fun. But remember—good sex is safe sex.'

'So just shag around and see what happens?' Robbie didn't sound heartbroken at the prospect of seeing some other girls. True love was on ice.

'You really do have a way with words, Robbie. I'm surprised there isn't a queue...'

It was too much for the production team. Phil snorted into Lizzie's headset, and out of the corner of her eye she could see the researchers laughing in the phone room. 'And a top tip from me—maybe if you don't call it "shagging around", you might just find that there are more girls interested in spending some time with you. '

Ben was the only one of the team suffering a sense of humour failure, and he shook his head firmly at her. Lizzie shrugged her shoulders and mouthed 'tosser' at Ben, but Ben always had been a bit of a goody-goody. Lizzie knew that plenty of her listeners would approve of the sarcastic approach in this instance. And she was sure Robbie could take it—assuming, of course, he'd even got it in the first place.

'OK, then.' Robbie seemed unfazed. She didn't get the impression that he was particularly well endowed in the grey matter department, or indeed in any area. 'And Lizzie?'

'Yup?'

'One more thing.'

Oh, no. Lizzie was sure she didn't want to hear this, but she couldn't just cut him off... Phil could, though. She nodded at Phil and mimed cutting her throat with her finger, but he was obviously doing something technical and wasn't looking. Damn.

'I'd love to buy you a beer... It's about time someone gave you a night to remember. You're single now aren't you? Forget married men. What you need is a younger model.'

It was no good. Phil lost it totally, and as he fell about in the studio Lizzie could see the researcher who'd briefed Robbie tearing her hair out in the phone gallery at the way it was all going. He obviously hadn't sounded like a total wanker when she'd taken the call earlier.

'Yeah, Robbie—whatever. Don't wait up.'

Time to move it all on. Lizzie glanced at the studio clock and her running order. 'Right it's 8:22 and you're listening to City FM on 99.9. Coming up after the adverts is a man with a voice to soothe and a soul to die for. Mr Bill Withers and "Lean on Me". Stay with us. We'll be back right after these.'

It was all cued up. Lizzie took her headphones off for a minute. Her ears needed some air. Ben's body language indicated he was limbering up for a rant.

'Steady on, Liz. He rang in for advice, not a dressing down.'

'He was a jumped-up little wanker, Ben, and you know it.'

'You know you just have to be nice, though. It's still the first half-hour of the show and you never know who's listening.'

'Ease up.' Phil came to Lizzie's defence. 'He was a total twat...probably wanks himself to sleep over her publicity shot...'

'Thanks.' His intentions might have been honourable but Lizzie didn't appreciate the mental picture that Phil had just painted. It was too sordid for her female mind to want to visualise. Men.

'Don't worry, mate.' Phil hadn't finished yet. 'Seriously, I doubt he was listening...and even if he was I bet he was having a bloody good laugh. You have to draw the line somewhere.'

Ben was always paranoid until 9:00 p.m. as he had it on good authority—i.e. he had slept with the controller's PA's best friend on more than one occasion—that big boss Richard Drake often listened to the first part of her show on a Tuesday, when he was at the gym. Lizzie hoped he had been mid-sit-up during her mini-outburst, just in case he, like Ben, had failed to see the funny side.

'Sorry.' It wouldn't have registered on even the most sensitive apology scale but it seemed to do the trick for now. Just sometimes Lizzie had to handle things her way.

Phil mixed back to the studio a few seconds early and Lizzie was miles away, with Bill Withers and a bunch of flowers. It was only a split-second silence, but enough to get Ben waving his arms quite strenuously. Lizzie dipped her head to apologise silently while burbling away into her microphone on automatic pilot.

'How was that for you? I love that song. Restores my faith in human nature. Remember, you can always lean on us if you need anything. The number, just to remind you, is 0990 99 88 77 and the time is 8:26. I'm Lizzie Ford. You're listening to City FM and this is *The Agony and the Ecstasy.*'

As she was going through her spiel Ben's voice cut into her headphones. 'Lost Sam on line six; instead going to line five. A man. Won't give his name. Wing it and for Christ's sake be gentle. Only three minutes thirty-two to the news.'

'Now, we have a mystery man on line five who'd rather not give us his name.'

Could it be? Lizzie was an irrepressible optimist.

'Hello, line five.' She was as cheery as you could be if you didn't know who you were about to speak to and were hoping for the man of your daydream to surprise you. Her heart skipped a beat in the momentary silence before he spoke.

'Hello, Lizzie.'

It wasn't the voice she'd been hoping to hear. She fought off disappointment. No wonder she always felt let down. Her expectations were obviously far too high.

'I need a bit of a female perspective.'

'I can certainly help you with that...' He sounded normal enough, and thankfully a million miles from Planet Robbie at any rate.

'It all sounds a bit pathetic, really, but I didn't know who else to call. The thing is I've had a bit of a fight with my girlfriend. I'm thirty-two and we've been together for just over a year and a half now, and it's all been going really well. Then, in a fit of jealousy, I went and accused her of something she hasn't done. She denied it, but I wouldn't take no for an answer, so she packed me a bag, took my keys and threw me out of the flat. Now she won't have me back because she says that she can't share her life with a man who doesn't trust her.'

'You can see her point. Why didn't you believe her the first time?'

'Oh, all the usual recipes for disaster. I'd had a couple of beers; I'd been wound up by my mates. I just lost it, I'm afraid. I realise now that I was totally out of order. I love her and I want to make it up to her. She means the world to me. But typically every time I try and apologise something goes wrong, and now she won't even answer my calls. I leave messages every time. I've even dropped in to see her but she never answers the door.'

'Maybe she's out.'

'Maybe. Either way, I just don't know what to do next.'

'If I were you I'd lay off the heavy-handed approach...stop pestering her with calls and visits. Don't take this the wrong way, but right now she's probably worrying that you're some sort of nutter. If you keep this up she'll think she's had a lucky escape.'

They were running up to the news. Ben had just started counting down twenty seconds in her eyeline. Pushed for time and thinking about Matt, Lizzie knew exactly what to suggest.

'Send her some flowers and a simple message and then sit tight. If she still doesn't get in touch wait a few days, then give her a call—just the one, though. Tell her how you feel, but make sure you give her time to come round. Don't bombard her with attention. There's a fine line between stalking and caring. Let her miss you and just remember that to be there for her you don't need to be sitting on her doorstep when she gets back from work every day. Give her space, but don't give up. No one said women were easy, but we're worth it.'

There was a smile in her voice and this time she got a thumbs-up from Ben, who seemed to have forgiven her for her vacant moment at the top of the link. Lizzie was in good spirits. The mystery man thanked her as they came off the air for the news, but she had really only been half speaking to him.

For the first time in weeks Lizzie was talking to him; Matt was sure of it. He grabbed his mobile from the passenger seat and pressed 'call'. Engaged. 'Redial'. Still no joy. He dialled Lizzie's mobile and it went straight to answer-phone. He swung his car into a U-turn and, leaving a symphony of horns in his wake, put his foot down as he accelerated towards the studios. He knew the other drivers were probably calling him all sorts of names—and, yes, they were right, he probably did look like a poseur in his white T-shirt, sunglasses and classic convertible. But what did he have to lose? Traffic permitting, he'd find out soon enough.

The news was over and according to the running order they had another two minutes of ads. Ben was giving Lizzie the low-down on the next couple of callers while the researcher who'd vetted Robbie had gone to chainsmoke herself into the recovery position.

Ben stopped mid-sentence as the white light on the wall started flashing silently. The private studio phone was ringing, which usually only meant one thing. Richard Drake had been listening and had a pearl of wisdom that he wished to impart on 'his' team. He only called at inopportune moments and always expected undivided attention. He didn't seem to understand the way live radio worked, even though he proudly told anyone who wanted to know—and quite a few others—that he'd worked his way to the top from the very bottom.

Phil answered it in the sound gallery. The team could see him through the soundproof glass studio divider, and although they couldn't hear what he was saying his face was definitely registering concern.

There was a click as he opened up studio talkback and pointed at Lizzie through the window. 'Hey, Ford, it's for you.'

Ben's shoulders visibly relaxed as the tension passed on to his presenter.

'Who is it?' Lizzie folded her arms across her chest defensively. Still seated, she propelled herself to the private phone courtesy of her executive chair, and while she waited for Phil to patch it through she braced herself for the worst.

Thinking back, she knew she shouldn't have been quite so tetchy with that Robbie bloke. But she could have been a lot worse, and she certainly didn't want to have to make some gormless apology on air. Shit. Why did Richard have to be listening tonight? She really didn't want to have to do the humble pie, yes sir, no sir routine... She wasn't in the mood.

She was about to pick up the receiver when Phil's voice cut into the studio again. 'They've gone. It was Security. Apparently you've got a visitor. Male. White. Um...that's about all they could tell me. A guy asked for you at the front desk, then it seems got bored of the whole red tape thing and just jumped the gate and headed straight for the lifts. They just wanted to warn you in case he gets here before they do. They're going to try and intercept him at fourth floor reception.'

Lizzie's pulse raced. Maybe Robbie had been some sort of psycho caller.

'Thirty seconds.' Apparently unperturbed that his presenter's life might be in danger, Ben reminded Lizzie that she still had a show to do.

Nervously she put on her headphones, shutting out the outside world. She didn't have a lot of faith in station security. They never seemed to be even remotely on the ball. She wondered whether the studio window into the corridor was bulletproof as well as soundproof, and wished she hadn't stayed up watching some trigger-happy-good-guy-gets-shot American-made-for-TV-action-movie last night.

'Coming to you in ten, nine, eight...' the studio clock was ominously counting down in red seconds '...seven, six...fuck... nutter alert.'

Lizzie swung round in her chair and was about to throw herself to the floor with her hands over her head to protect her from the now almost inevitable—in her overactive imagination, at least—spray of bullets, when her heart stopped. There on the other side of the soundproof glass was a very familiar face, shortly joined by two security guards who grabbed an arm each. Lizzie squealed.

'Two, one...cue Lizzie.'

She was on air and speechless. Not a winning combination. Her eyes fixed on Matt, she found her voice a few seconds later and luckily for her career something vaguely appropriate came out before all the listeners fiddled with their radios in search of a station which actually had some output. Ben looked as if he was watching Wimbledon as he desperately tried to work out what the hell was going on and why it had to happen during his show.

'Um...sorry about that...everything seems to have gone a bit haywire at our end. Right...welcome back. I'm Lizzie Ford and this is City FM...' Lizzie took a deep breath. Her chest was tight with a cocktail of excitement, fear and emotion. Now she could understand how people had heart attacks from shock. 'More calls and music in a minute, but first of all let me share something with you. Phil, mike up my visitor, will you?'

She winked at Matt, who was now face to face with her, give or take several inches of glass. He was smiling apprehensively. He couldn't believe he was actually standing there, but he was ecstatic to see that Lizzie looked pleased—make that *very* pleased—to see him.

Security loosened their grip and he walked to the studio door as fast as his suddenly shaky legs would allow.

'Now, I know some of you are familiar with the events of my love life over recent months. By no means my finest hour in terms of doing the right thing, but for a few precious weeks the best example I will probably ever be able to find of following your heart...'

Matt could feel himself melting. He wanted to have his arms full of Lizzie, but instead he had some guy clipping a microphone onto his T-shirt a few frustrating metres from where he wanted to be. He took a deep breath.

'As you know it was all over—for the best, I told myself. I told him to go and he disappeared...back to his wife, I presumed. I heard nothing. I dealt with the overwhelming disappointment as best I could, did my best to move on, and then today I discovered that he's been sending me flowers for weeks. My flatmate had been intercepting them. To protect me from myself. But I found out. And now, just a minute ago, he arrived here at the studio, out of the blue...'

Lizzie wished she could find a modicum of privacy for her and Matt. She looked across to Ben, who was just staring at her, as was Phil, as were the researchers from the phone gallery. It was like something out of a Musical Statues masterclass. She was going to have to carry on. Against her better judgement, she was going to have to finish what she'd started.

'I'm not sure what he wants, or what's changed, but I just have to find out. So please excuse me for this moment of total self-indulgence and let me introduce you to him. Matt—hello.'

'Hi...'

He said it really slowly. Lizzie had an overwhelming urge to tear her headphones off and kiss him.

It was just like a scene from a film. Matt wondered who he'd want to play his character... He wasn't sure about this whole live on the radio thing, but he didn't really have much choice now. 'I'm not sure what I'm doing here, but something made me come. I've been trying to get in touch with you for weeks. So much has changed...'

Lizzie smiled at him, her eyes searching his, begging him to say what she wanted to hear. His surroundings blurred into insignificance. As far as he was concerned there was only one person he wanted to speak to and she was right in front of him. This was his chance.

Clare's mobile rang in her bag. She blushed as she rummaged for the source of the noise and wished she had opted for the original ring rather than the electronic version of the *Happy Days* theme tune which had seemed such a good idea at the time. She was sure she'd turned if off when they'd sat down. As she reached to silence it she spotted the caller ID and, apologetically mouthing 'sorry' to Ed, answered it as discreetly as she could, willing none of the other diners or waiting staff to lynch her at the table.

'Hello? Annie? Is everything OK?'

'Are you listening?'

'Yup. Go ahead.' Clare half covered her mouth with her hand in an attempt to keep the noise to a minimum.

'No. Are you *listening*? To her show?'

'No. I'm in a restaurant.' God, Annie could be demanding. Clare was a person in her own right, and her life continued on Tuesday and Thursday evenings whether she liked it or not. She might share a flat with her daughter but she wasn't married to her.

'Well, get yourself to a radio now. He's on—with her. It's—well...it's gripping. Do you know? I think it all might work out.'

'Who's on...?' And then it dawned on her 'Matt...on the radio...with Lizzie?' Clare forgot about being quiet. Her volume settings were suddenly all over the place. 'How? When?' She stood up without thinking and then sat down again very quickly, her voice a whisper as her cheeks reddened. 'What's he said so far?'

'He just turned up while she was doing her show. Seems keen. I haven't been able to get through. But anyway, I'm sure I'm the last person she wants to speak to right now. I think little Lizzie has got her hands quite full enough at the moment.'

'I don't believe it.' Clare was genuinely excited for Lizzie. 'Has he left Rachel? Has he said?' Talk about timing. A couple of minutes ago she'd been on a genuine date for the first time in years, and now she was going to have leave before it had even started.

Ed, who to Clare's amusement up until now had been trying to pretend that he was absorbed in his menu and not really listening, finally gave up and cocked an eyebrow inquisitively. Clare nodded to confirm that his hearing had indeed been perfect and, still on the phone, instinctively stood up to go. Apparently unruffled by the unorthodox behaviour of his date, Ed slipped a credit card to the waiter, told him they'd be back, and then, taking Clare's hand, led her out of the restaurant. She relaxed at his touch. It was great to have someone else taking charge for a change.

'Listen, Clare, I've got to go. I don't want to miss any of it.'

'Thanks for letting me know. We're on our way to the car to listen now.' But Annie had already gone.

As she sat in the passenger seat of Ed's car on the second floor of the NCP car park on Brewer Street she couldn't help but beam at the world around her. It was all working out perfectly.

The incoming lines were flashing madly. Ben wasn't surprised; the atmosphere in the studio was electric. Relieved to have a purpose, he went into the phone gallery to see what they wanted. A few seconds later he flicked his mike on and whispered into Lizzie's ear. 'Terrific stuff. Listeners desperate to speak to you. Lines two and three cued up. Take them as and when.' He scrunched his running order into a ball and tossed it into the bin. You couldn't plan radio like this.

'So, you see, I have so much to thank you for...' Matt paused. Lizzie was motionless. Suspended in time. He was hers. He had left. Weeks ago. She allowed herself to dream the happy ending. Warning bells sounded all over her body. If he let her down again she wasn't sure that she'd recover. Mind you, neither would he if Clare got to him first. What happened now? She couldn't find words. Thankfully Ben was paying attention and helped her out with a timely interjection.

'Phil on standby with music and ads, and callers on line two and three for you. Two is someone who claims to know you. Clare from Putney, is it? Anyway, she says "Go for it".'

Lizzie nodded silently as her heart soared. A lone tear escaped and hit the top of her smile as she clamped her lips together to prevent a full-blown sob escaping. To Ben's horror she took her headphones off and leaned across, away from the mike, ready to receive the kiss that Matt was about to give her. She melted into his lips. It was time for Ben to take the initiative and earn his salary.

At 8:46 and twenty-one seconds the listeners of *The Agony and the Ecstasy* were treated to a medley of jingles followed by three songs in a row, thanks to the humane spontaneity and whizz-kid versatility of Phil, who could see that their resident agony aunt was in no fit state to speak to anyone.

He'd worked on the show for long enough to know how much Lizzie valued her own space, and by the look of it Lizzie and Matt needed a couple of minutes to themselves. Not that they'd really noticed that there was anyone around anyway. They were caught up in a moment—a moment Lizzie deserved—and Phil wasn't going to be the one to spoil it.

Neither was Ben. His lips were working overtime, but unknown to him Phil had faded his microphone to nothing while he concentrated on picking a handful of suitable tunes to take them through to the news.

On sale in January from Red Dress Ink…

Spanish Disco

Erica Orloff

Prescription for heartburn:
Avoid spicy foods, alcohol, coffee and stress.

Prescription for heartache:
Avoid feeling sorry for yourself.

Too bad for editor Cassie Hayes, she's got a bad case of both. And now that her publishing company is in dire straits, she's stuck on an island with an epic poem that was supposed to be a long-awaited sequel, a cook who goes a little heavy on the cayenne, a nasty coffee addiction, a predilection for tequila and a reclusive author more than happy to ply her with beer. There's little doubt that she'll survive the adventure, but will you?

RED DRESS INK
TM

RDI0103-TR

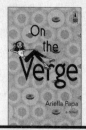

Strapless

Leigh Riker

Australia or Bust!

Darcie Baxter is given a once-in-a-lifetime
chance to open a new lingerie shop in Sydney.
So she packs up and moves to Australia,
leaving New York City, her grandmother and
her possessed cat behind. A whirlwind affair
with an Australian sheep rancher sends her into
panic mode, fleeing Australia with a bad case of
the noncommittals. Who wants to be barefoot
and pregnant in the Outback? But don't worry—
she won't get away that easily!

**RED
DRESS
INK**
TM

Visit us at www.reddressink.com

RDI0802R-TR